MANGA SHAKESPEARE™

KING LEAR

ADAPTED BY
RICHARD APPIGNANESI

ILLUSTRATED BY
ILYA

Amulet Books, New York

HISTORICAL NOTE:

This manga recreation of King Lear is set on the American frontier during the colonial wars of the 1750s, between the French and British settlers, and the Iroquois Confederacy – the six tribes of the Mohawk, the Oneida, the Onondaga, the Cayuga, the Seneca, and the Tuscarora. The artist has extensively researched Native American costume, jewellery and tattoo. Though some details have been combined for artistic purposes, the cultural references to the Iroquois Six Nations of the period are as accurate as possible. For a full list of sources for these depictions, see: www.mangashakespeare.com.

Cataloging-in-Publication Data has been applied for and may be obtained from the Library of Congress.
ISBN 978-0-8109-4222-6

Copyright © 2009 SelfMadeHero, a division of MetroMedia Ltd

Originally published in the U.K. by SelfMadeHero
(www.selfmadehero.com)

Illustrator: Ilya
Text Adaptor: Richard Appignanesi
Designer: Andy Huckle
Textual Consultant: Nick de Somogyi
Publisher: Emma Hayley

Printed and bound in China
10 9 8 7 6 5 4 3 2 1

ABRAMS
THE ART OF BOOKS SINCE 1949

115 West 18th Street
New York, NY 10011
www.abramsbooks.com

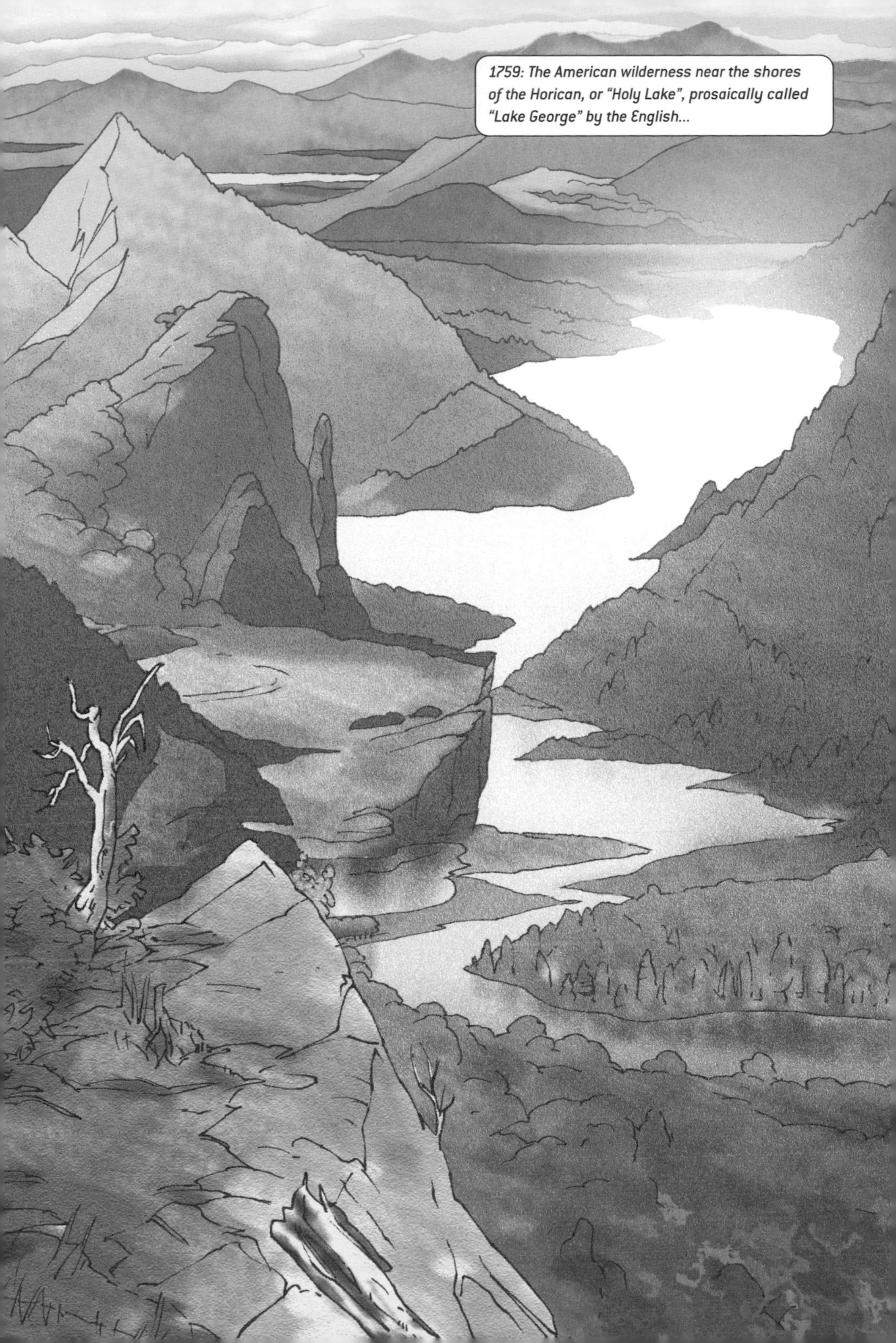
1759: The American wilderness near the shores of the Horican, or "Holy Lake", prosaically called "Lake George" by the English...

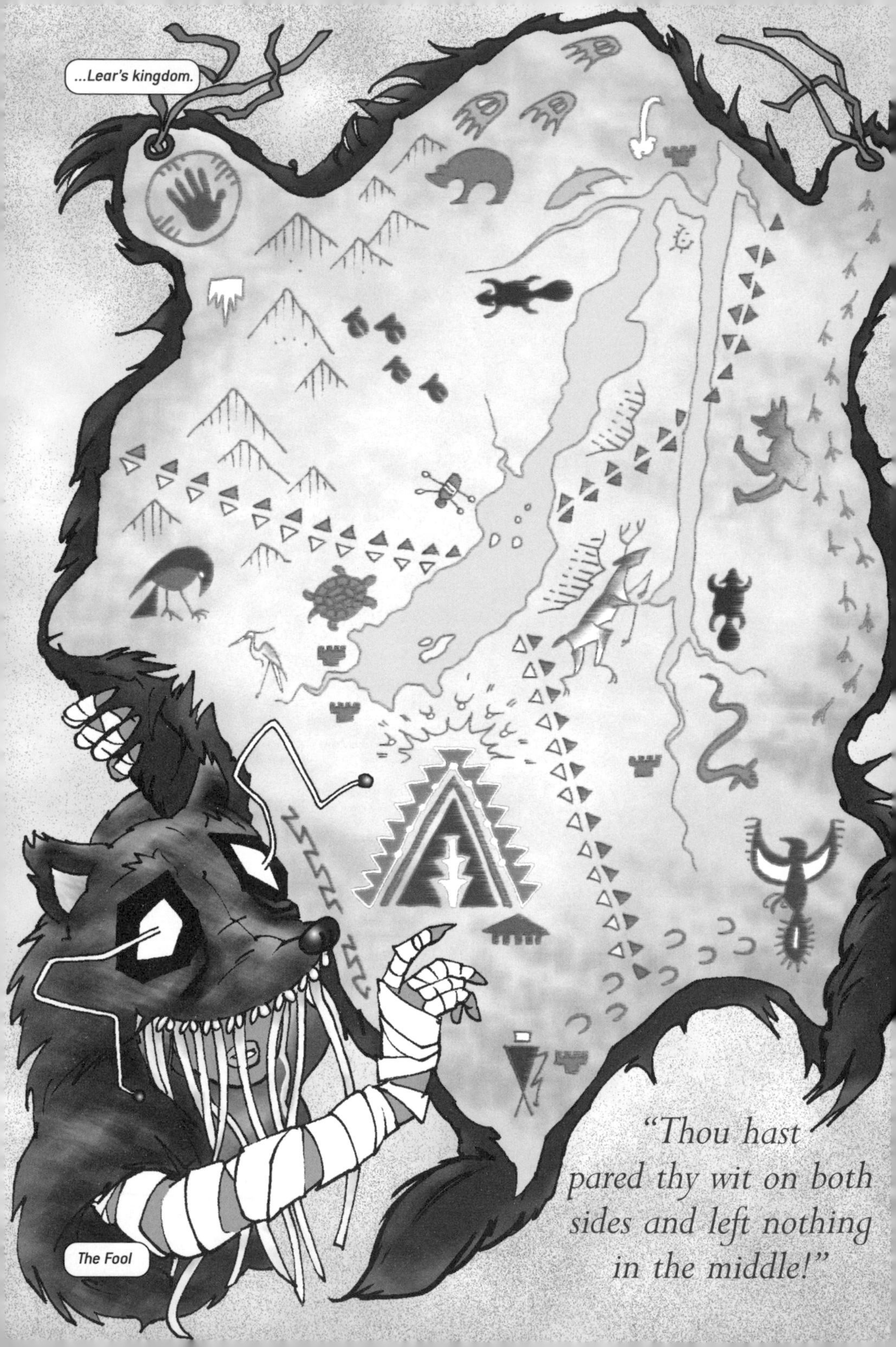
...Lear's kingdom.
The Fool
"Thou hast pared thy wit on both sides and left nothing in the middle!"

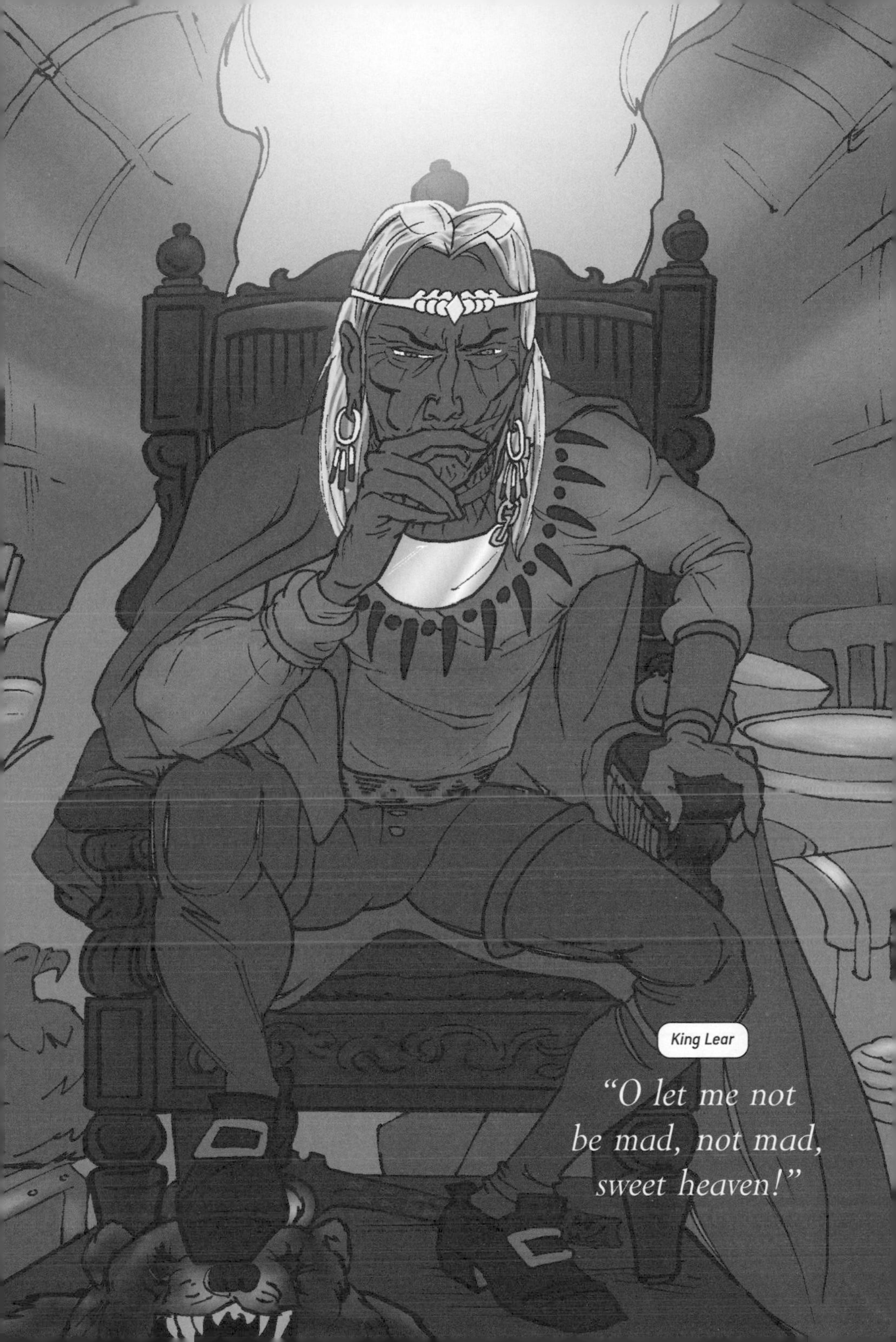
King Lear
"O let me not
be mad, not mad,
sweet heaven!"

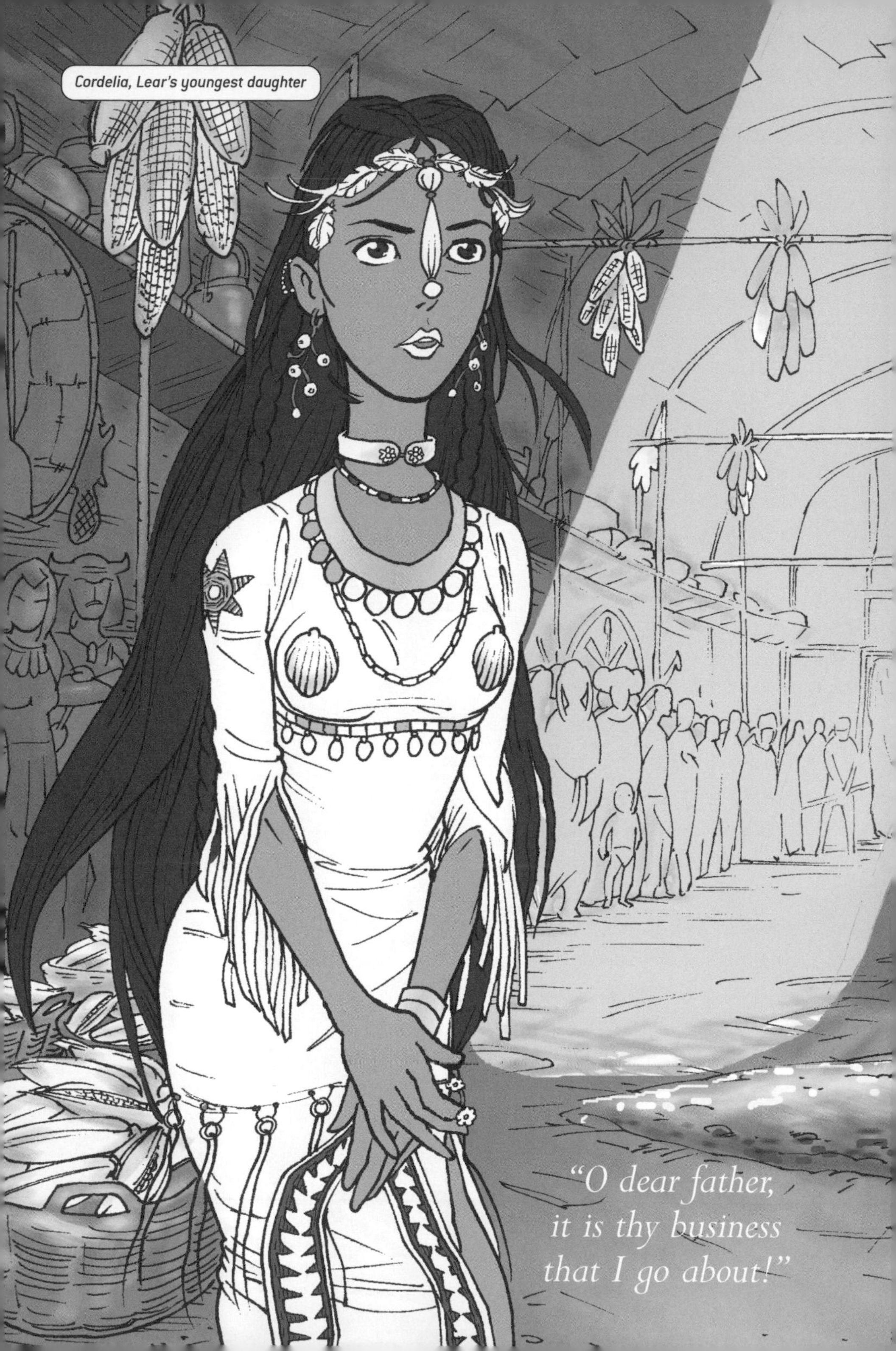
Cordelia, Lear's youngest daughter
"O dear father, it is thy business that I go about!"

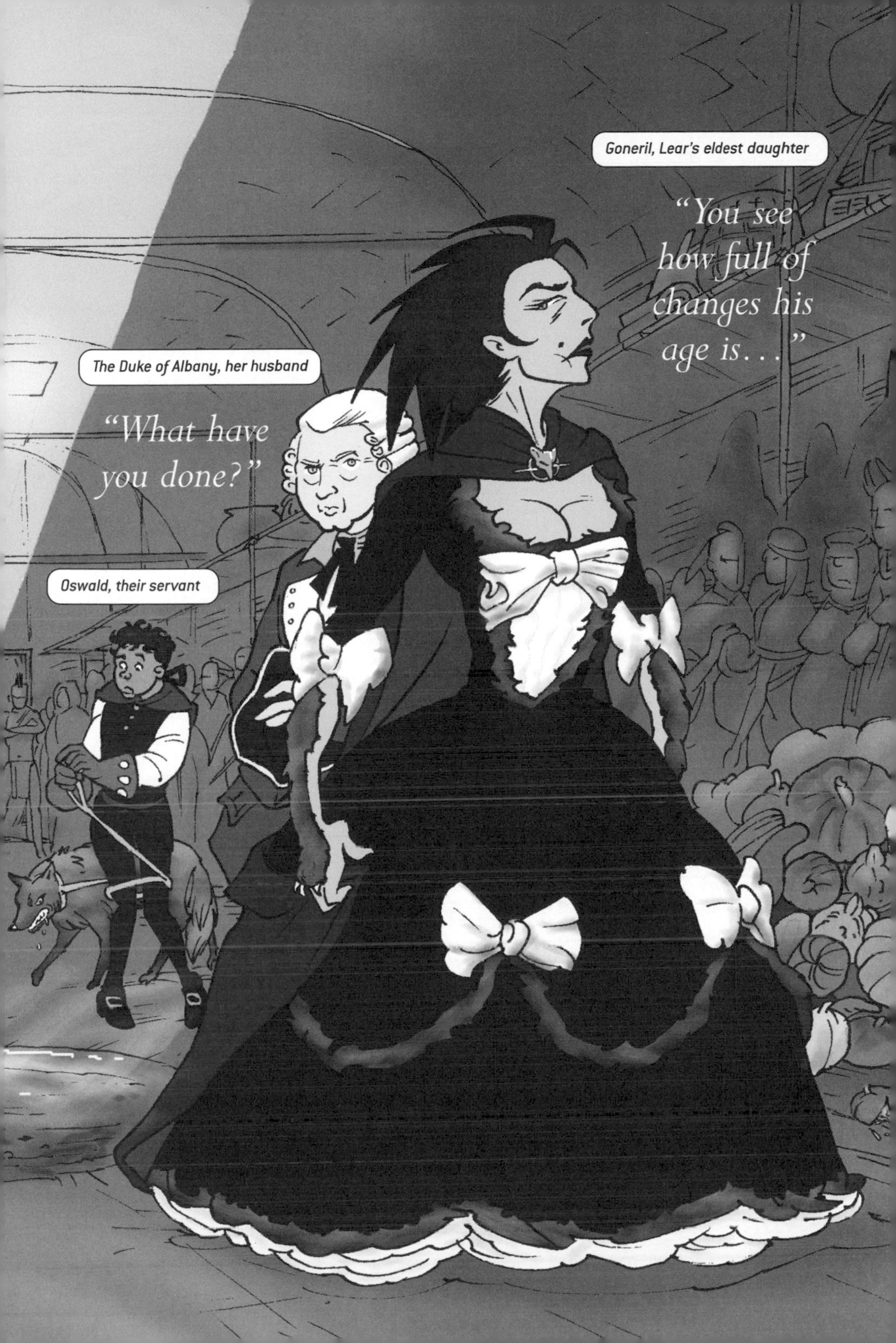
Goneril, Lear's eldest daughter
"You see how full of changes his age is. . ."
The Duke of Albany, her husband
"What have you done?"
Oswald, their servant

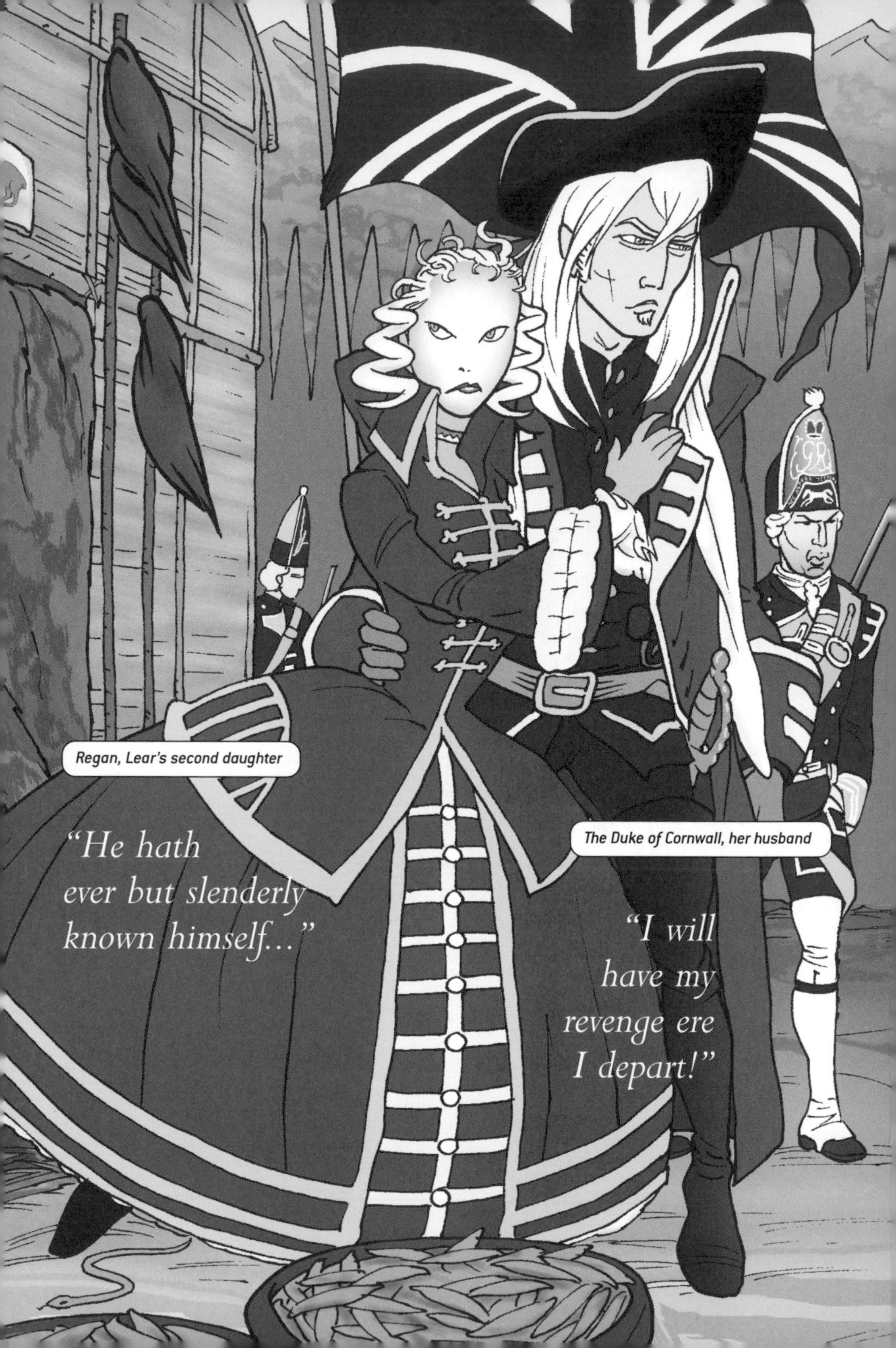
Regan, Lear's second daughter
"He hath ever but slenderly known himself..."
The Duke of Cornwall, her husband
"I will have my revenge ere I depart!"

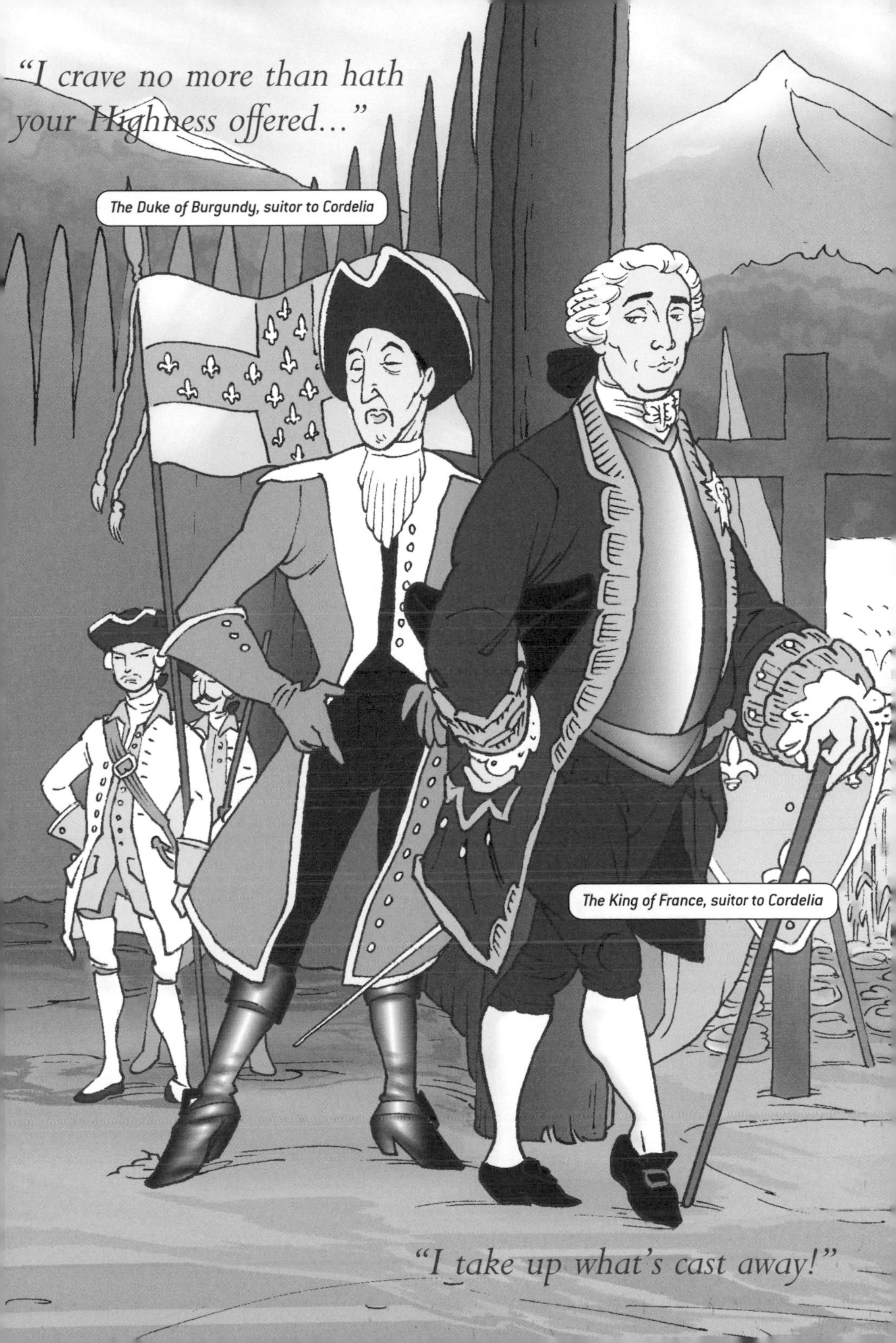
"I crave no more than hath your Highness offered..."
The Duke of Burgundy, suitor to Cordelia
The King of France, suitor to Cordelia
"I take up what's cast away!"

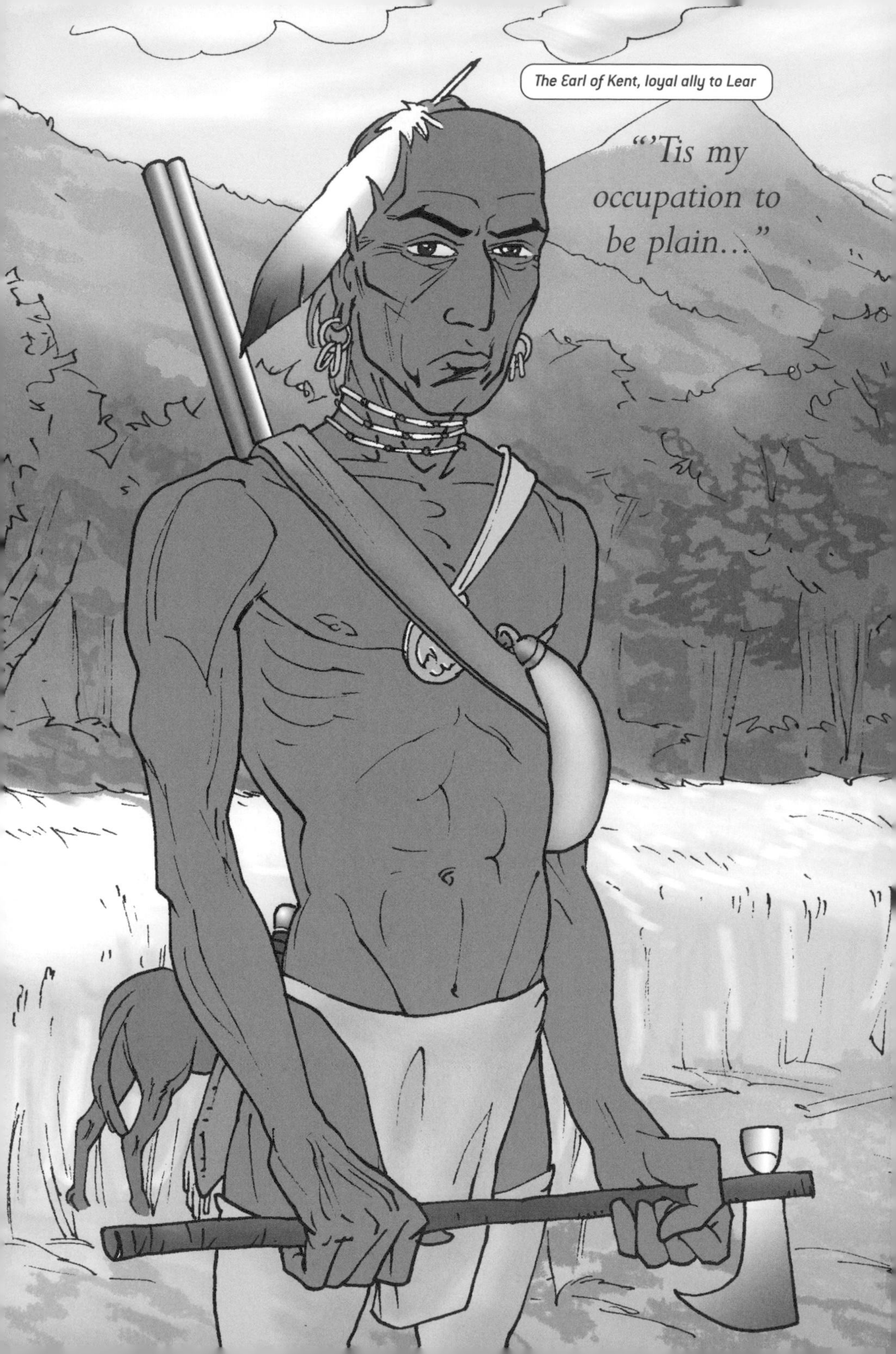
The Earl of Kent, loyal ally to Lear
"'Tis my occupation to be plain..."

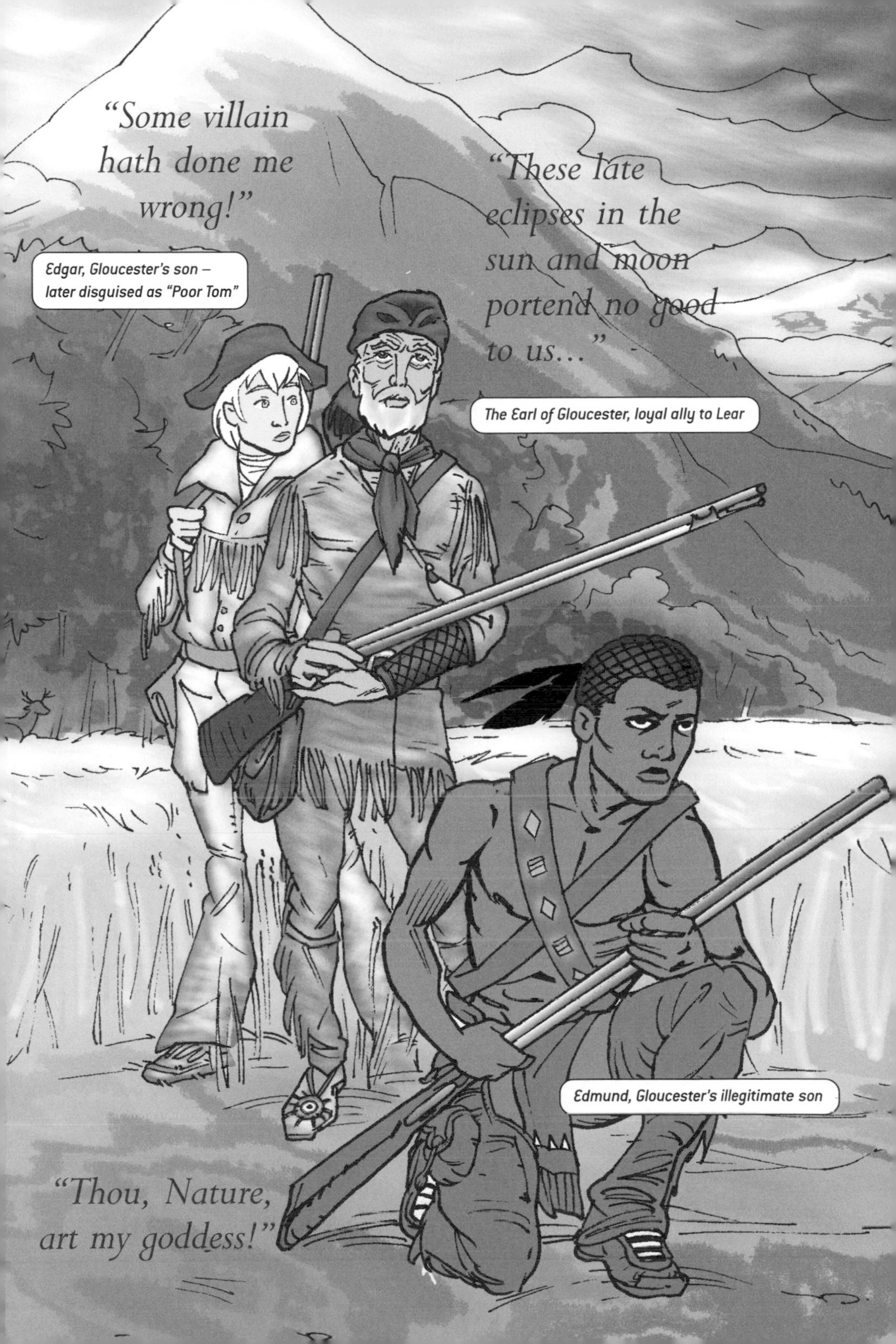
"Some villain hath done me wrong!"
Edgar, Gloucester's son – later disguised as "Poor Tom"
"These late eclipses in the sun and moon portend no good to us…"
The Earl of Gloucester, loyal ally to Lear
Edmund, Gloucester's illegitimate son
"Thou, Nature, art my goddess!"

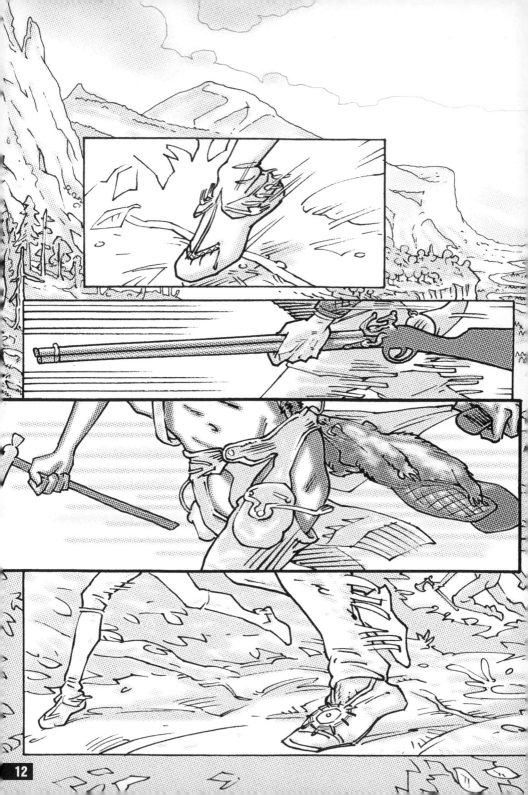

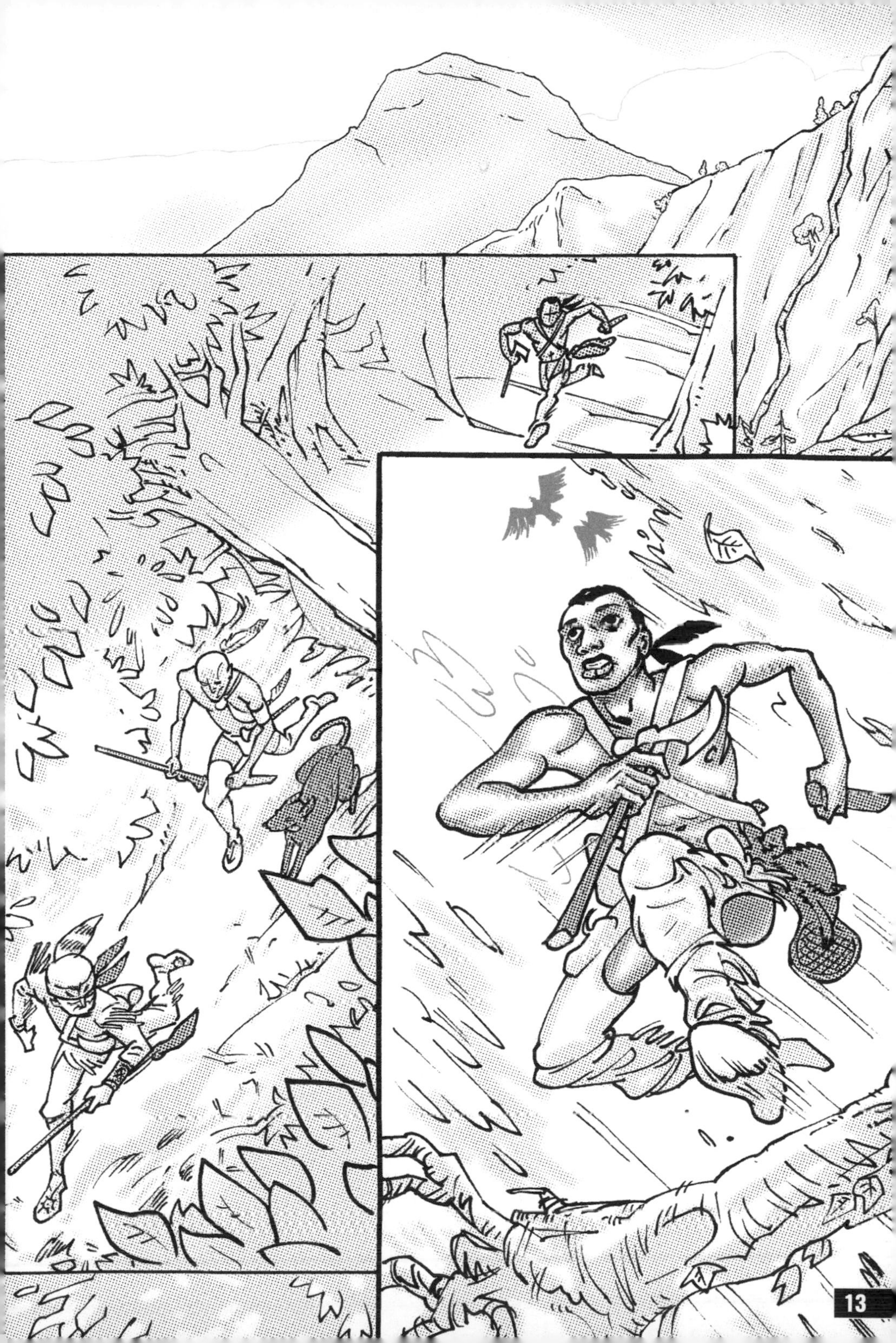

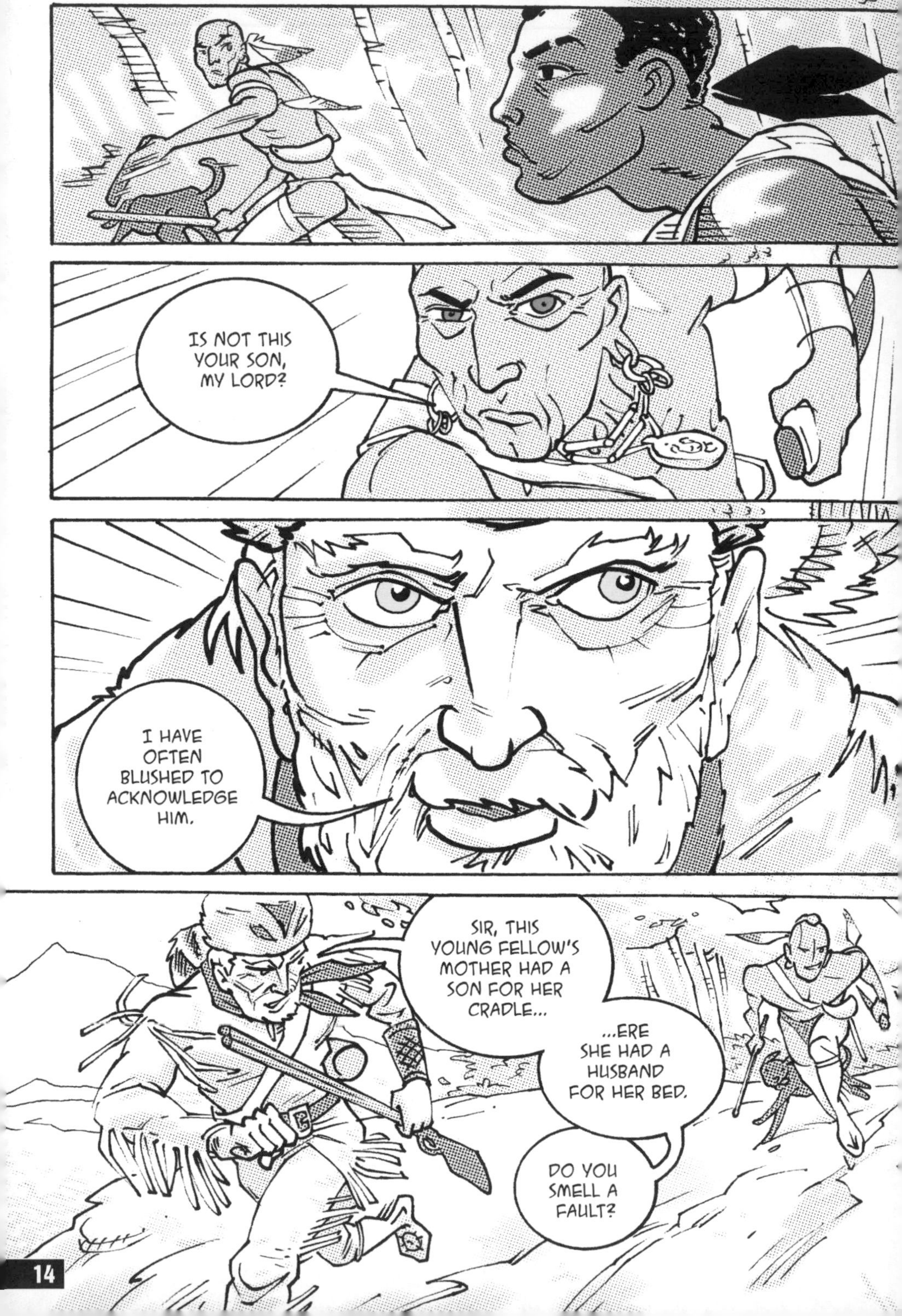
IS NOT THIS YOUR SON, MY LORD?
I HAVE OFTEN BLUSHED TO ACKNOWLEDGE HIM.
SIR, THIS YOUNG FELLOW'S MOTHER HAD A SON FOR HER CRADLE...
...ERE SHE HAD A HUSBAND FOR HER BED.
DO YOU SMELL A FAULT?

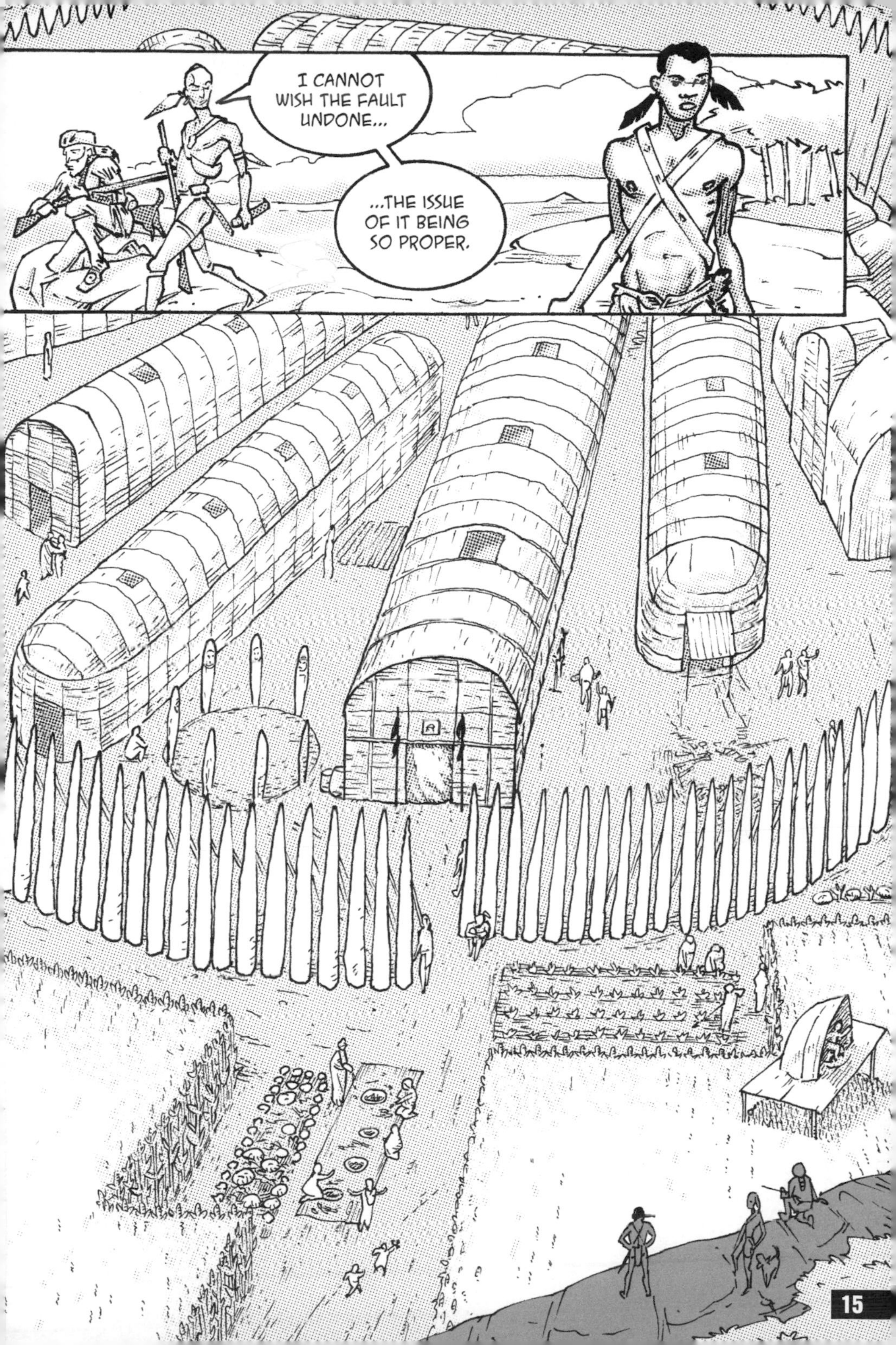
I CANNOT WISH THE FAULT UNDONE...
...THE ISSUE OF IT BEING SO PROPER.

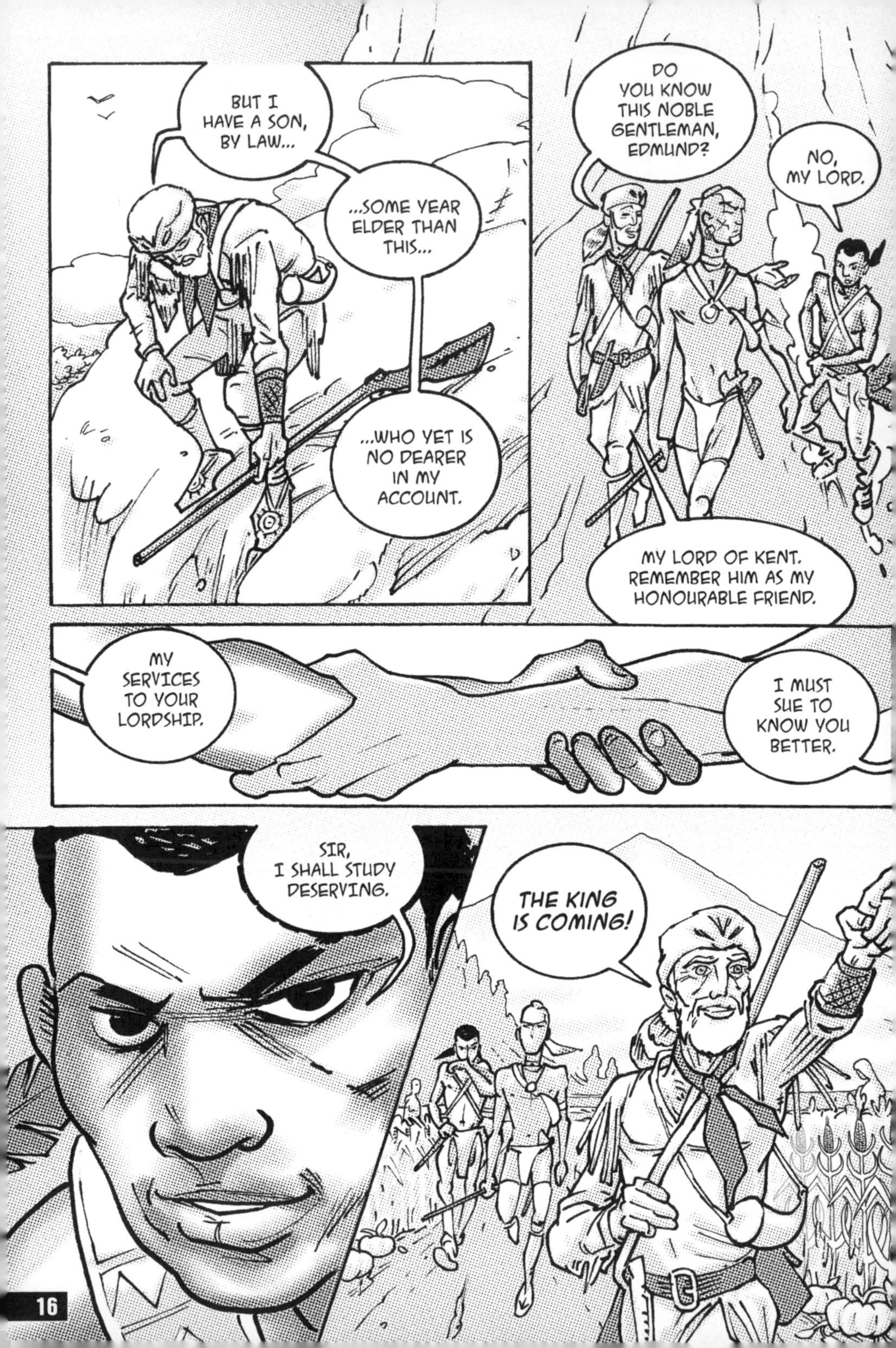
BUT I HAVE A SON, BY LAW...
...SOME YEAR ELDER THAN THIS...
...WHO YET IS NO DEARER IN MY ACCOUNT.
DO YOU KNOW THIS NOBLE GENTLEMAN, EDMUND?
NO, MY LORD.
MY LORD OF KENT. REMEMBER HIM AS MY HONOURABLE FRIEND.
MY SERVICES TO YOUR LORDSHIP.
I MUST SUE TO KNOW YOU BETTER.
SIR, I SHALL STUDY DESERVING.
THE KING IS COMING!

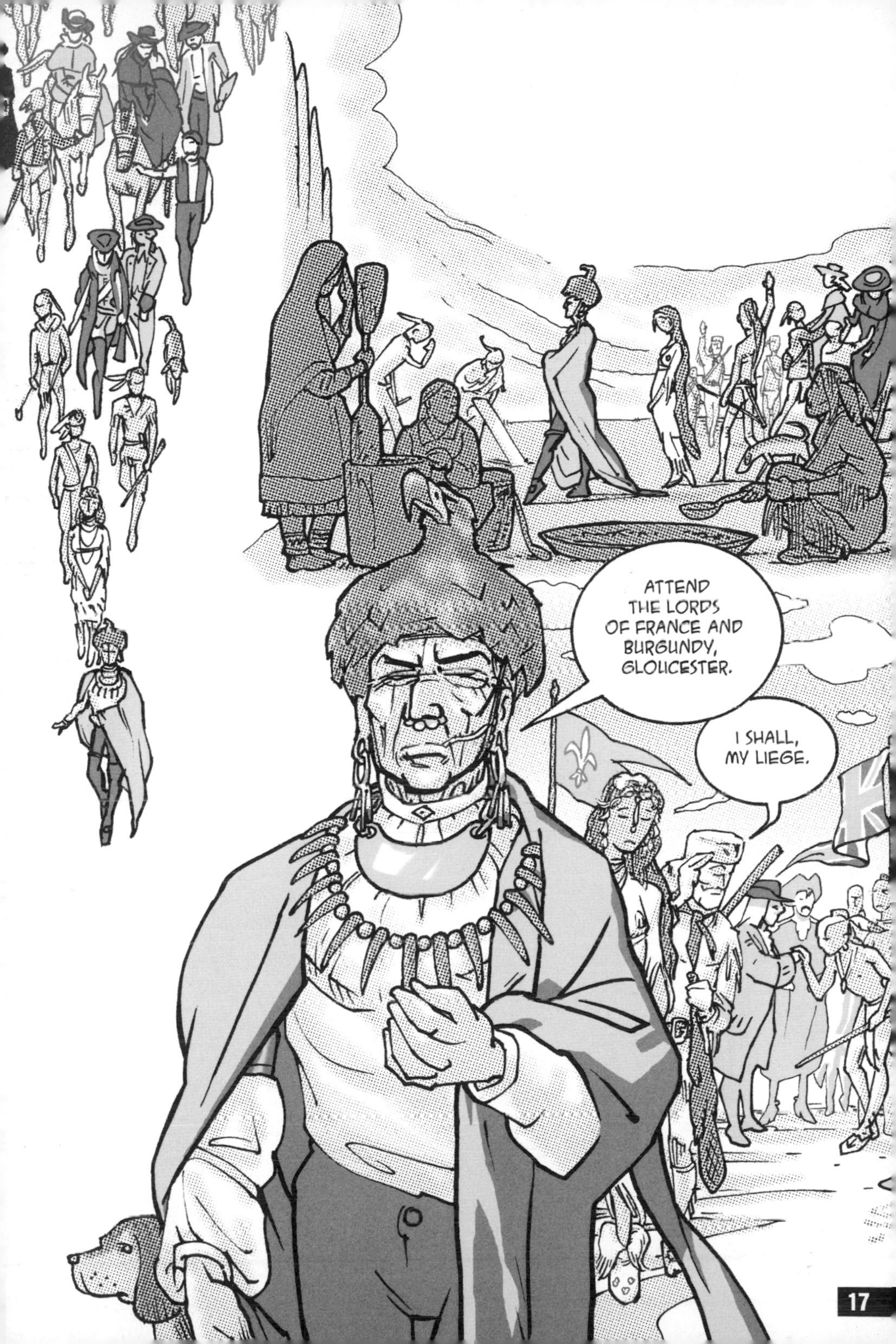
ATTEND THE LORDS OF FRANCE AND BURGUNDY, GLOUCESTER.
I SHALL, MY LIEGE.

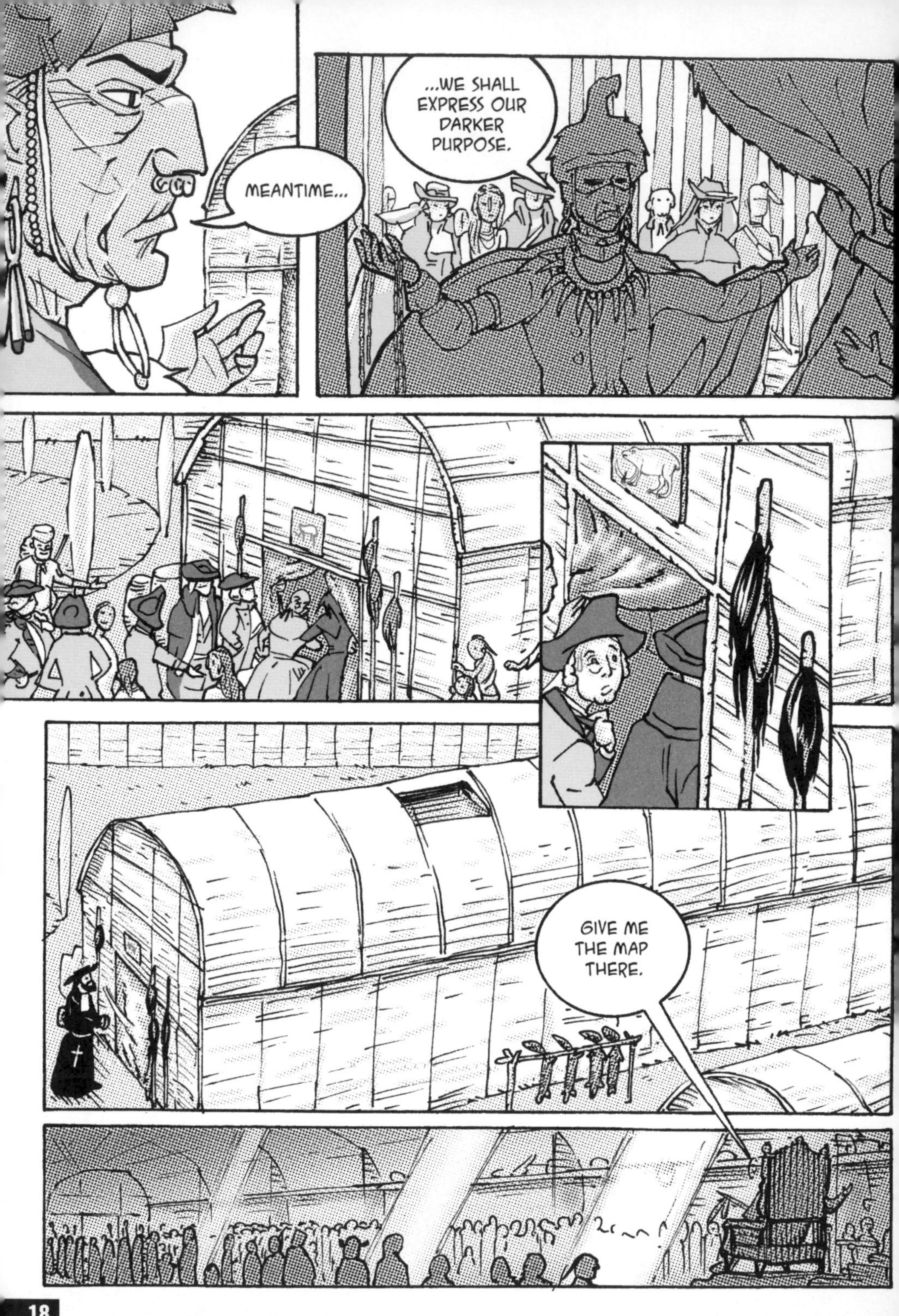
MEANTIME...
...WE SHALL EXPRESS OUR DARKER PURPOSE.
GIVE ME THE MAP THERE.

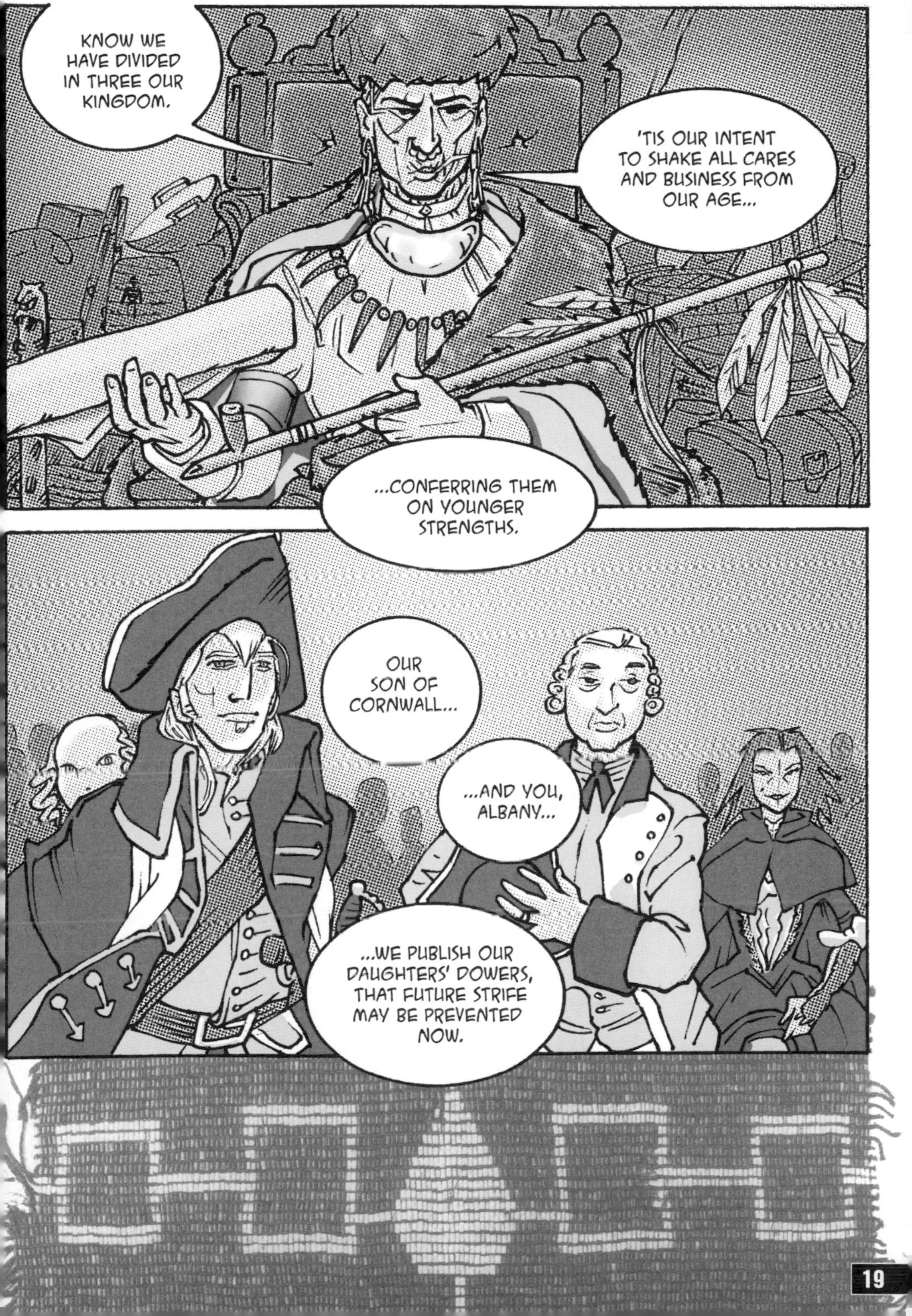
KNOW WE HAVE DIVIDED IN THREE OUR KINGDOM.
'TIS OUR INTENT TO SHAKE ALL CARES AND BUSINESS FROM OUR AGE...
...CONFERRING THEM ON YOUNGER STRENGTHS.
OUR SON OF CORNWALL...
...AND YOU, ALBANY...
...WE PUBLISH OUR DAUGHTERS' DOWERS, THAT FUTURE STRIFE MAY BE PREVENTED NOW.

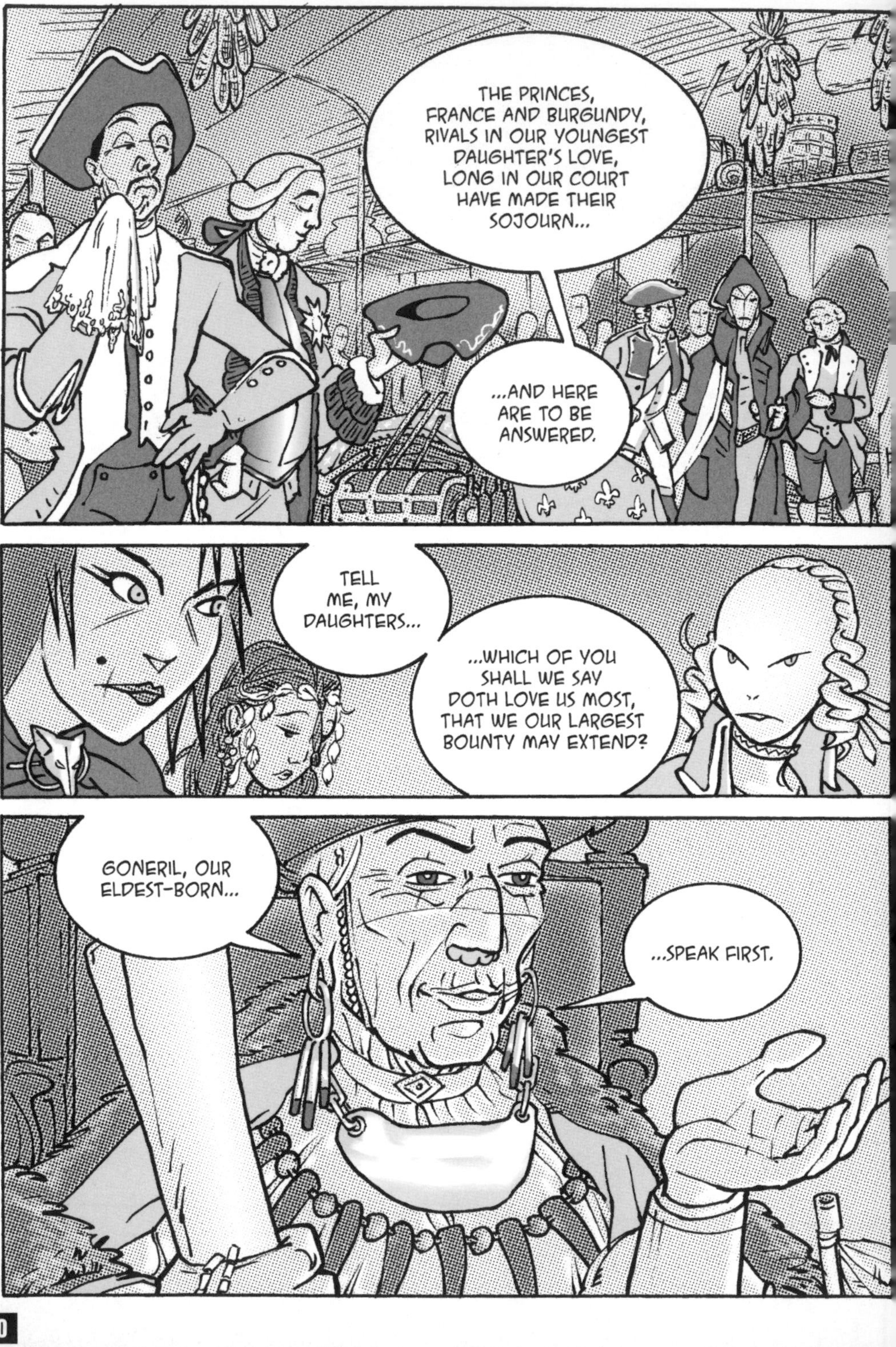
THE PRINCES, FRANCE AND BURGUNDY, RIVALS IN OUR YOUNGEST DAUGHTER'S LOVE, LONG IN OUR COURT HAVE MADE THEIR SOJOURN...
...AND HERE ARE TO BE ANSWERED.
TELL ME, MY DAUGHTERS...
...WHICH OF YOU SHALL WE SAY DOTH LOVE US MOST, THAT WE OUR LARGEST BOUNTY MAY EXTEND?
GONERIL, OUR ELDEST-BORN...
...SPEAK FIRST.

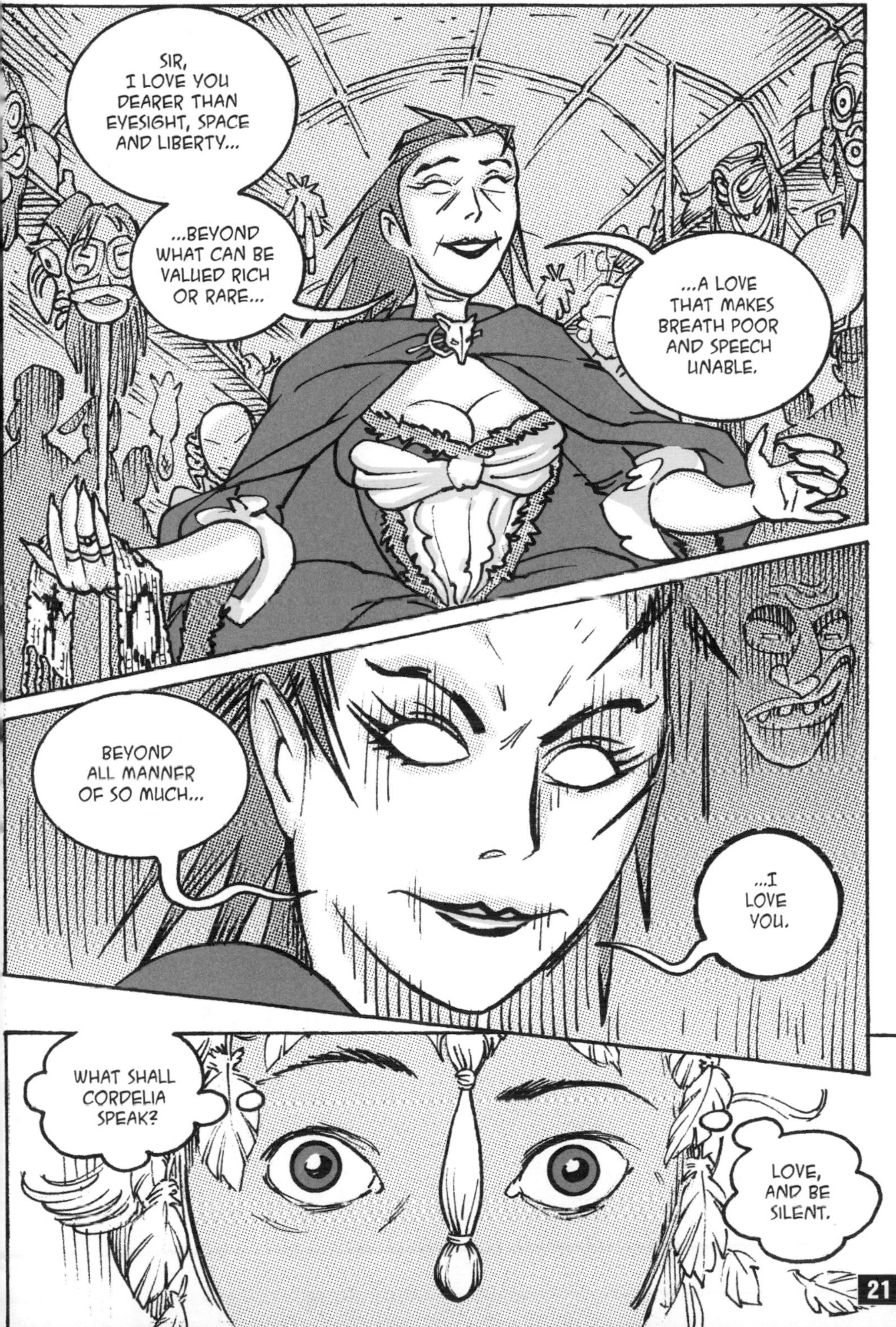
SIR, I LOVE YOU DEARER THAN EYESIGHT, SPACE AND LIBERTY...
...BEYOND WHAT CAN BE VALUED RICH OR RARE...
...A LOVE THAT MAKES BREATH POOR AND SPEECH UNABLE.
BEYOND ALL MANNER OF SO MUCH...
...I LOVE YOU.
WHAT SHALL CORDELIA SPEAK?
LOVE, AND BE SILENT.

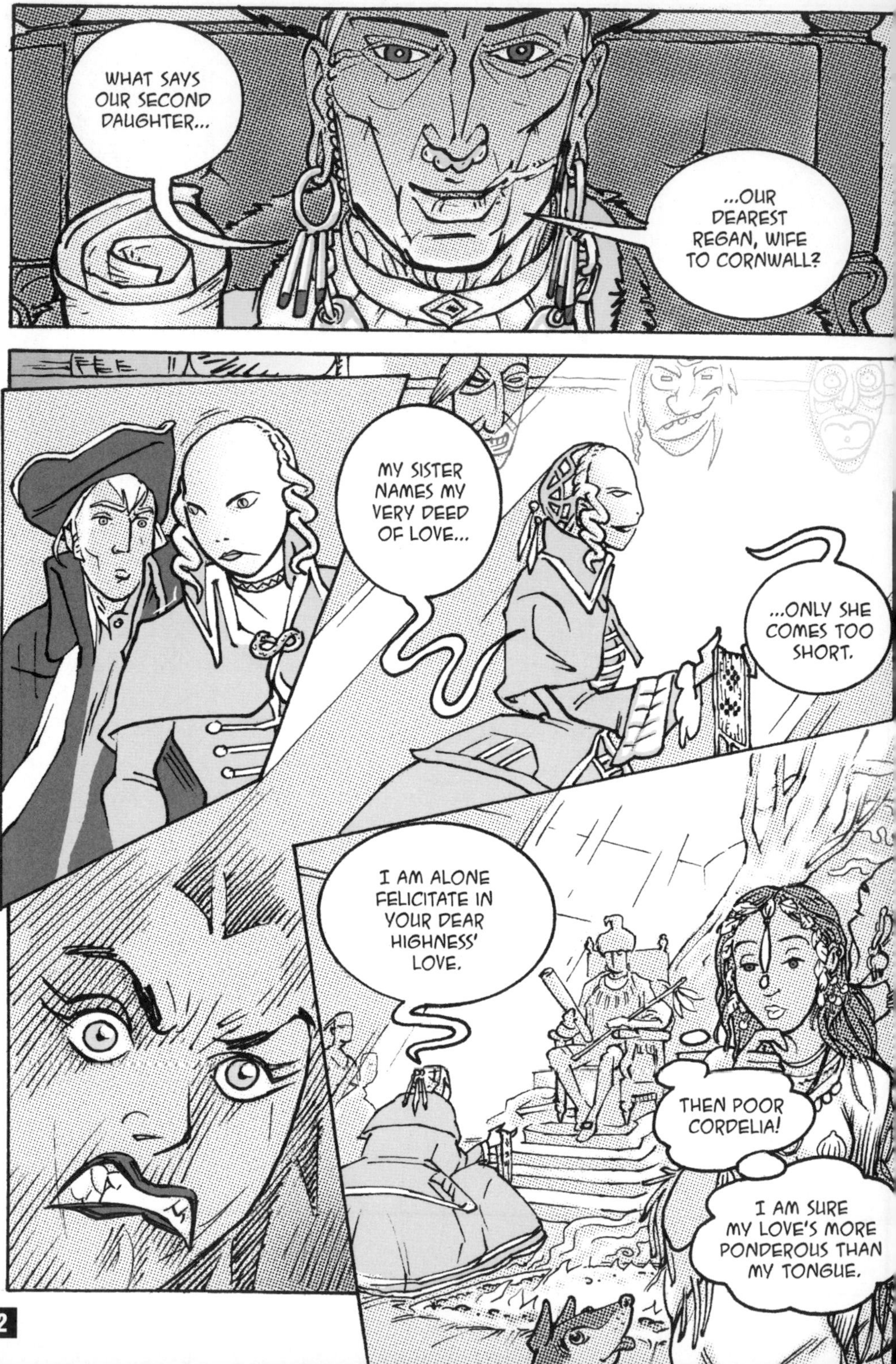
WHAT SAYS OUR SECOND DAUGHTER...
...OUR DEAREST REGAN, WIFE TO CORNWALL?
MY SISTER NAMES MY VERY DEED OF LOVE...
...ONLY SHE COMES TOO SHORT.
I AM ALONE FELICITATE IN YOUR DEAR HIGHNESS' LOVE.
THEN POOR CORDELIA!
I AM SURE MY LOVE'S MORE PONDEROUS THAN MY TONGUE.

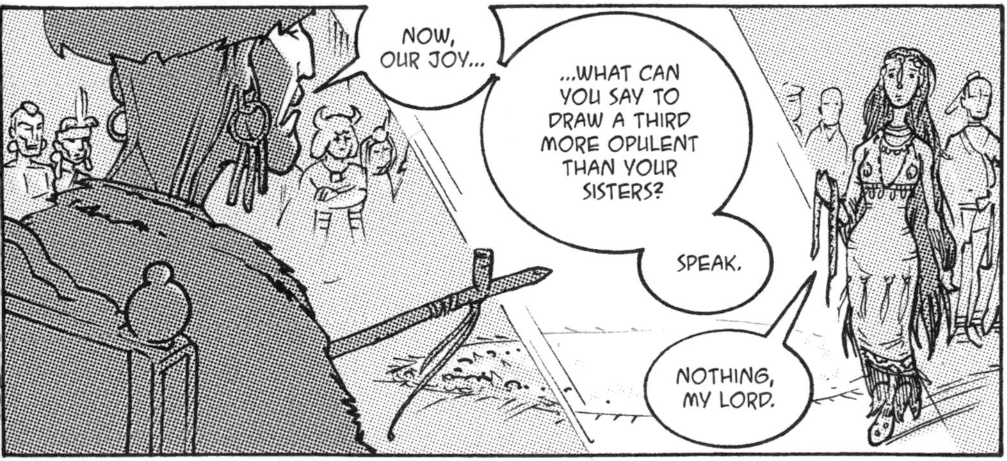
NOW, OUR JOY...
...WHAT CAN YOU SAY TO DRAW A THIRD MORE OPULENT THAN YOUR SISTERS?
SPEAK.
NOTHING, MY LORD.
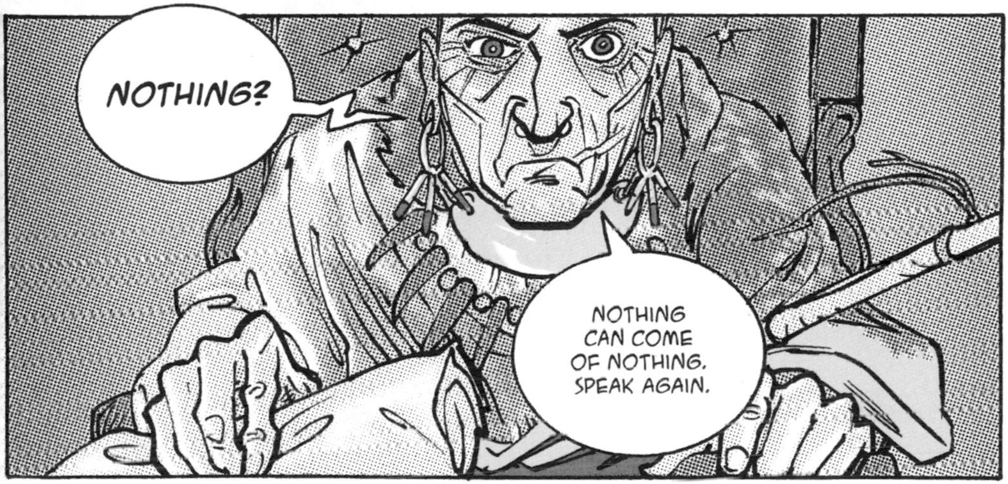
NOTHING?
NOTHING CAN COME OF NOTHING. SPEAK AGAIN.
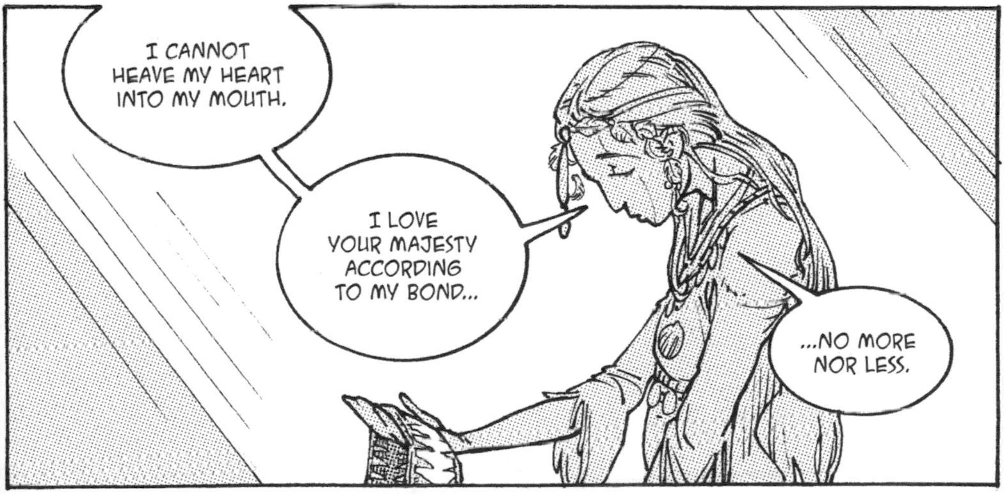
I CANNOT HEAVE MY HEART INTO MY MOUTH.
I LOVE YOUR MAJESTY ACCORDING TO MY BOND...
...NO MORE NOR LESS.

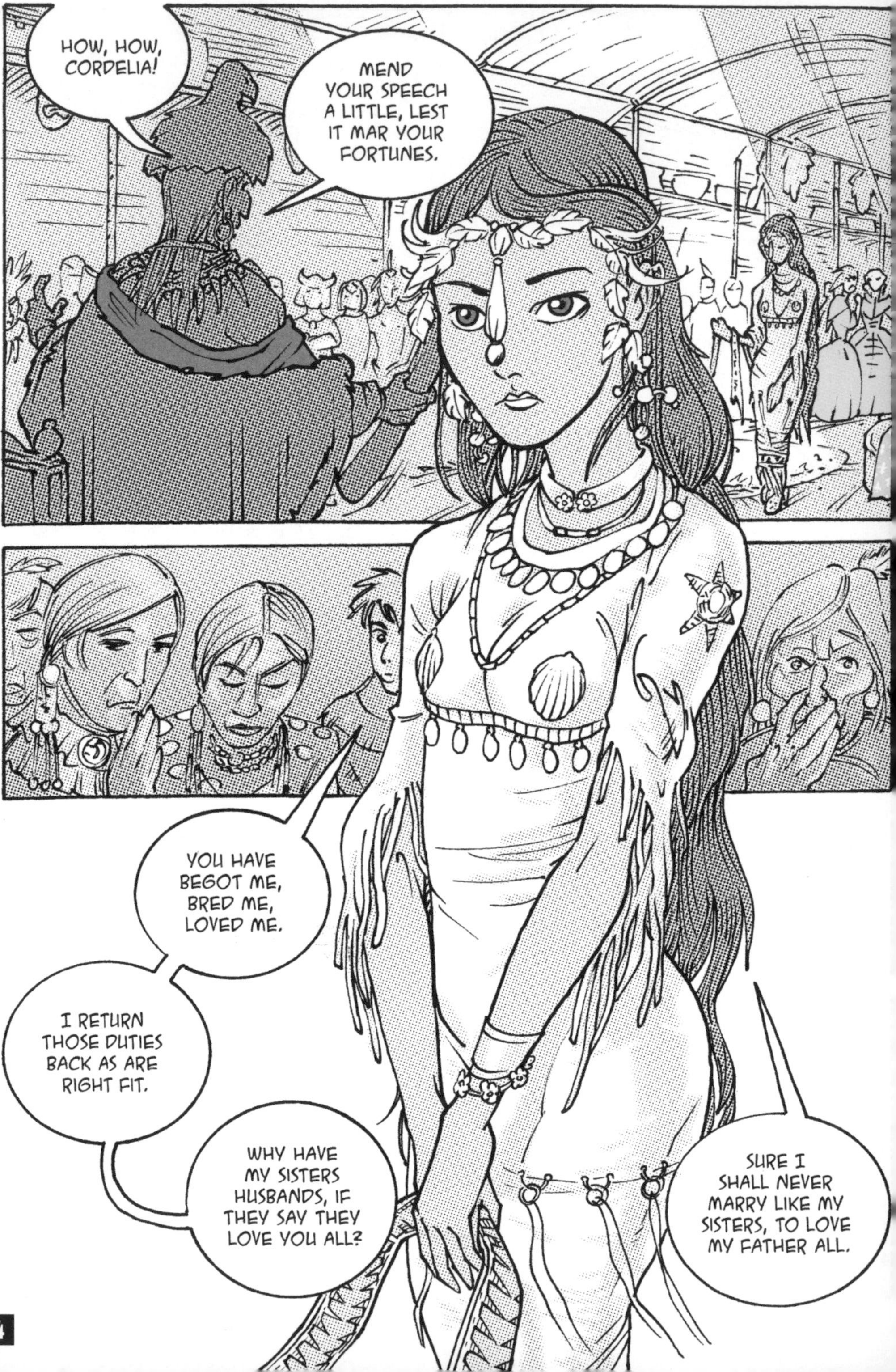
HOW, HOW, CORDELIA!
MEND YOUR SPEECH A LITTLE, LEST IT MAR YOUR FORTUNES.
YOU HAVE BEGOT ME, BRED ME, LOVED ME.
I RETURN THOSE DUTIES BACK AS ARE RIGHT FIT.
WHY HAVE MY SISTERS HUSBANDS, IF THEY SAY THEY LOVE YOU ALL?
SURE I SHALL NEVER MARRY LIKE MY SISTERS, TO LOVE MY FATHER ALL.

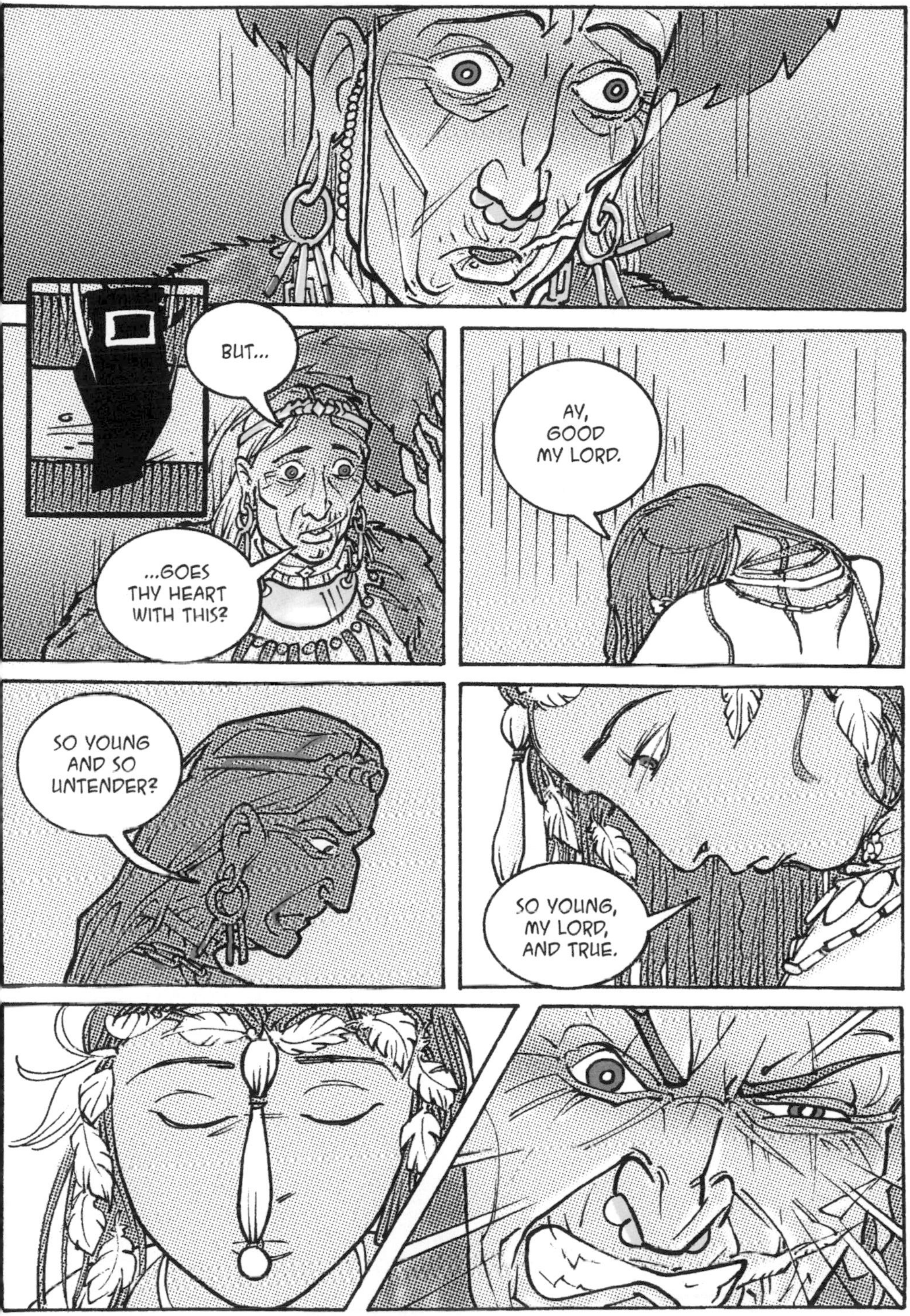
BUT...
...GOES THY HEART WITH THIS?
AY, GOOD MY LORD.
SO YOUNG AND SO UNTENDER?
SO YOUNG, MY LORD, AND TRUE.

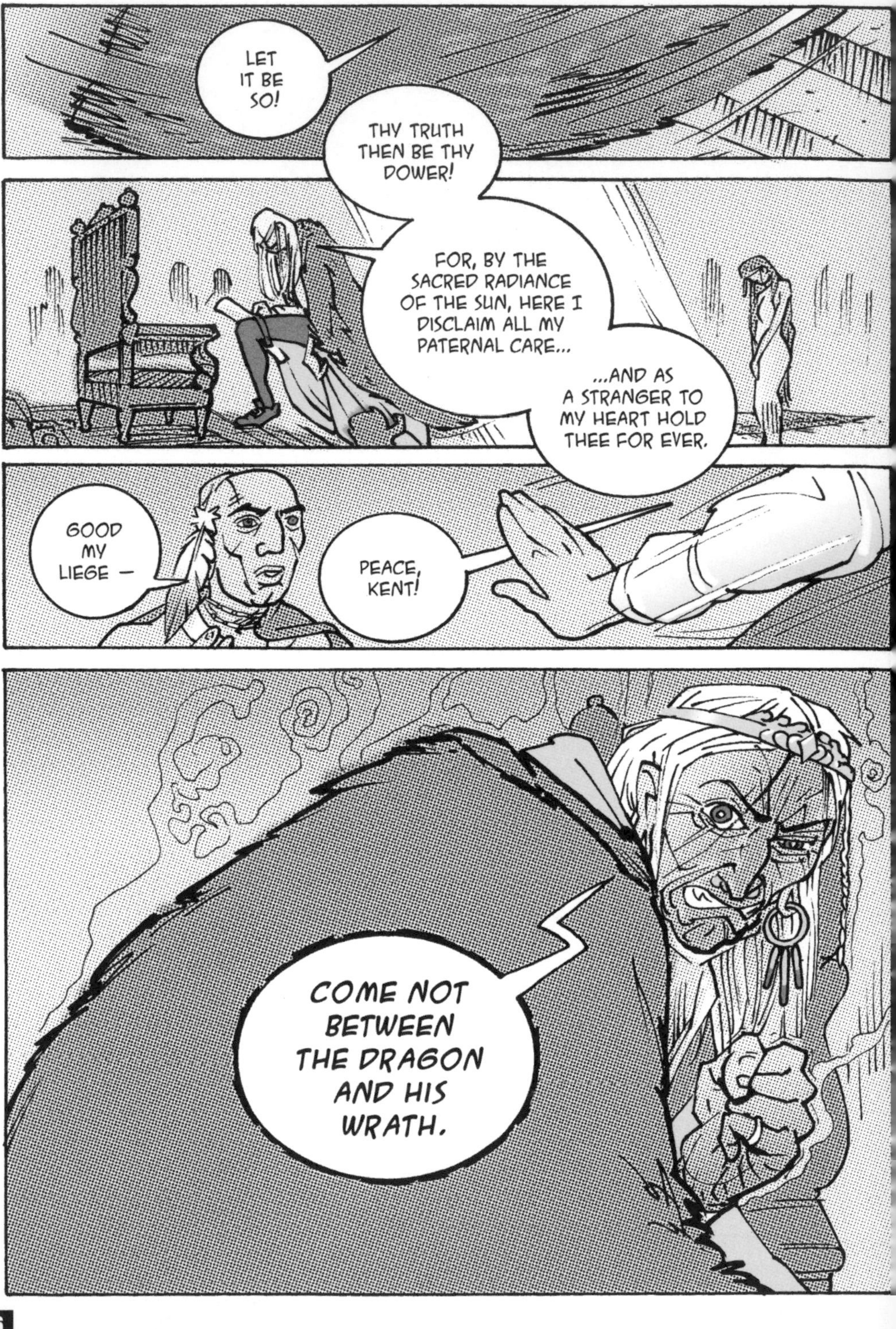
LET IT BE SO!
THY TRUTH THEN BE THY DOWER!
FOR, BY THE SACRED RADIANCE OF THE SUN, HERE I DISCLAIM ALL MY PATERNAL CARE...
...AND AS A STRANGER TO MY HEART HOLD THEE FOR EVER.
GOOD MY LIEGE —
PEACE, KENT!
COME NOT BETWEEN THE DRAGON AND HIS WRATH.

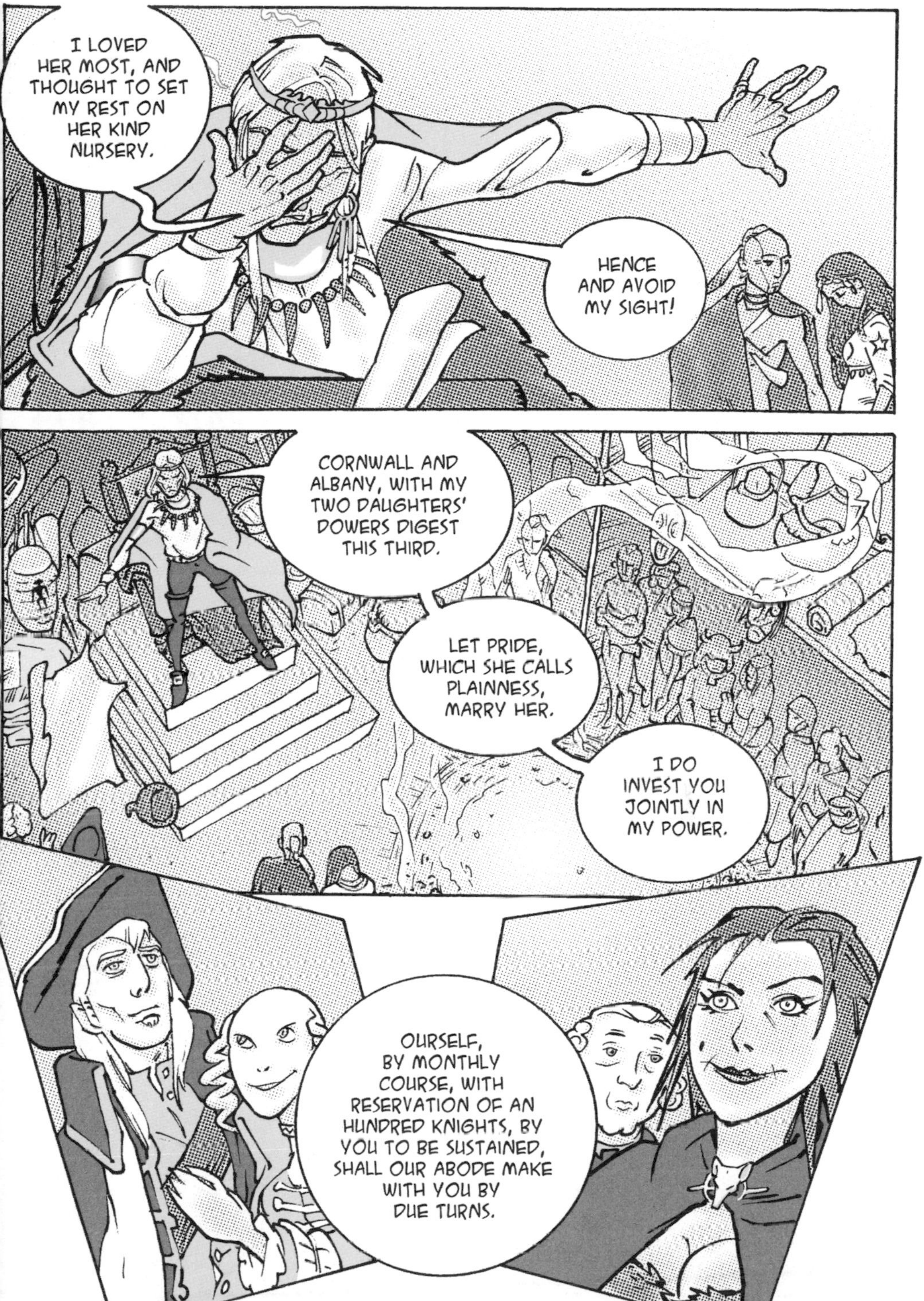
I LOVED HER MOST, AND THOUGHT TO SET MY REST ON HER KIND NURSERY.
HENCE AND AVOID MY SIGHT!
CORNWALL AND ALBANY, WITH MY TWO DAUGHTERS' DOWERS DIGEST THIS THIRD.
LET PRIDE, WHICH SHE CALLS PLAINNESS, MARRY HER.
I DO INVEST YOU JOINTLY IN MY POWER.
OURSELF, BY MONTHLY COURSE, WITH RESERVATION OF AN HUNDRED KNIGHTS, BY YOU TO BE SUSTAINED, SHALL OUR ABODE MAKE WITH YOU BY DUE TURNS.

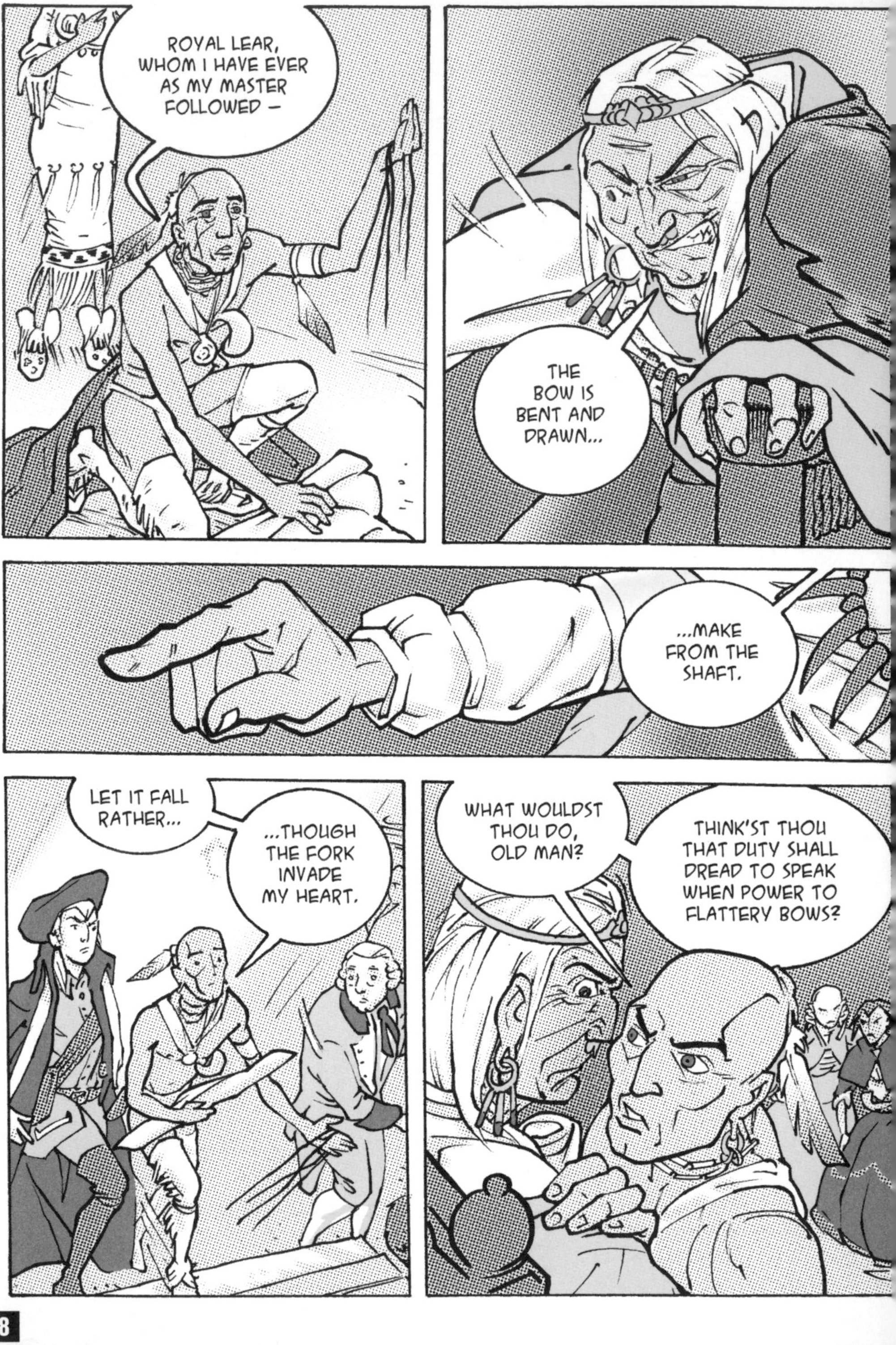
ROYAL LEAR, WHOM I HAVE EVER AS MY MASTER FOLLOWED –
THE BOW IS BENT AND DRAWN...
...MAKE FROM THE SHAFT.
LET IT FALL RATHER...
...THOUGH THE FORK INVADE MY HEART.
WHAT WOULDST THOU DO, OLD MAN?
THINK'ST THOU THAT DUTY SHALL DREAD TO SPEAK WHEN POWER TO FLATTERY BOWS?

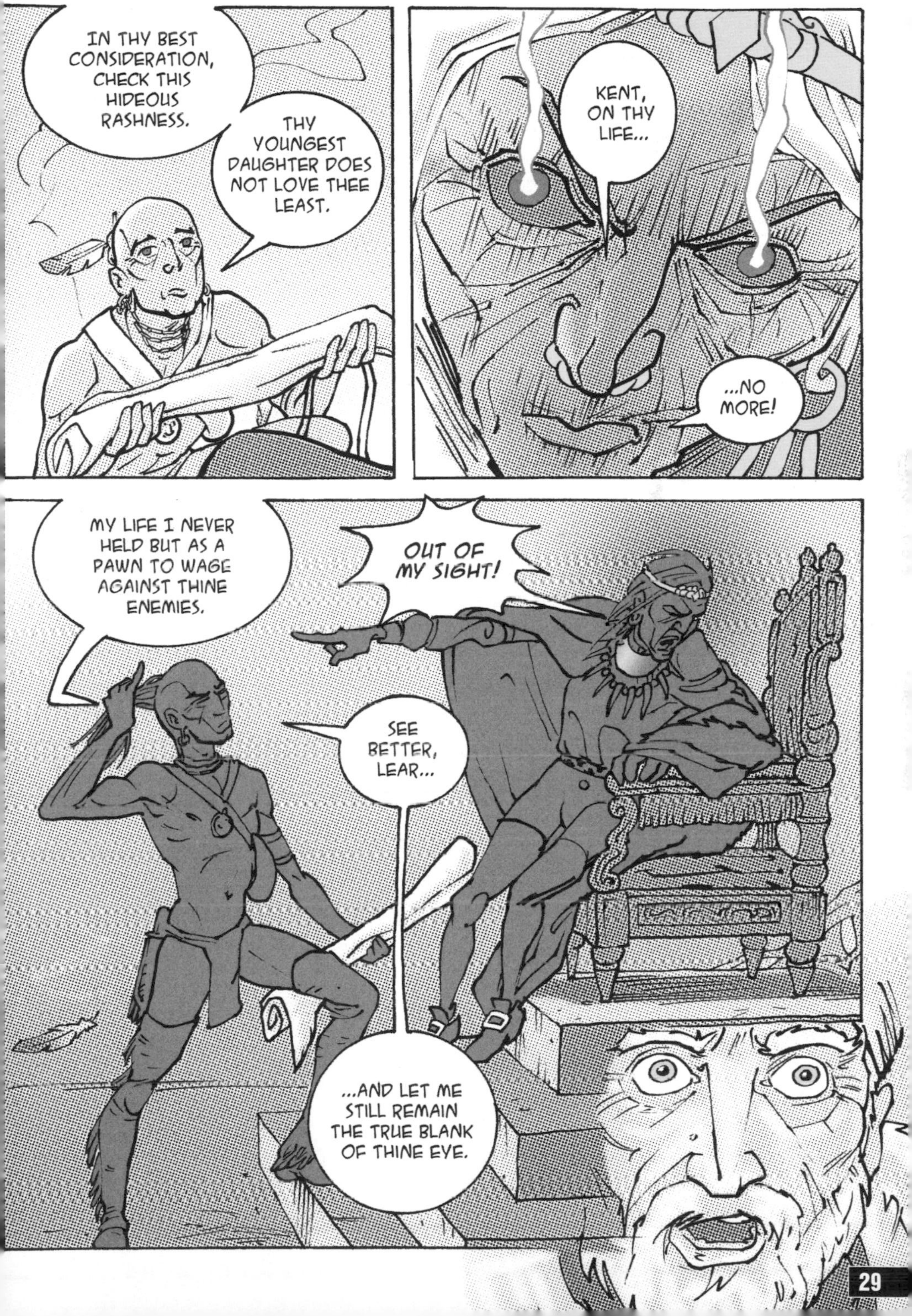
IN THY BEST CONSIDERATION, CHECK THIS HIDEOUS RASHNESS.
THY YOUNGEST DAUGHTER DOES NOT LOVE THEE LEAST.
KENT, ON THY LIFE...
...NO MORE!
MY LIFE I NEVER HELD BUT AS A PAWN TO WAGE AGAINST THINE ENEMIES.
OUT OF MY SIGHT!
SEE BETTER, LEAR...
...AND LET ME STILL REMAIN THE TRUE BLANK OF THINE EYE.

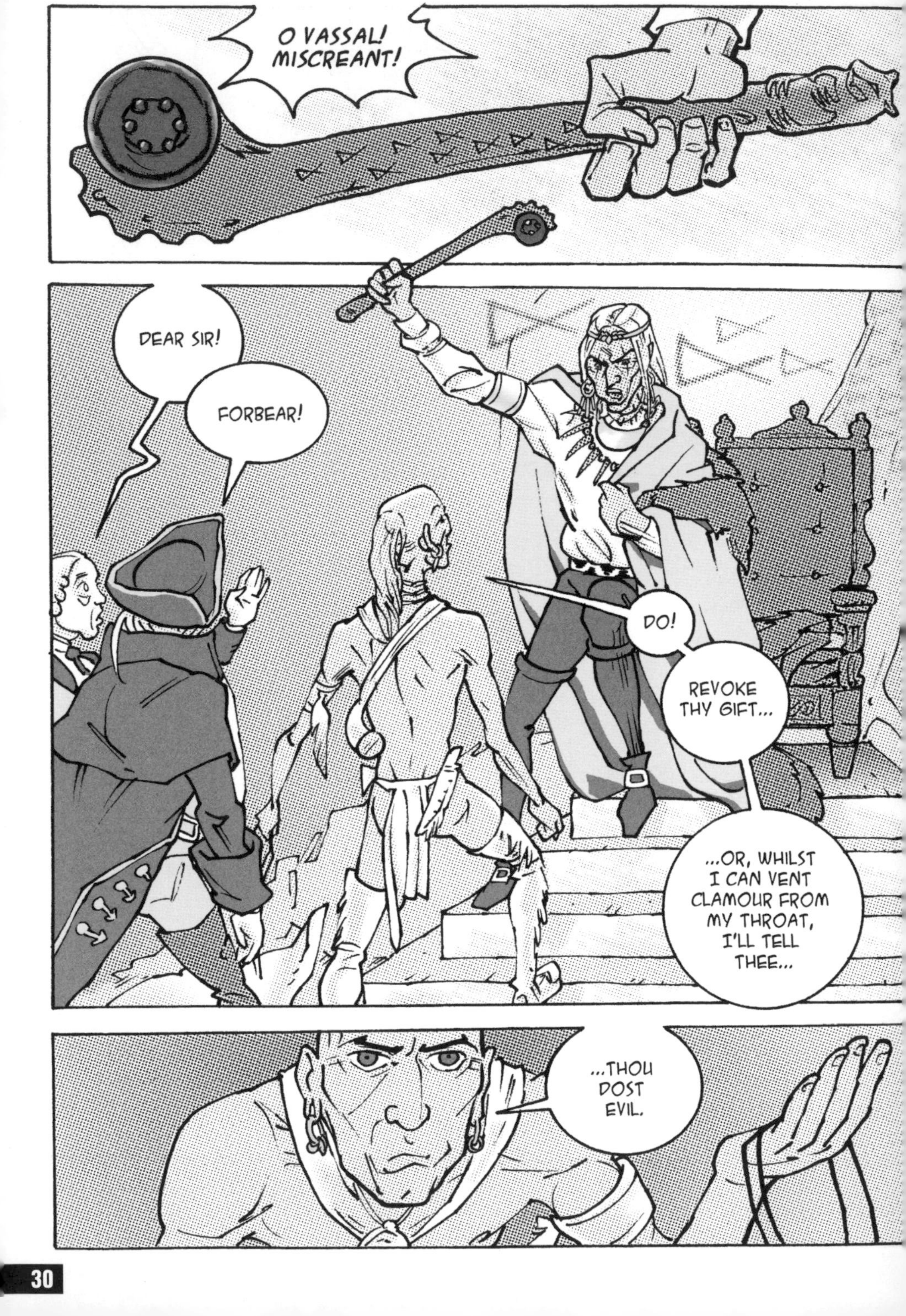
O VASSAL! MISCREANT!
DEAR SIR!
FORBEAR!
DO!
REVOKE THY GIFT...
...OR, WHILST I CAN VENT CLAMOUR FROM MY THROAT, I'LL TELL THEE...
...THOU DOST EVIL.

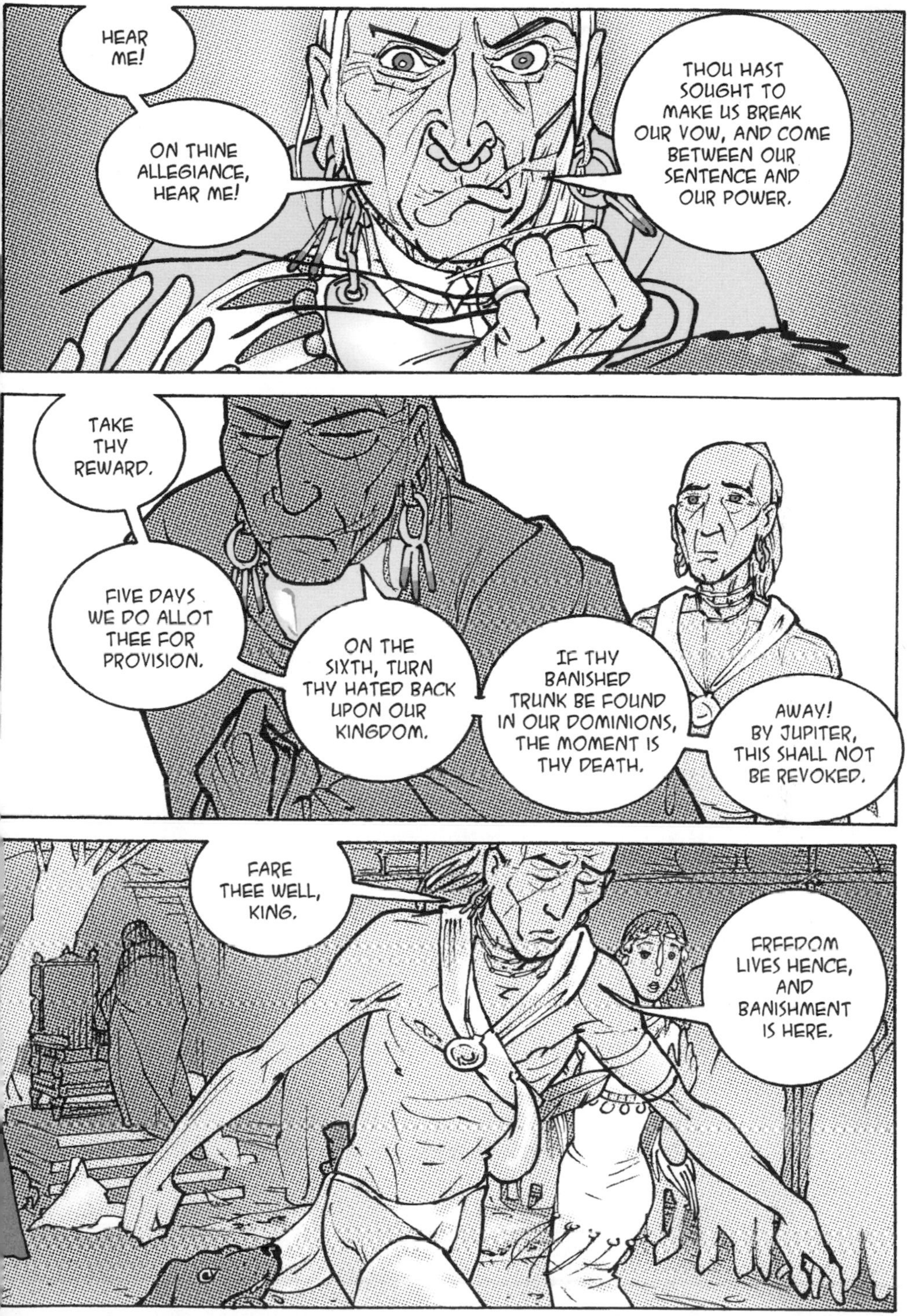
HEAR ME!
ON THINE ALLEGIANCE, HEAR ME!
THOU HAST SOUGHT TO MAKE US BREAK OUR VOW, AND COME BETWEEN OUR SENTENCE AND OUR POWER.
TAKE THY REWARD.
FIVE DAYS WE DO ALLOT THEE FOR PROVISION.
ON THE SIXTH, TURN THY HATED BACK UPON OUR KINGDOM.
IF THY BANISHED TRUNK BE FOUND IN OUR DOMINIONS, THE MOMENT IS THY DEATH.
AWAY! BY JUPITER, THIS SHALL NOT BE REVOKED.
FARE THEE WELL, KING.
FREEDOM LIVES HENCE, AND BANISHMENT IS HERE.

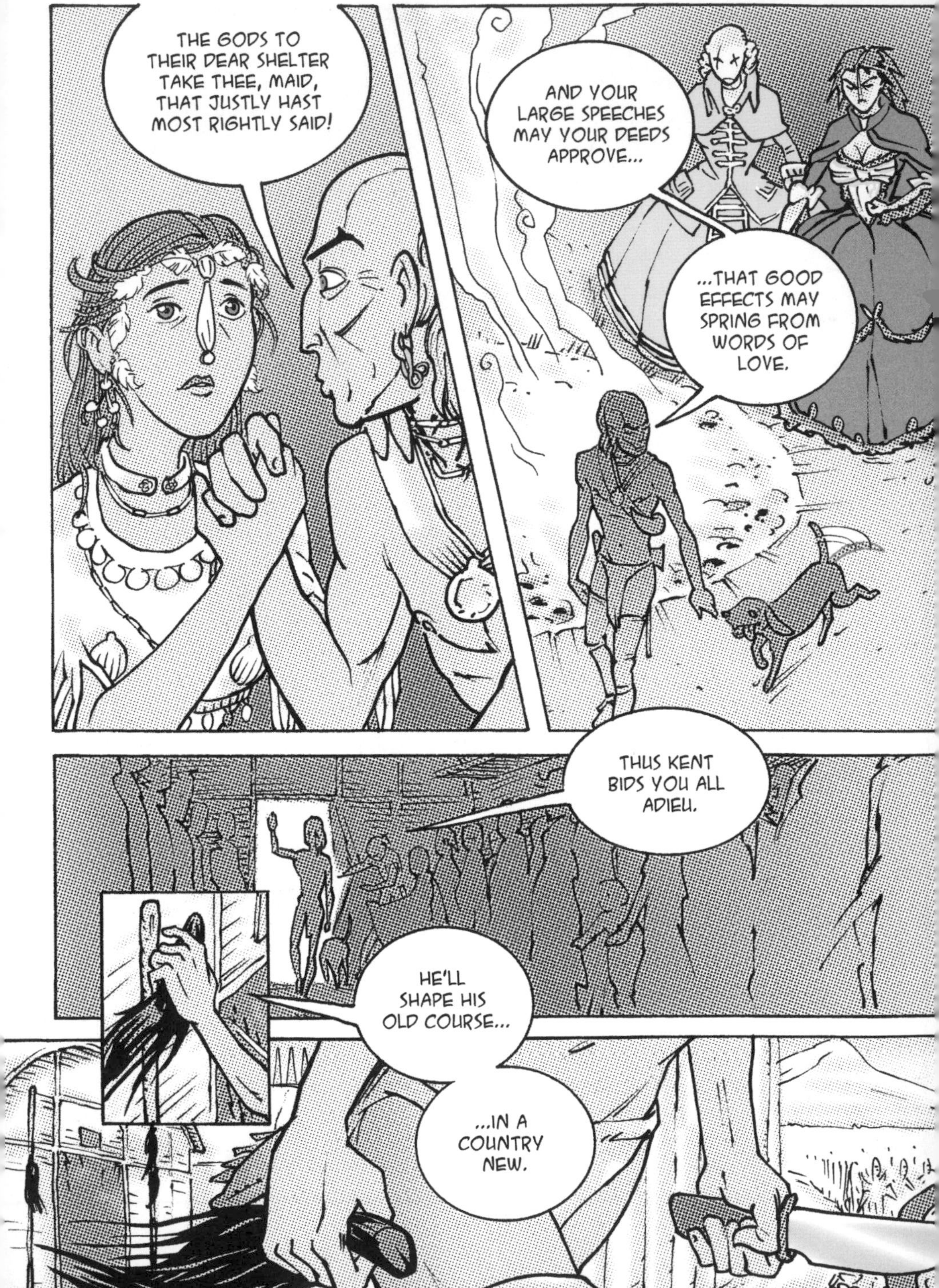
THE GODS TO THEIR DEAR SHELTER TAKE THEE, MAID, THAT JUSTLY HAST MOST RIGHTLY SAID!
AND YOUR LARGE SPEECHES MAY YOUR DEEDS APPROVE...
...THAT GOOD EFFECTS MAY SPRING FROM WORDS OF LOVE.
THUS KENT BIDS YOU ALL ADIEU.
HE'LL SHAPE HIS OLD COURSE...
...IN A COUNTRY NEW.

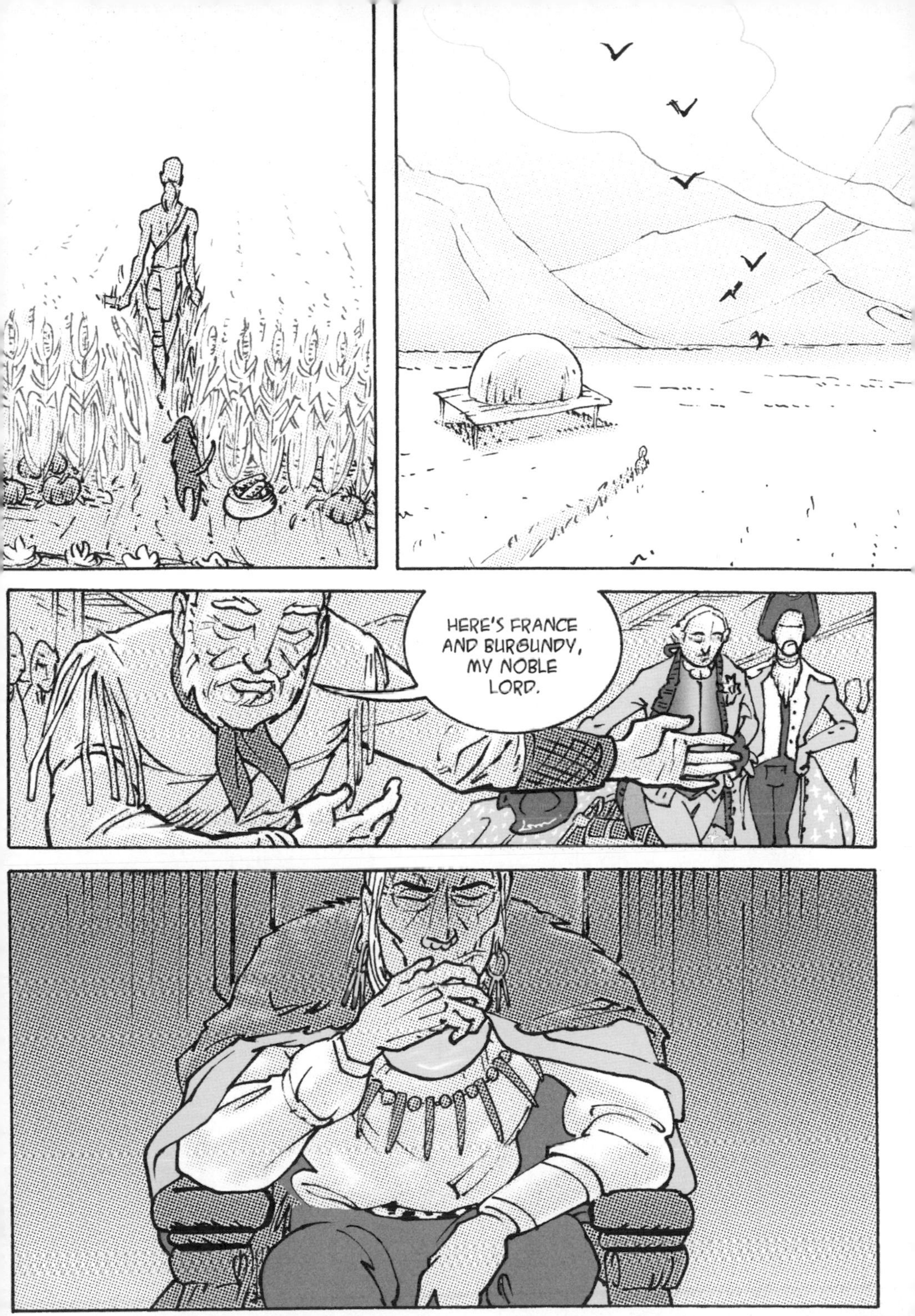
HERE'S FRANCE AND BURGUNDY, MY NOBLE LORD.

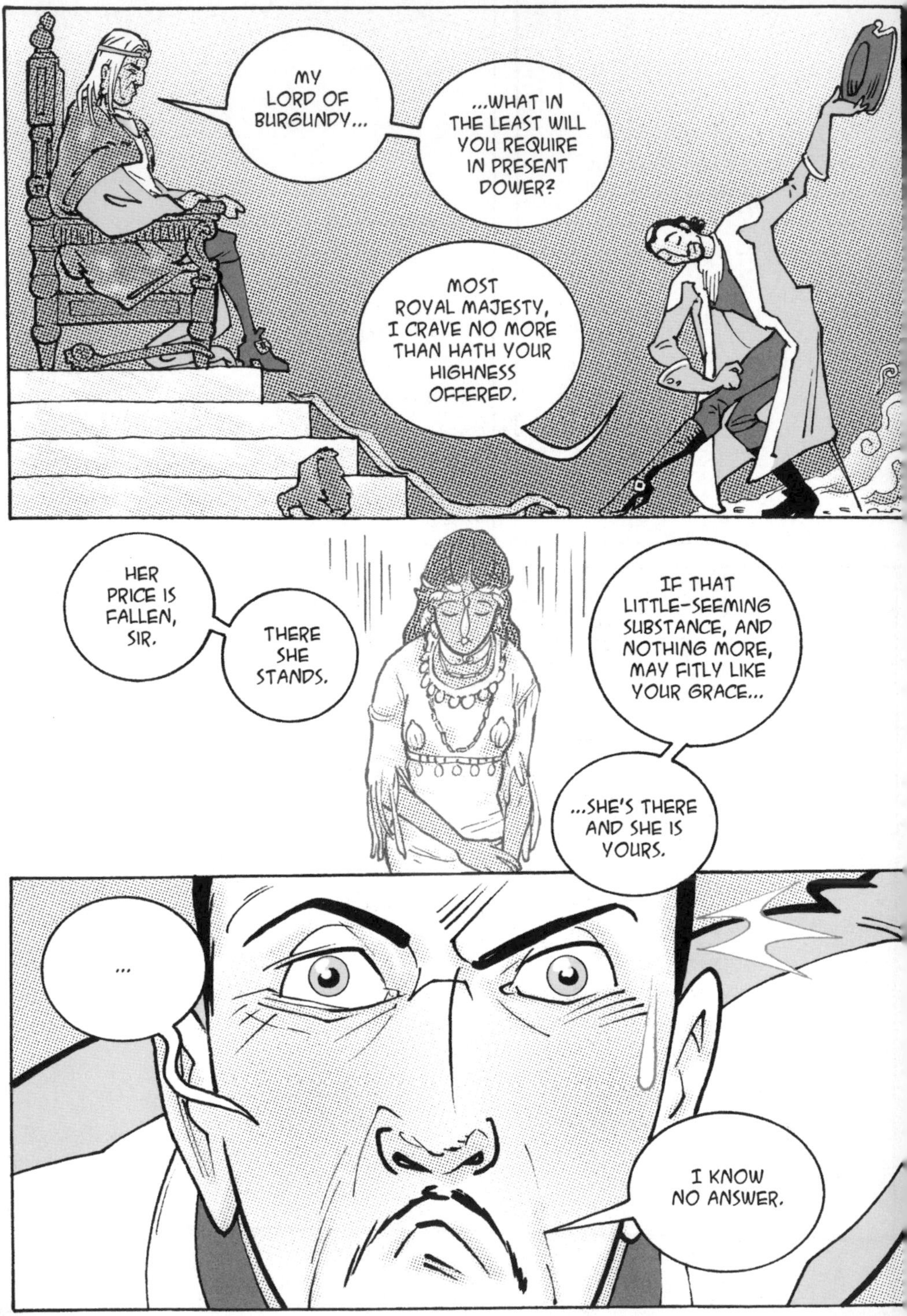
MY LORD OF BURGUNDY...
...WHAT IN THE LEAST WILL YOU REQUIRE IN PRESENT DOWER?
MOST ROYAL MAJESTY, I CRAVE NO MORE THAN HATH YOUR HIGHNESS OFFERED.
HER PRICE IS FALLEN, SIR.
THERE SHE STANDS.
IF THAT LITTLE-SEEMING SUBSTANCE, AND NOTHING MORE, MAY FITLY LIKE YOUR GRACE...
...SHE'S THERE AND SHE IS YOURS.
...
I KNOW NO ANSWER.

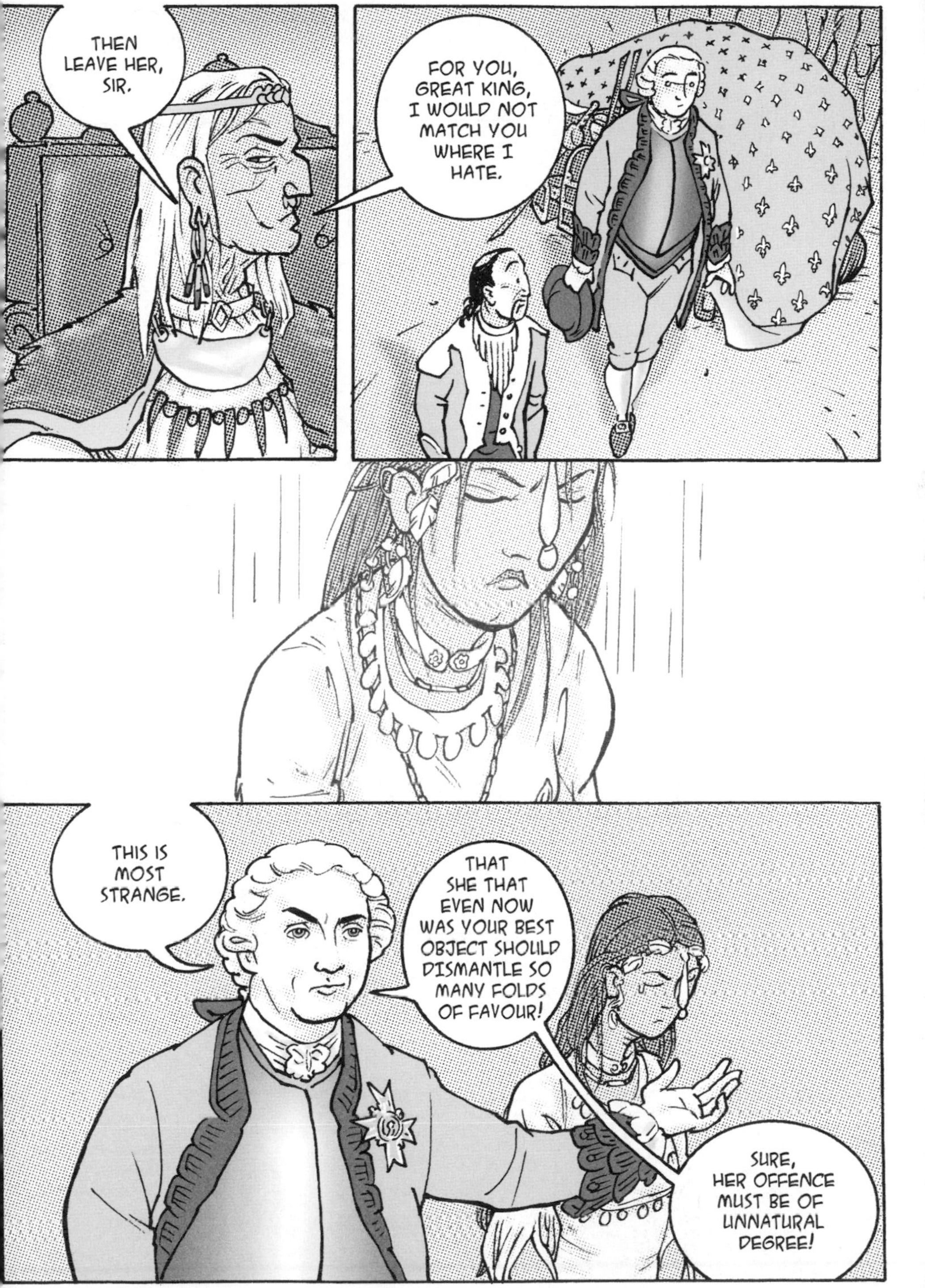
THEN LEAVE HER, SIR.
FOR YOU, GREAT KING, I WOULD NOT MATCH YOU WHERE I HATE.
THIS IS MOST STRANGE.
THAT SHE THAT EVEN NOW WAS YOUR BEST OBJECT SHOULD DISMANTLE SO MANY FOLDS OF FAVOUR!
SURE, HER OFFENCE MUST BE OF UNNATURAL DEGREE!

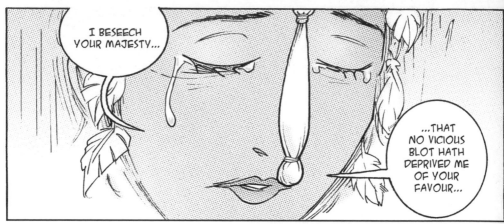

I BESEECH YOUR MAJESTY...

...THAT NO VICIOUS BLOT HATH DEPRIVED ME OF YOUR FAVOUR...

...BUT FOR WANT OF SUCH A TONGUE AS I AM GLAD I HAVE NOT, THOUGH NOT TO HAVE IT HATH LOST ME IN YOUR LIKING.

BETTER THOU HADST NOT BEEN BORN THAN NOT TO HAVE PLEASED ME BETTER.

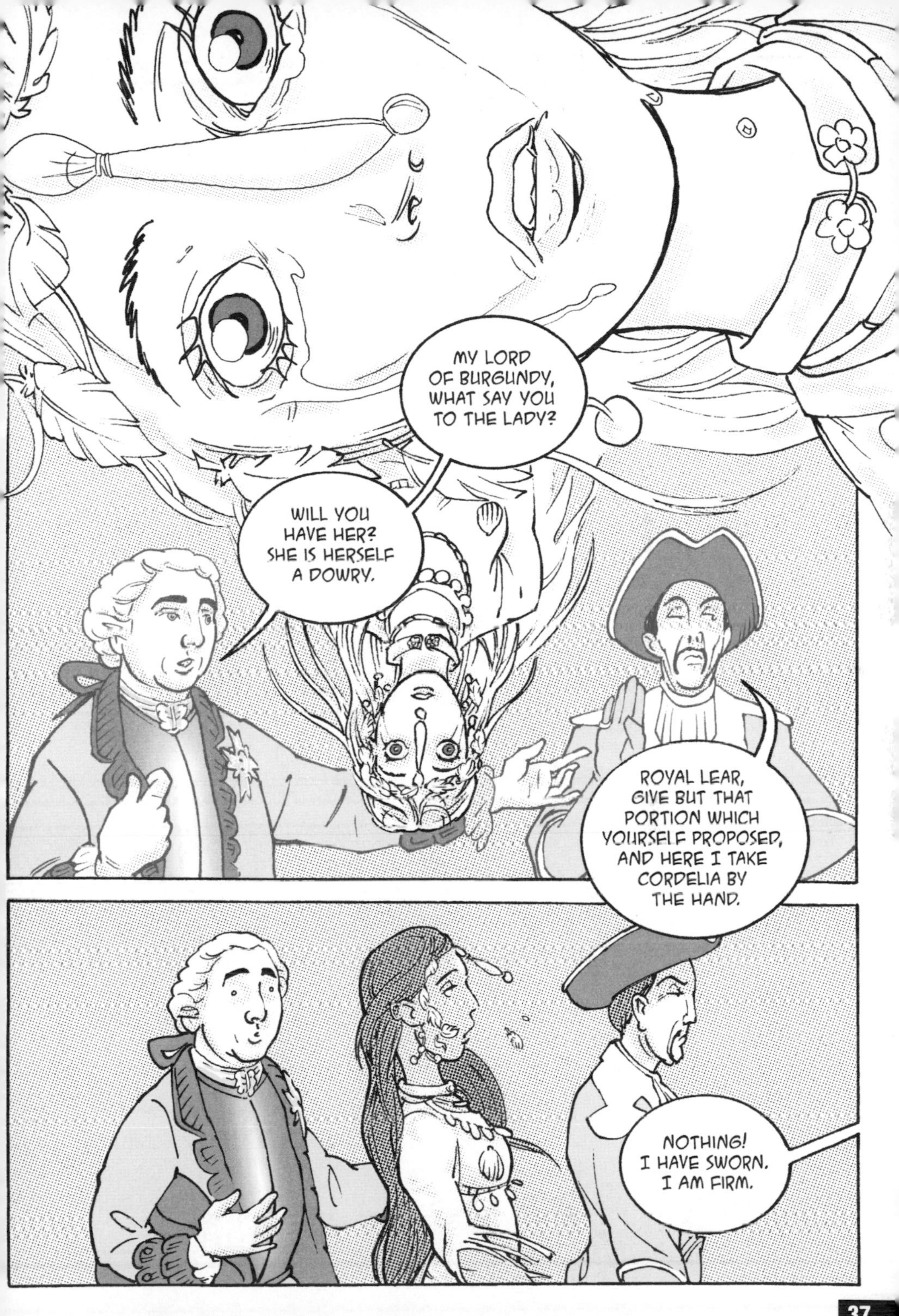
MY LORD OF BURGUNDY, WHAT SAY YOU TO THE LADY?
WILL YOU HAVE HER? SHE IS HERSELF A DOWRY.
ROYAL LEAR, GIVE BUT THAT PORTION WHICH YOURSELF PROPOSED, AND HERE I TAKE CORDELIA BY THE HAND.
NOTHING! I HAVE SWORN. I AM FIRM.

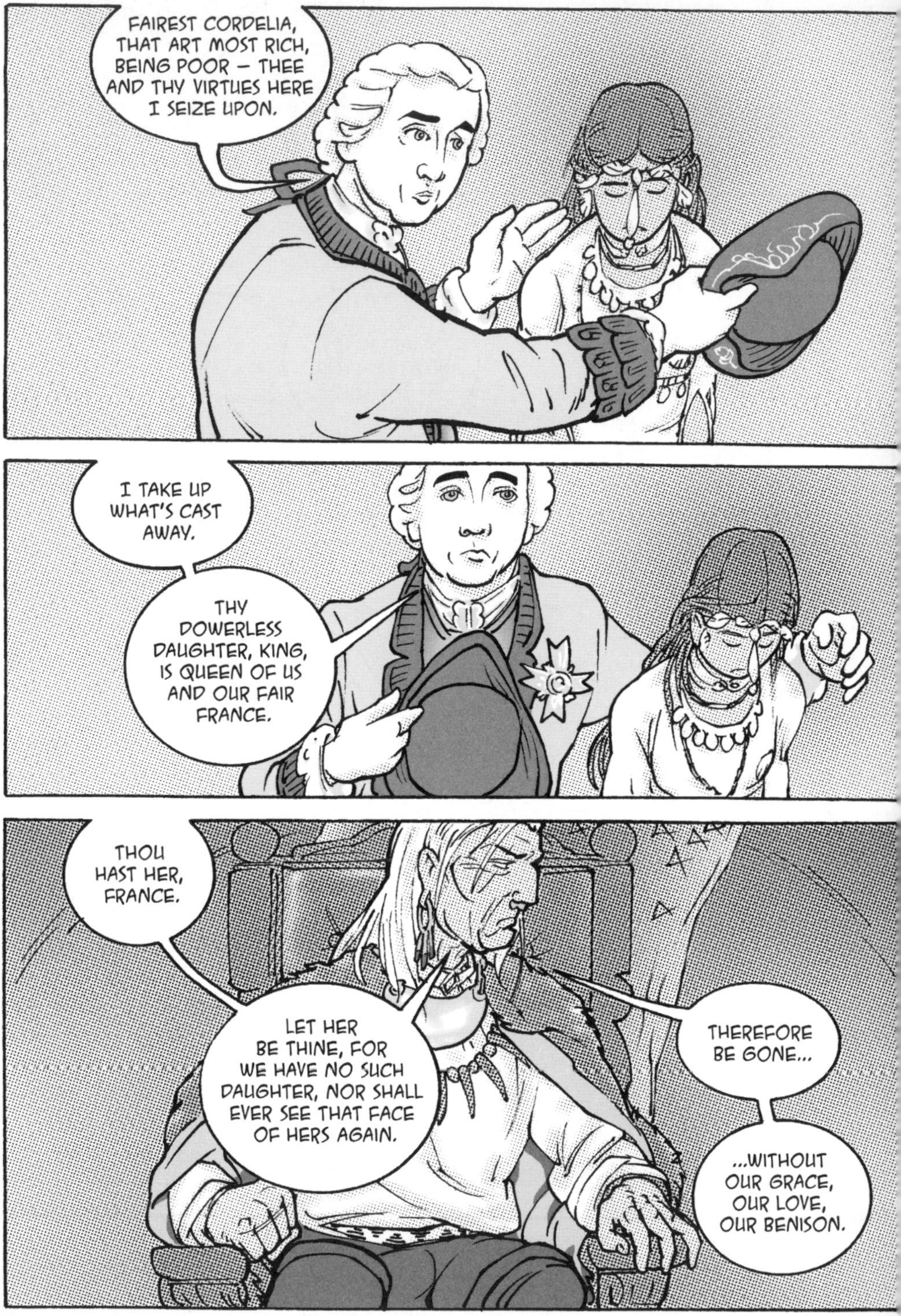
FAIREST CORDELIA, THAT ART MOST RICH, BEING POOR – THEE AND THY VIRTUES HERE I SEIZE UPON.
I TAKE UP WHAT'S CAST AWAY.
THY DOWERLESS DAUGHTER, KING, IS QUEEN OF US AND OUR FAIR FRANCE.
THOU HAST HER, FRANCE.
LET HER BE THINE, FOR WE HAVE NO SUCH DAUGHTER, NOR SHALL EVER SEE THAT FACE OF HERS AGAIN.
THEREFORE BE GONE...
...WITHOUT OUR GRACE, OUR LOVE, OUR BENISON.

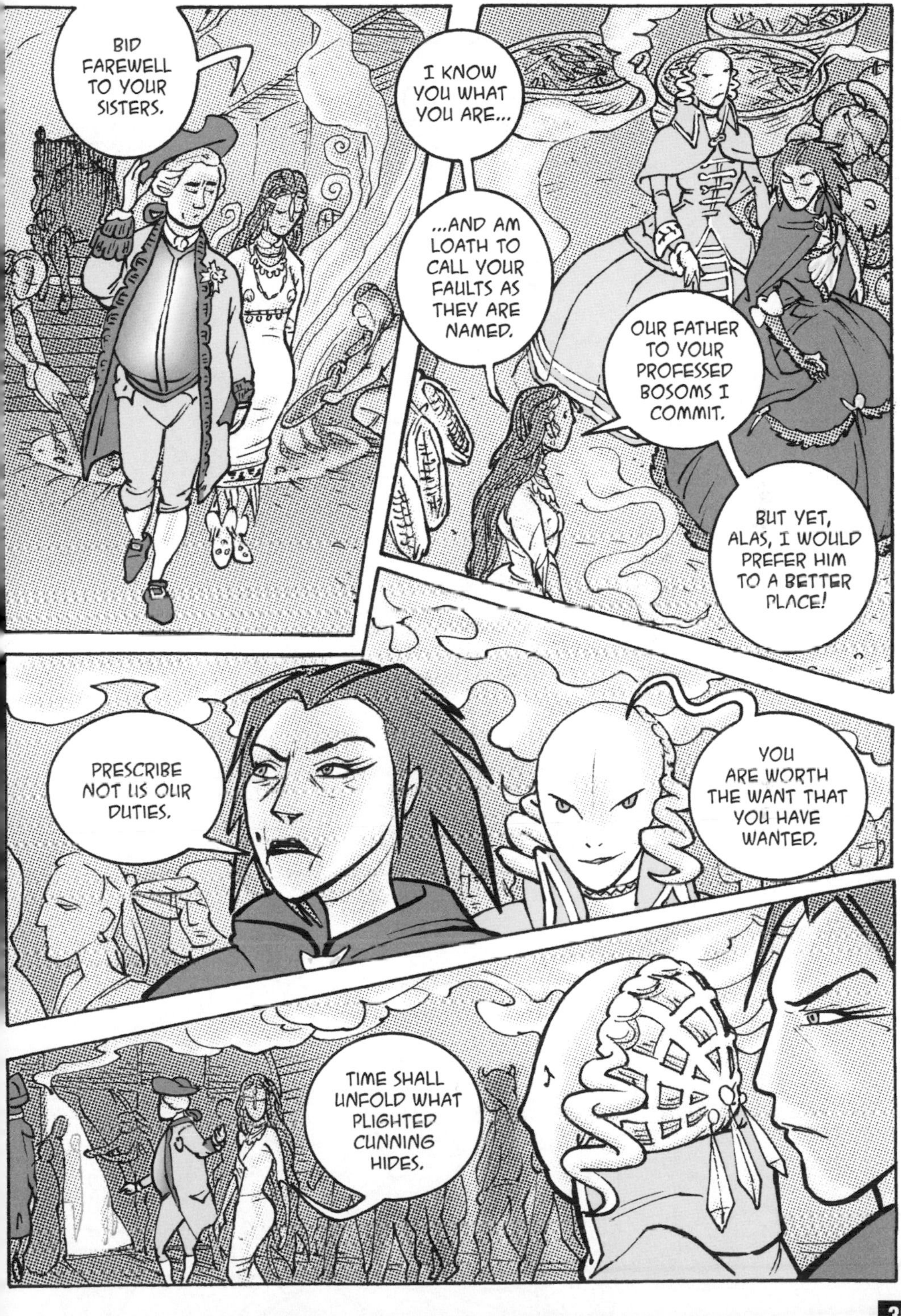
BID FAREWELL TO YOUR SISTERS.
I KNOW YOU WHAT YOU ARE...
...AND AM LOATH TO CALL YOUR FAULTS AS THEY ARE NAMED.
OUR FATHER TO YOUR PROFESSED BOSOMS I COMMIT.
BUT YET, ALAS, I WOULD PREFER HIM TO A BETTER PLACE!
PRESCRIBE NOT US OUR DUTIES.
YOU ARE WORTH THE WANT THAT YOU HAVE WANTED.
TIME SHALL UNFOLD WHAT PLIGHTED CUNNING HIDES.

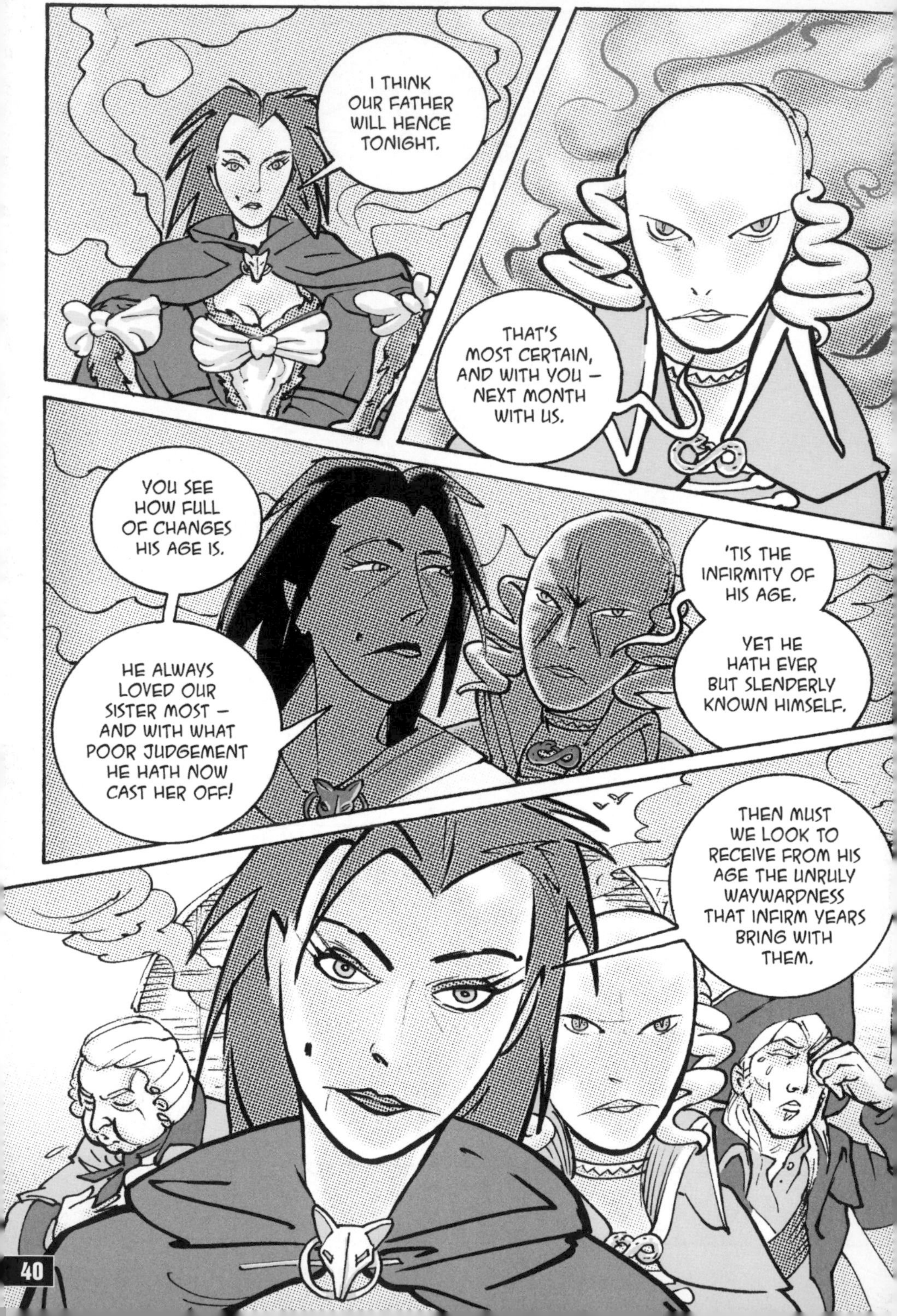
I THINK OUR FATHER WILL HENCE TONIGHT.
THAT'S MOST CERTAIN, AND WITH YOU – NEXT MONTH WITH US.
YOU SEE HOW FULL OF CHANGES HIS AGE IS.
HE ALWAYS LOVED OUR SISTER MOST – AND WITH WHAT POOR JUDGEMENT HE HATH NOW CAST HER OFF!
'TIS THE INFIRMITY OF HIS AGE.
YET HE HATH EVER BUT SLENDERLY KNOWN HIMSELF.
THEN MUST WE LOOK TO RECEIVE FROM HIS AGE THE UNRULY WAYWARDNESS THAT INFIRM YEARS BRING WITH THEM.

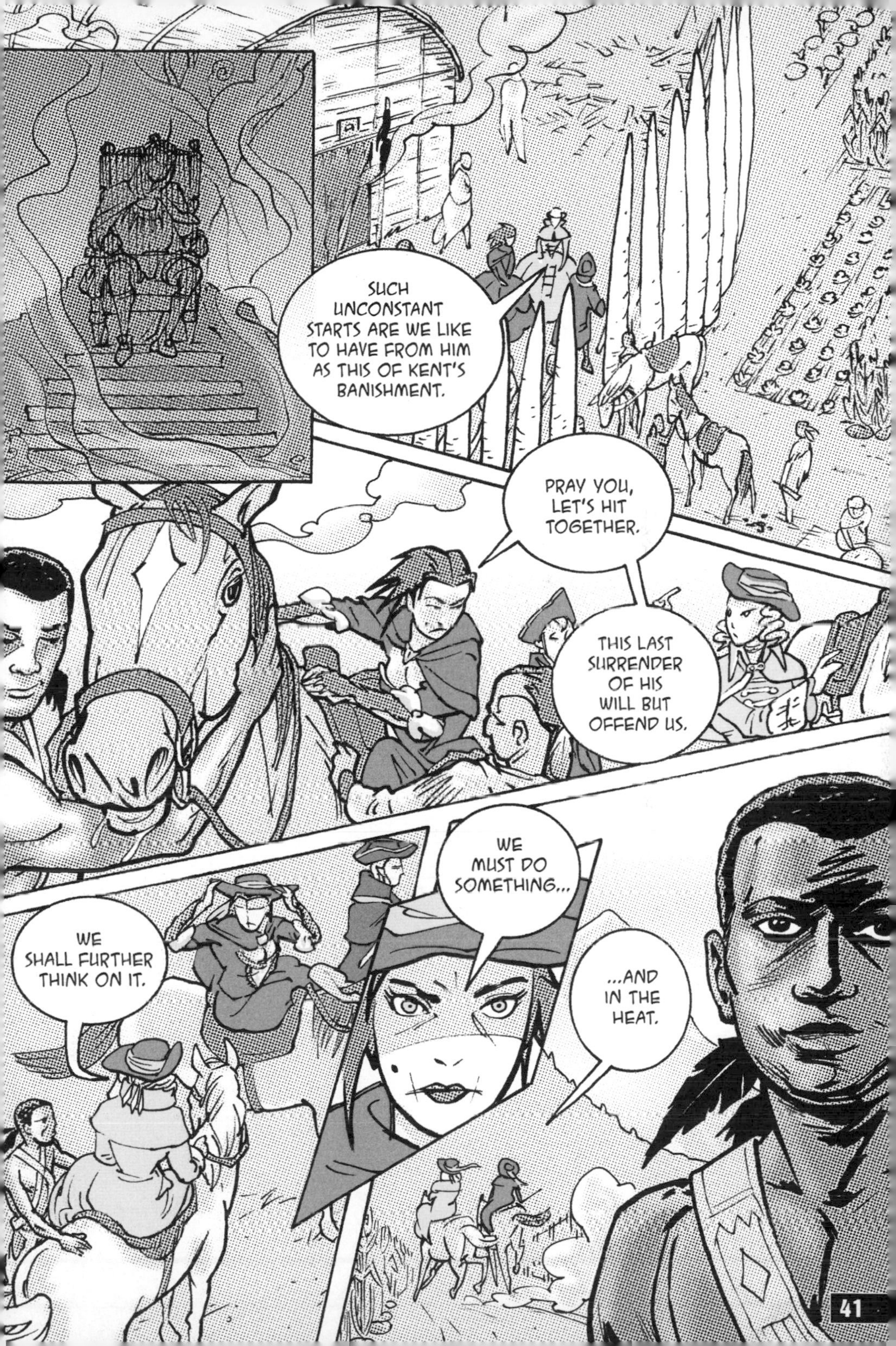
SUCH UNCONSTANT STARTS ARE WE LIKE TO HAVE FROM HIM AS THIS OF KENT'S BANISHMENT.
PRAY YOU, LET'S HIT TOGETHER.
THIS LAST SURRENDER OF HIS WILL BUT OFFEND US.
WE SHALL FURTHER THINK ON IT.
WE MUST DO SOMETHING...
...AND IN THE HEAT.

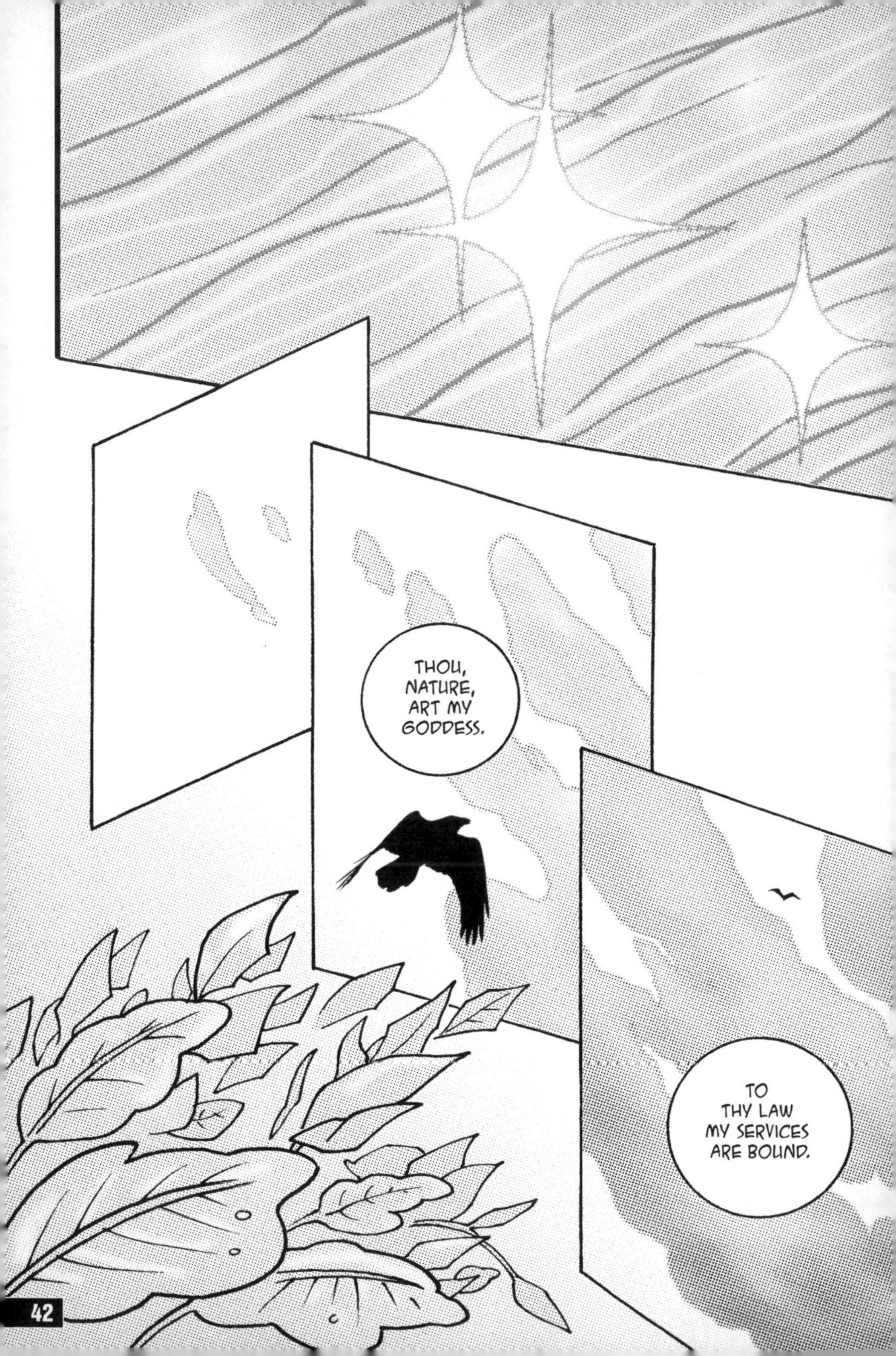
THOU, NATURE, ART MY GODDESS.
TO THY LAW MY SERVICES ARE BOUND.

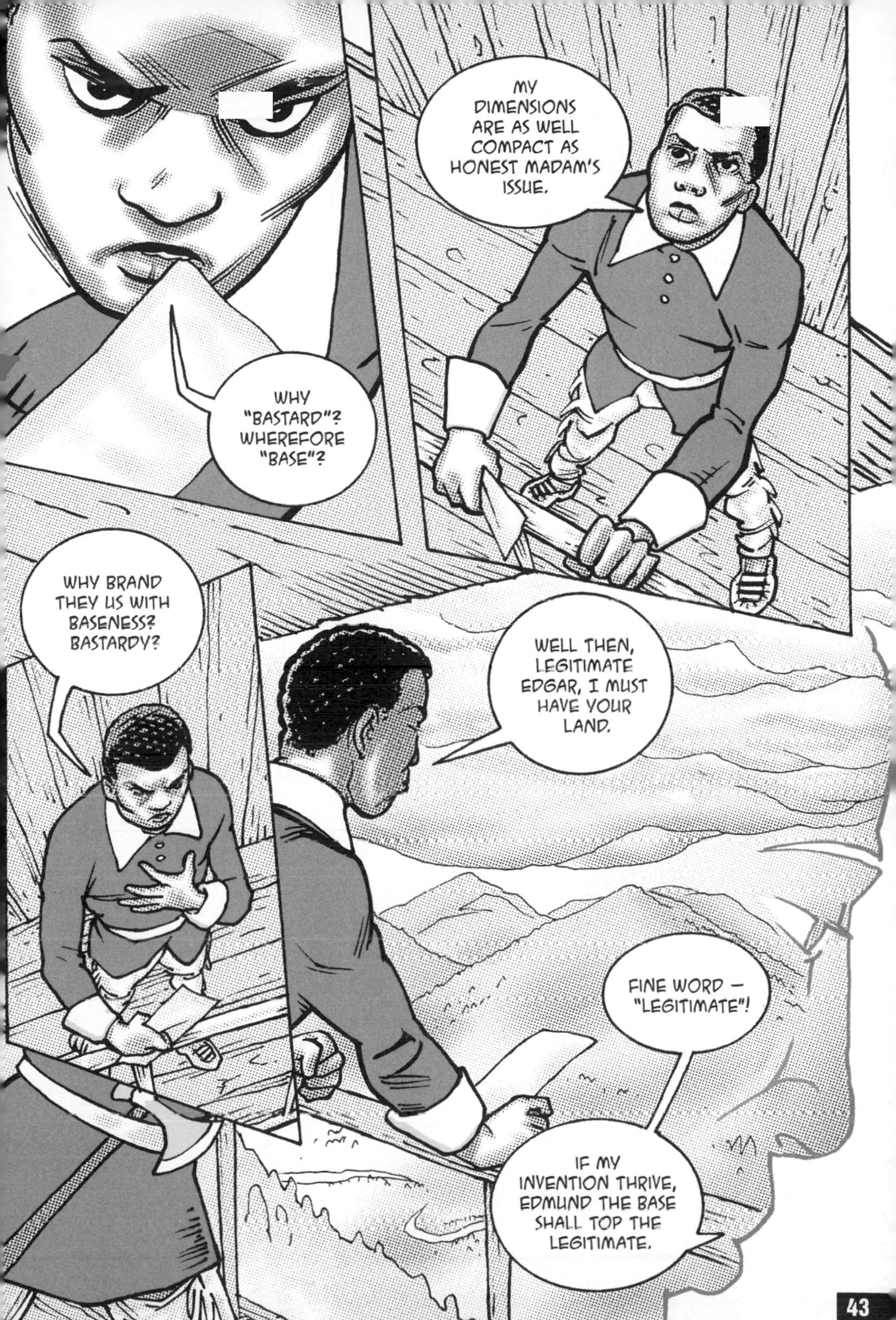
WHY "BASTARD"? WHEREFORE "BASE"?
MY DIMENSIONS ARE AS WELL COMPACT AS HONEST MADAM'S ISSUE.
WHY BRAND THEY US WITH BASENESS? BASTARDY?
WELL THEN, LEGITIMATE EDGAR, I MUST HAVE YOUR LAND.
FINE WORD — "LEGITIMATE"!
IF MY INVENTION THRIVE, EDMUND THE BASE SHALL TOP THE LEGITIMATE.

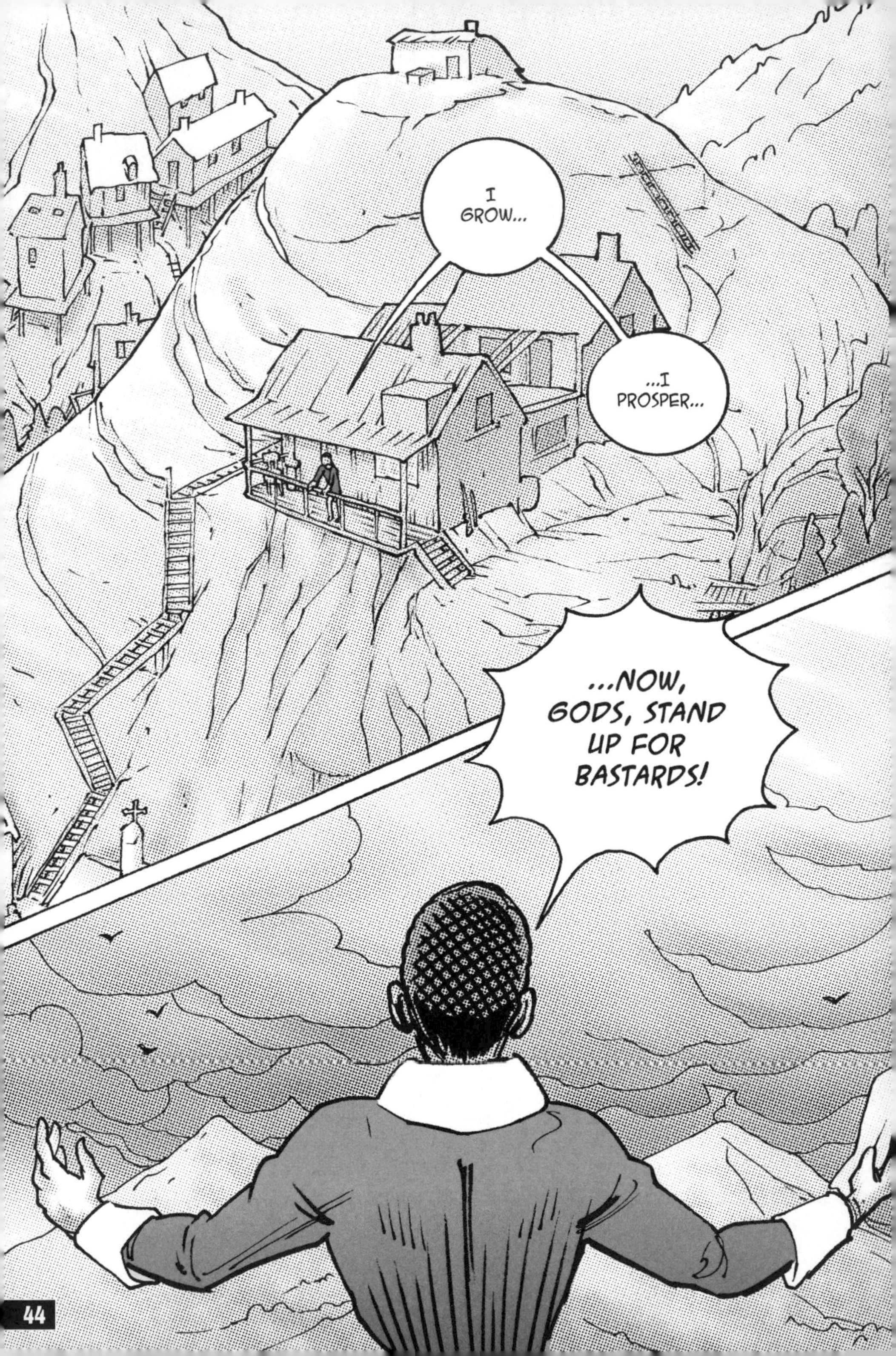
I GROW...
...I PROSPER...
...NOW, GODS, STAND UP FOR BASTARDS!

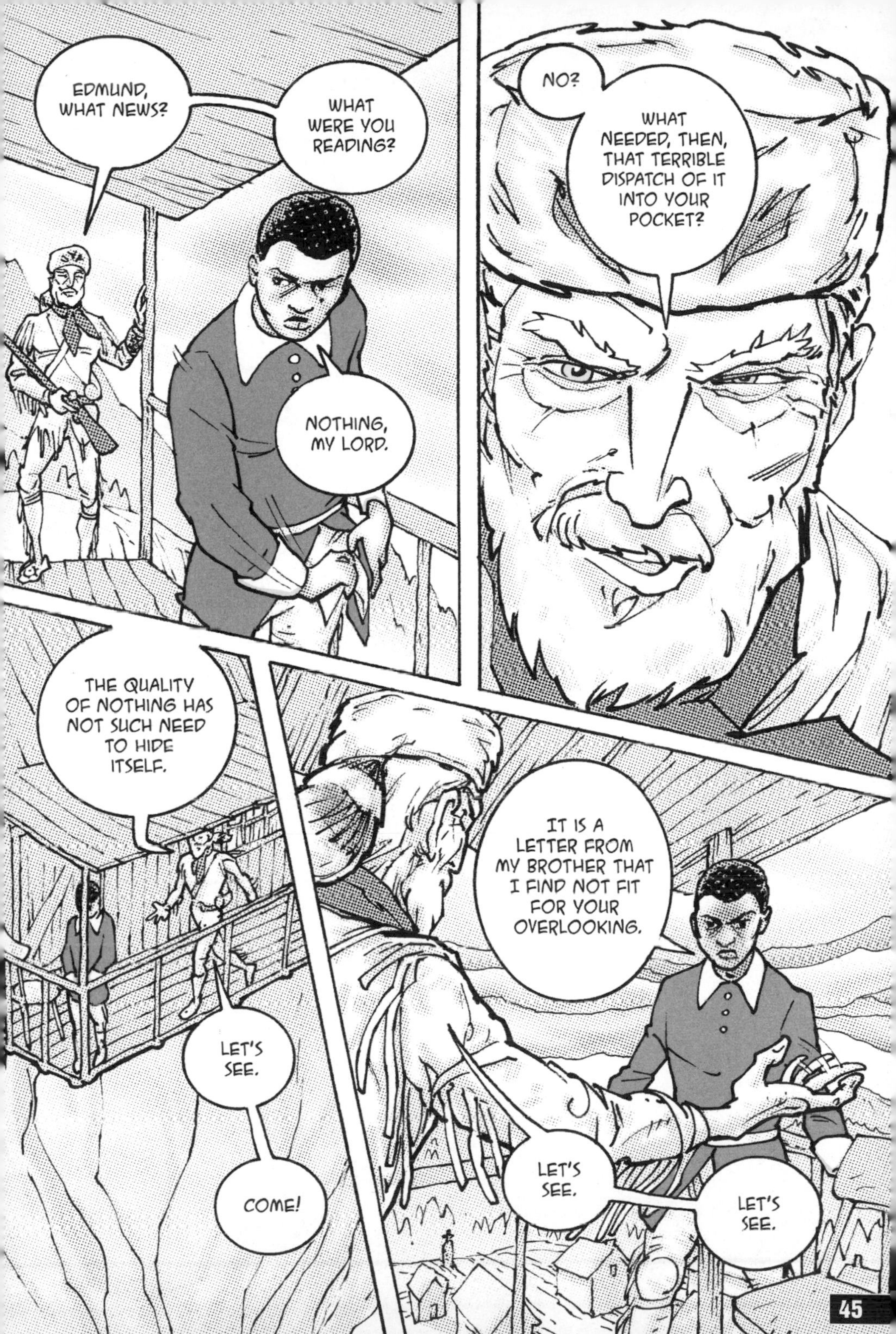
EDMUND, WHAT NEWS?
WHAT WERE YOU READING?
NOTHING, MY LORD.
NO?
WHAT NEEDED, THEN, THAT TERRIBLE DISPATCH OF IT INTO YOUR POCKET?
THE QUALITY OF NOTHING HAS NOT SUCH NEED TO HIDE ITSELF.
LET'S SEE.
COME!
IT IS A LETTER FROM MY BROTHER THAT I FIND NOT FIT FOR YOUR OVERLOOKING.
LET'S SEE.
LET'S SEE.

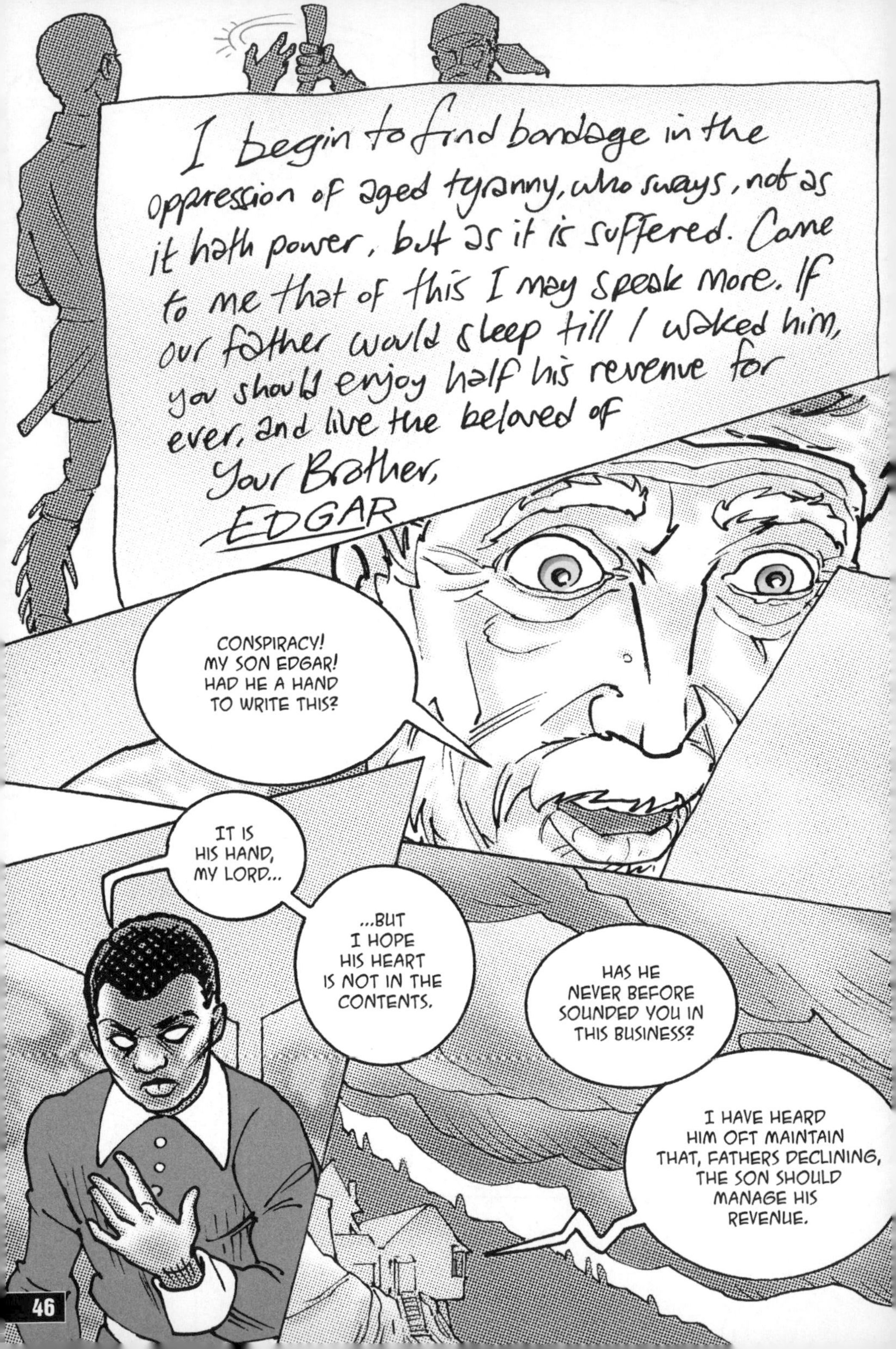
I begin to find bondage in the oppression of aged tyranny, who sways, not as it hath power, but as it is suffered. Come to me that of this I may speak more. If our father would sleep till I waked him, you should enjoy half his revenue for ever, and live the beloved of
Your Brother,
EDGAR
CONSPIRACY! MY SON EDGAR! HAD HE A HAND TO WRITE THIS?
IT IS HIS HAND, MY LORD...
...BUT I HOPE HIS HEART IS NOT IN THE CONTENTS.
HAS HE NEVER BEFORE SOUNDED YOU IN THIS BUSINESS?
I HAVE HEARD HIM OFT MAINTAIN THAT, FATHERS DECLINING, THE SON SHOULD MANAGE HIS REVENUE.

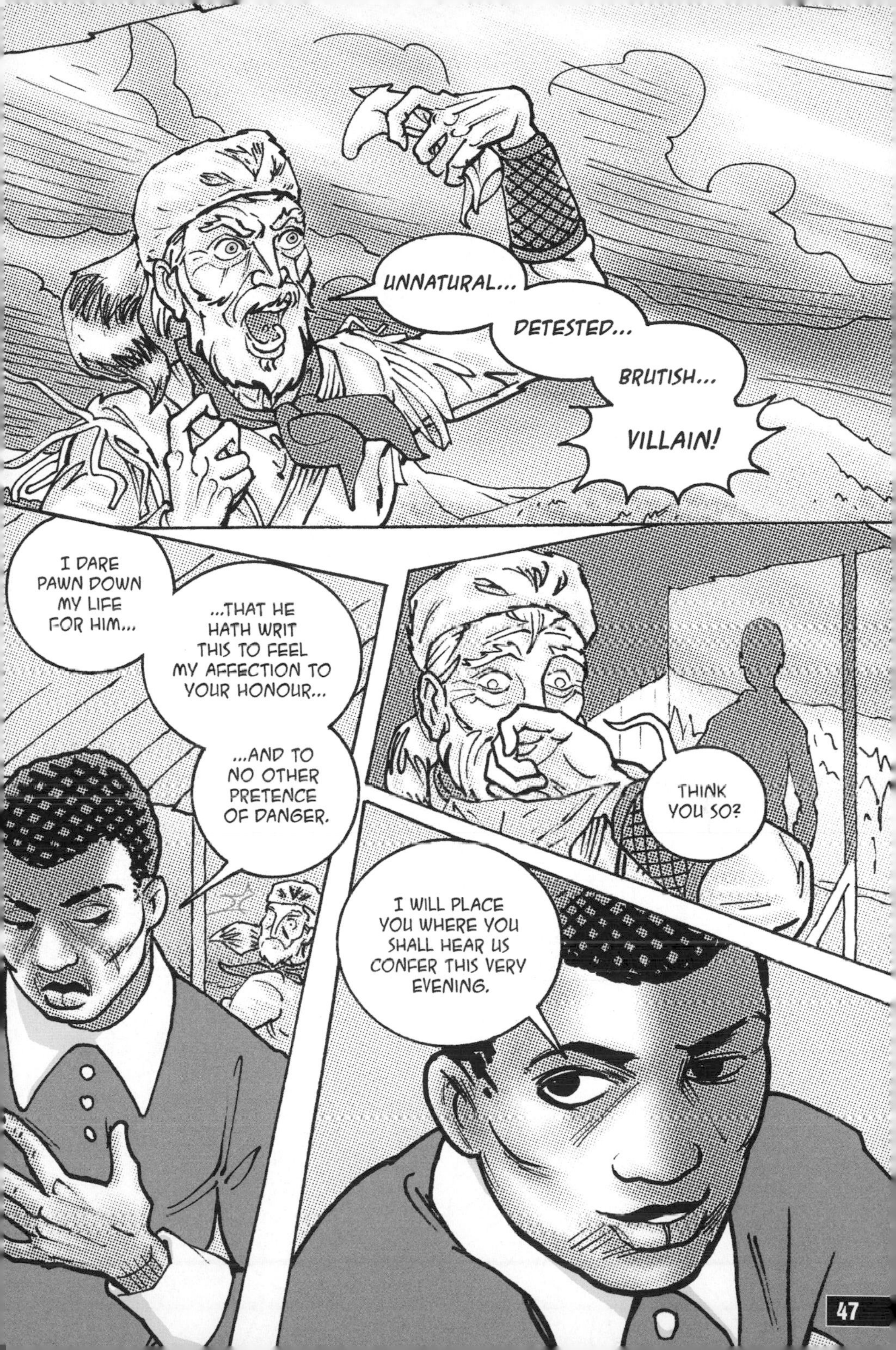
UNNATURAL...
DETESTED...
BRUTISH...
VILLAIN!
I DARE PAWN DOWN MY LIFE FOR HIM...
...THAT HE HATH WRIT THIS TO FEEL MY AFFECTION TO YOUR HONOUR...
...AND TO NO OTHER PRETENCE OF DANGER.
THINK YOU SO?
I WILL PLACE YOU WHERE YOU SHALL HEAR US CONFER THIS VERY EVENING.

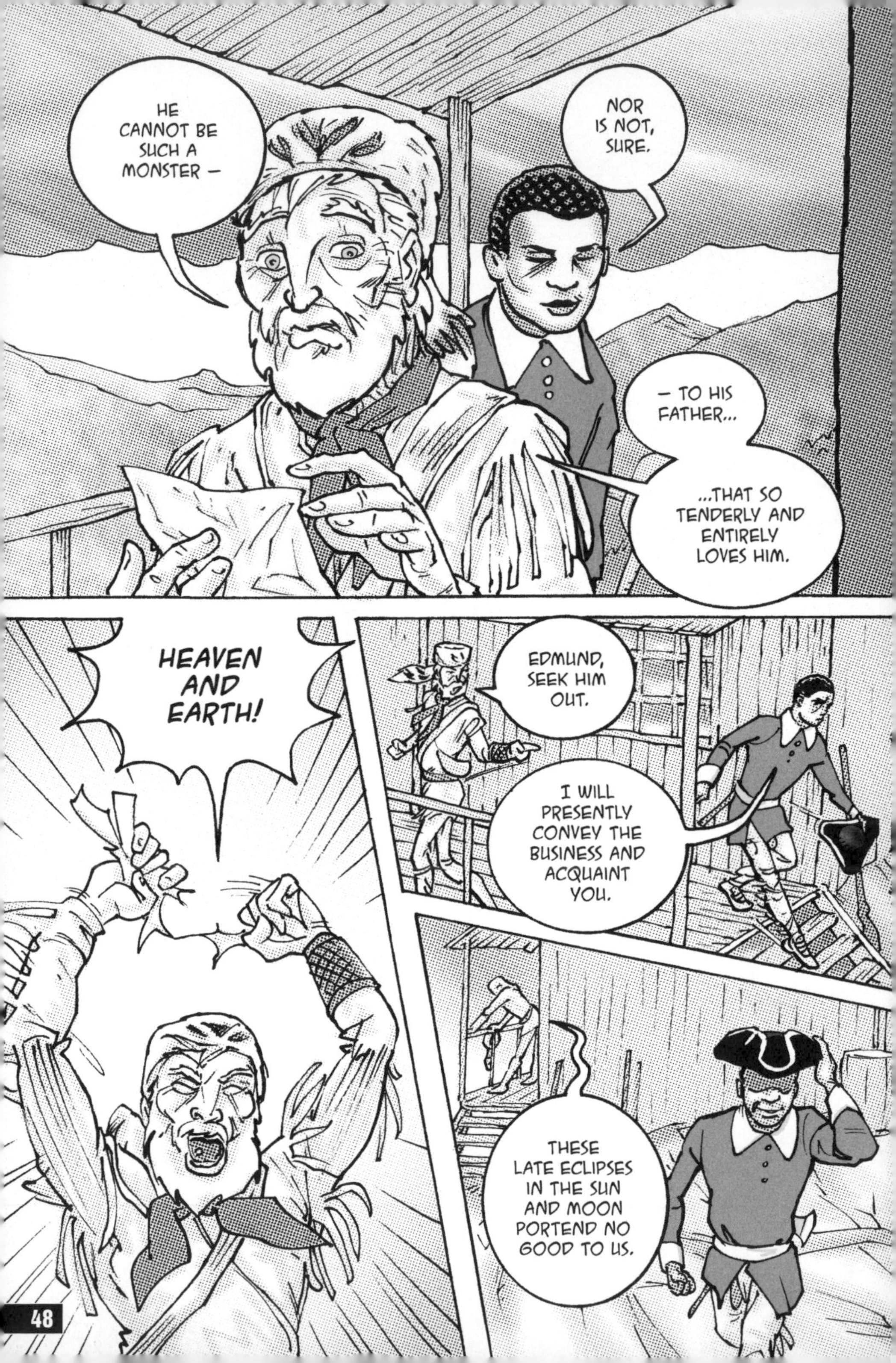

HE CANNOT BE SUCH A MONSTER —
NOR IS NOT, SURE.
— TO HIS FATHER...
...THAT SO TENDERLY AND ENTIRELY LOVES HIM.
HEAVEN AND EARTH!
EDMUND, SEEK HIM OUT.
I WILL PRESENTLY CONVEY THE BUSINESS AND ACQUAINT YOU.
THESE LATE ECLIPSES IN THE SUN AND MOON PORTEND NO GOOD TO US.

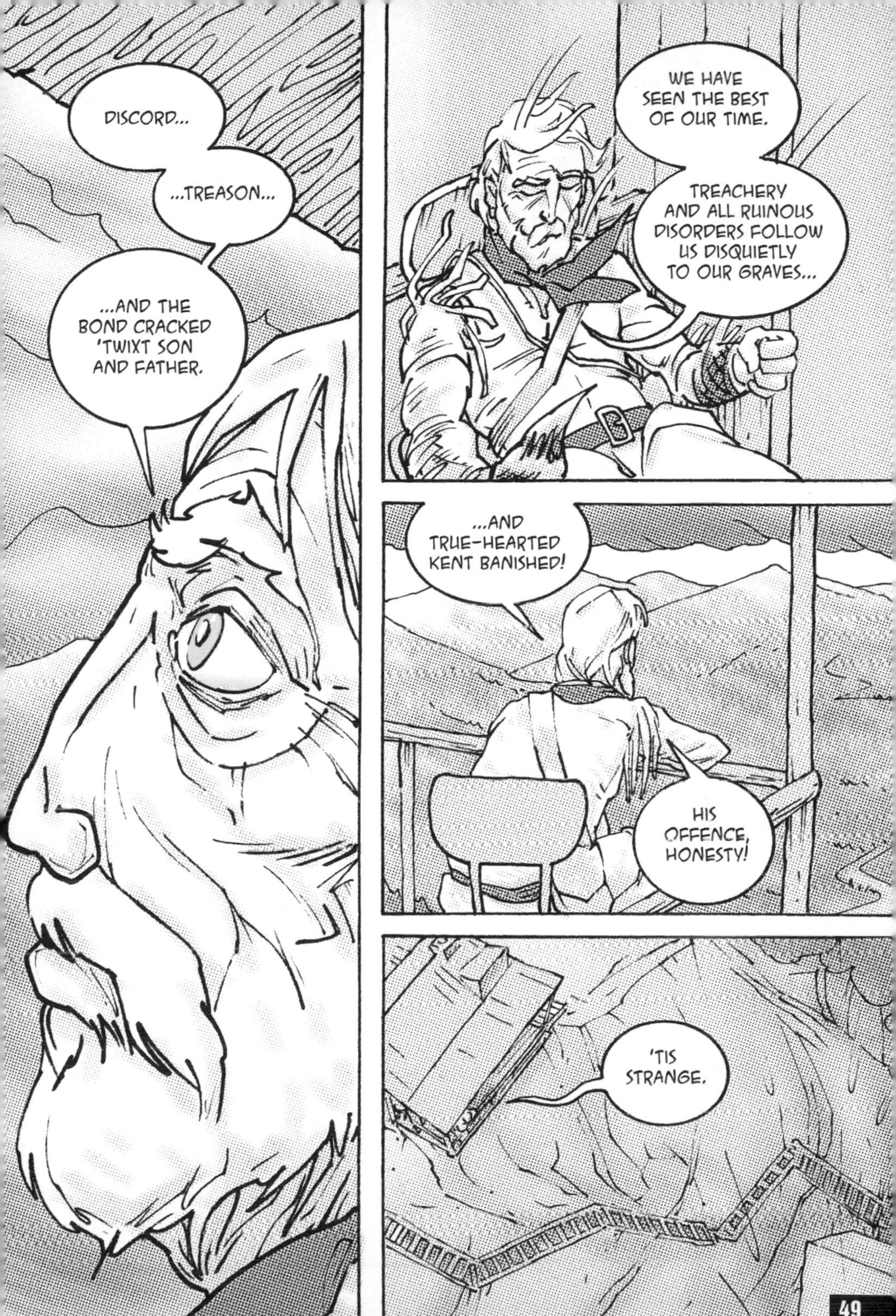
DISCORD...
...TREASON...
...AND THE BOND CRACKED 'TWIXT SON AND FATHER.
WE HAVE SEEN THE BEST OF OUR TIME.
TREACHERY AND ALL RUINOUS DISORDERS FOLLOW US DISQUIETLY TO OUR GRAVES...
...AND TRUE-HEARTED KENT BANISHED!
HIS OFFENCE, HONESTY!
'TIS STRANGE.

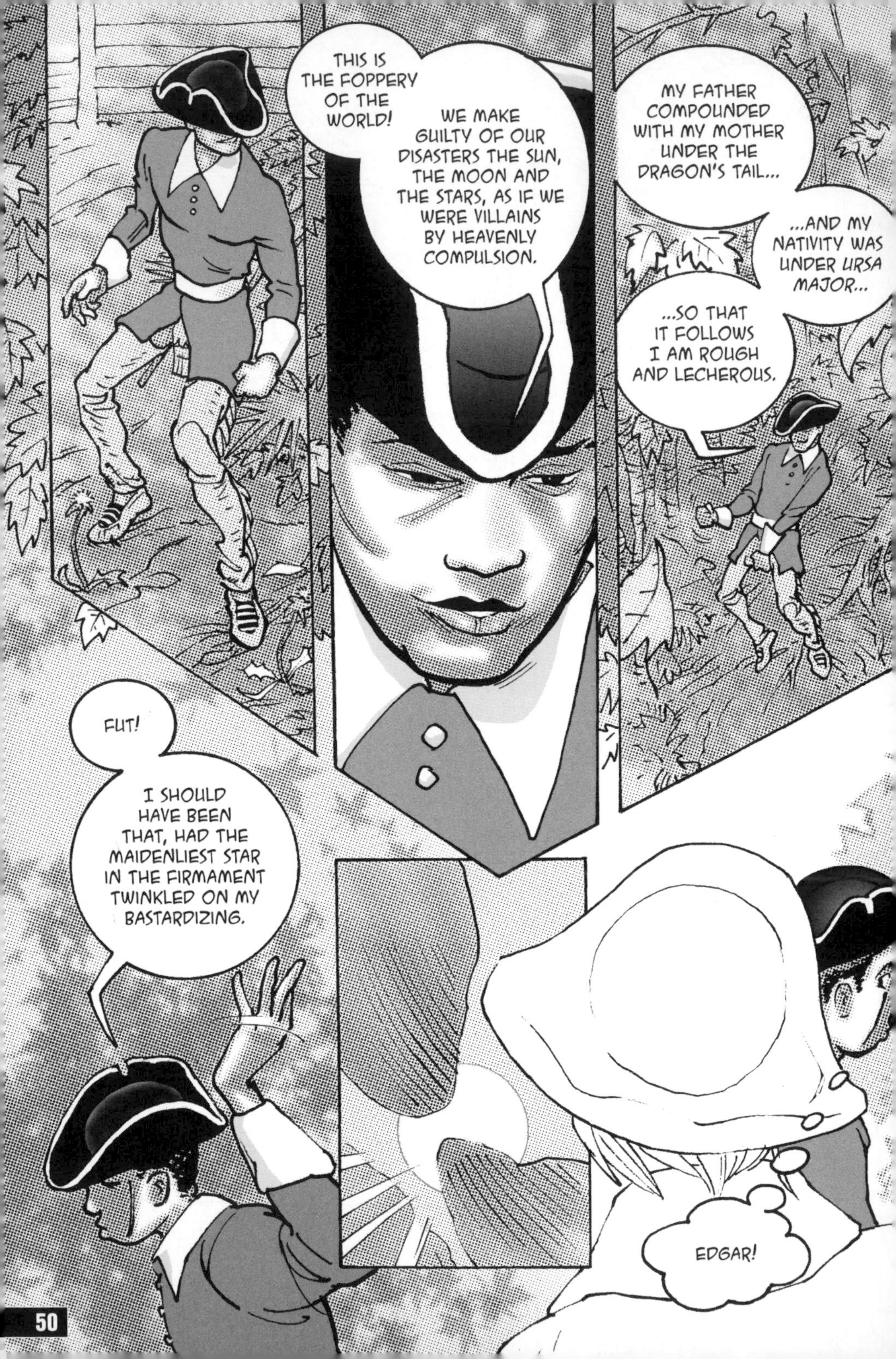
THIS IS THE FOPPERY OF THE WORLD!
WE MAKE GUILTY OF OUR DISASTERS THE SUN, THE MOON AND THE STARS, AS IF WE WERE VILLAINS BY HEAVENLY COMPULSION.
MY FATHER COMPOUNDED WITH MY MOTHER UNDER THE DRAGON'S TAIL...
...AND MY NATIVITY WAS UNDER URSA MAJOR...
...SO THAT IT FOLLOWS I AM ROUGH AND LECHEROUS.
FUT!
I SHOULD HAVE BEEN THAT, HAD THE MAIDENLIEST STAR IN THE FIRMAMENT TWINKLED ON MY BASTARDIZING.
EDGAR!

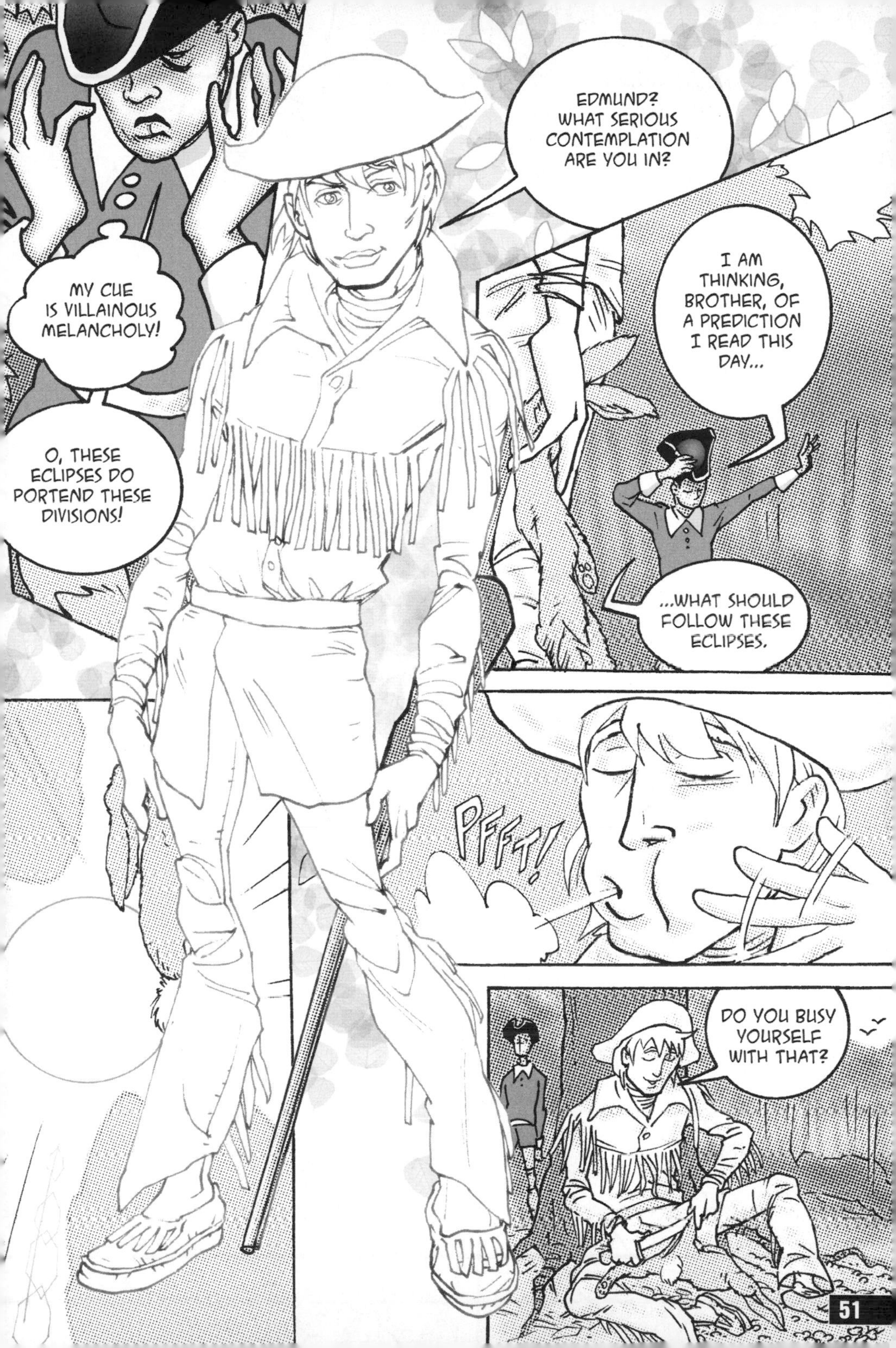

MY CUE IS VILLAINOUS MELANCHOLY!
O, THESE ECLIPSES DO PORTEND THESE DIVISIONS!
EDMUND? WHAT SERIOUS CONTEMPLATION ARE YOU IN?
I AM THINKING, BROTHER, OF A PREDICTION I READ THIS DAY...
...WHAT SHOULD FOLLOW THESE ECLIPSES.
PFFT!
DO YOU BUSY YOURSELF WITH THAT?

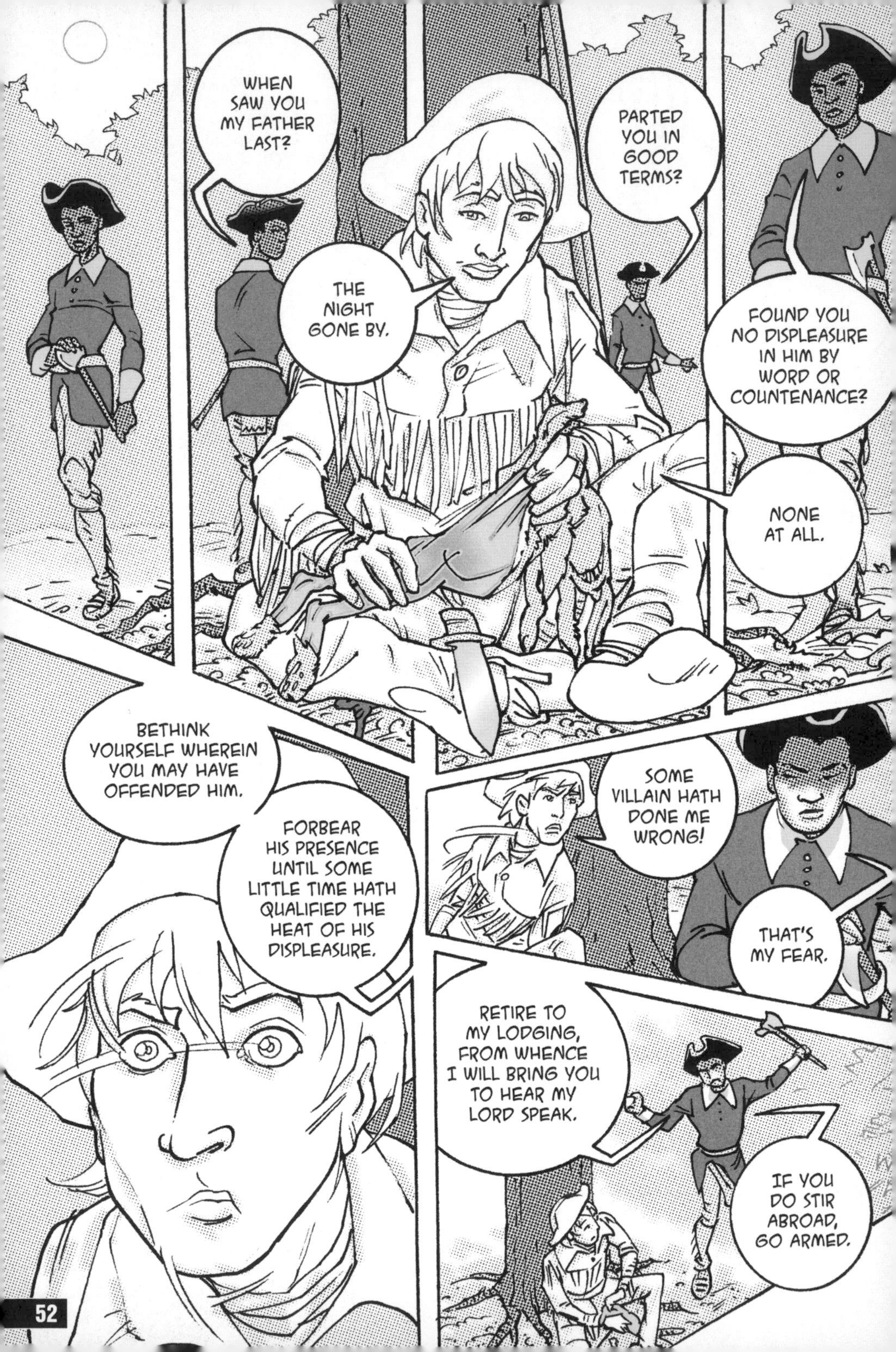

WHEN SAW YOU MY FATHER LAST?
THE NIGHT GONE BY.
PARTED YOU IN GOOD TERMS?
FOUND YOU NO DISPLEASURE IN HIM BY WORD OR COUNTENANCE?
NONE AT ALL.
BETHINK YOURSELF WHEREIN YOU MAY HAVE OFFENDED HIM.
FORBEAR HIS PRESENCE UNTIL SOME LITTLE TIME HATH QUALIFIED THE HEAT OF HIS DISPLEASURE.
SOME VILLAIN HATH DONE ME WRONG!
THAT'S MY FEAR.
RETIRE TO MY LODGING, FROM WHENCE I WILL BRING YOU TO HEAR MY LORD SPEAK.
IF YOU DO STIR ABROAD, GO ARMED.

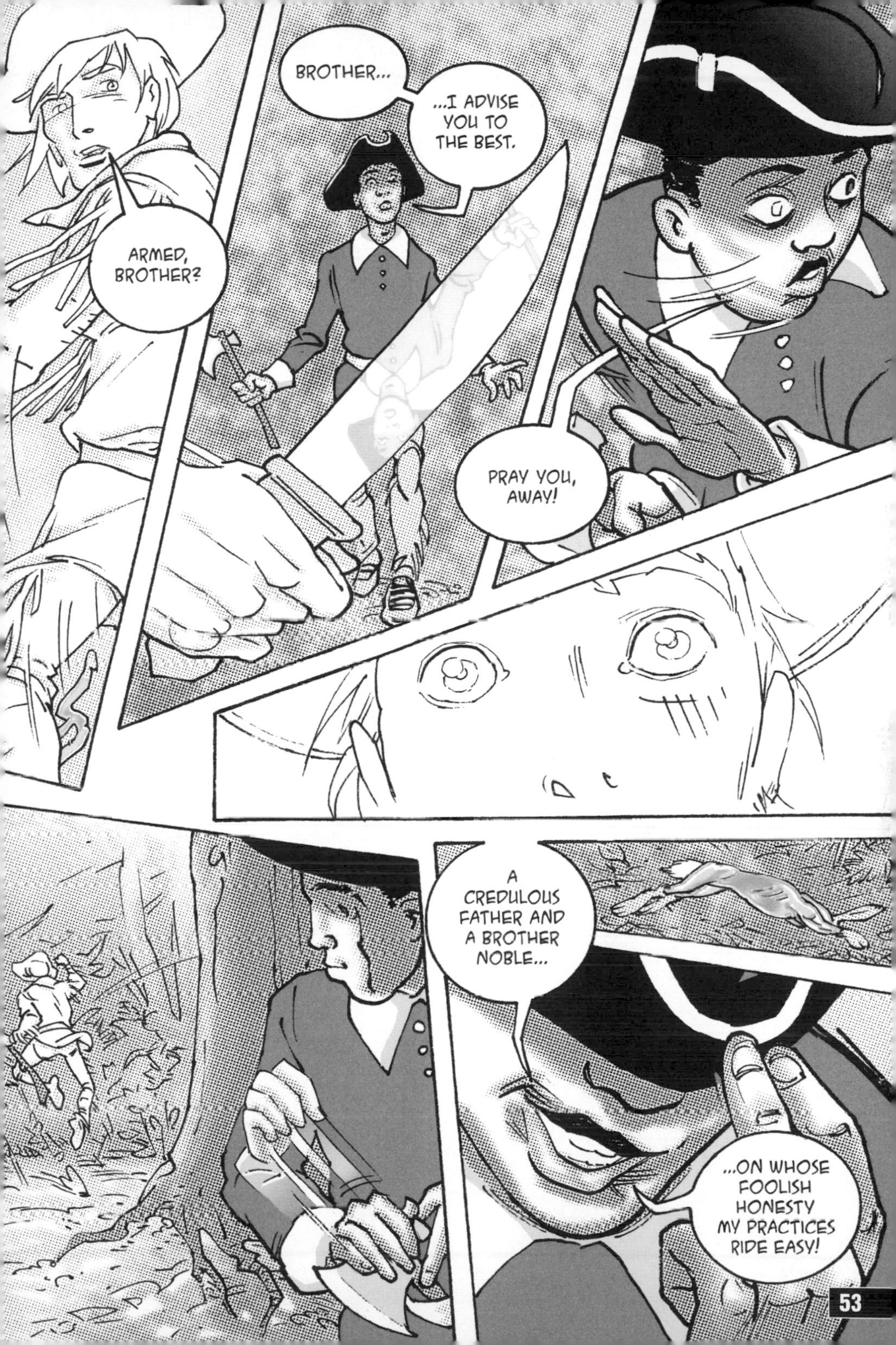
ARMED, BROTHER?
BROTHER...
...I ADVISE YOU TO THE BEST.
PRAY YOU, AWAY!
A CREDULOUS FATHER AND A BROTHER NOBLE...
...ON WHOSE FOOLISH HONESTY MY PRACTICES RIDE EASY!

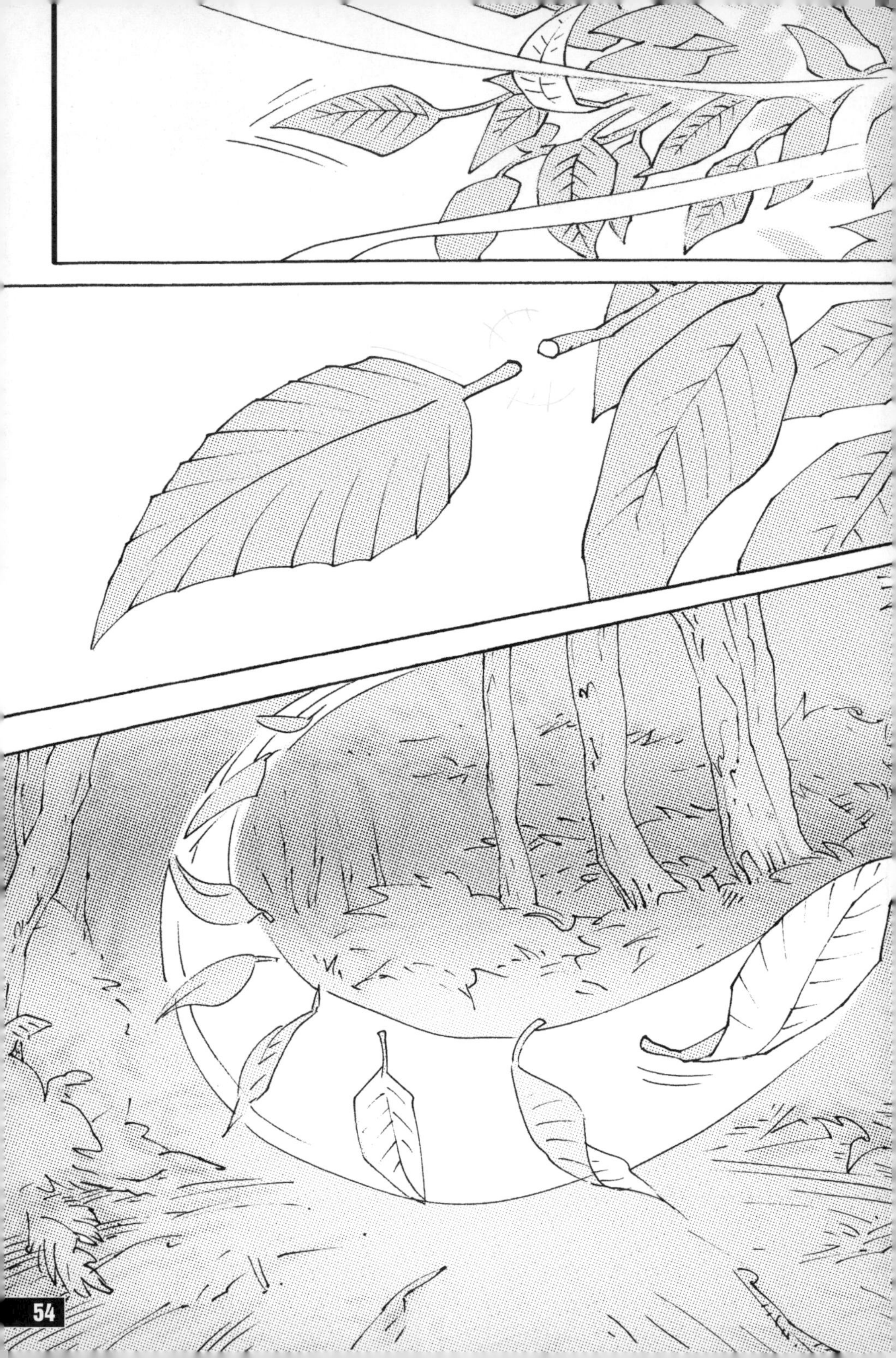

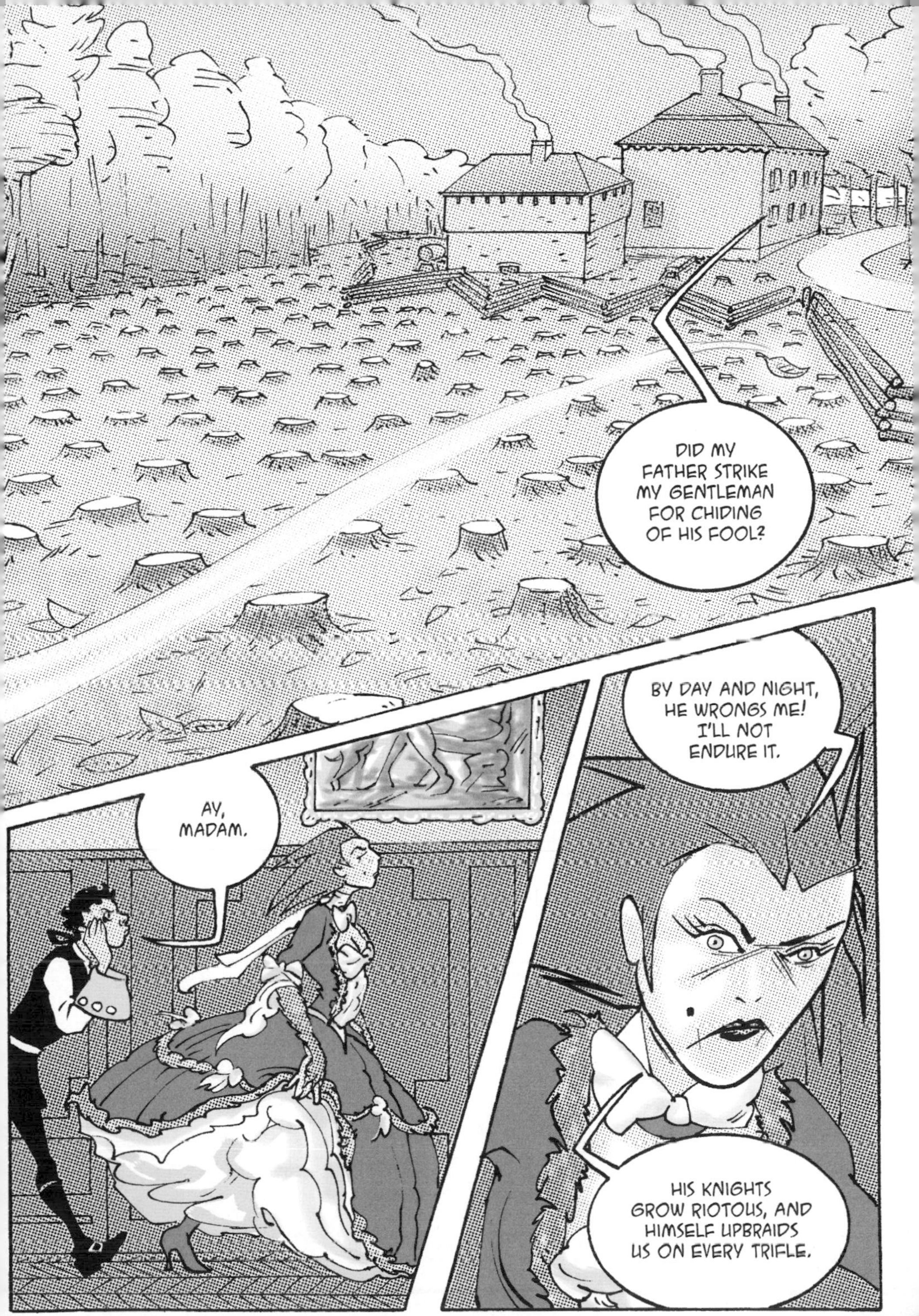
DID MY FATHER STRIKE MY GENTLEMAN FOR CHIDING OF HIS FOOL?
AY, MADAM.
BY DAY AND NIGHT, HE WRONGS ME! I'LL NOT ENDURE IT.
HIS KNIGHTS GROW RIOTOUS, AND HIMSELF UPBRAIDS US ON EVERY TRIFLE.

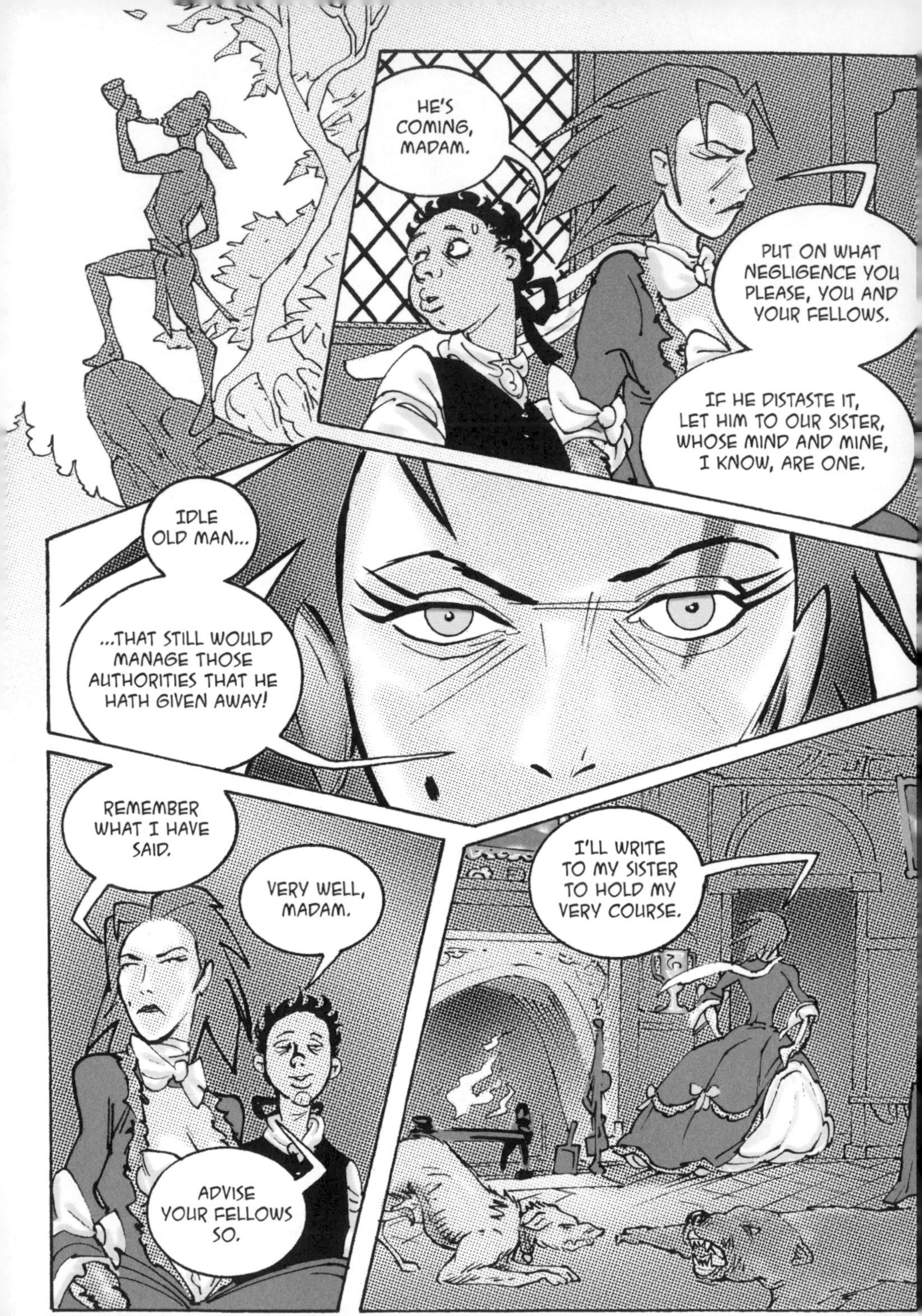
HE'S COMING, MADAM.
PUT ON WHAT NEGLIGENCE YOU PLEASE, YOU AND YOUR FELLOWS.
IF HE DISTASTE IT, LET HIM TO OUR SISTER, WHOSE MIND AND MINE, I KNOW, ARE ONE.
IDLE OLD MAN...
...THAT STILL WOULD MANAGE THOSE AUTHORITIES THAT HE HATH GIVEN AWAY!
REMEMBER WHAT I HAVE SAID.
VERY WELL, MADAM.
ADVISE YOUR FELLOWS SO.
I'LL WRITE TO MY SISTER TO HOLD MY VERY COURSE.

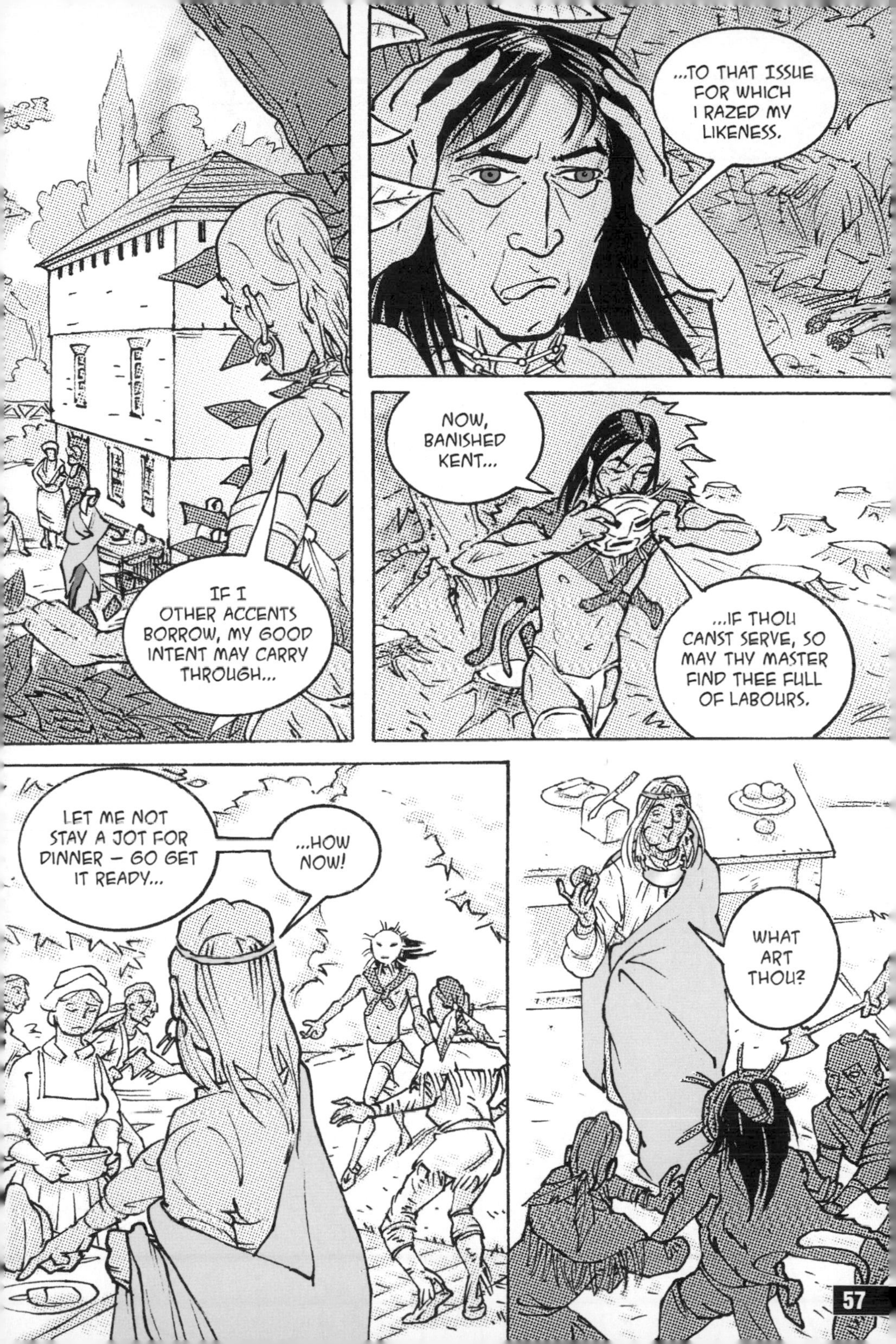
IF I OTHER ACCENTS BORROW, MY GOOD INTENT MAY CARRY THROUGH...
...TO THAT ISSUE FOR WHICH I RAZED MY LIKENESS.
NOW, BANISHED KENT...
...IF THOU CANST SERVE, SO MAY THY MASTER FIND THEE FULL OF LABOURS.
LET ME NOT STAY A JOT FOR DINNER – GO GET IT READY...
...HOW NOW!
WHAT ART THOU?

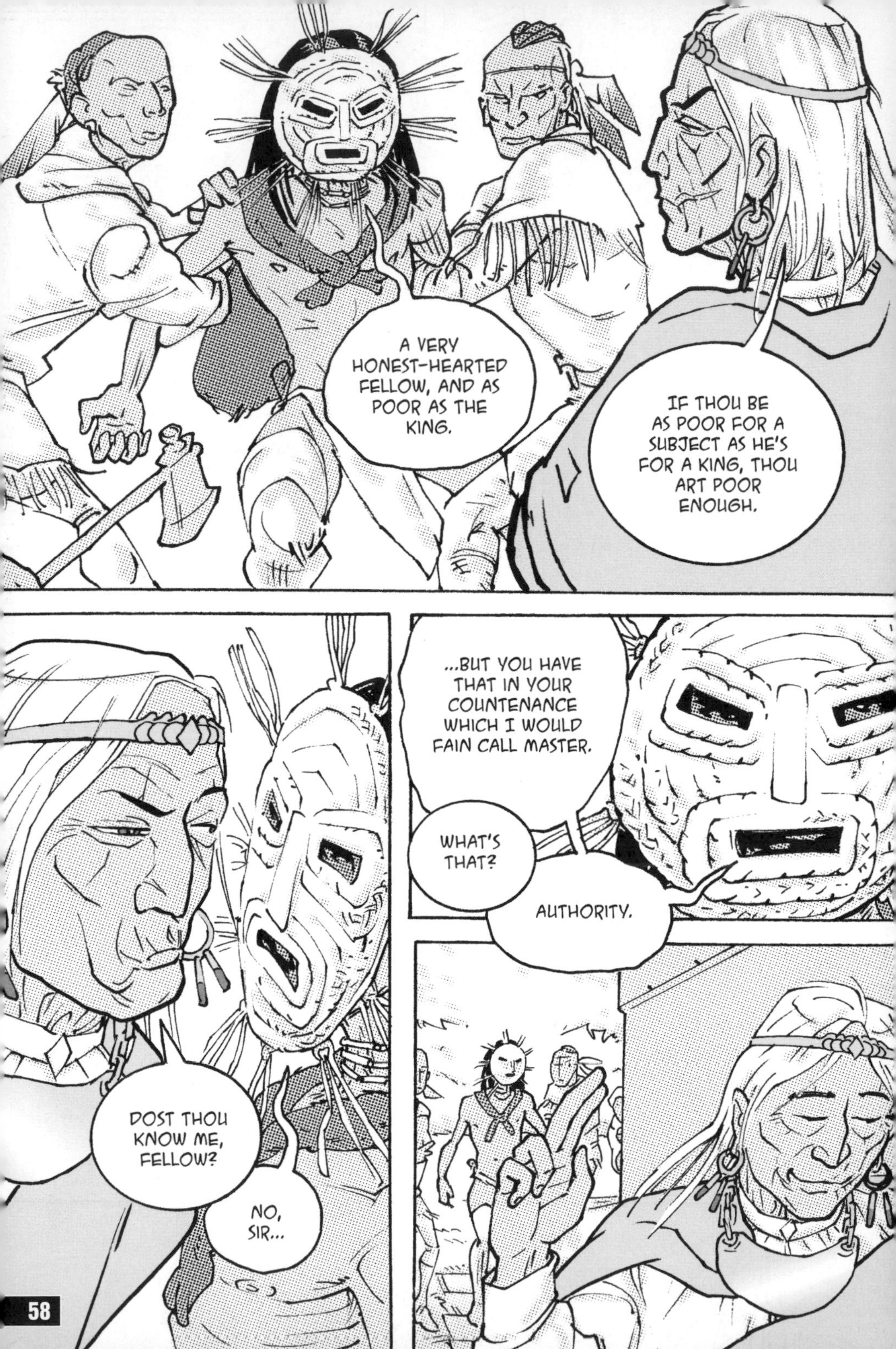
A VERY HONEST-HEARTED FELLOW, AND AS POOR AS THE KING.
IF THOU BE AS POOR FOR A SUBJECT AS HE'S FOR A KING, THOU ART POOR ENOUGH.
DOST THOU KNOW ME, FELLOW?
NO, SIR...
...BUT YOU HAVE THAT IN YOUR COUNTENANCE WHICH I WOULD FAIN CALL MASTER.
WHAT'S THAT?
AUTHORITY.

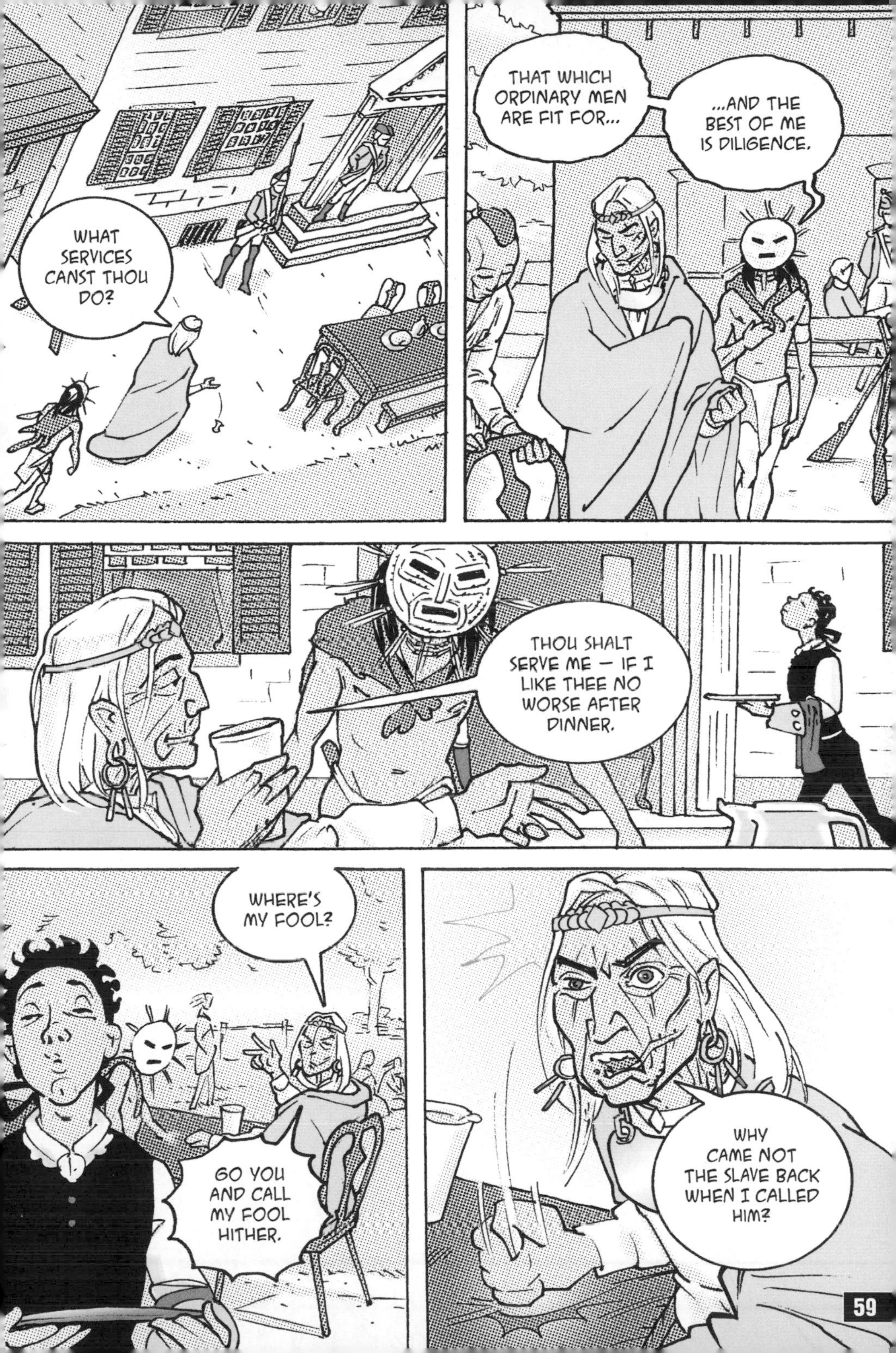
WHAT SERVICES CANST THOU DO?
THAT WHICH ORDINARY MEN ARE FIT FOR...
...AND THE BEST OF ME IS DILIGENCE.
THOU SHALT SERVE ME — IF I LIKE THEE NO WORSE AFTER DINNER.
WHERE'S MY FOOL?
GO YOU AND CALL MY FOOL HITHER.
WHY CAME NOT THE SLAVE BACK WHEN I CALLED HIM?

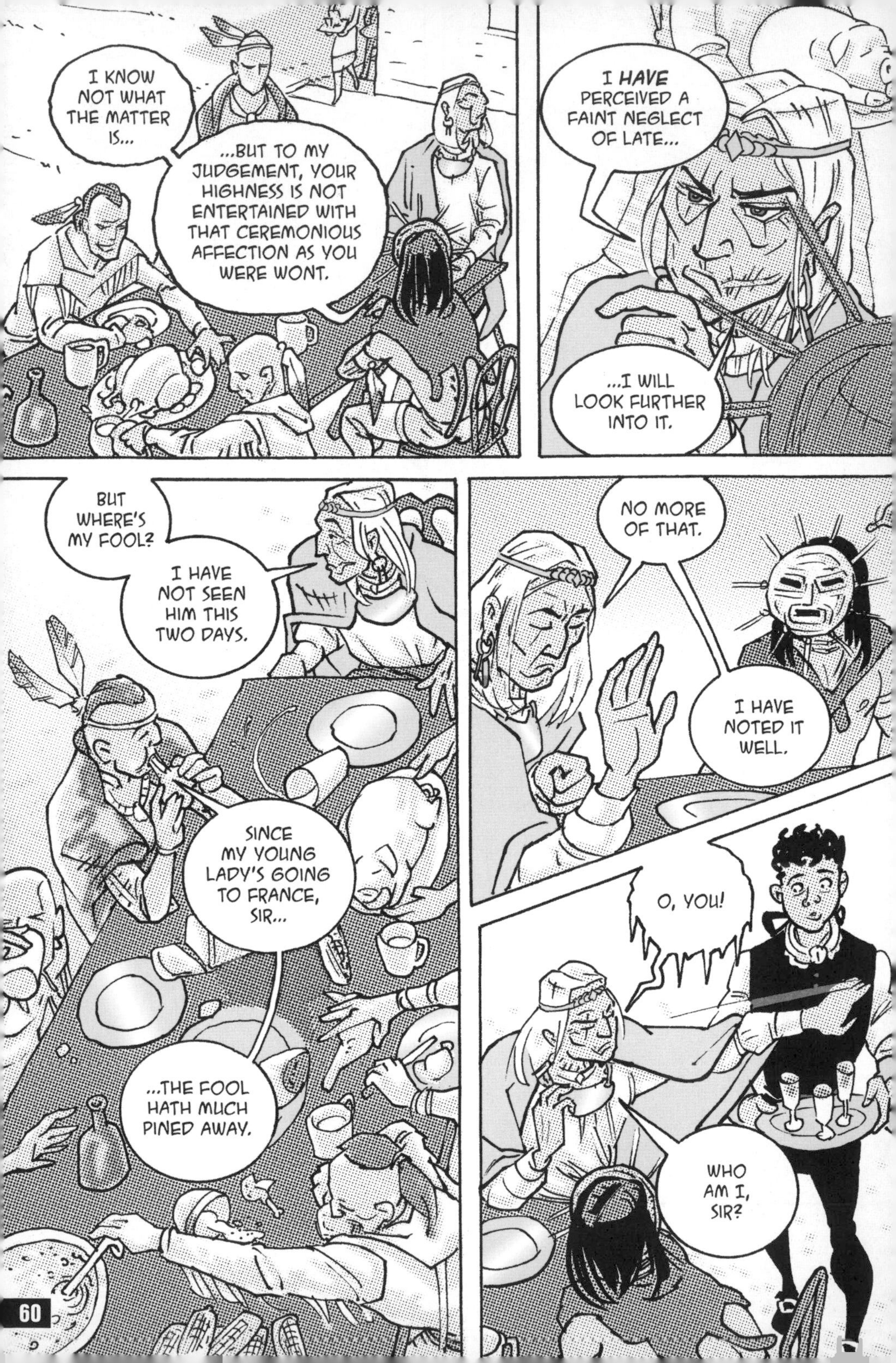
I KNOW NOT WHAT THE MATTER IS...
...BUT TO MY JUDGEMENT, YOUR HIGHNESS IS NOT ENTERTAINED WITH THAT CEREMONIOUS AFFECTION AS YOU WERE WONT.
I **HAVE** PERCEIVED A FAINT NEGLECT OF LATE...
...I WILL LOOK FURTHER INTO IT.
BUT WHERE'S MY FOOL?
I HAVE NOT SEEN HIM THIS TWO DAYS.
SINCE MY YOUNG LADY'S GOING TO FRANCE, SIR...
...THE FOOL HATH MUCH PINED AWAY.
NO MORE OF THAT.
I HAVE NOTED IT WELL.
O, YOU!
WHO AM I, SIR?

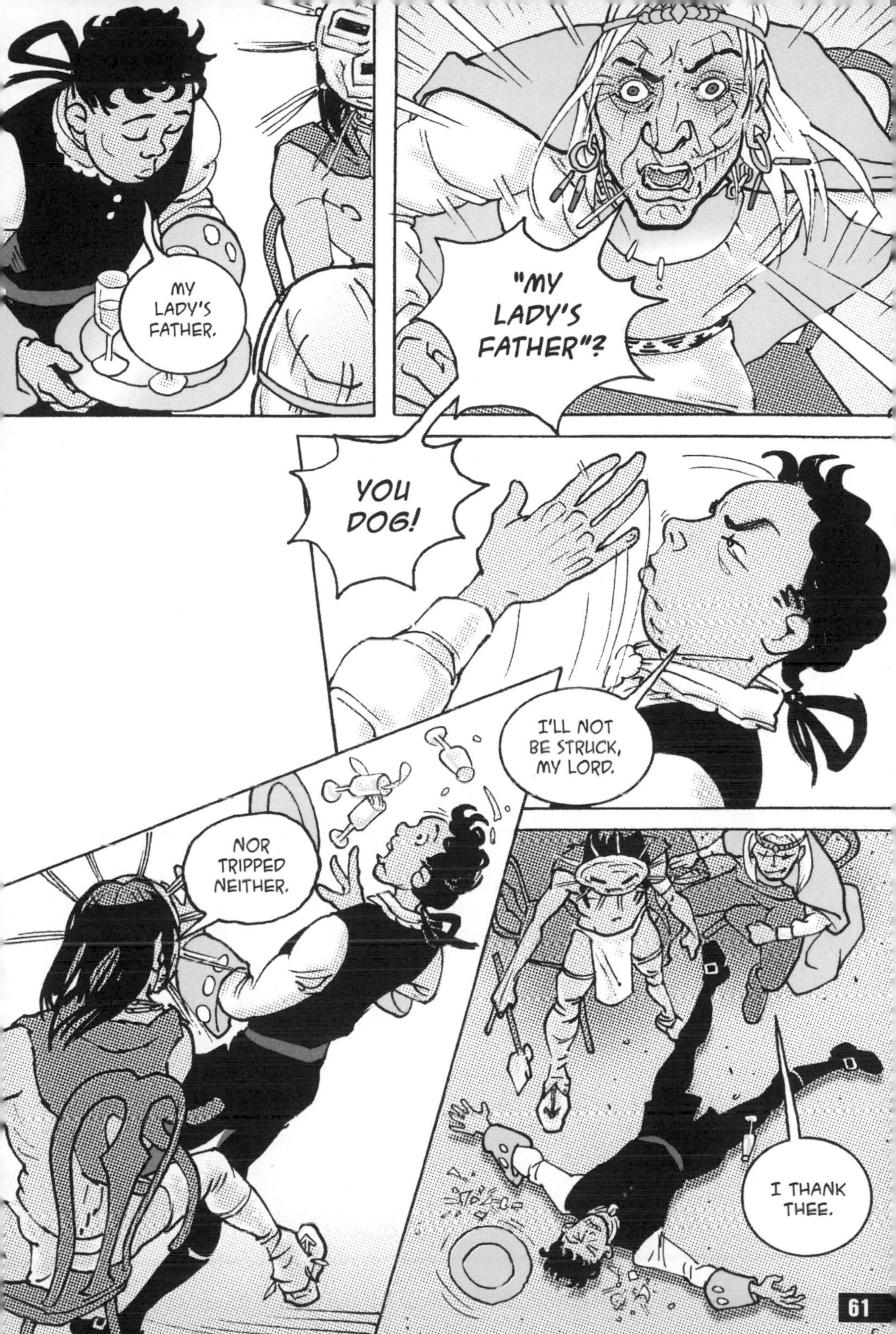
MY LADY'S FATHER.
"MY LADY'S FATHER"?
YOU DOG!
I'LL NOT BE STRUCK, MY LORD.
NOR TRIPPED NEITHER.
I THANK THEE.

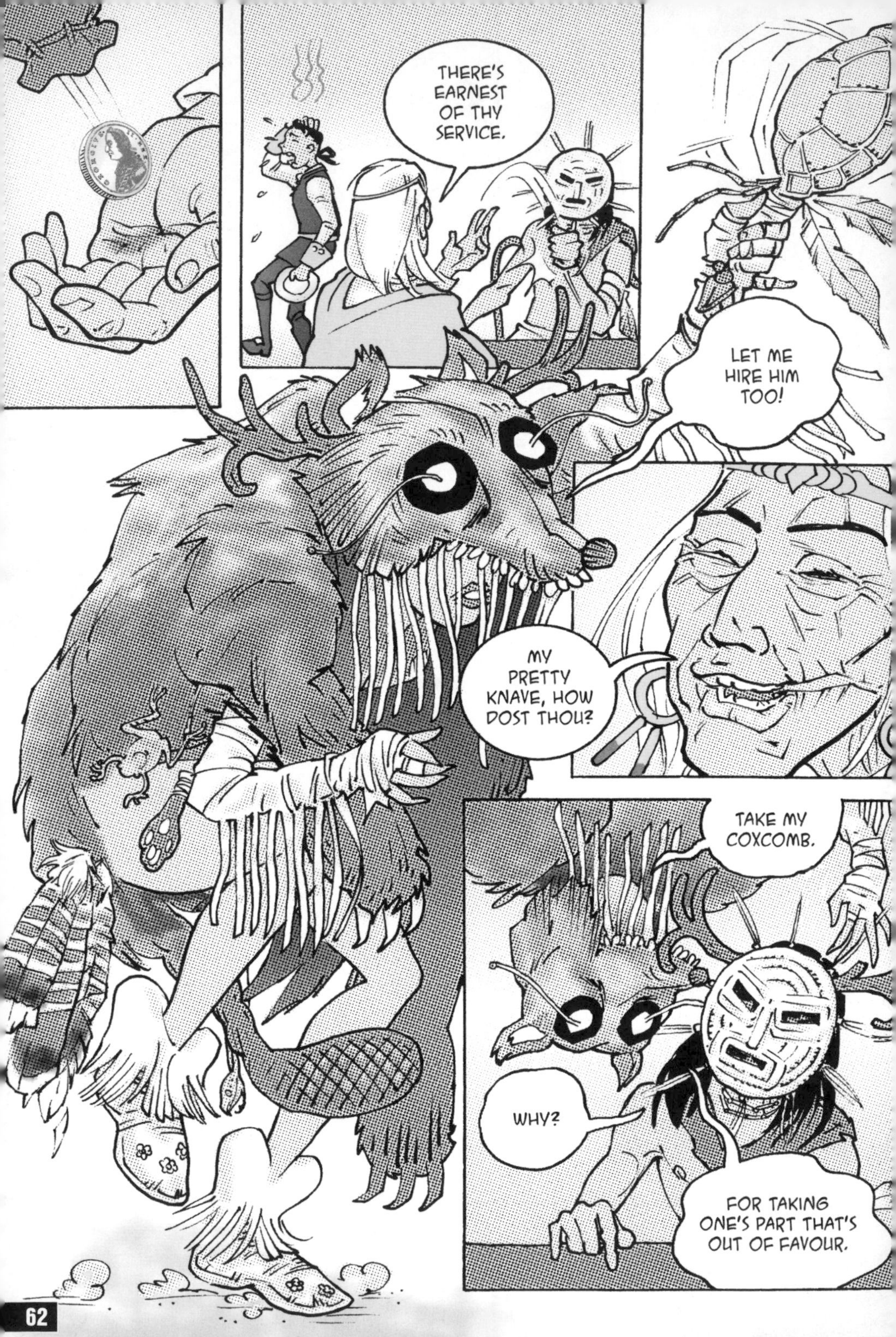
THERE'S EARNEST OF THY SERVICE.
LET ME HIRE HIM TOO!
MY PRETTY KNAVE, HOW DOST THOU?
TAKE MY COXCOMB.
WHY?
FOR TAKING ONE'S PART THAT'S OUT OF FAVOUR.

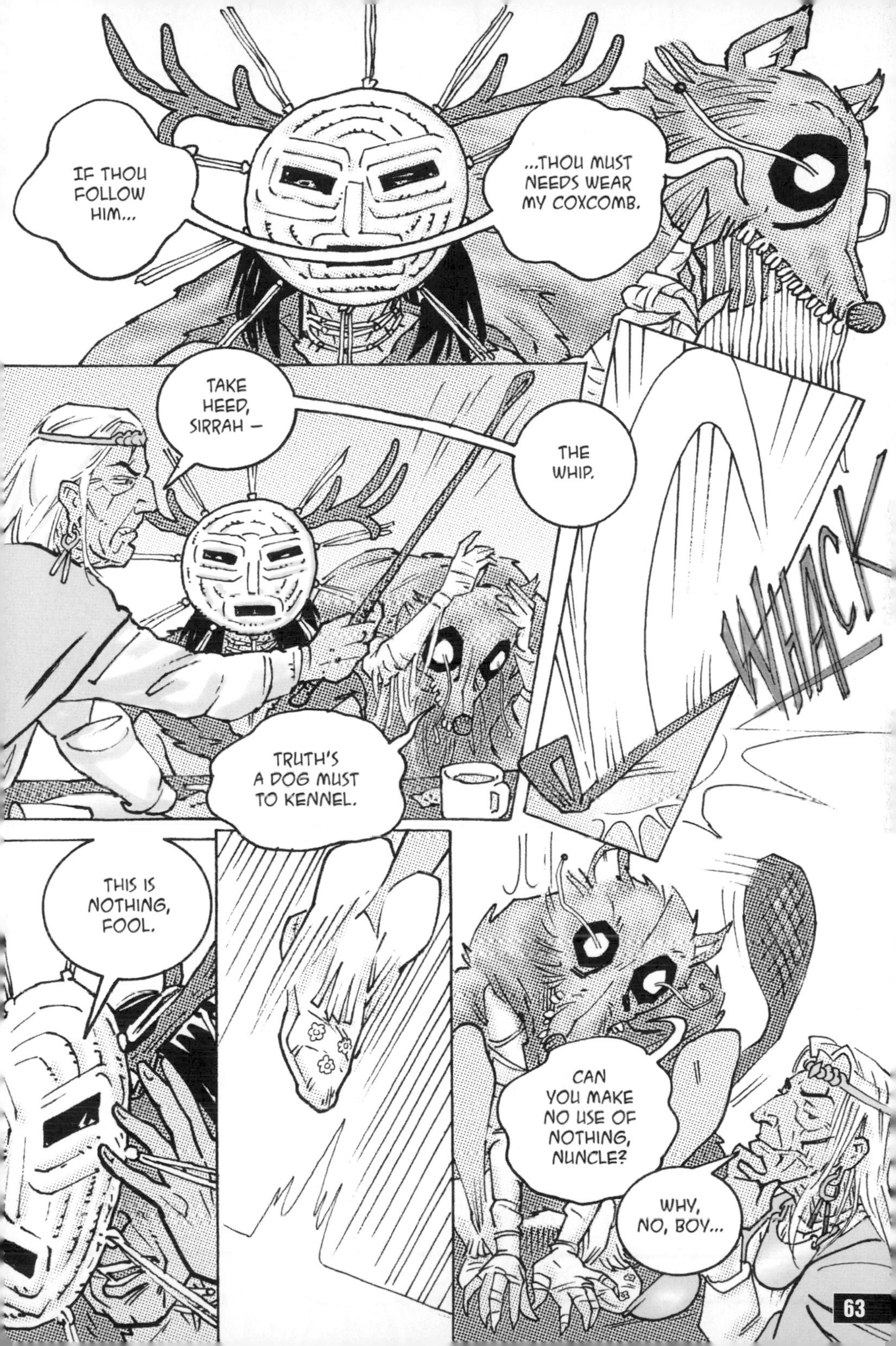
IF THOU FOLLOW HIM...
...THOU MUST NEEDS WEAR MY COXCOMB.
TAKE HEED, SIRRAH —
THE WHIP.
WHACK
TRUTH'S A DOG MUST TO KENNEL.
THIS IS NOTHING, FOOL.
CAN YOU MAKE NO USE OF NOTHING, NUNCLE?
WHY, NO, BOY...

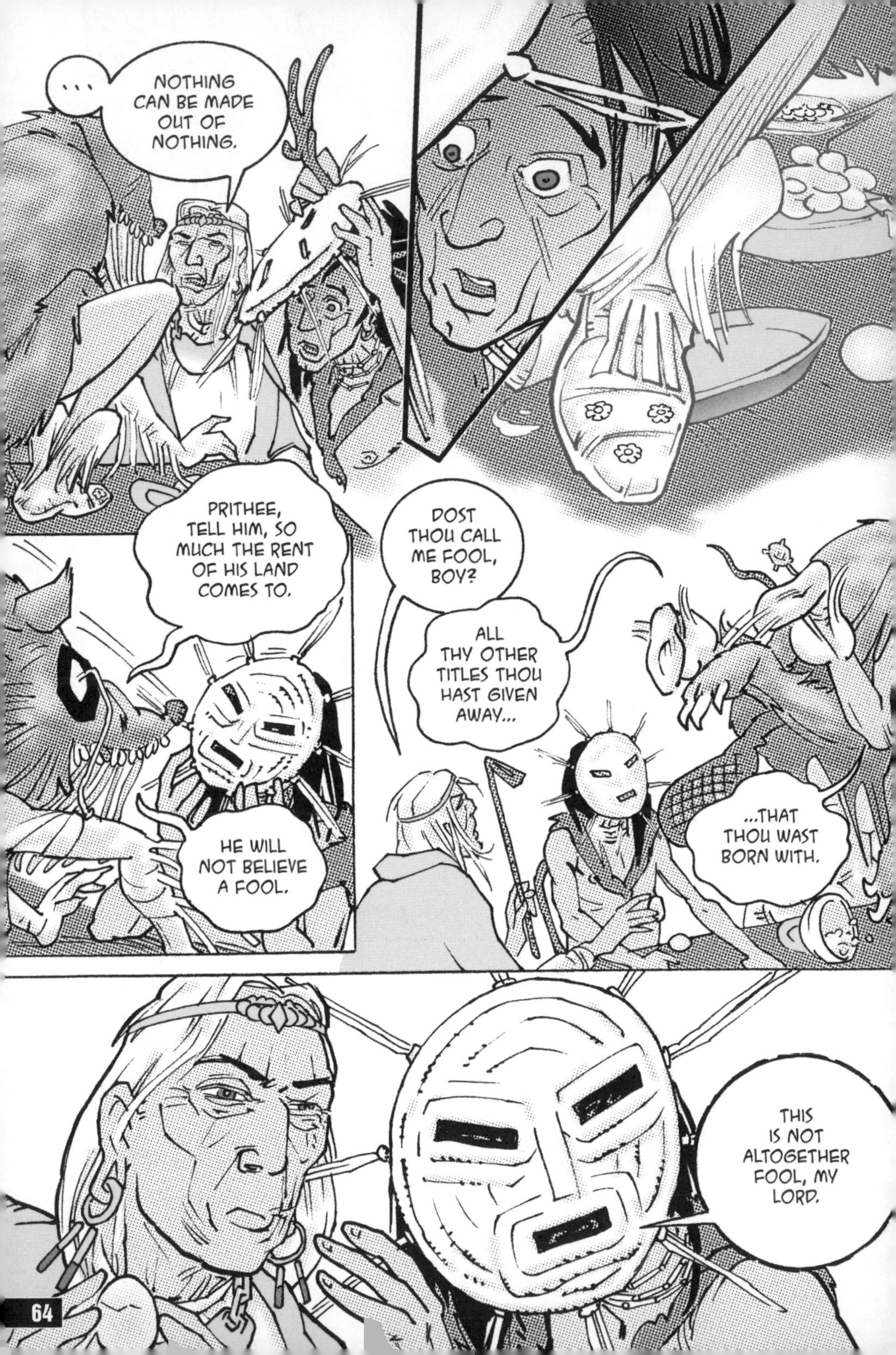
...
NOTHING CAN BE MADE OUT OF NOTHING.
PRITHEE, TELL HIM, SO MUCH THE RENT OF HIS LAND COMES TO.
HE WILL NOT BELIEVE A FOOL.
DOST THOU CALL ME FOOL, BOY?
ALL THY OTHER TITLES THOU HAST GIVEN AWAY...
...THAT THOU WAST BORN WITH.
THIS IS NOT ALTOGETHER FOOL, MY LORD.

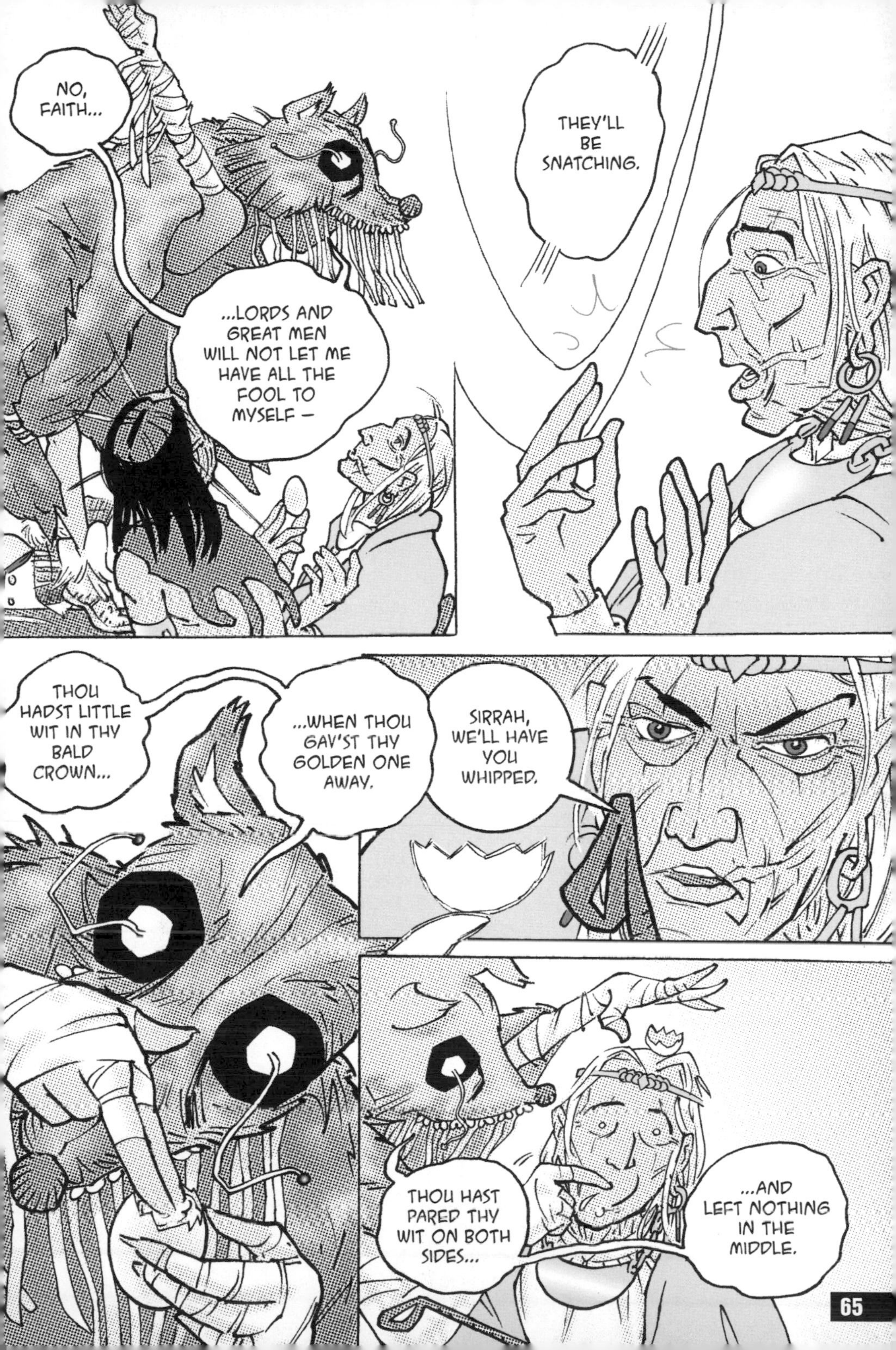
NO, FAITH...
...LORDS AND GREAT MEN WILL NOT LET ME HAVE ALL THE FOOL TO MYSELF –
THEY'LL BE SNATCHING.
THOU HADST LITTLE WIT IN THY BALD CROWN...
...WHEN THOU GAV'ST THY GOLDEN ONE AWAY.
SIRRAH, WE'LL HAVE YOU WHIPPED.
THOU HAST PARED THY WIT ON BOTH SIDES...
...AND LEFT NOTHING IN THE MIDDLE.

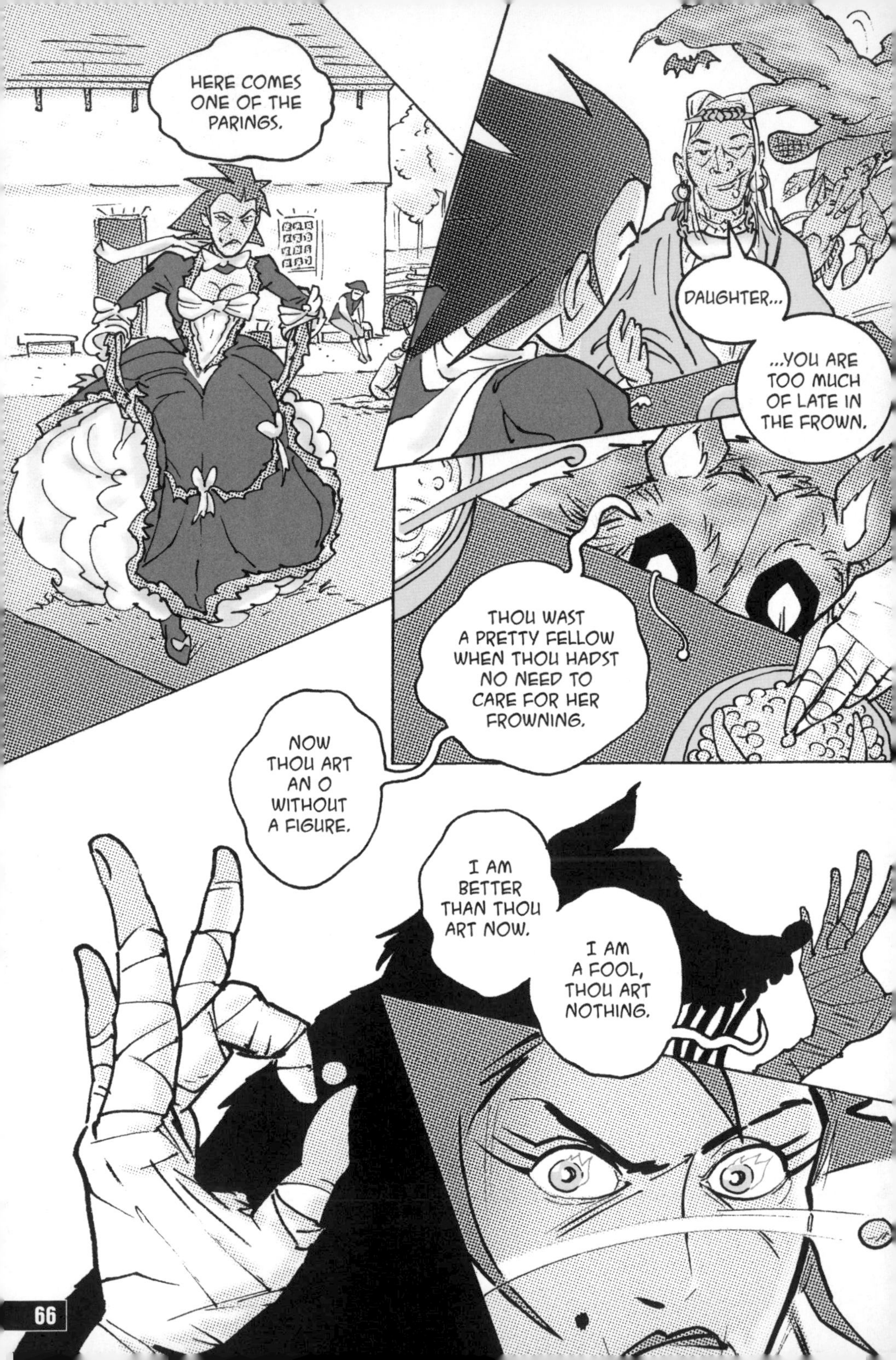
HERE COMES ONE OF THE PARINGS.
DAUGHTER...
...YOU ARE TOO MUCH OF LATE IN THE FROWN.
THOU WAST A PRETTY FELLOW WHEN THOU HADST NO NEED TO CARE FOR HER FROWNING.
NOW THOU ART AN O WITHOUT A FIGURE.
I AM BETTER THAN THOU ART NOW.
I AM A FOOL, THOU ART NOTHING.

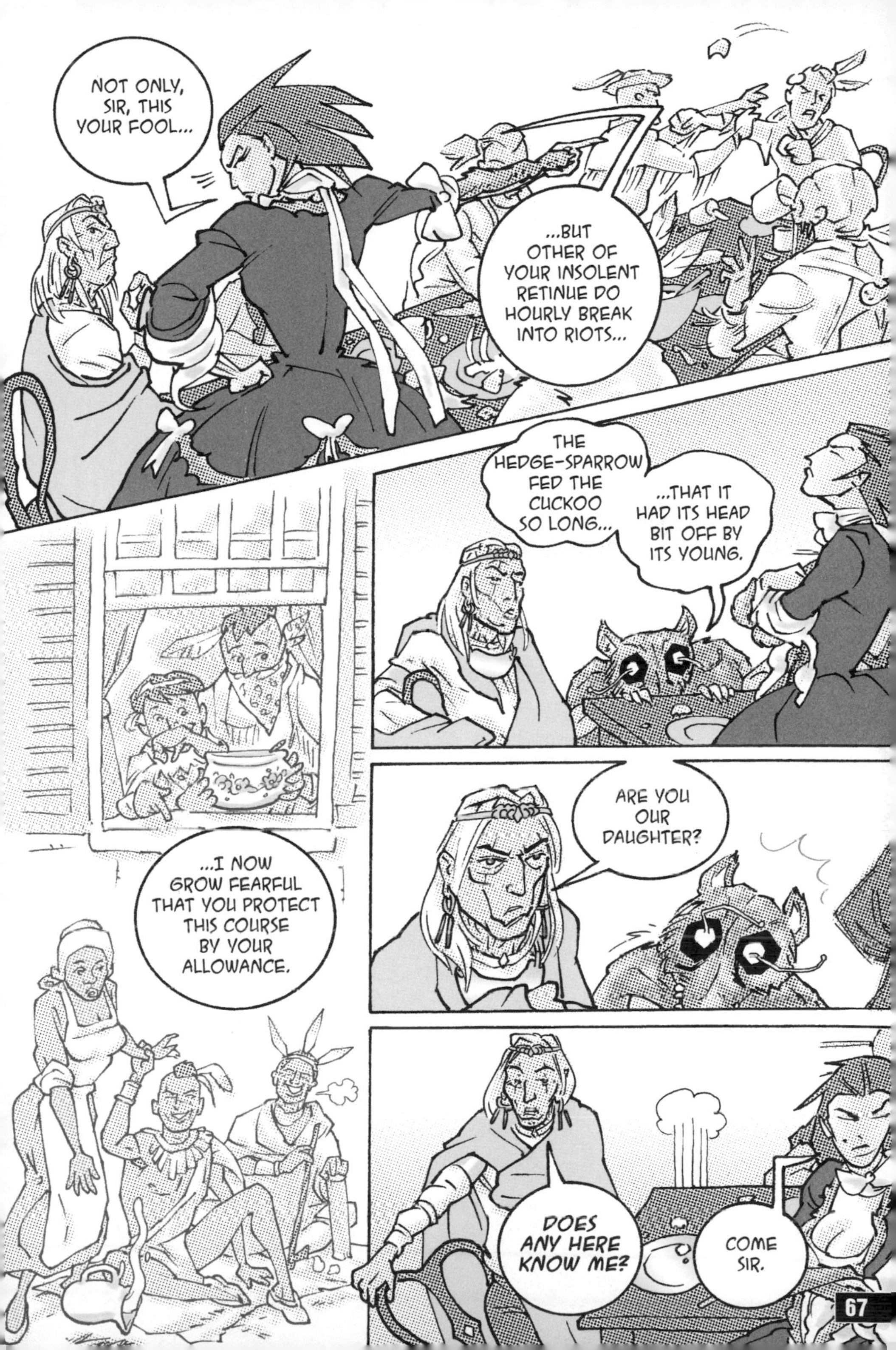
NOT ONLY, SIR, THIS YOUR FOOL...
...BUT OTHER OF YOUR INSOLENT RETINUE DO HOURLY BREAK INTO RIOTS...
...I NOW GROW FEARFUL THAT YOU PROTECT THIS COURSE BY YOUR ALLOWANCE.
THE HEDGE-SPARROW FED THE CUCKOO SO LONG...
...THAT IT HAD ITS HEAD BIT OFF BY ITS YOUNG.
ARE YOU OUR DAUGHTER?
DOES ANY HERE KNOW ME?
COME SIR.

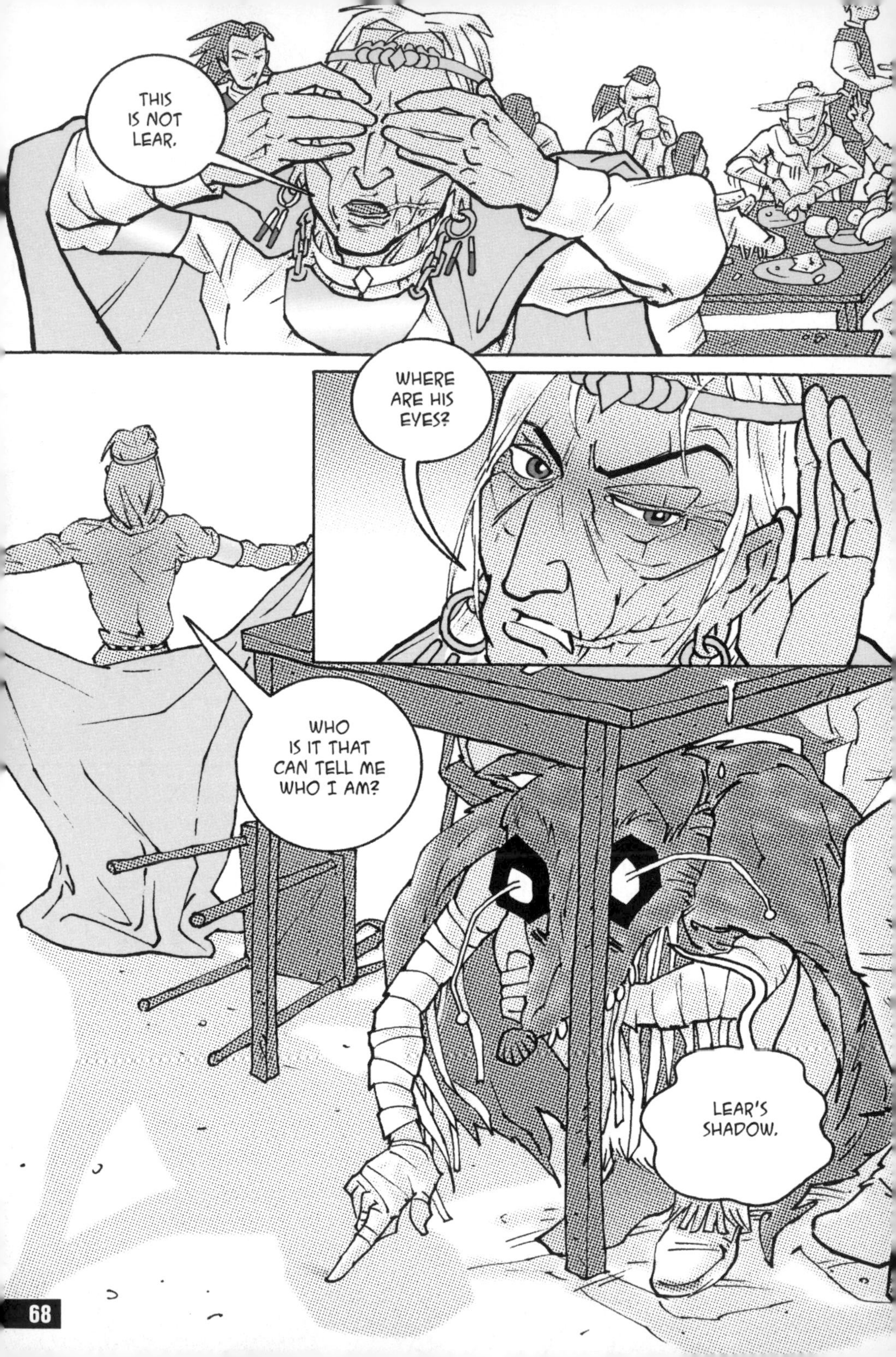

THIS IS NOT LEAR.
WHERE ARE HIS EYES?
WHO IS IT THAT CAN TELL ME WHO I AM?
LEAR'S SHADOW.

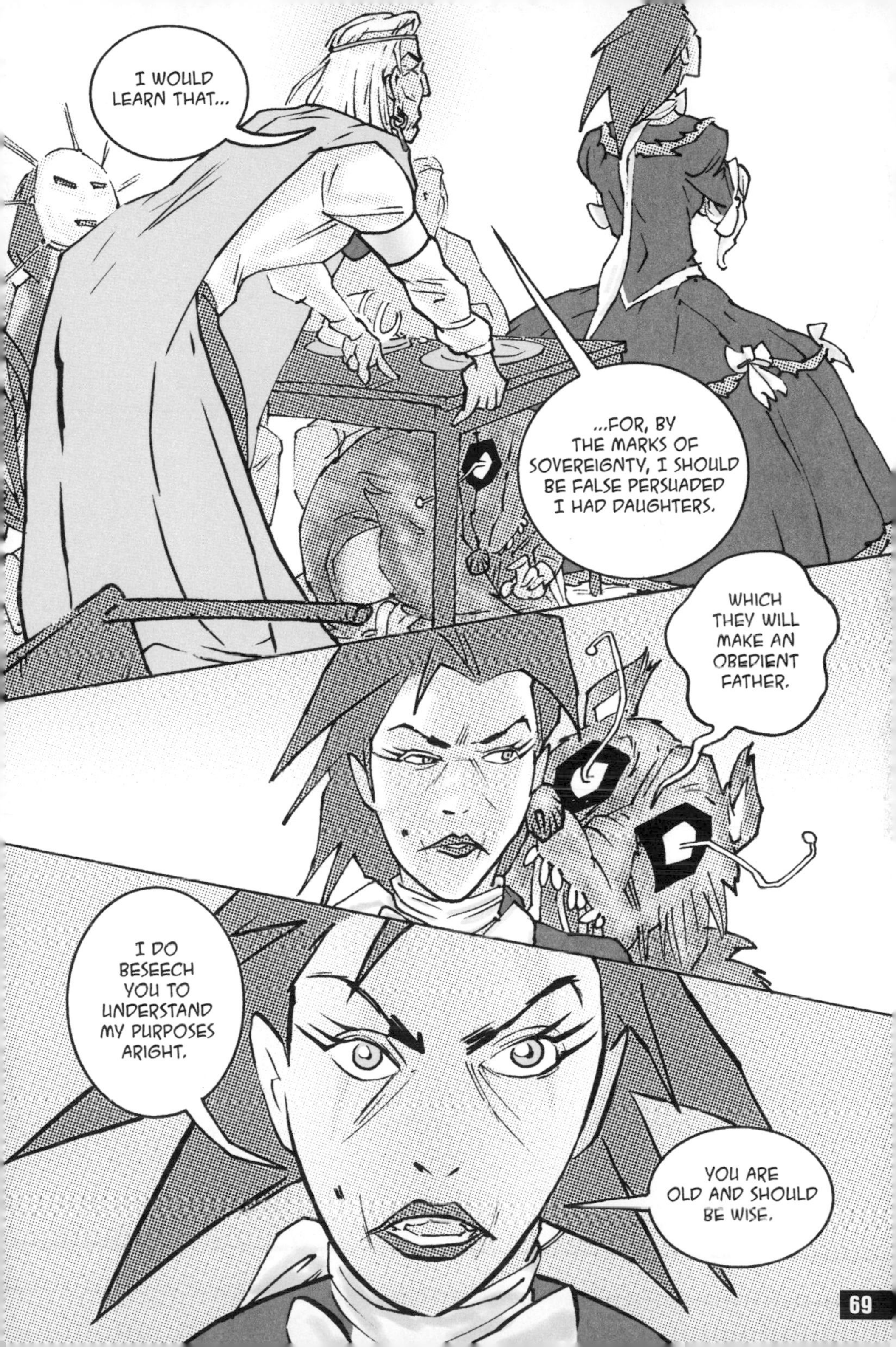
I WOULD LEARN THAT...
...FOR, BY THE MARKS OF SOVEREIGNTY, I SHOULD BE FALSE PERSUADED I HAD DAUGHTERS.
WHICH THEY WILL MAKE AN OBEDIENT FATHER.
I DO BESEECH YOU TO UNDERSTAND MY PURPOSES ARIGHT.
YOU ARE OLD AND SHOULD BE WISE.

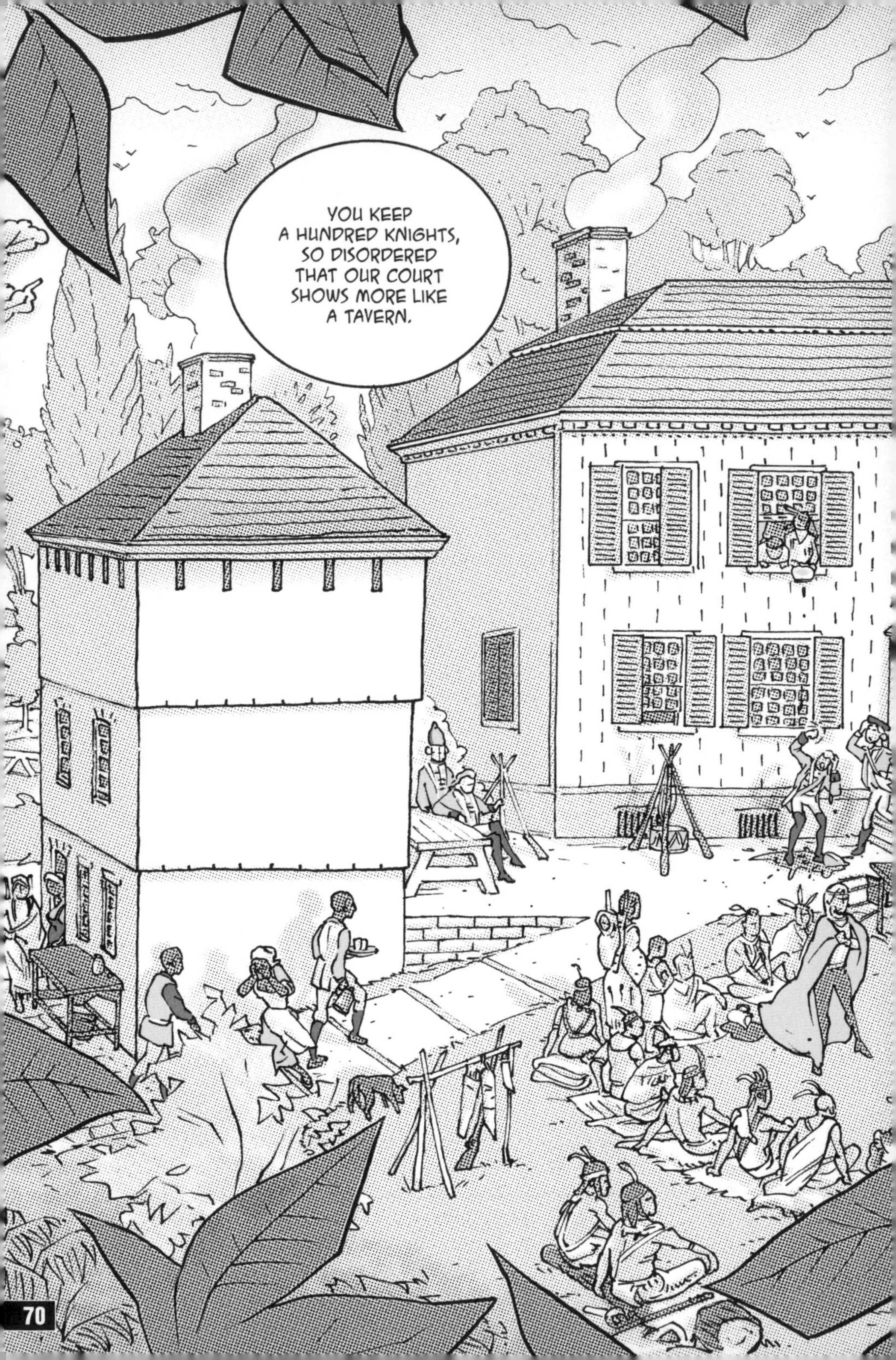
YOU KEEP A HUNDRED KNIGHTS, SO DISORDERED THAT OUR COURT SHOWS MORE LIKE A TAVERN.

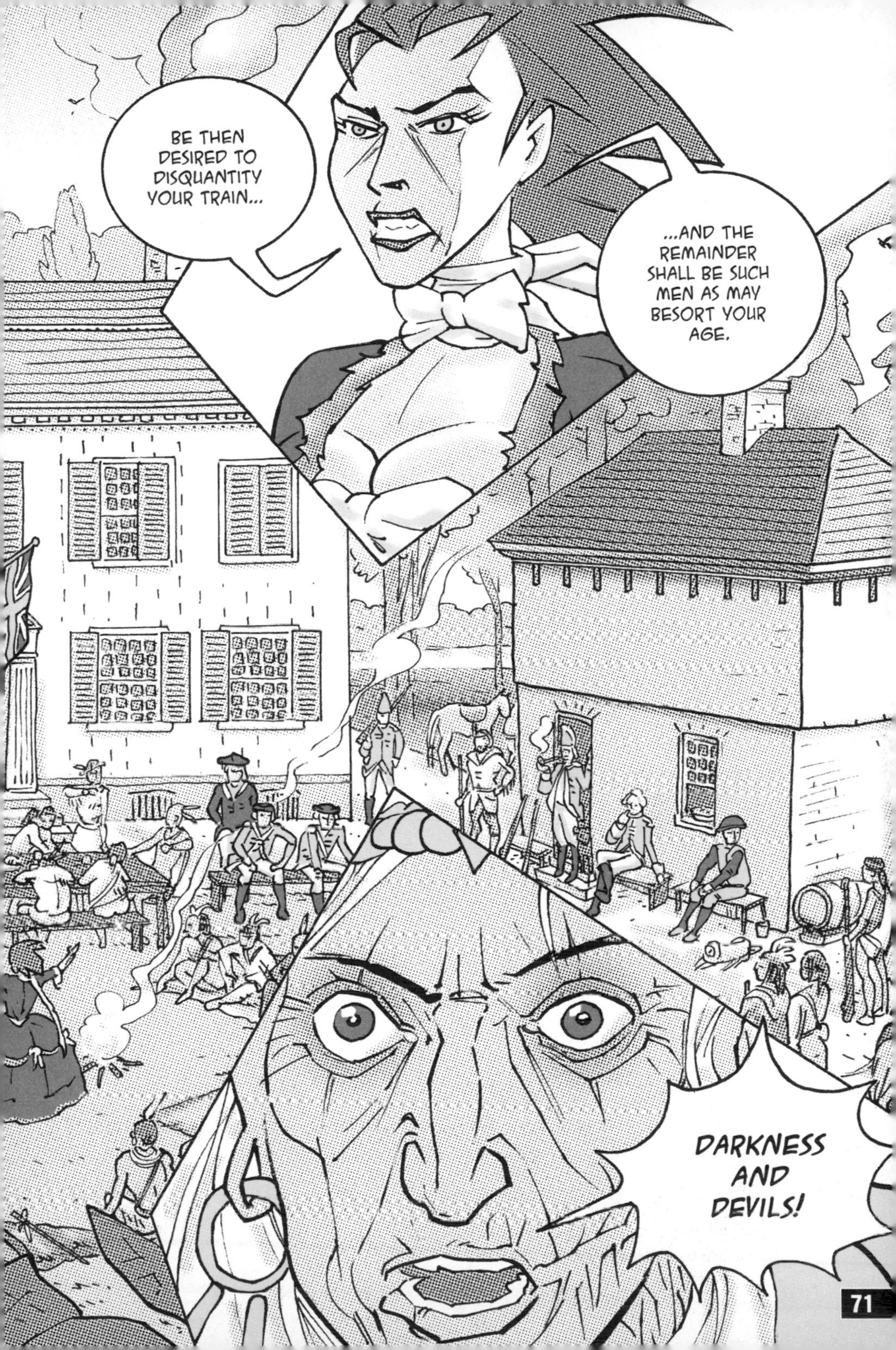
BE THEN DESIRED TO DISQUANTITY YOUR TRAIN...
...AND THE REMAINDER SHALL BE SUCH MEN AS MAY BESORT YOUR AGE.
DARKNESS AND DEVILS!

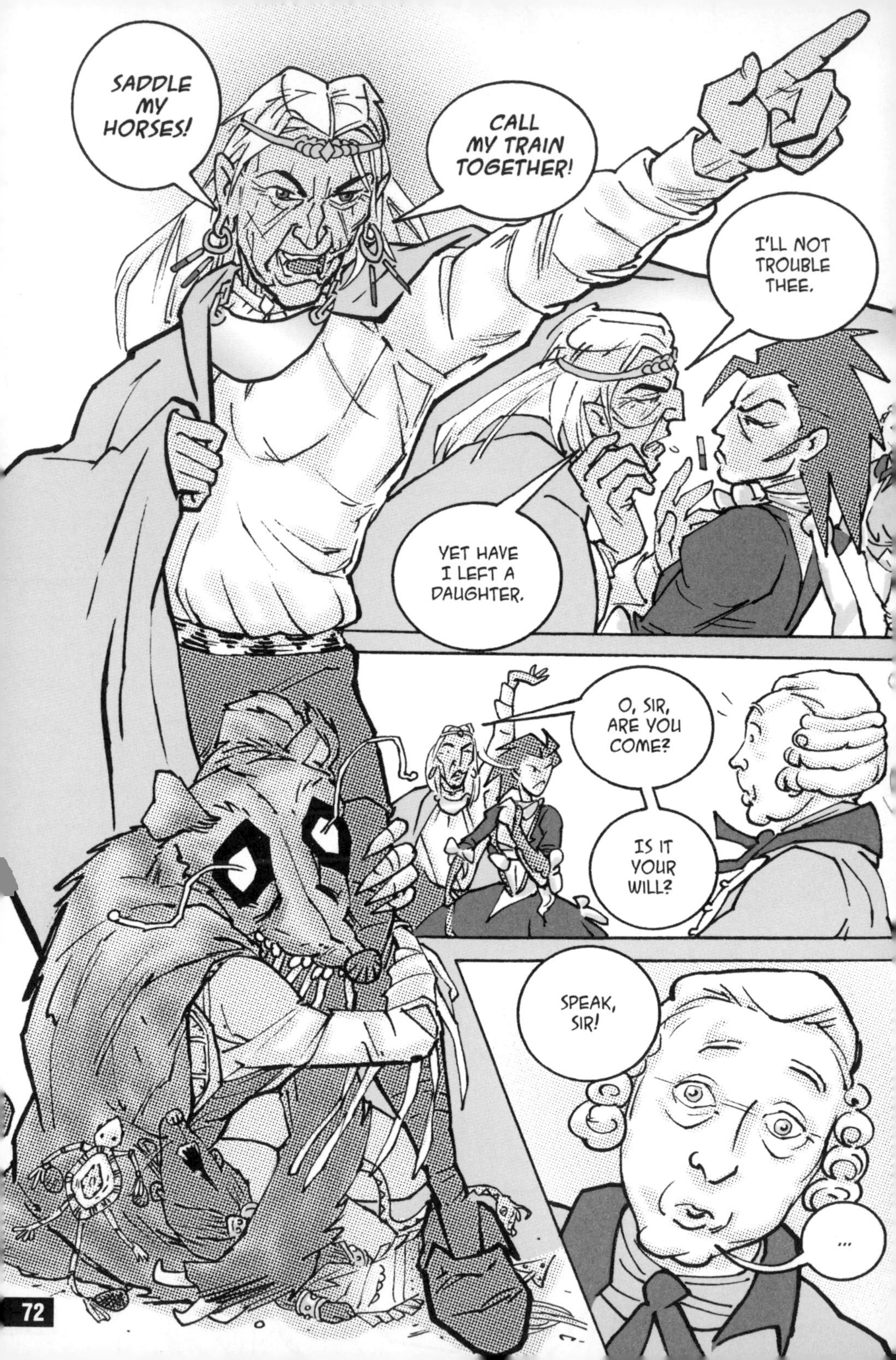

SADDLE MY HORSES!
CALL MY TRAIN TOGETHER!
I'LL NOT TROUBLE THEE.
YET HAVE I LEFT A DAUGHTER.
O, SIR, ARE YOU COME?
IS IT YOUR WILL?
SPEAK, SIR!
...

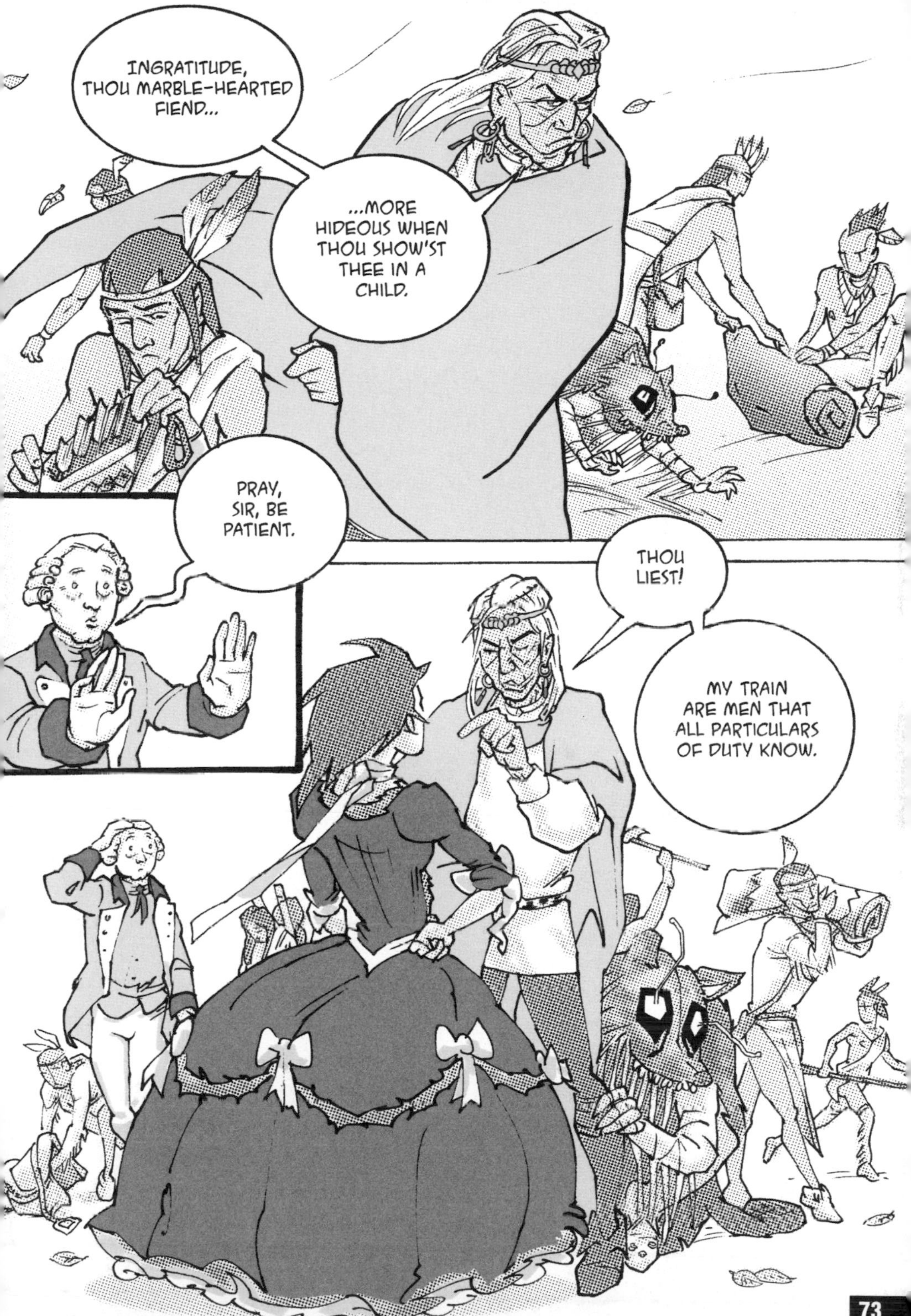
INGRATITUDE, THOU MARBLE-HEARTED FIEND...
...MORE HIDEOUS WHEN THOU SHOW'ST THEE IN A CHILD.
PRAY, SIR, BE PATIENT.
THOU LIEST!
MY TRAIN ARE MEN THAT ALL PARTICULARS OF DUTY KNOW.

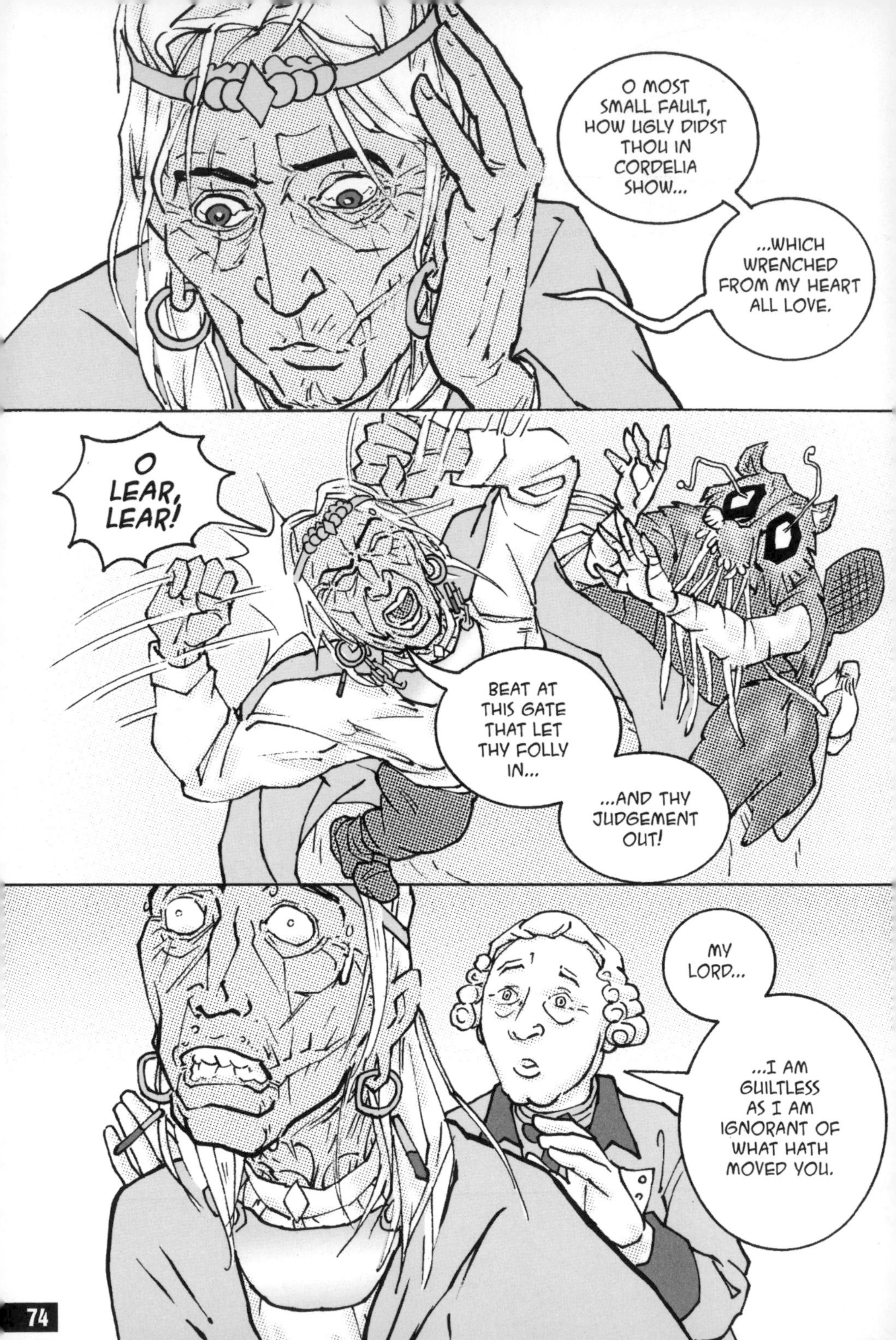
O MOST SMALL FAULT, HOW UGLY DIDST THOU IN CORDELIA SHOW...
...WHICH WRENCHED FROM MY HEART ALL LOVE.
O LEAR, LEAR!
BEAT AT THIS GATE THAT LET THY FOLLY IN...
...AND THY JUDGEMENT OUT!
MY LORD...
...I AM GUILTLESS AS I AM IGNORANT OF WHAT HATH MOVED YOU.

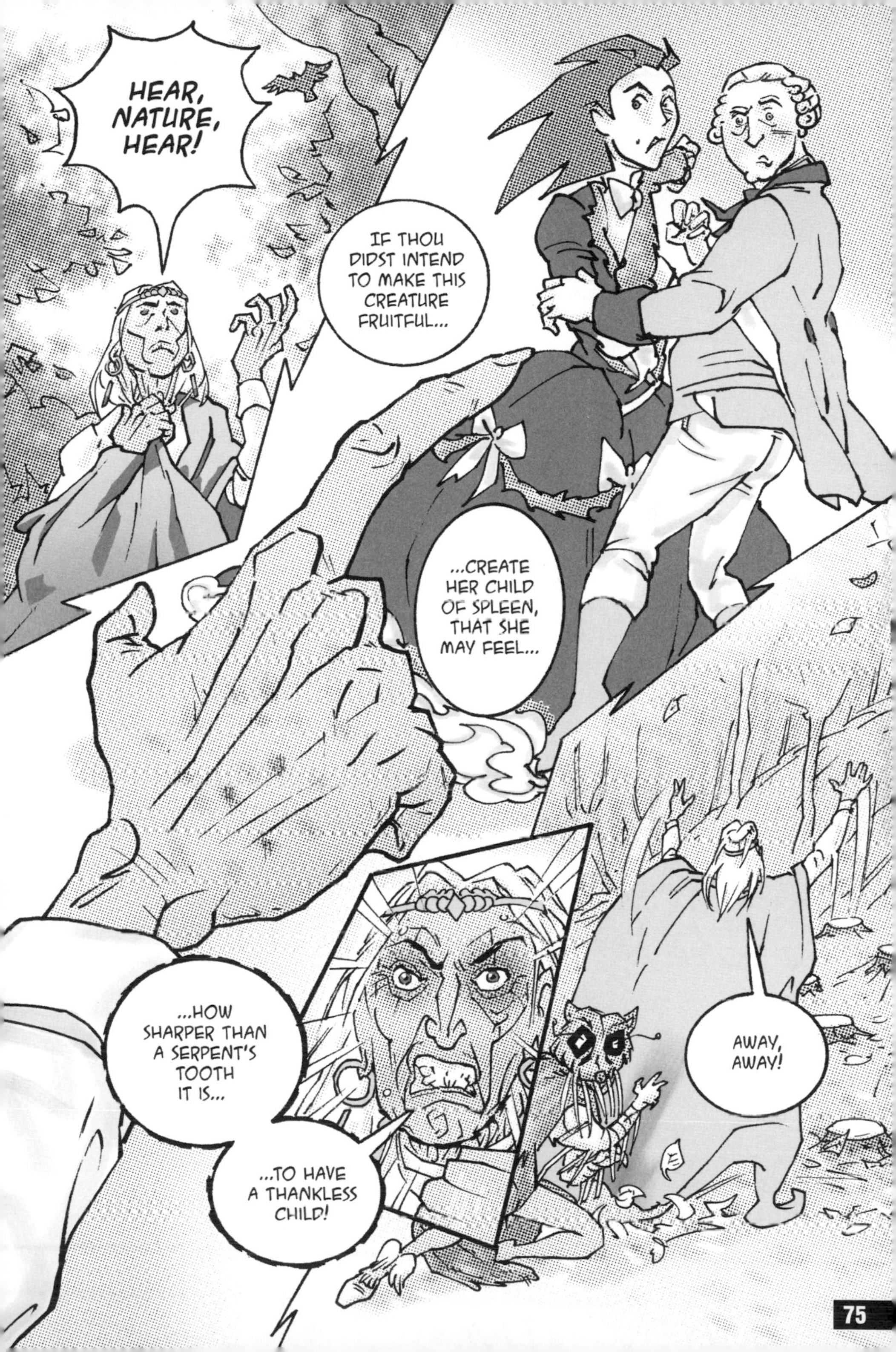
HEAR, NATURE, HEAR!
IF THOU DIDST INTEND TO MAKE THIS CREATURE FRUITFUL...
...CREATE HER CHILD OF SPLEEN, THAT SHE MAY FEEL...
...HOW SHARPER THAN A SERPENT'S TOOTH IT IS...
...TO HAVE A THANKLESS CHILD!
AWAY, AWAY!

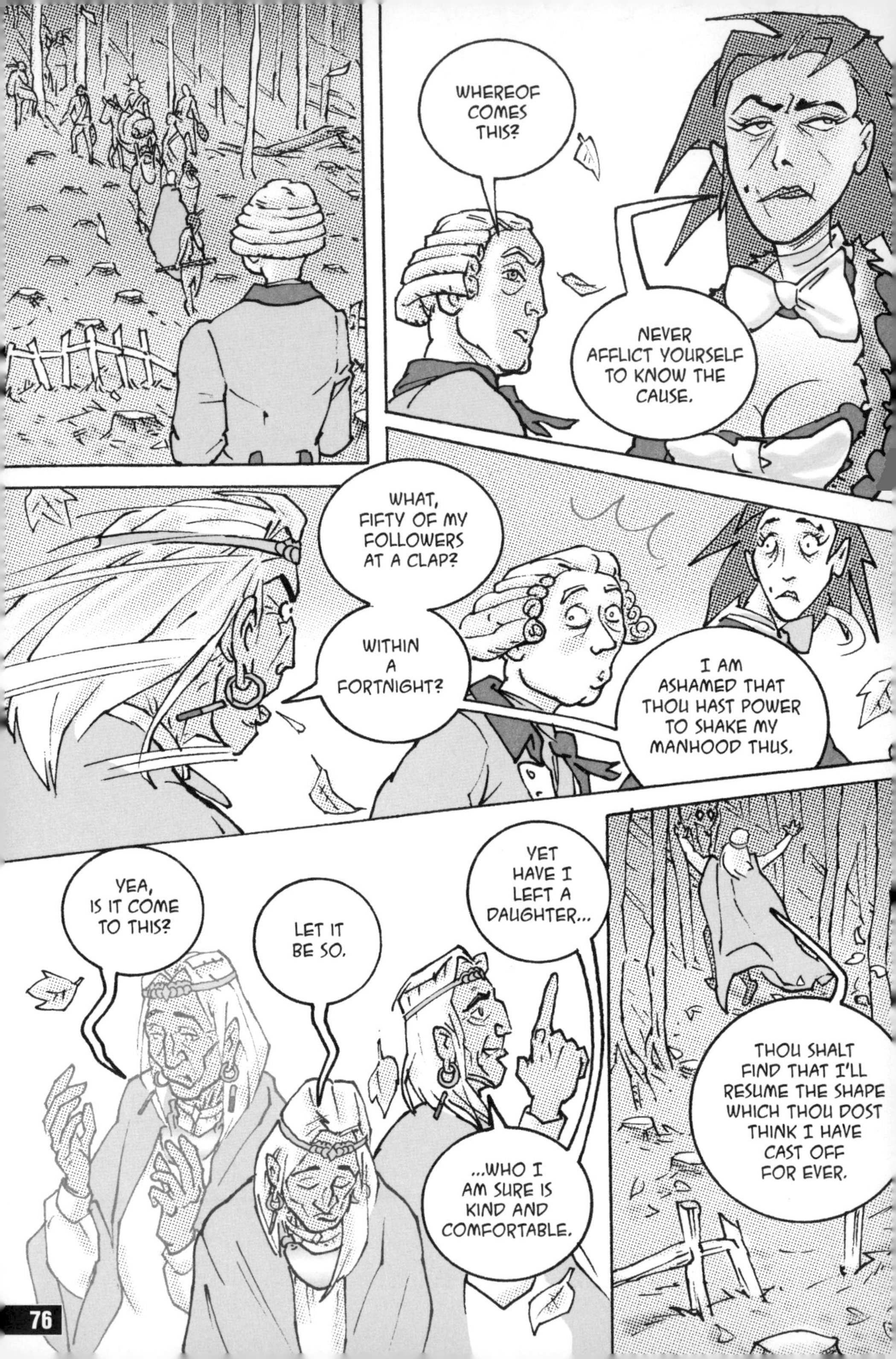
WHEREOF COMES THIS?
NEVER AFFLICT YOURSELF TO KNOW THE CAUSE.
WHAT, FIFTY OF MY FOLLOWERS AT A CLAP?
WITHIN A FORTNIGHT?
I AM ASHAMED THAT THOU HAST POWER TO SHAKE MY MANHOOD THUS.
YEA, IS IT COME TO THIS?
LET IT BE SO.
YET HAVE I LEFT A DAUGHTER...
...WHO I AM SURE IS KIND AND COMFORTABLE.
THOU SHALT FIND THAT I'LL RESUME THE SHAPE WHICH THOU DOST THINK I HAVE CAST OFF FOR EVER.

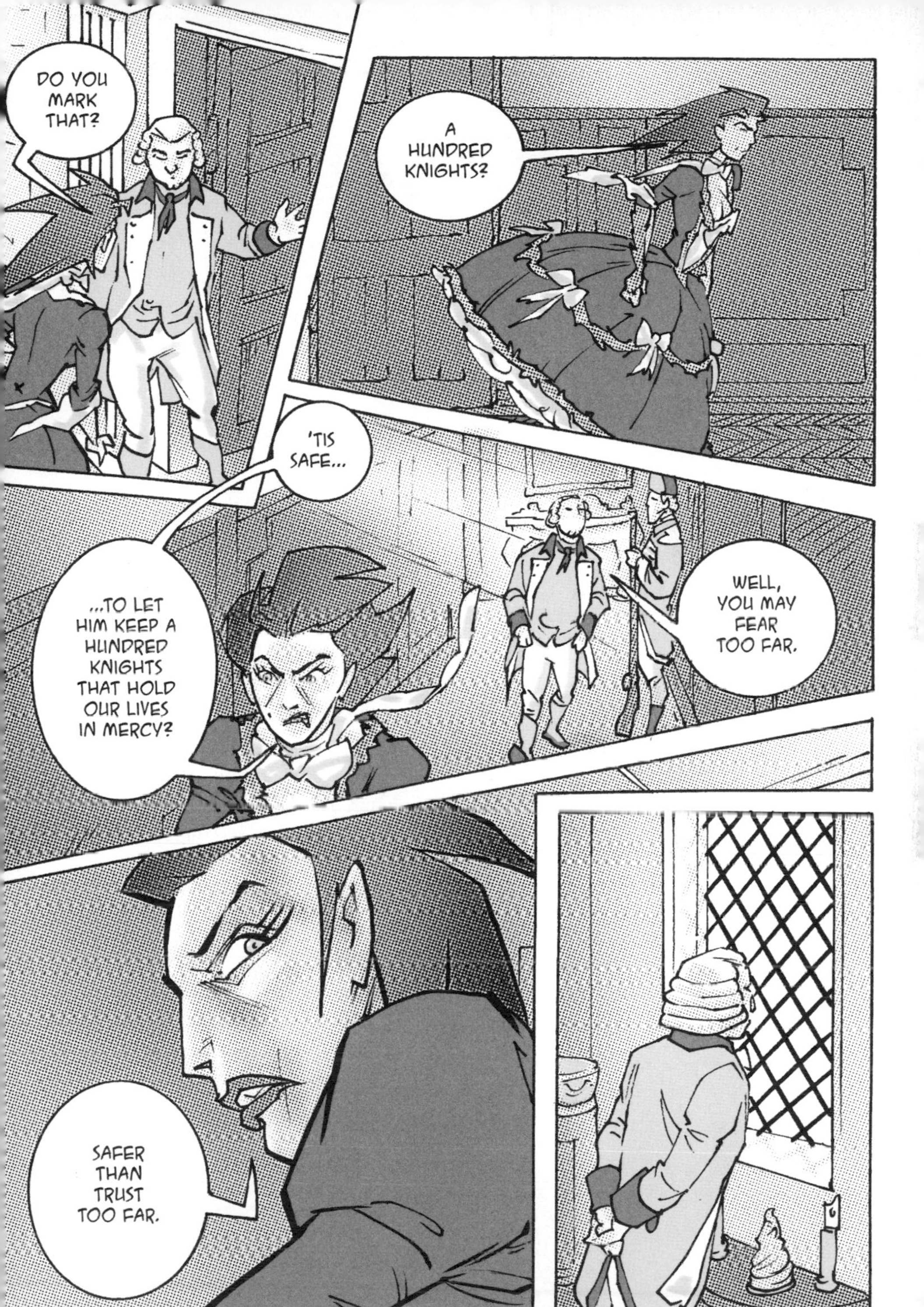
DO YOU MARK THAT?
A HUNDRED KNIGHTS?
'TIS SAFE...
...TO LET HIM KEEP A HUNDRED KNIGHTS THAT HOLD OUR LIVES IN MERCY?
WELL, YOU MAY FEAR TOO FAR.
SAFER THAN TRUST TOO FAR.

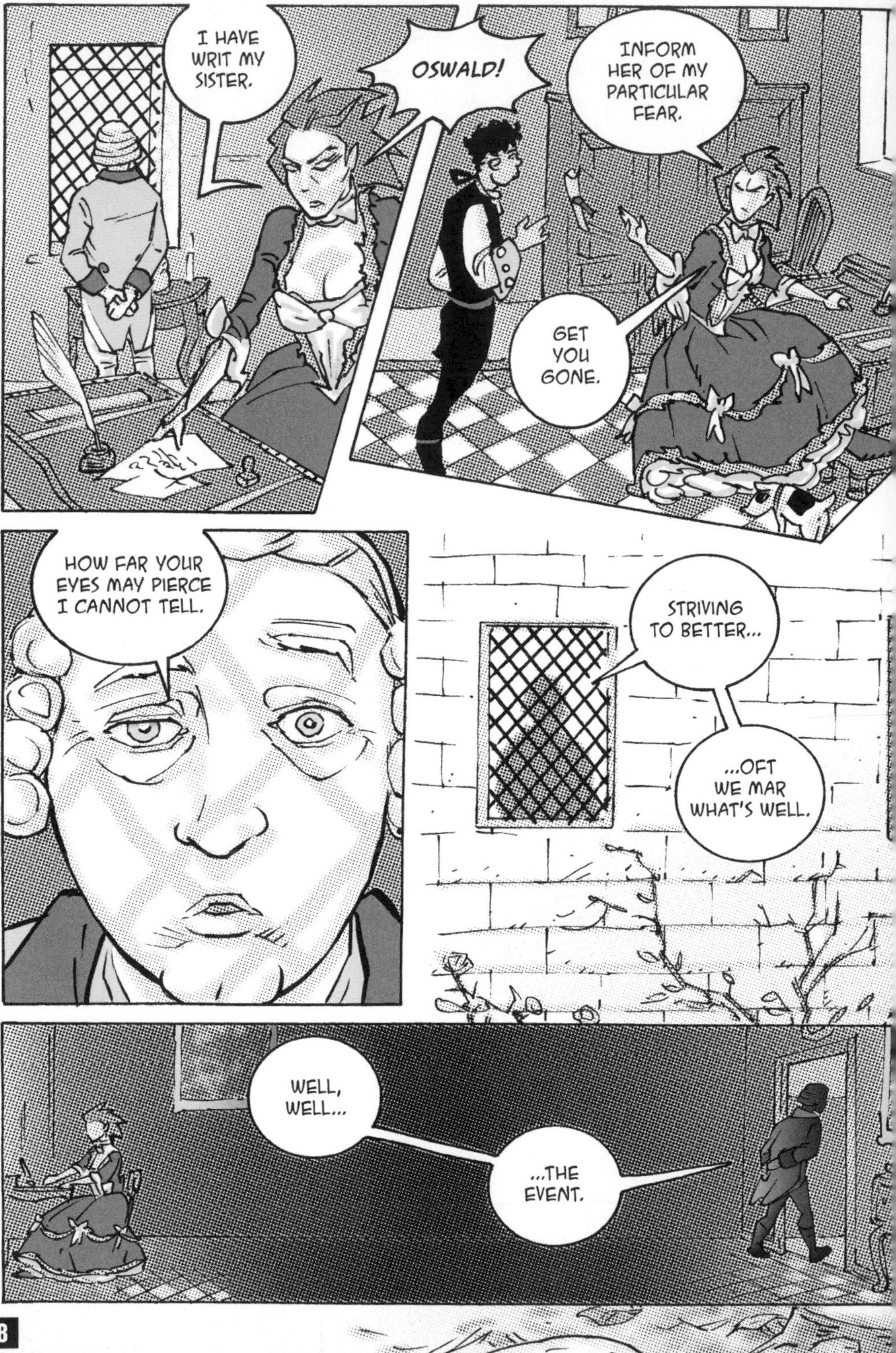
I HAVE WRIT MY SISTER.
OSWALD!
INFORM HER OF MY PARTICULAR FEAR.
GET YOU GONE.
HOW FAR YOUR EYES MAY PIERCE I CANNOT TELL.
STRIVING TO BETTER...
...OFT WE MAR WHAT'S WELL.
WELL, WELL...
...THE EVENT.

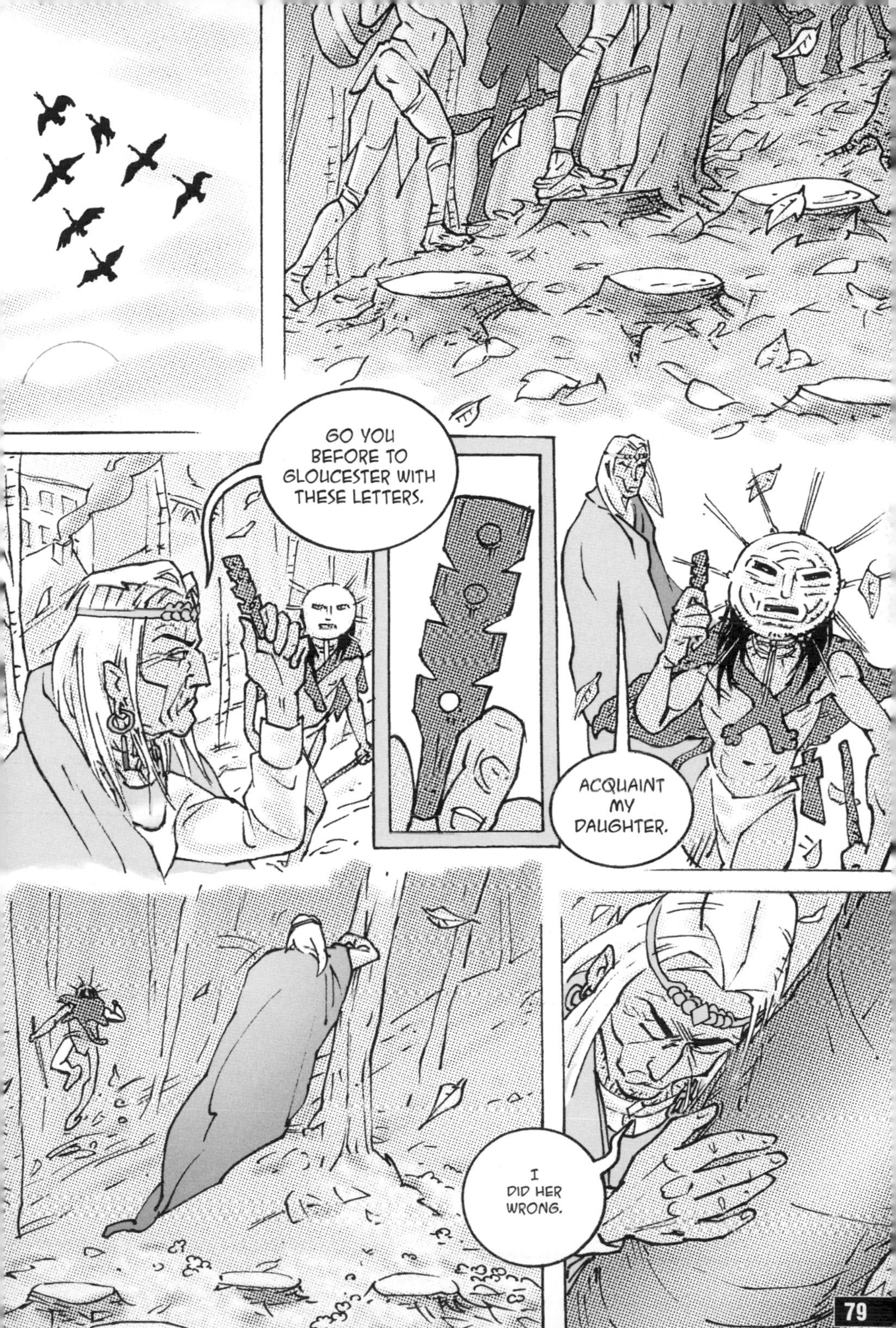
GO YOU BEFORE TO GLOUCESTER WITH THESE LETTERS.
ACQUAINT MY DAUGHTER.
I DID HER WRONG.

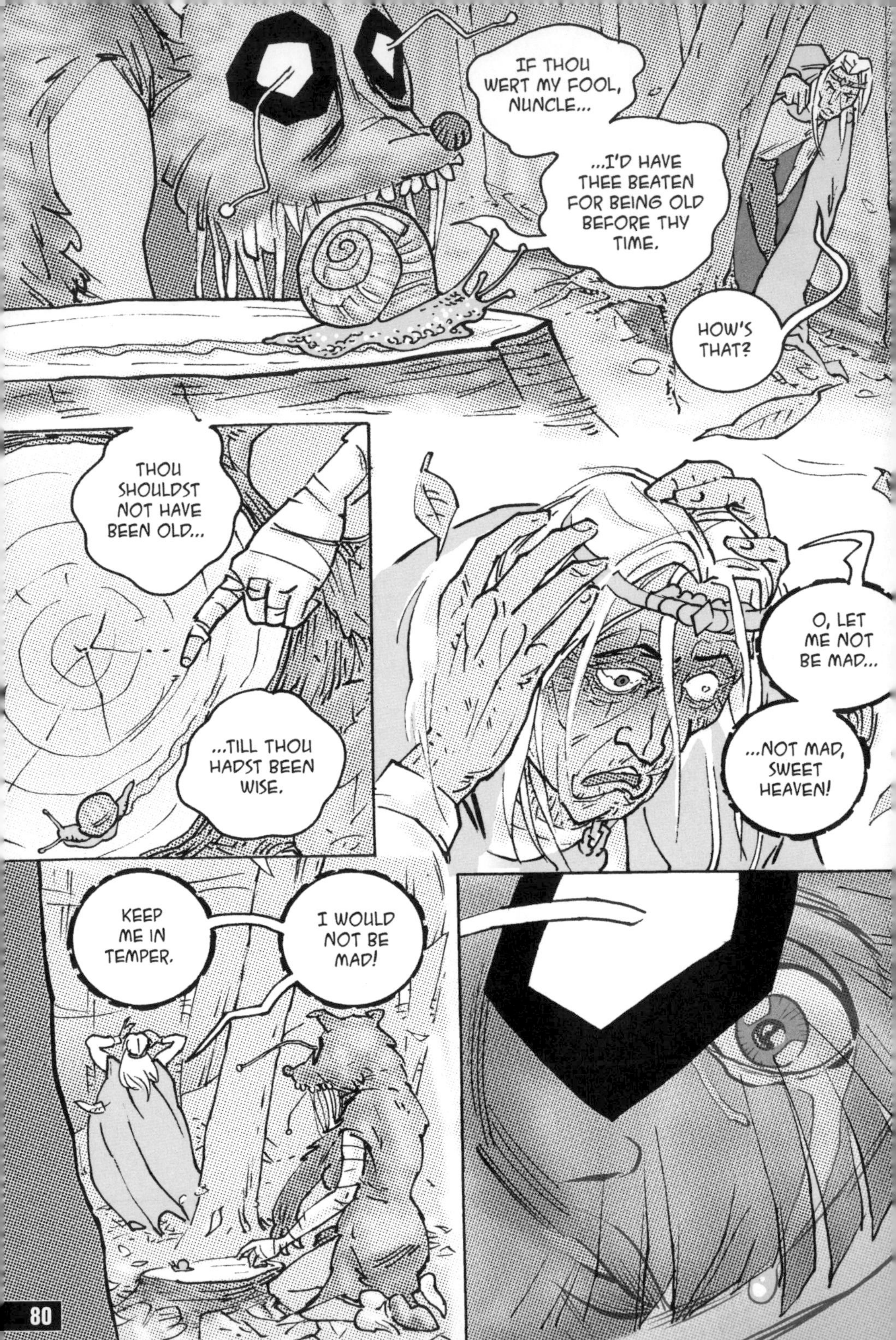
IF THOU WERT MY FOOL, NUNCLE...
...I'D HAVE THEE BEATEN FOR BEING OLD BEFORE THY TIME.
HOW'S THAT?
THOU SHOULDST NOT HAVE BEEN OLD...
...TILL THOU HADST BEEN WISE.
O, LET ME NOT BE MAD...
...NOT MAD, SWEET HEAVEN!
KEEP ME IN TEMPER.
I WOULD NOT BE MAD!

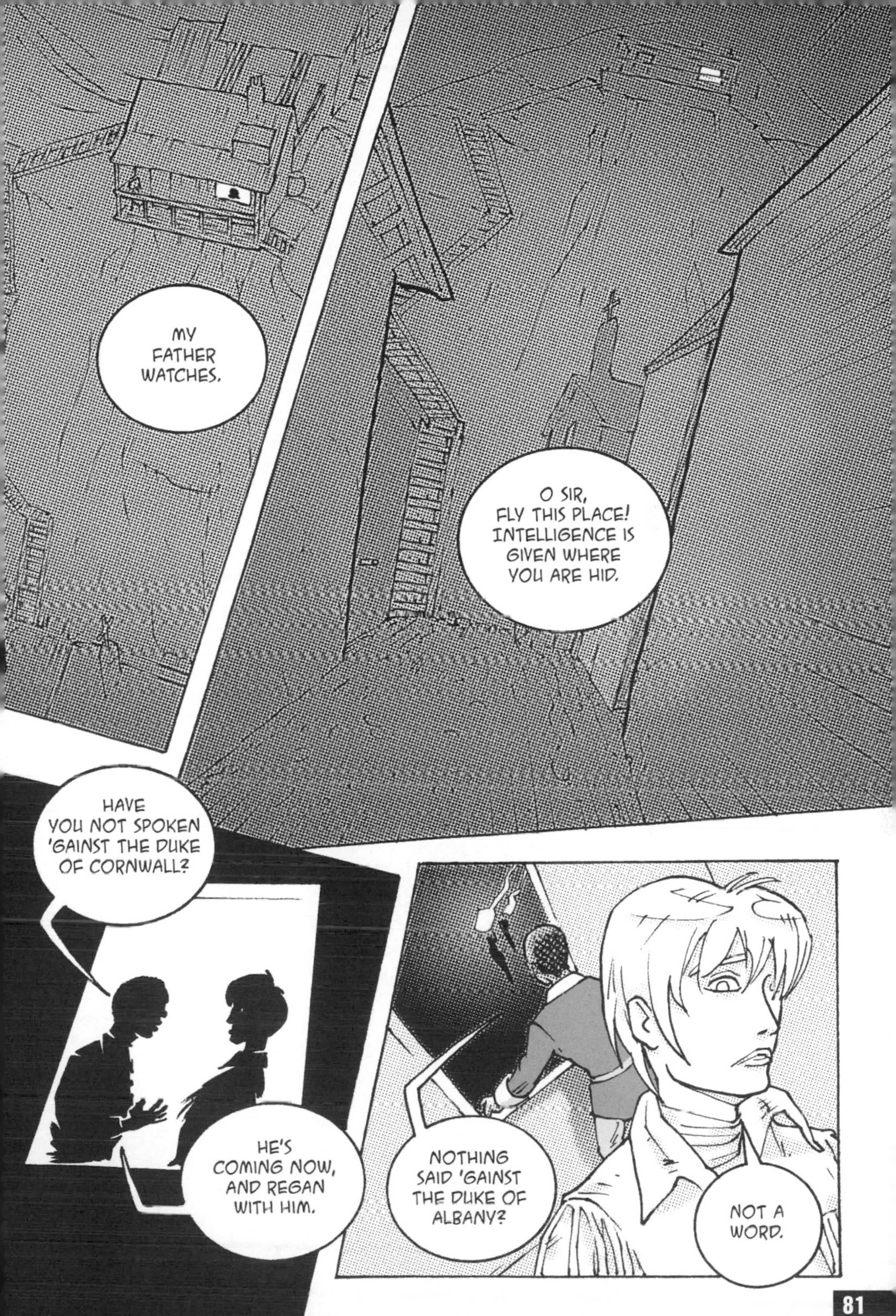
MY FATHER WATCHES.
O SIR, FLY THIS PLACE! INTELLIGENCE IS GIVEN WHERE YOU ARE HID.
HAVE YOU NOT SPOKEN 'GAINST THE DUKE OF CORNWALL?
HE'S COMING NOW, AND REGAN WITH HIM.
NOTHING SAID 'GAINST THE DUKE OF ALBANY?
NOT A WORD.

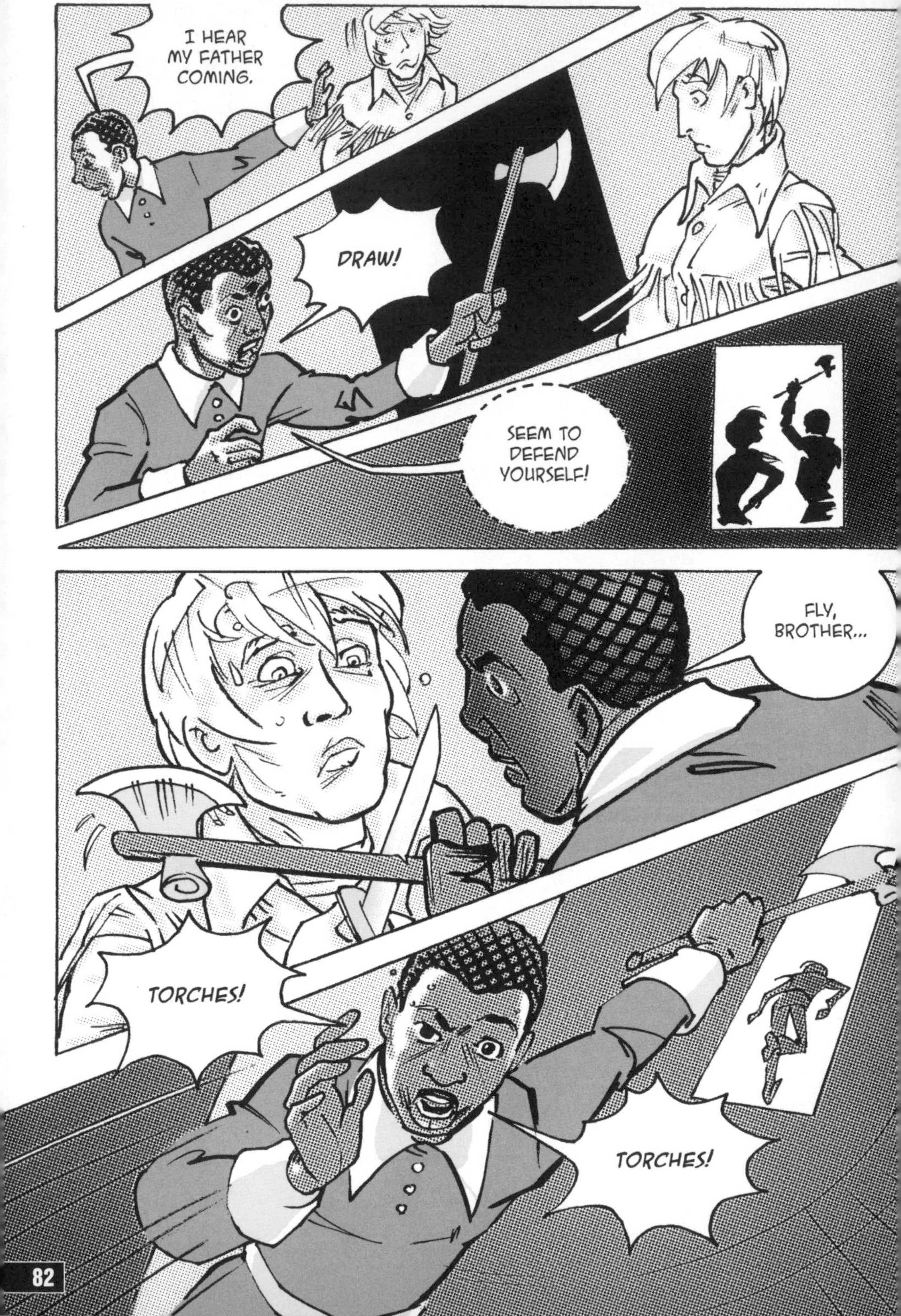
I HEAR MY FATHER COMING.
DRAW!
SEEM TO DEFEND YOURSELF!
FLY, BROTHER...
TORCHES!
TORCHES!

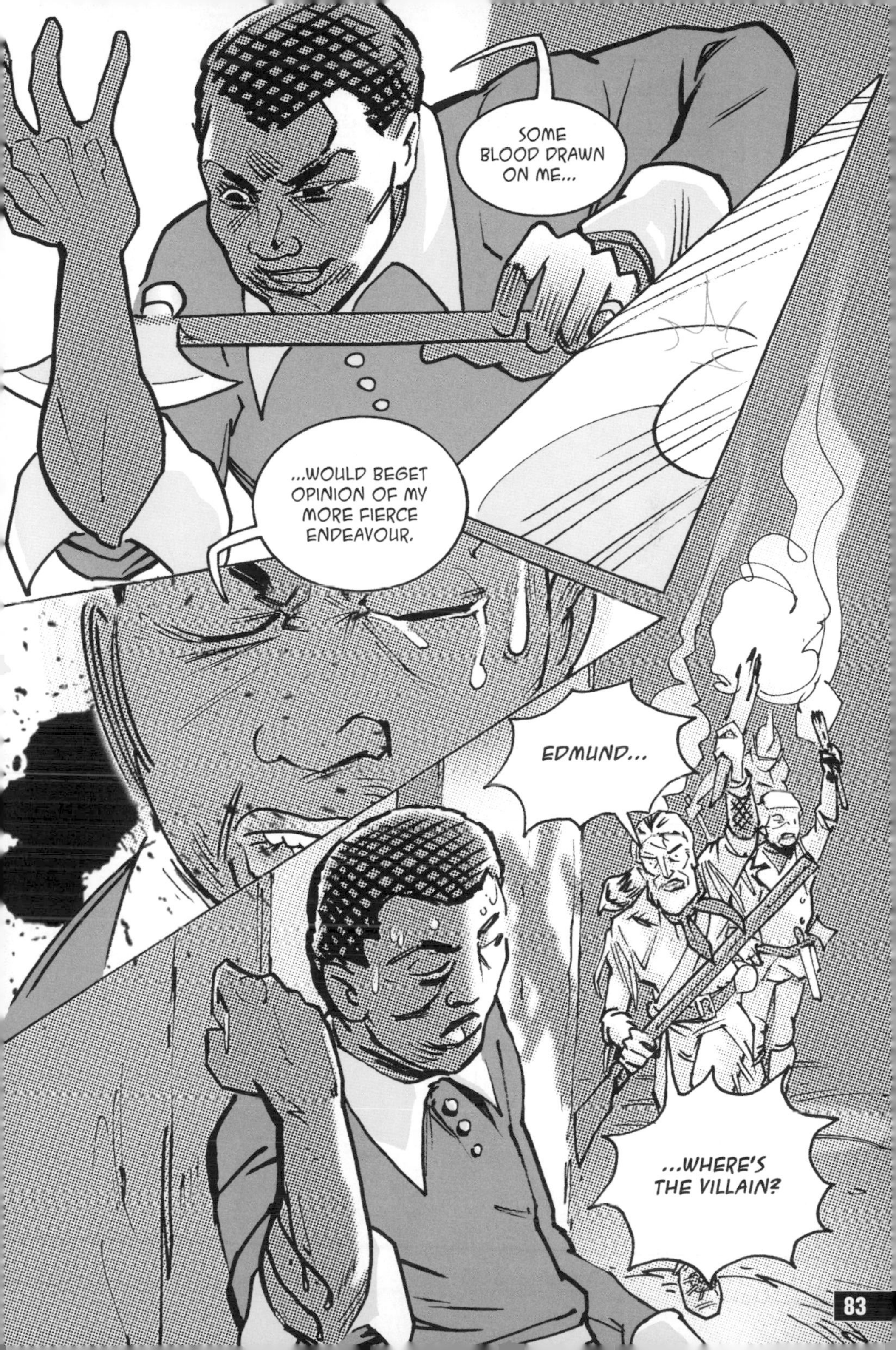
SOME BLOOD DRAWN ON ME...
...WOULD BEGET OPINION OF MY MORE FIERCE ENDEAVOUR.
EDMUND...
...WHERE'S THE VILLAIN?

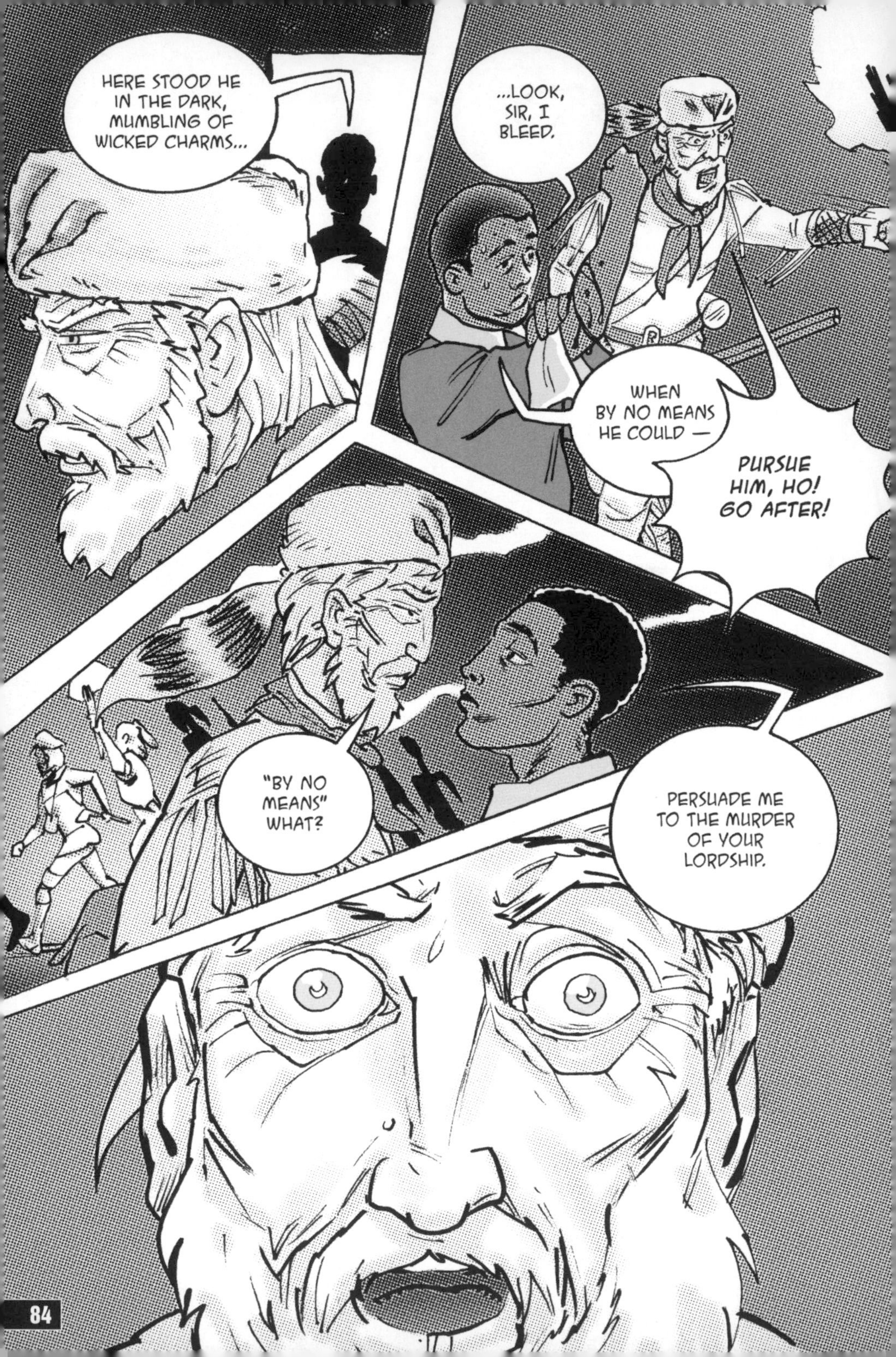
HERE STOOD HE IN THE DARK, MUMBLING OF WICKED CHARMS...
...LOOK, SIR, I BLEED.
WHEN BY NO MEANS HE COULD —
PURSUE HIM, HO! GO AFTER!
"BY NO MEANS" WHAT?
PERSUADE ME TO THE MURDER OF YOUR LORDSHIP.

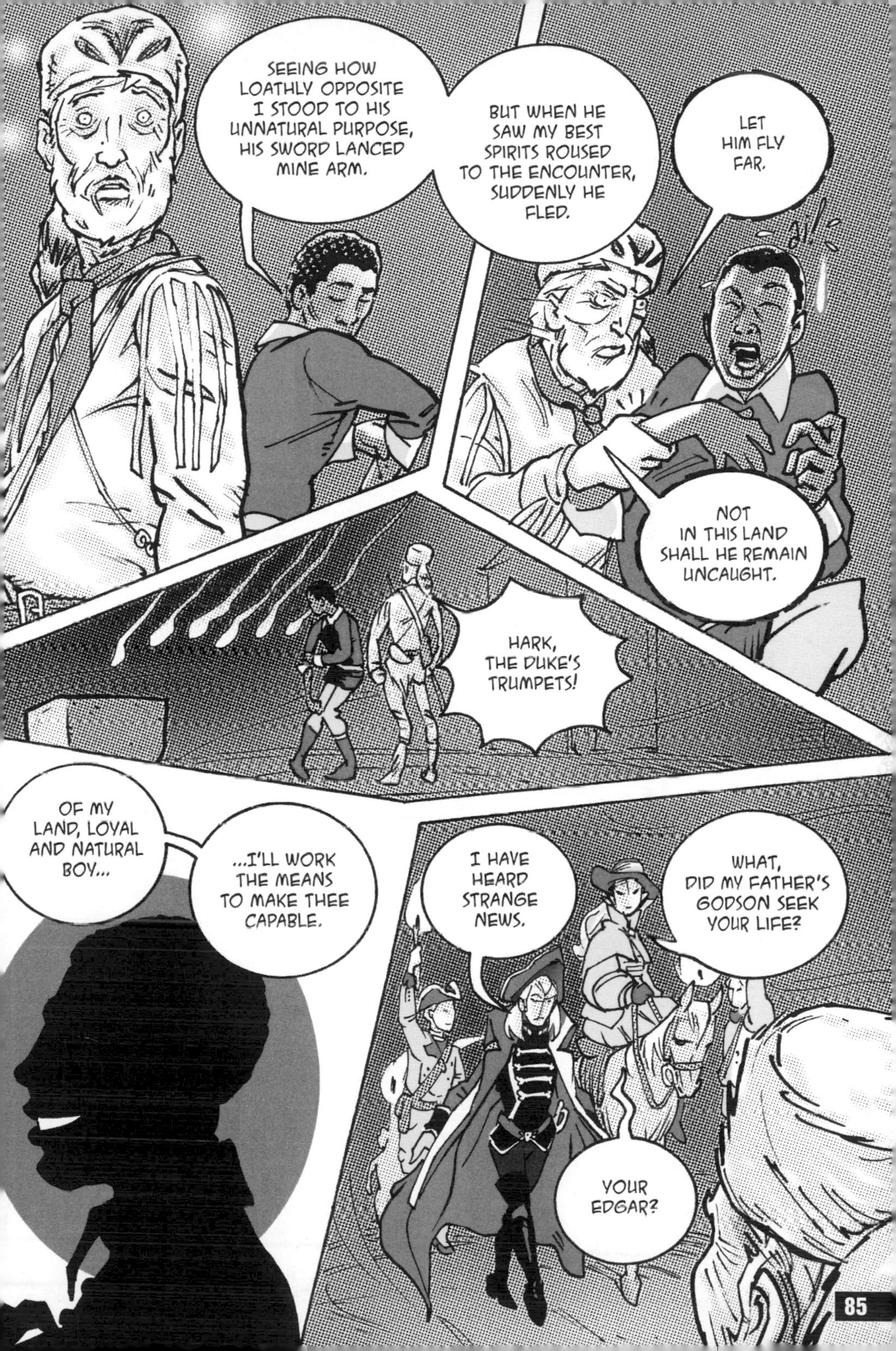
SEEING HOW LOATHLY OPPOSITE I STOOD TO HIS UNNATURAL PURPOSE, HIS SWORD LANCED MINE ARM.
BUT WHEN HE SAW MY BEST SPIRITS ROUSED TO THE ENCOUNTER, SUDDENLY HE FLED.
LET HIM FLY FAR.
NOT IN THIS LAND SHALL HE REMAIN UNCAUGHT.
HARK, THE DUKE'S TRUMPETS!
OF MY LAND, LOYAL AND NATURAL BOY...
...I'LL WORK THE MEANS TO MAKE THEE CAPABLE.
I HAVE HEARD STRANGE NEWS.
WHAT, DID MY FATHER'S GODSON SEEK YOUR LIFE?
YOUR EDGAR?

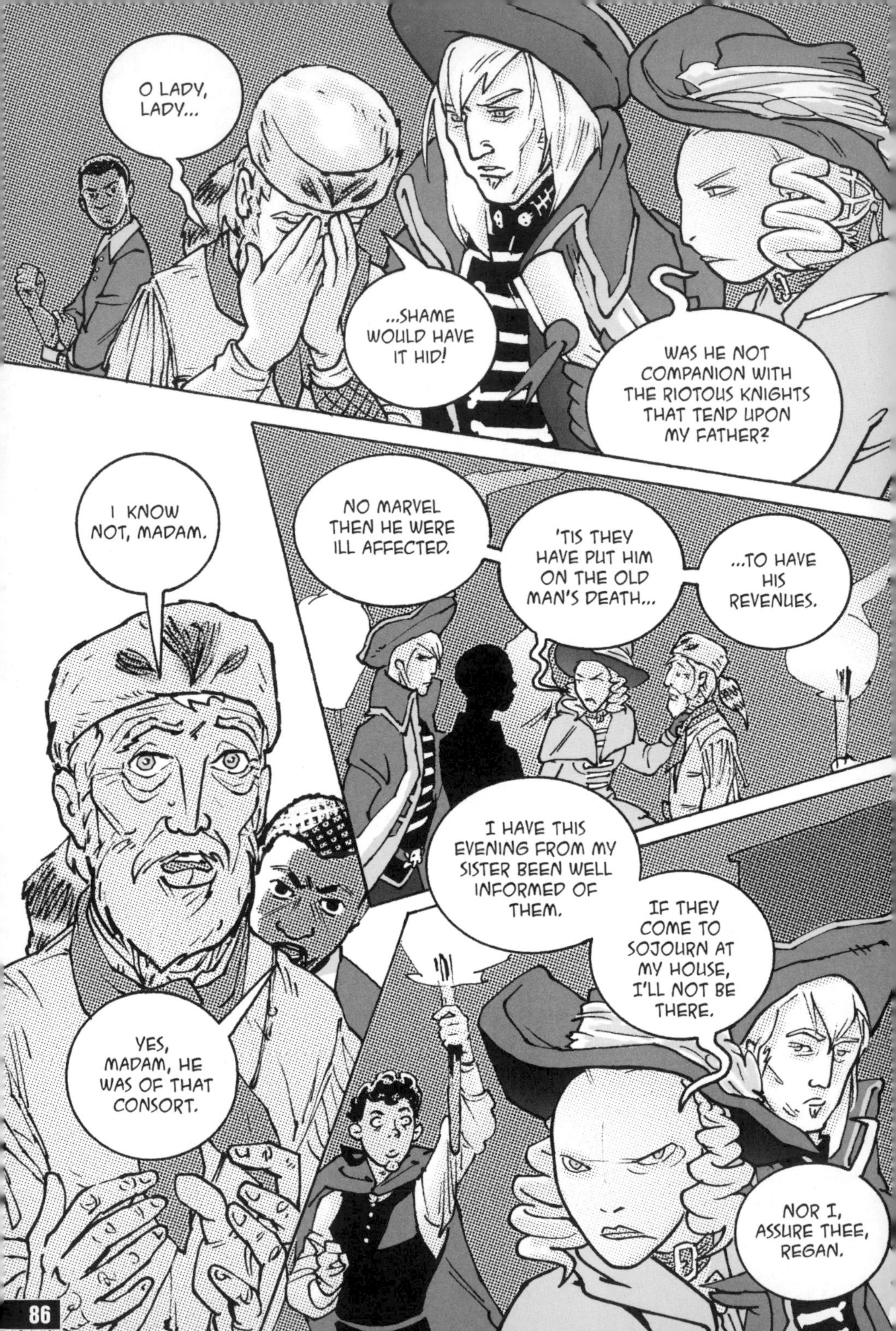
O LADY, LADY...
...SHAME WOULD HAVE IT HID!
WAS HE NOT COMPANION WITH THE RIOTOUS KNIGHTS THAT TEND UPON MY FATHER?
I KNOW NOT, MADAM.
YES, MADAM, HE WAS OF THAT CONSORT.
NO MARVEL THEN HE WERE ILL AFFECTED.
'TIS THEY HAVE PUT HIM ON THE OLD MAN'S DEATH...
...TO HAVE HIS REVENUES.
I HAVE THIS EVENING FROM MY SISTER BEEN WELL INFORMED OF THEM.
IF THEY COME TO SOJOURN AT MY HOUSE, I'LL NOT BE THERE.
NOR I, ASSURE THEE, REGAN.

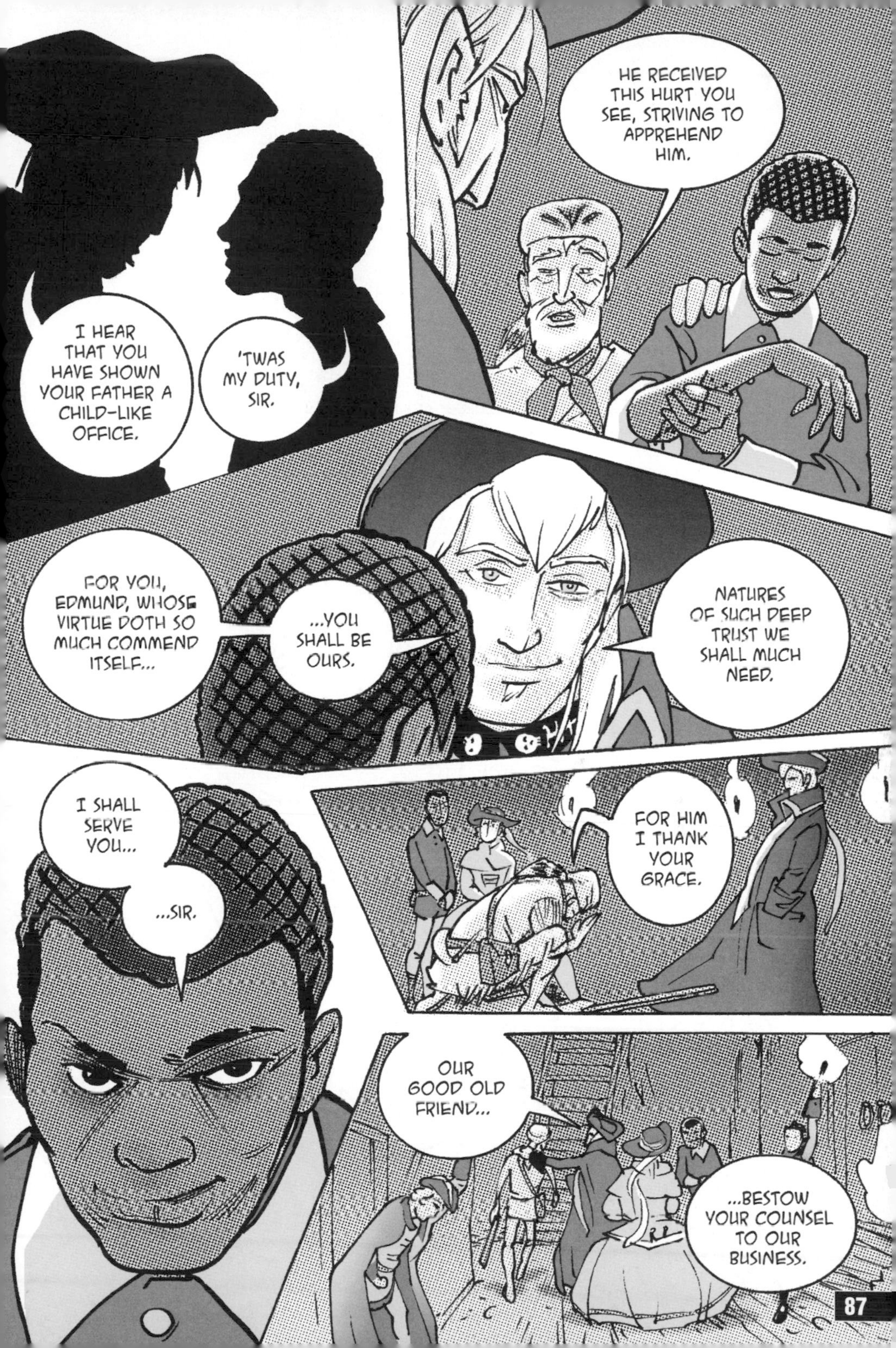
I HEAR THAT YOU HAVE SHOWN YOUR FATHER A CHILD-LIKE OFFICE.
'TWAS MY DUTY, SIR.
HE RECEIVED THIS HURT YOU SEE, STRIVING TO APPREHEND HIM.
FOR YOU, EDMUND, WHOSE VIRTUE DOTH SO MUCH COMMEND ITSELF...
...YOU SHALL BE OURS.
NATURES OF SUCH DEEP TRUST WE SHALL MUCH NEED.
I SHALL SERVE YOU...
...SIR.
FOR HIM I THANK YOUR GRACE.
OUR GOOD OLD FRIEND...
...BESTOW YOUR COUNSEL TO OUR BUSINESS.

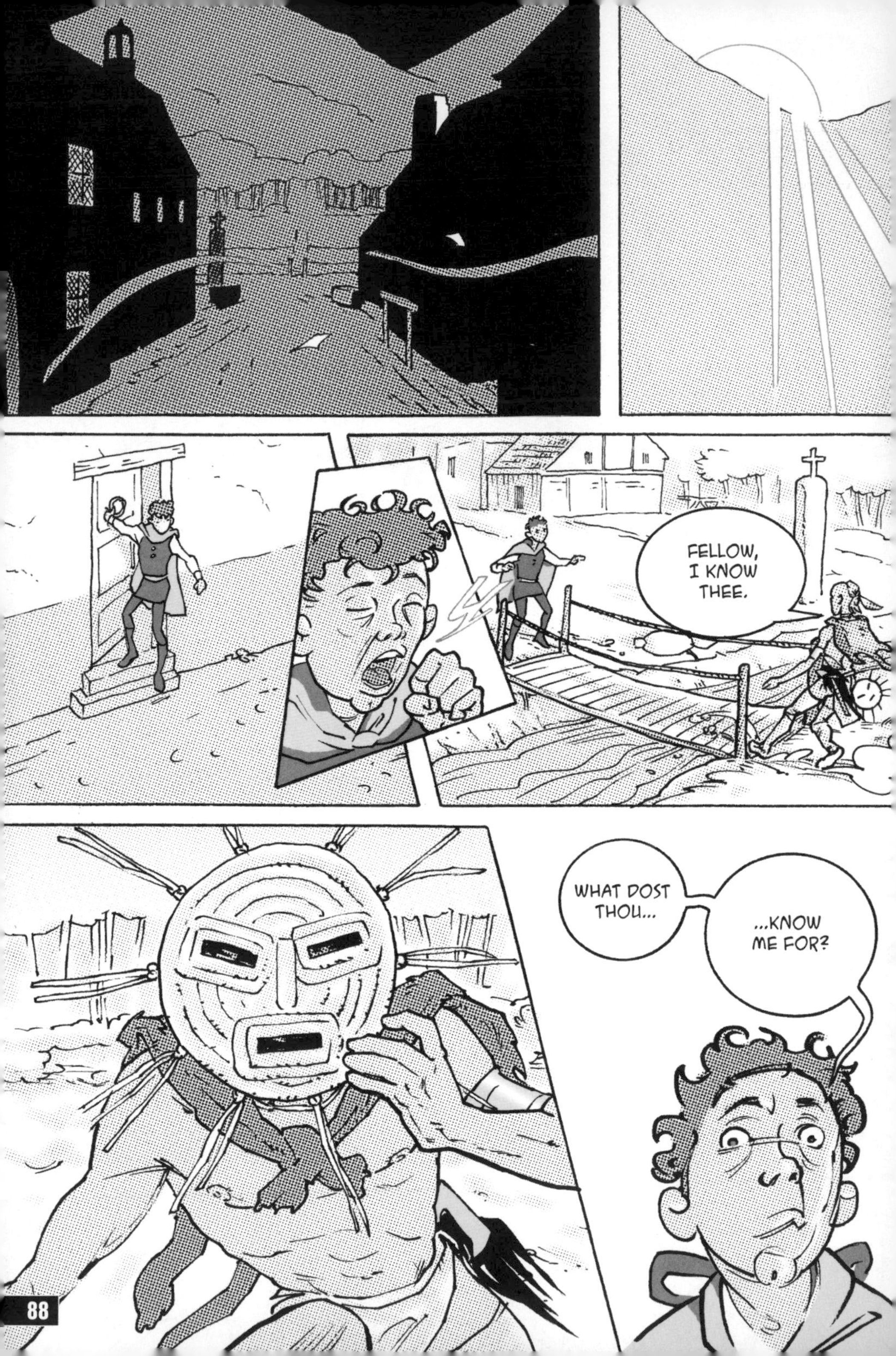
FELLOW, I KNOW THEE.
WHAT DOST THOU...
...KNOW ME FOR?

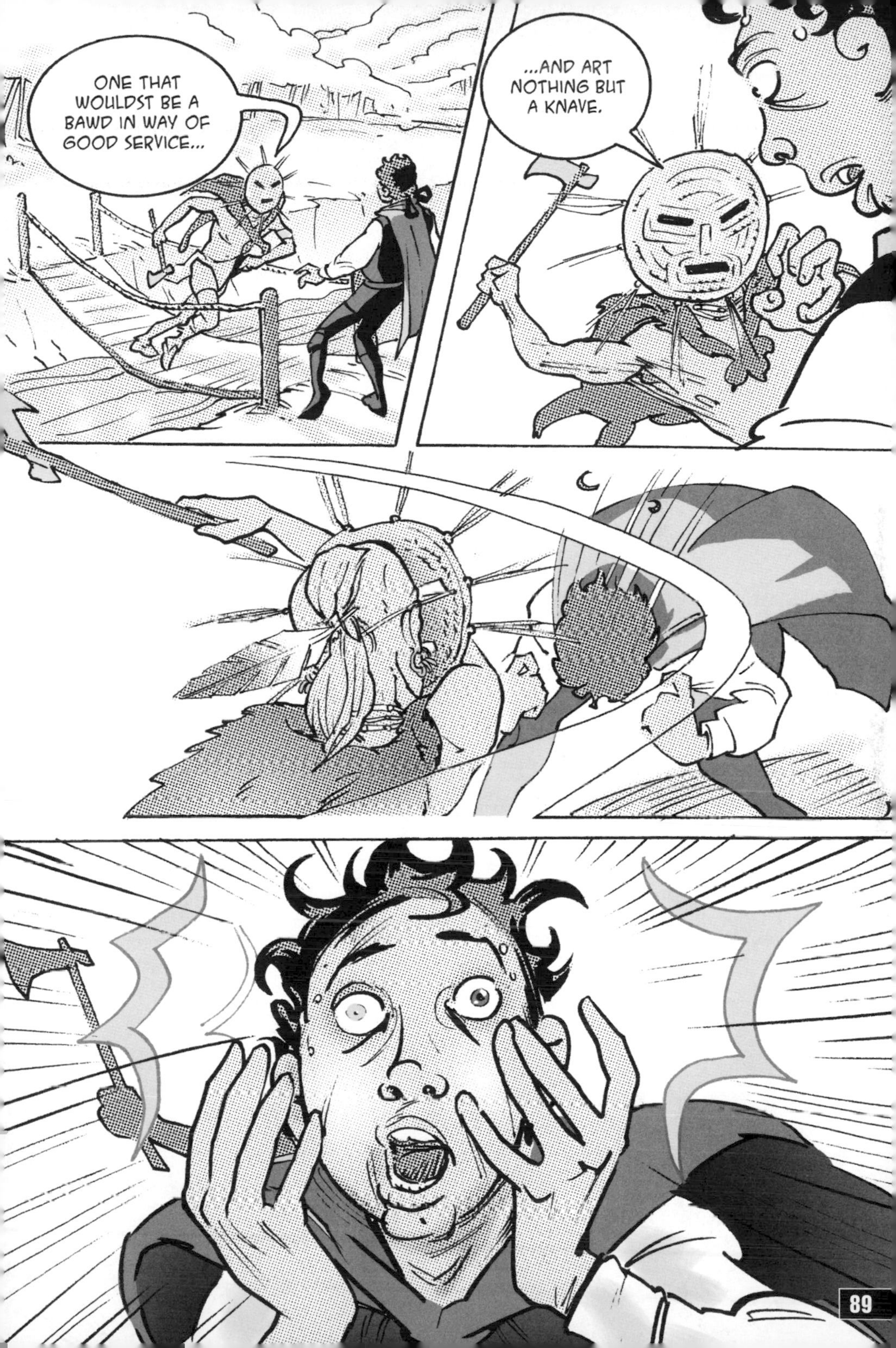
ONE THAT WOULDST BE A BAWD IN WAY OF GOOD SERVICE...
...AND ART NOTHING BUT A KNAVE.

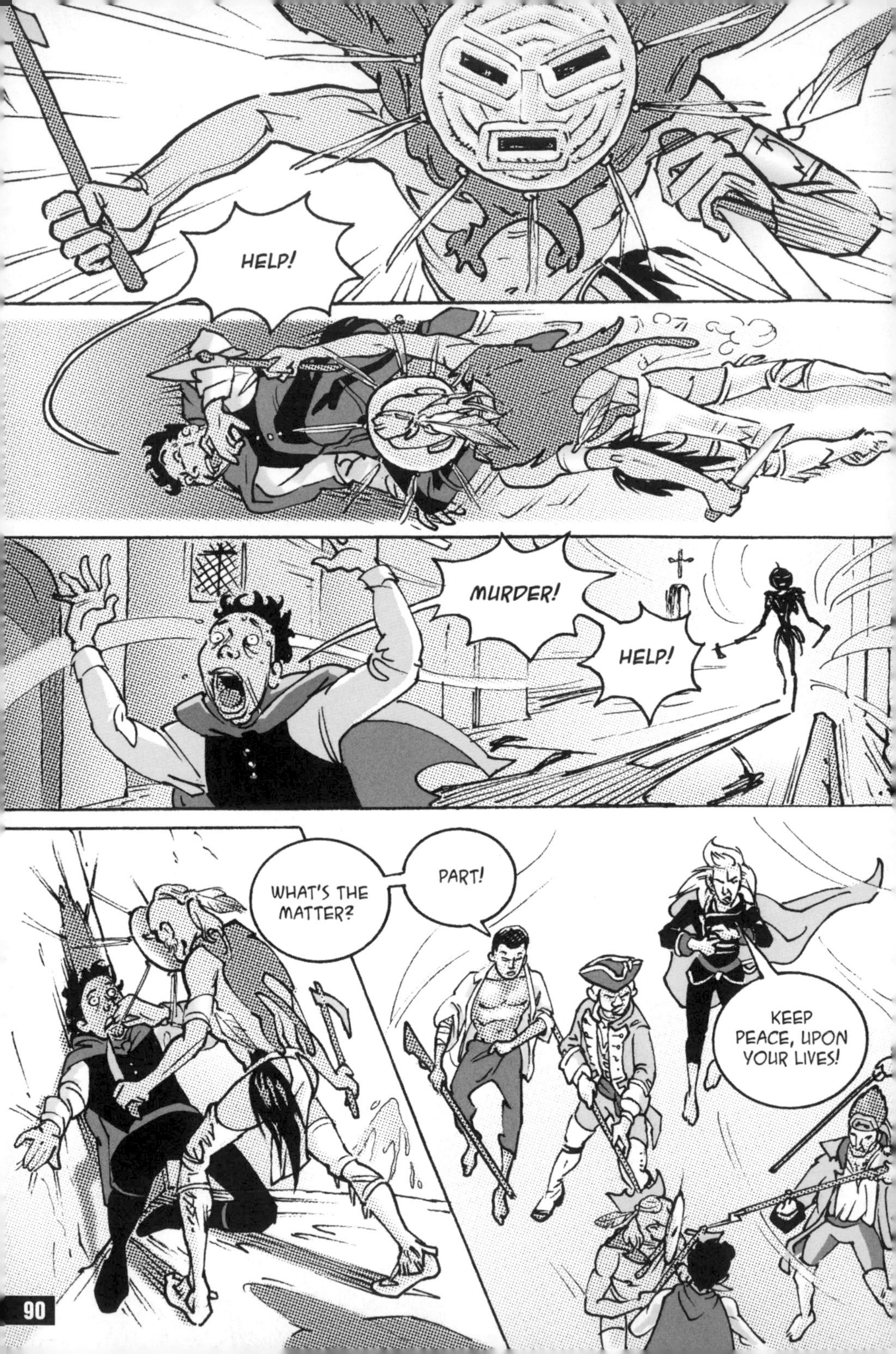
HELP!
MURDER!
HELP!
WHAT'S THE MATTER?
PART!
KEEP PEACE, UPON YOUR LIVES!

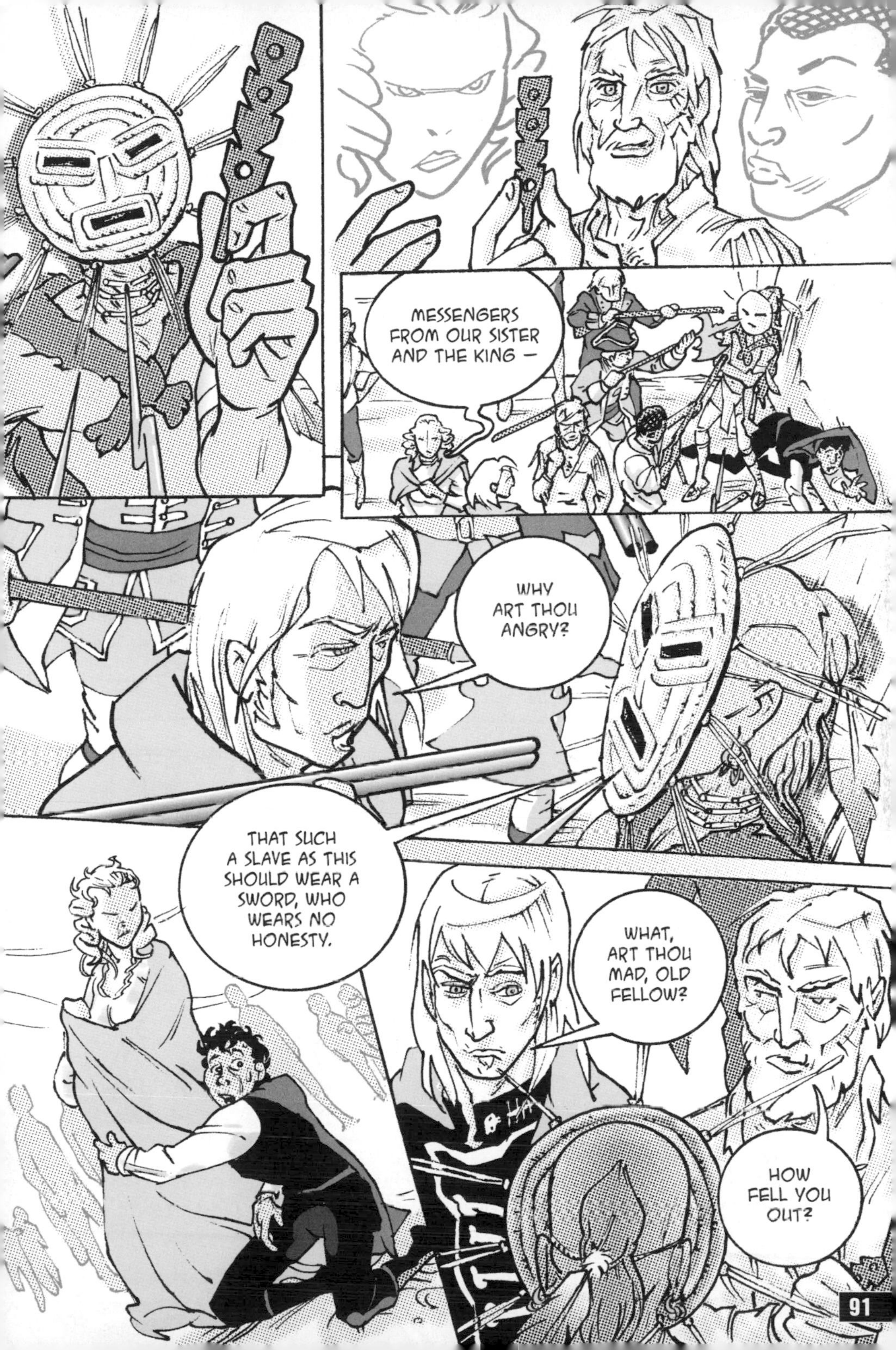
MESSENGERS FROM OUR SISTER AND THE KING —
WHY ART THOU ANGRY?
THAT SUCH A SLAVE AS THIS SHOULD WEAR A SWORD, WHO WEARS NO HONESTY.
WHAT, ART THOU MAD, OLD FELLOW?
HOW FELL YOU OUT?

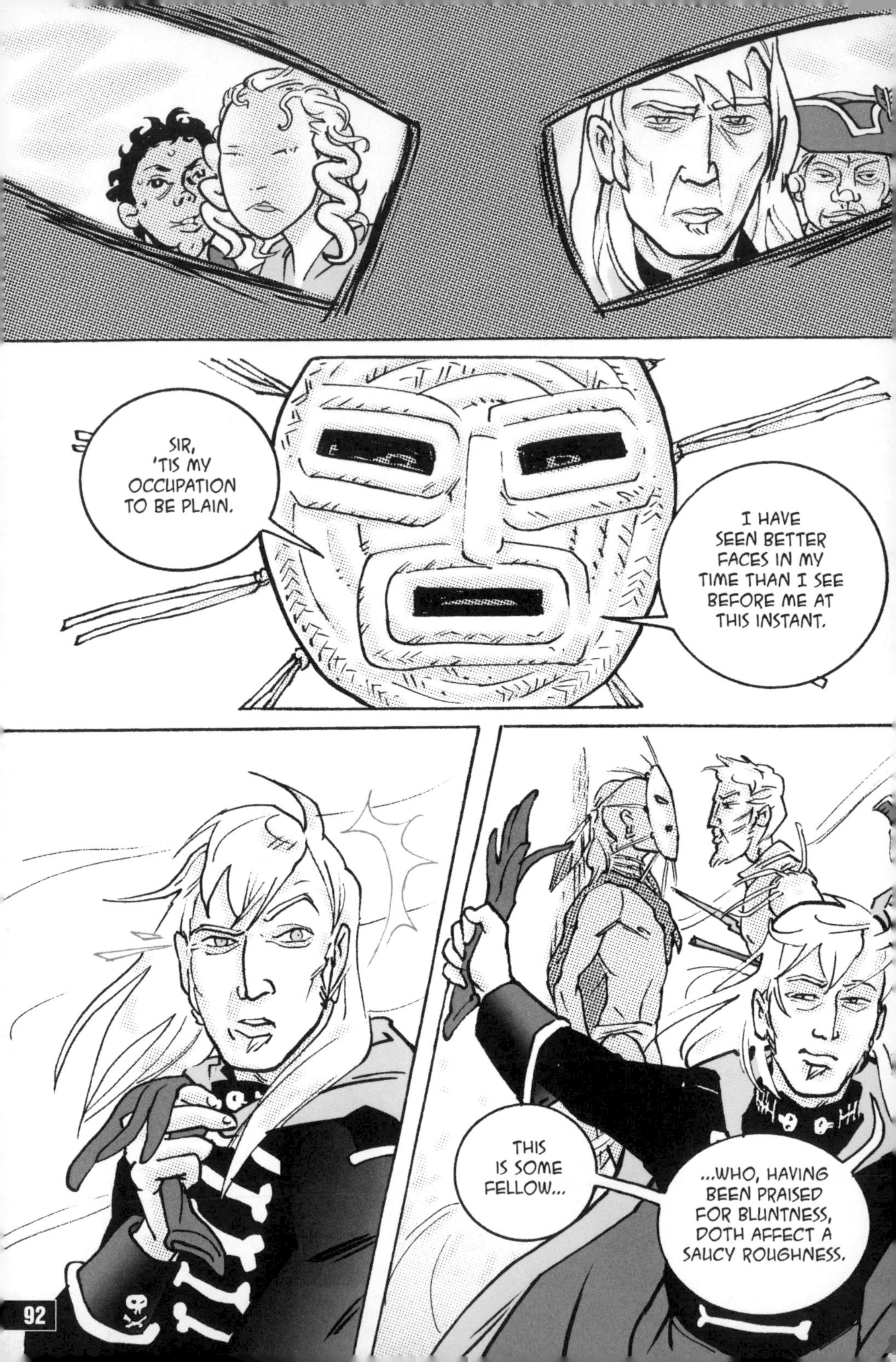
SIR, 'TIS MY OCCUPATION TO BE PLAIN.
I HAVE SEEN BETTER FACES IN MY TIME THAN I SEE BEFORE ME AT THIS INSTANT.
THIS IS SOME FELLOW...
...WHO, HAVING BEEN PRAISED FOR BLUNTNESS, DOTH AFFECT A SAUCY ROUGHNESS.

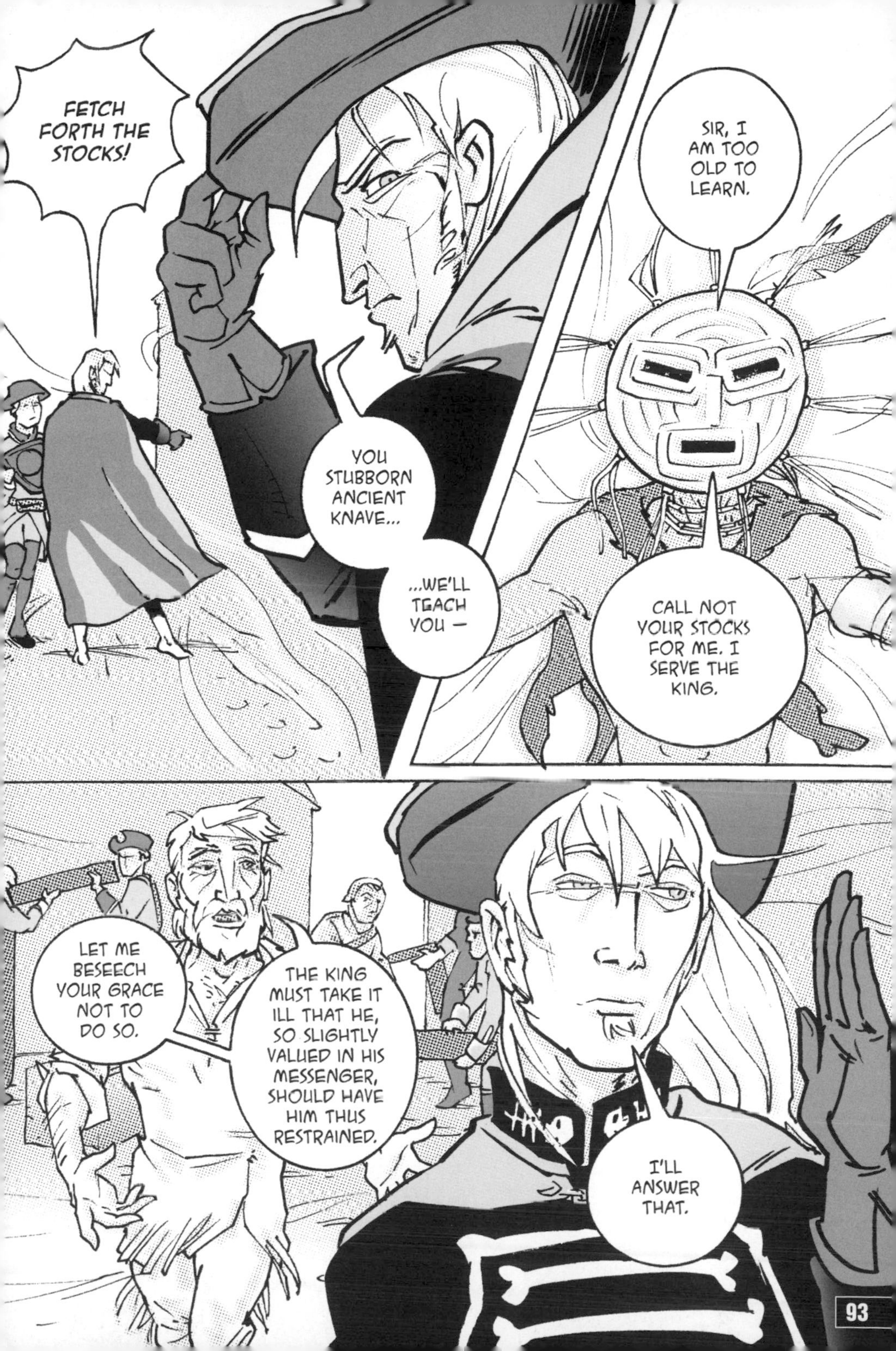
FETCH FORTH THE STOCKS!
YOU STUBBORN ANCIENT KNAVE...
...WE'LL TEACH YOU —
SIR, I AM TOO OLD TO LEARN.
CALL NOT YOUR STOCKS FOR ME. I SERVE THE KING.
LET ME BESEECH YOUR GRACE NOT TO DO SO.
THE KING MUST TAKE IT ILL THAT HE, SO SLIGHTLY VALUED IN HIS MESSENGER, SHOULD HAVE HIM THUS RESTRAINED.
I'LL ANSWER THAT.

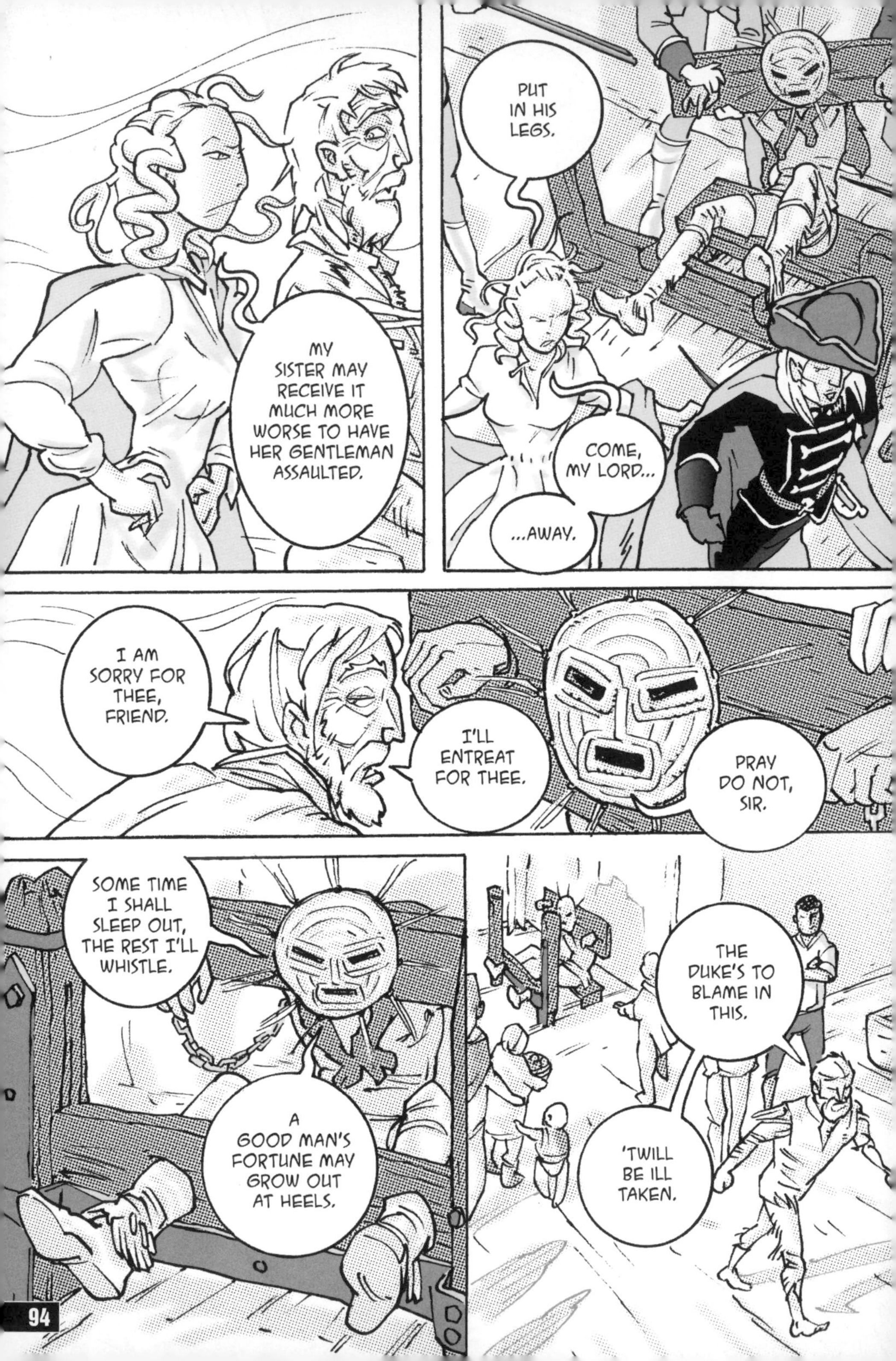
MY SISTER MAY RECEIVE IT MUCH MORE WORSE TO HAVE HER GENTLEMAN ASSAULTED.
PUT IN HIS LEGS.
COME, MY LORD...
...AWAY.
I AM SORRY FOR THEE, FRIEND.
I'LL ENTREAT FOR THEE.
PRAY DO NOT, SIR.
SOME TIME I SHALL SLEEP OUT, THE REST I'LL WHISTLE.
A GOOD MAN'S FORTUNE MAY GROW OUT AT HEELS.
THE DUKE'S TO BLAME IN THIS.
'TWILL BE ILL TAKEN.

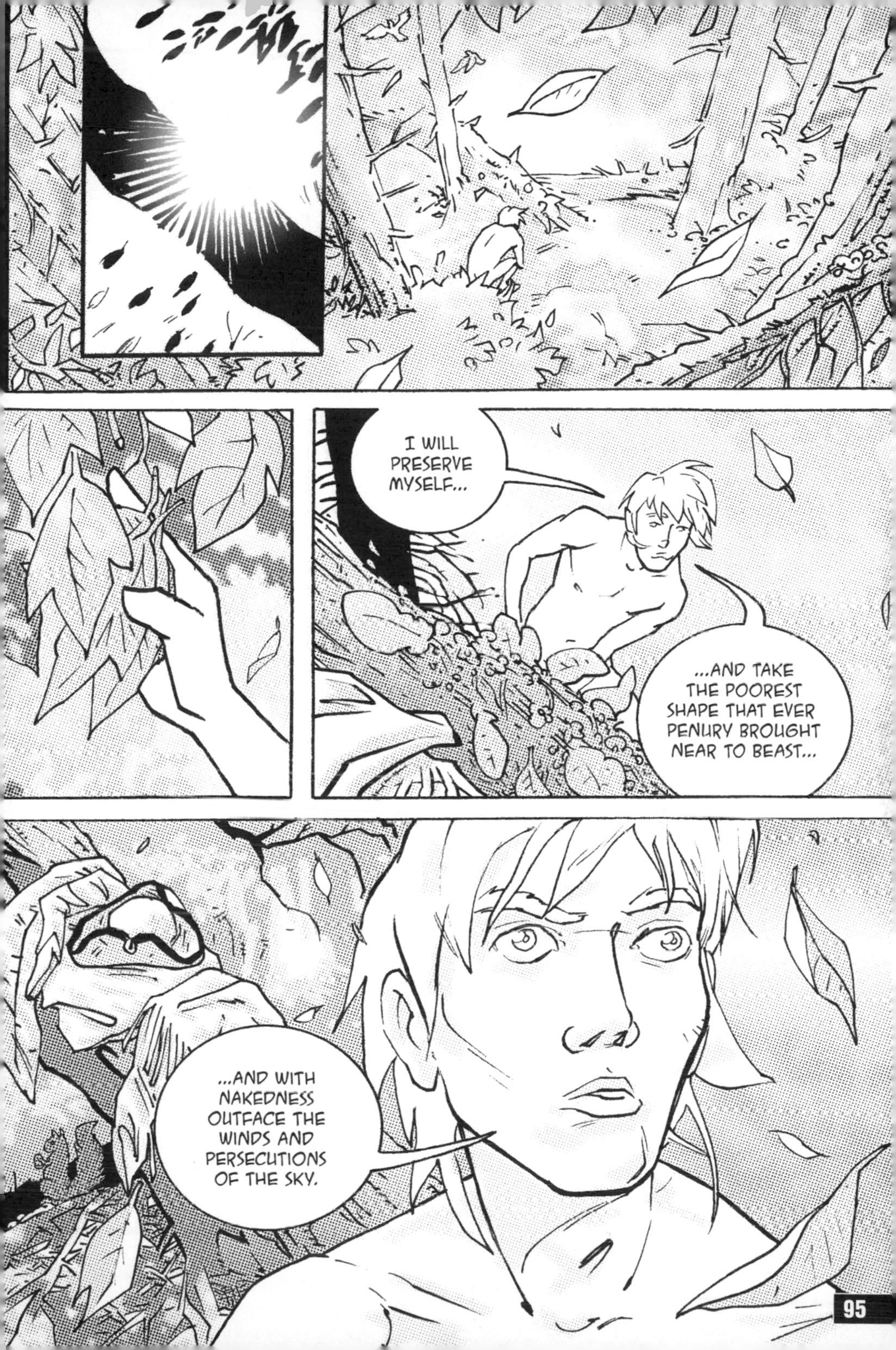
I WILL PRESERVE MYSELF...
...AND TAKE THE POOREST SHAPE THAT EVER PENURY BROUGHT NEAR TO BEAST...
...AND WITH NAKEDNESS OUTFACE THE WINDS AND PERSECUTIONS OF THE SKY.

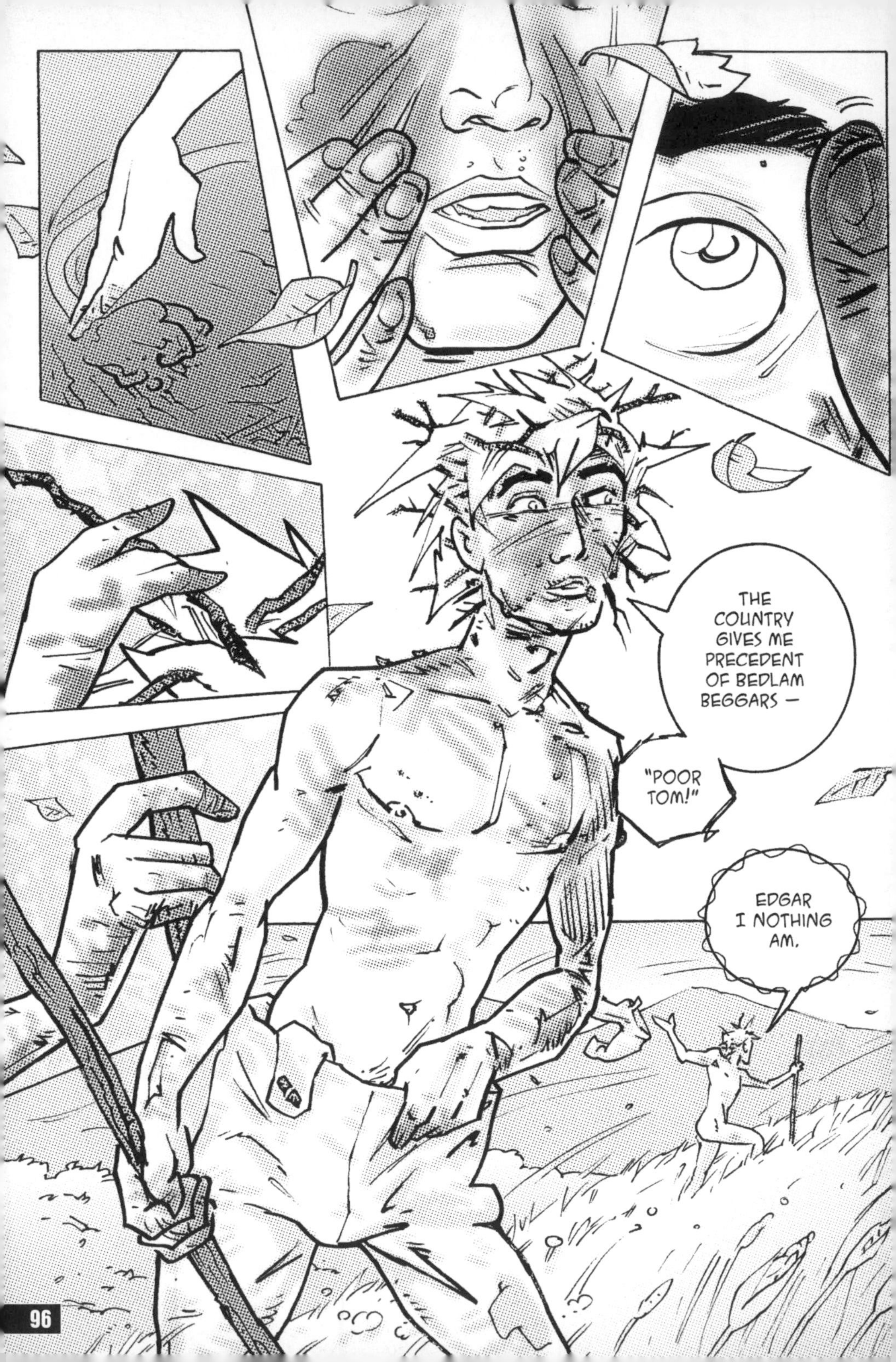
THE COUNTRY GIVES ME PRECEDENT OF BEDLAM BEGGARS —
"POOR TOM!"
EDGAR I NOTHING AM.

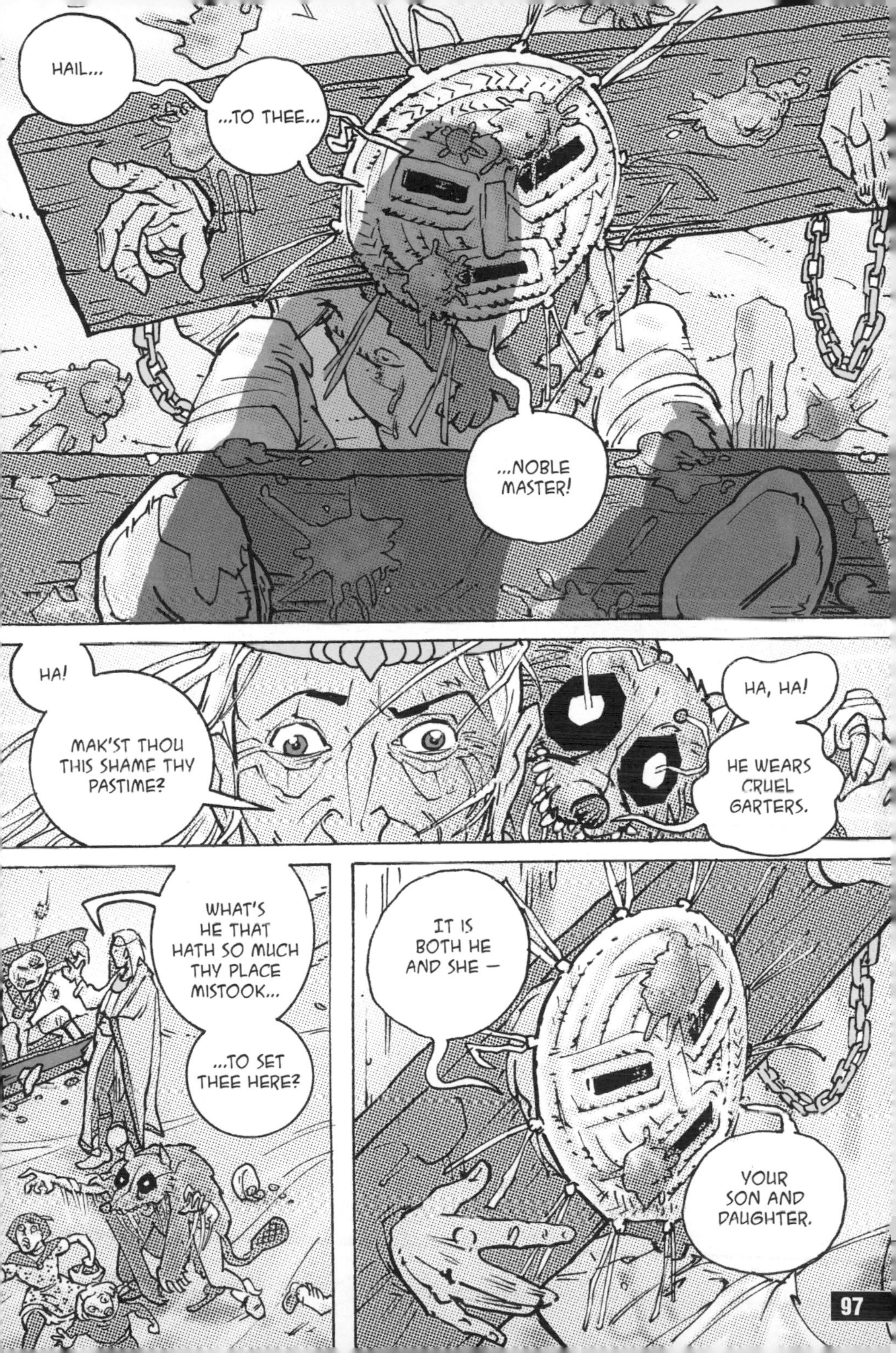
HAIL...
...TO THEE...
...NOBLE MASTER!
HA!
MAK'ST THOU THIS SHAME THY PASTIME?
HA, HA!
HE WEARS CRUEL GARTERS.
WHAT'S HE THAT HATH SO MUCH THY PLACE MISTOOK...
...TO SET THEE HERE?
IT IS BOTH HE AND SHE —
YOUR SON AND DAUGHTER.

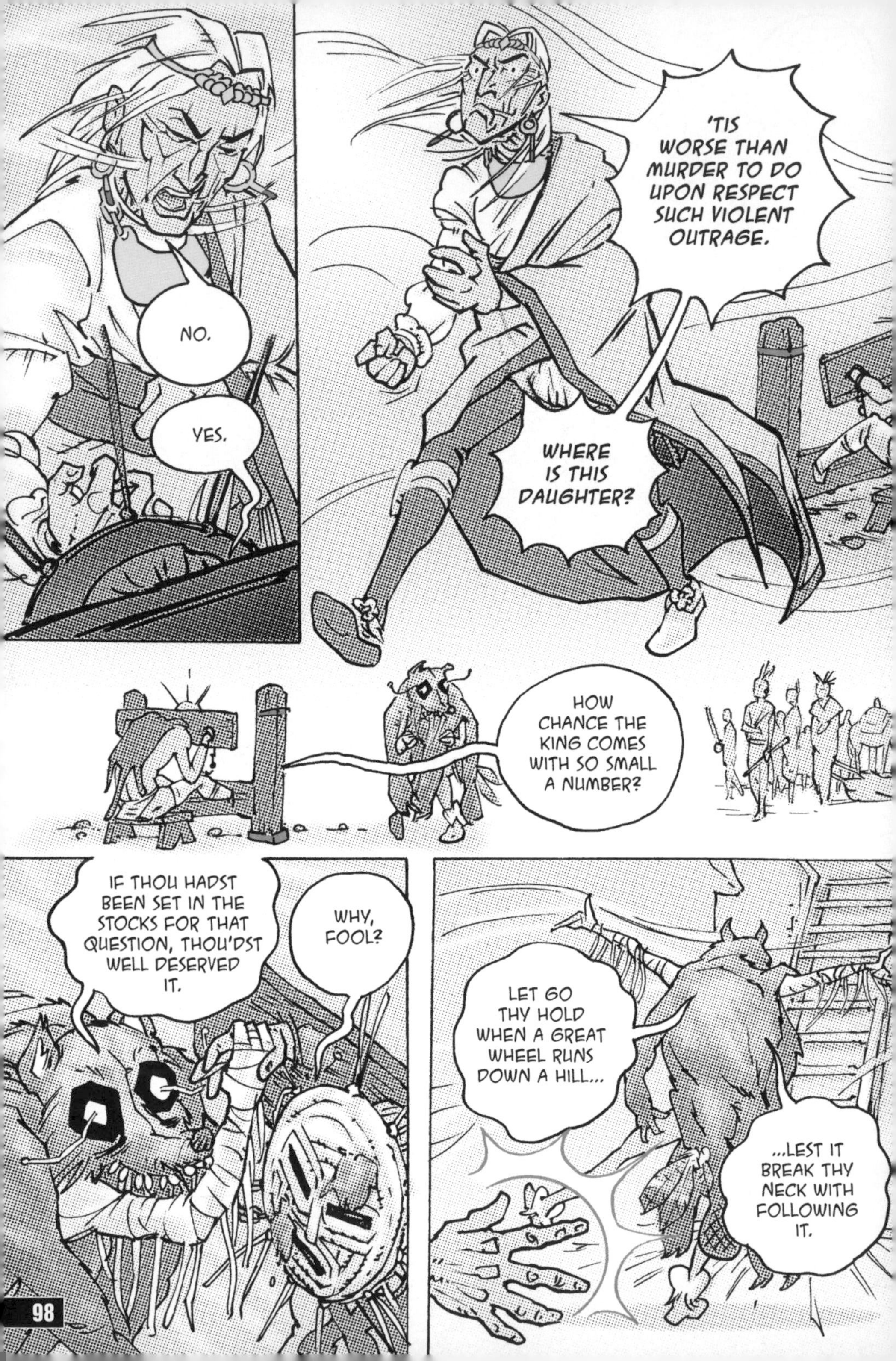
NO.
YES.
'TIS WORSE THAN MURDER TO DO UPON RESPECT SUCH VIOLENT OUTRAGE.
WHERE IS THIS DAUGHTER?
HOW CHANCE THE KING COMES WITH SO SMALL A NUMBER?
IF THOU HADST BEEN SET IN THE STOCKS FOR THAT QUESTION, THOU'DST WELL DESERVED IT.
WHY, FOOL?
LET GO THY HOLD WHEN A GREAT WHEEL RUNS DOWN A HILL...
...LEST IT BREAK THY NECK WITH FOLLOWING IT.

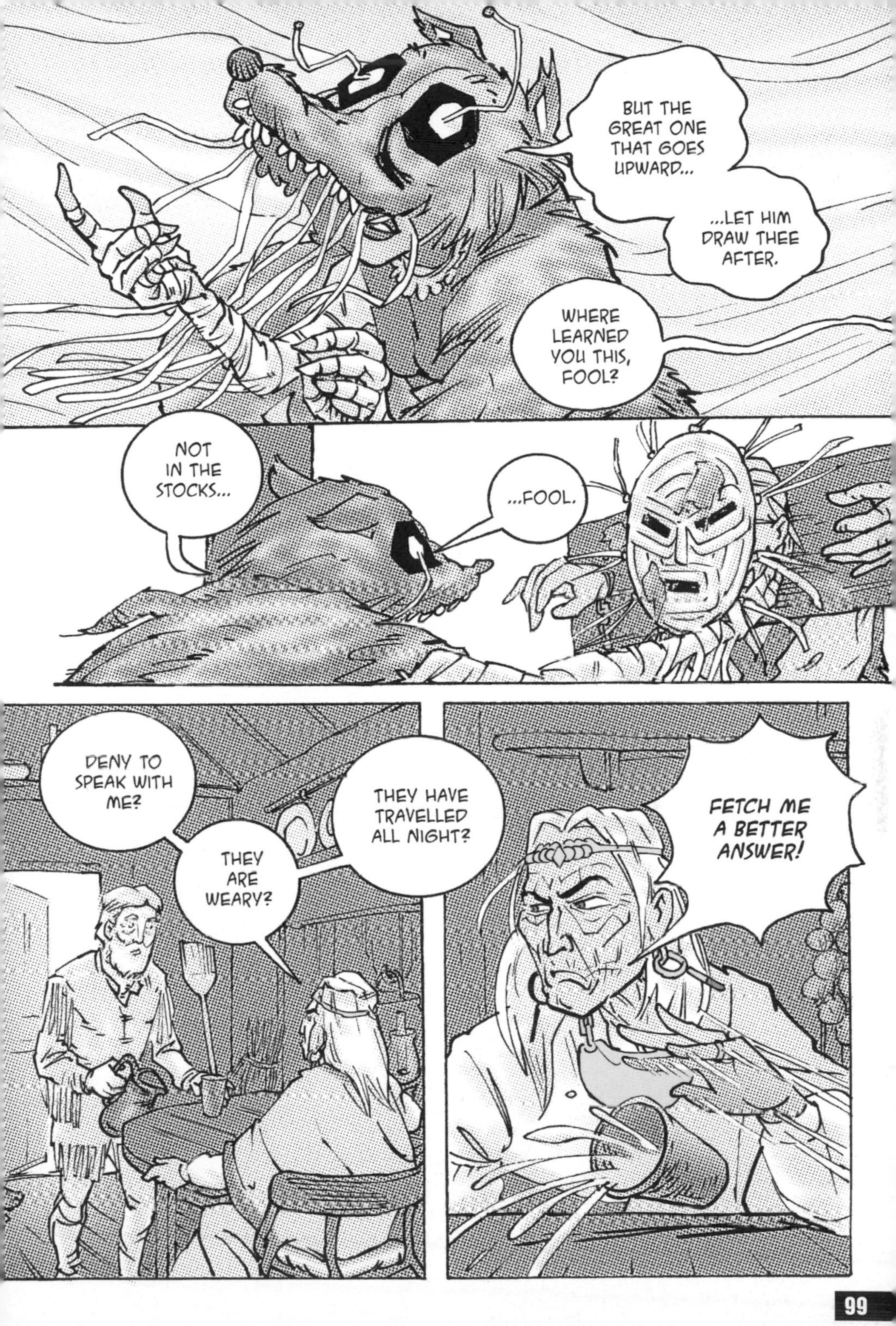
BUT THE GREAT ONE THAT GOES UPWARD...
...LET HIM DRAW THEE AFTER.
WHERE LEARNED YOU THIS, FOOL?
NOT IN THE STOCKS...
...FOOL.
DENY TO SPEAK WITH ME?
THEY ARE WEARY?
THEY HAVE TRAVELLED ALL NIGHT?
FETCH ME A BETTER ANSWER!

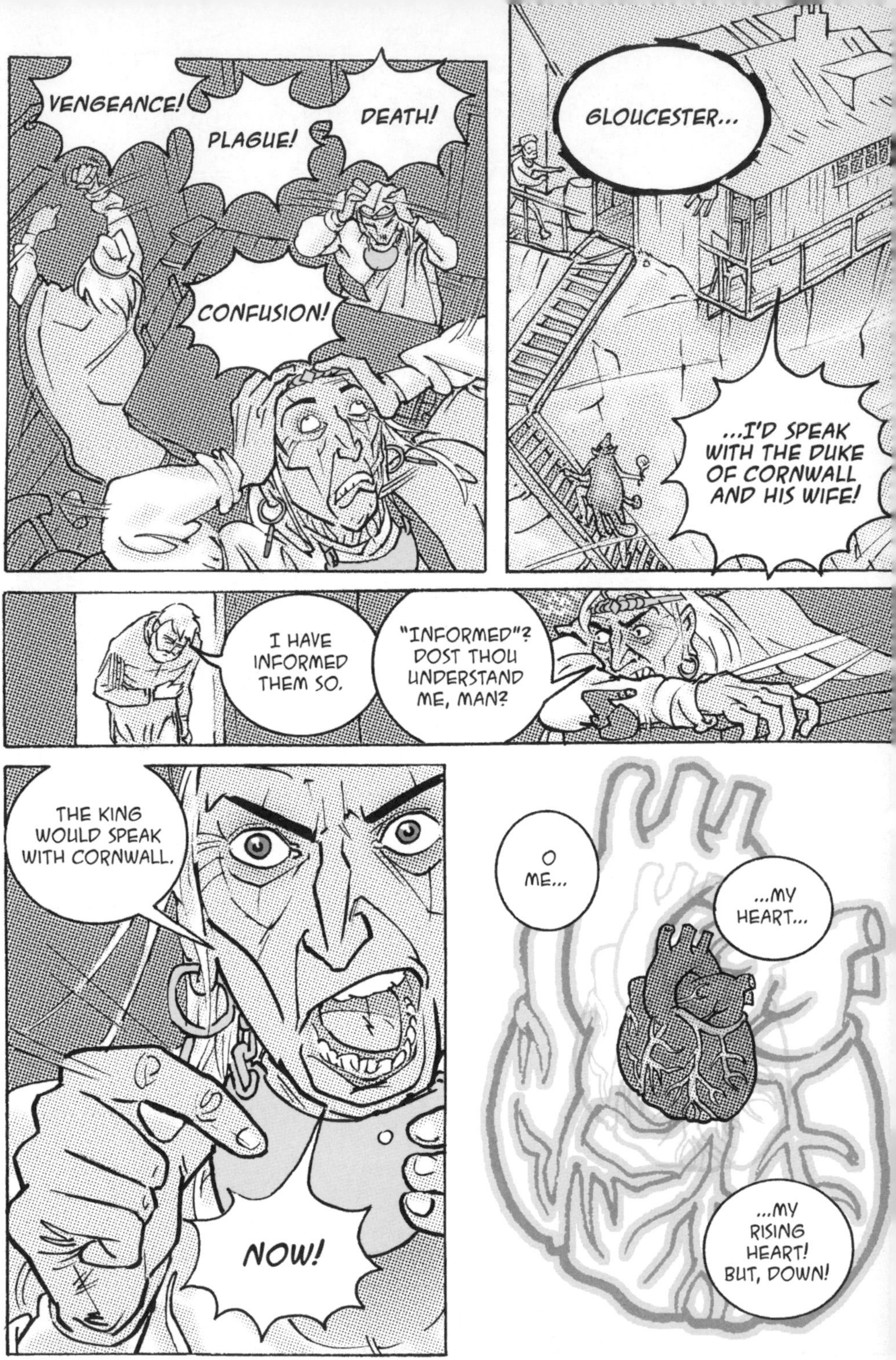
VENGEANCE!
PLAGUE!
DEATH!
CONFUSION!
GLOUCESTER...
...I'D SPEAK WITH THE DUKE OF CORNWALL AND HIS WIFE!
I HAVE INFORMED THEM SO.
"INFORMED"? DOST THOU UNDERSTAND ME, MAN?
THE KING WOULD SPEAK WITH CORNWALL.
NOW!
O ME...
...MY HEART...
...MY RISING HEART! BUT, DOWN!

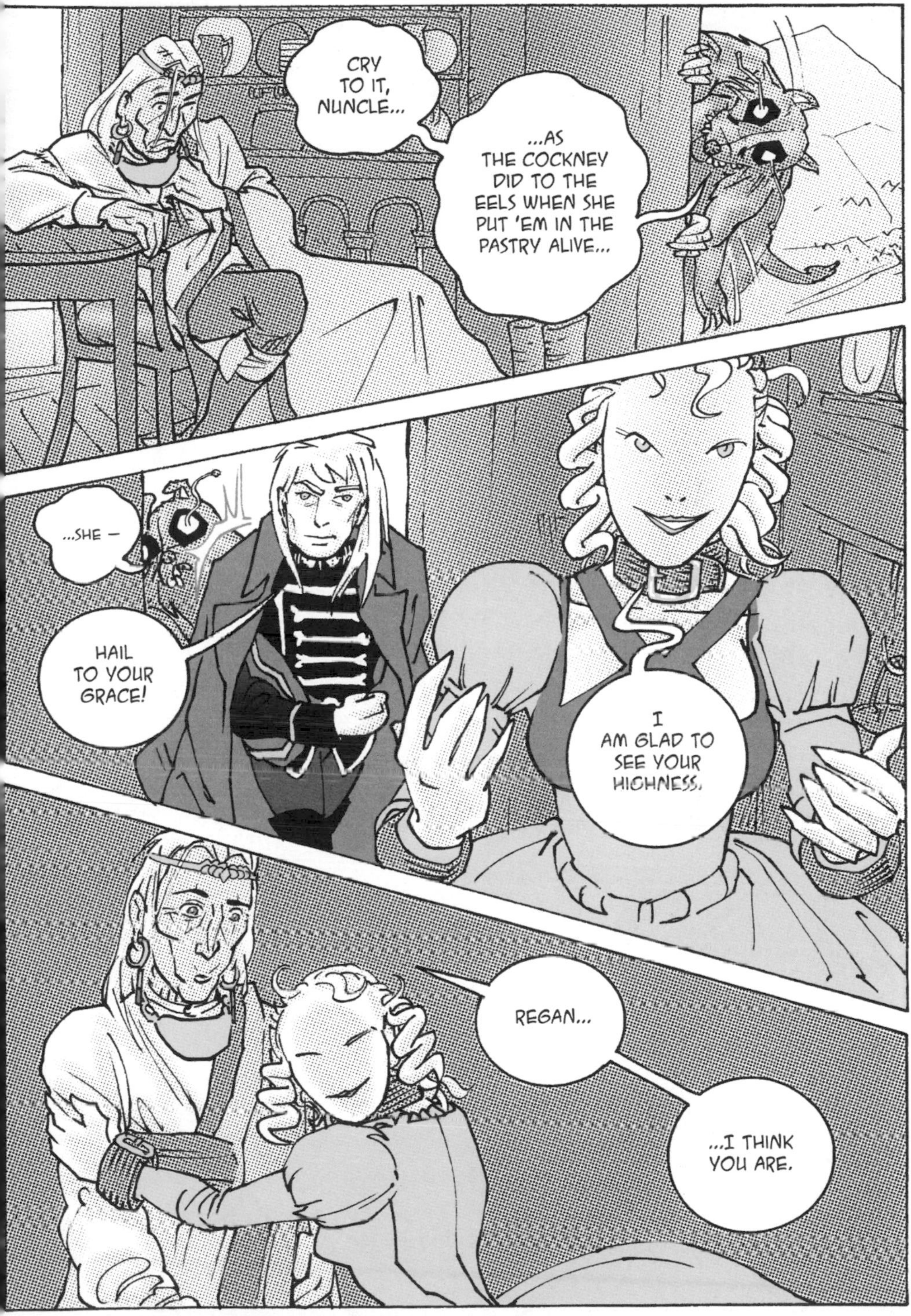
CRY TO IT, NUNCLE...
...AS THE COCKNEY DID TO THE EELS WHEN SHE PUT 'EM IN THE PASTRY ALIVE...
...SHE —
HAIL TO YOUR GRACE!
I AM GLAD TO SEE YOUR HIGHNESS.
REGAN...
...I THINK YOU ARE.

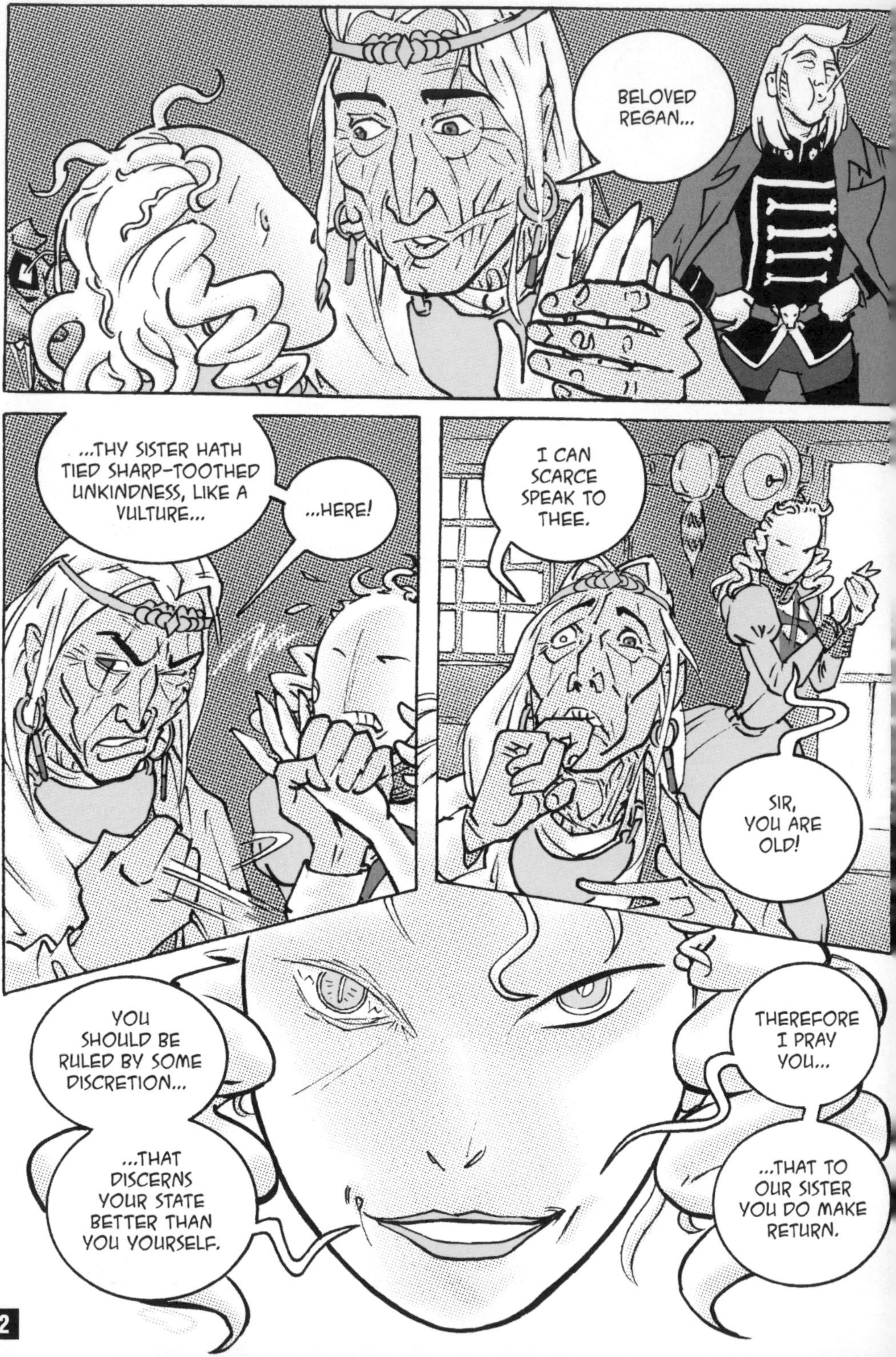
BELOVED REGAN...
...THY SISTER HATH TIED SHARP-TOOTHED UNKINDNESS, LIKE A VULTURE...
...HERE!
I CAN SCARCE SPEAK TO THEE.
SIR, YOU ARE OLD!
YOU SHOULD BE RULED BY SOME DISCRETION...
...THAT DISCERNS YOUR STATE BETTER THAN YOU YOURSELF.
THEREFORE I PRAY YOU...
...THAT TO OUR SISTER YOU DO MAKE RETURN.

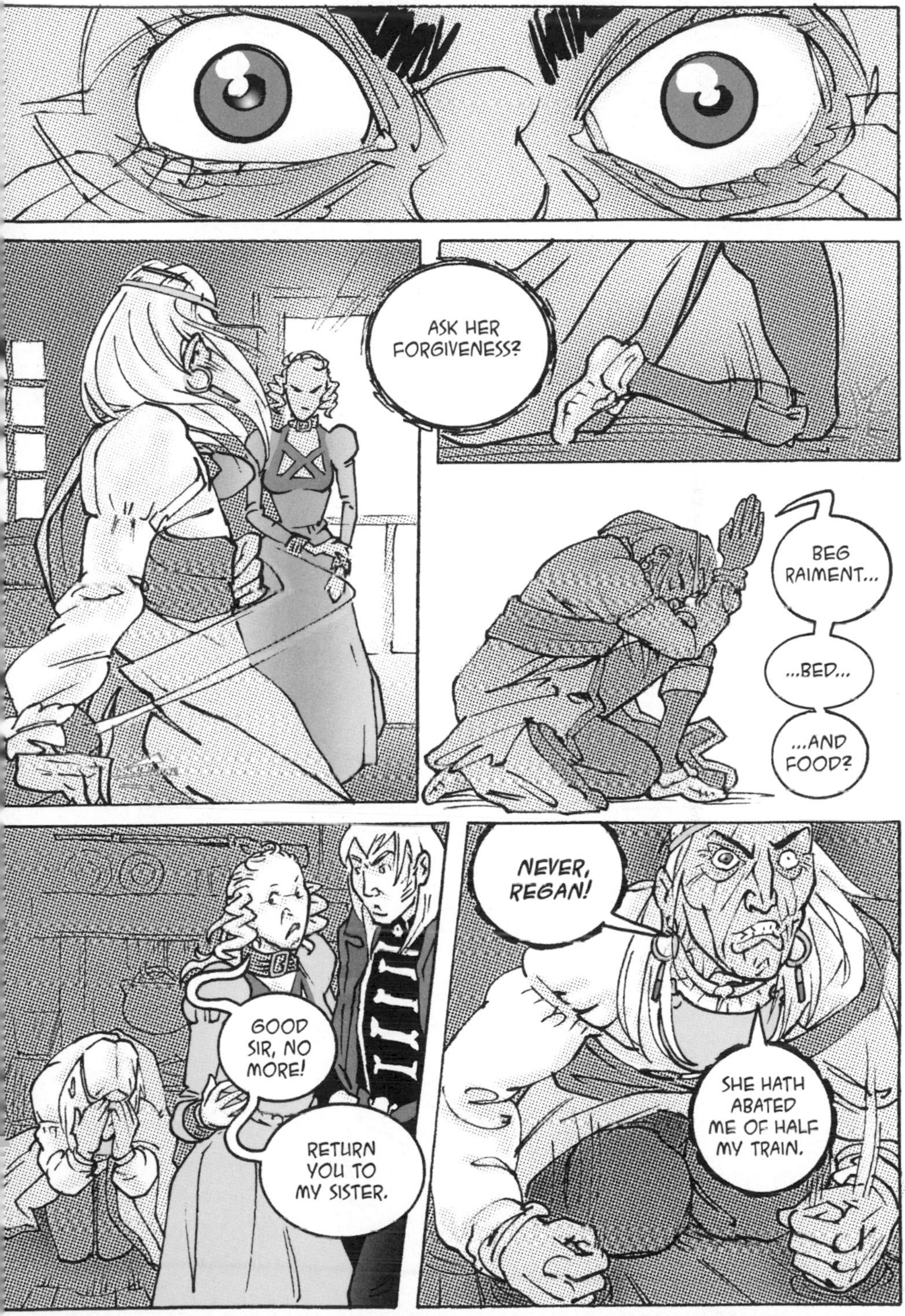
ASK HER FORGIVENESS?
BEG RAIMENT...
...BED...
...AND FOOD?
GOOD SIR, NO MORE!
RETURN YOU TO MY SISTER.
NEVER, REGAN!
SHE HATH ABATED ME OF HALF MY TRAIN.

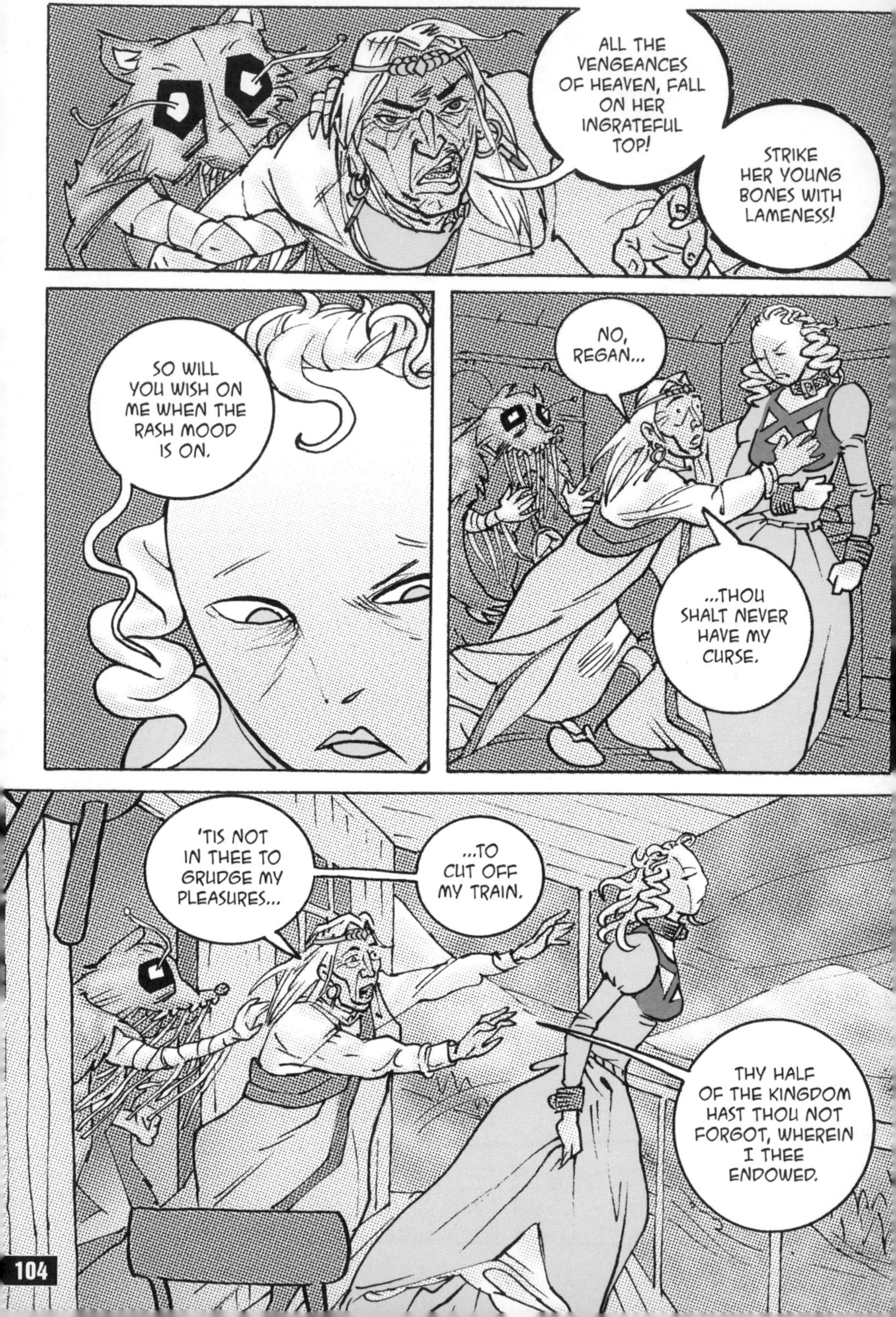
ALL THE VENGEANCES OF HEAVEN, FALL ON HER INGRATEFUL TOP!
STRIKE HER YOUNG BONES WITH LAMENESS!
SO WILL YOU WISH ON ME WHEN THE RASH MOOD IS ON.
NO, REGAN...
...THOU SHALT NEVER HAVE MY CURSE.
'TIS NOT IN THEE TO GRUDGE MY PLEASURES...
...TO CUT OFF MY TRAIN.
THY HALF OF THE KINGDOM HAST THOU NOT FORGOT, WHEREIN I THEE ENDOWED.

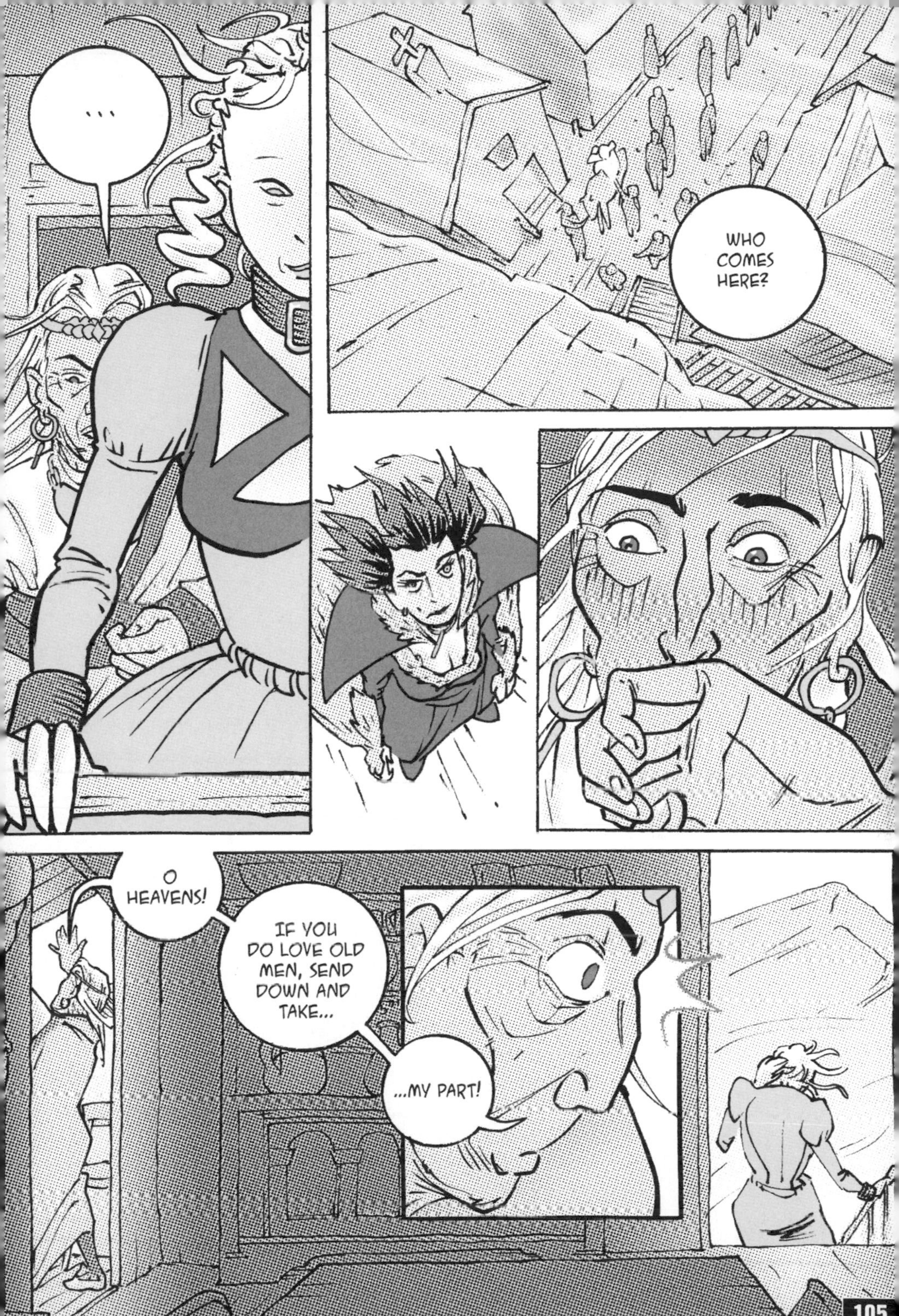
...
WHO COMES HERE?
O HEAVENS!
IF YOU DO LOVE OLD MEN, SEND DOWN AND TAKE...
...MY PART!

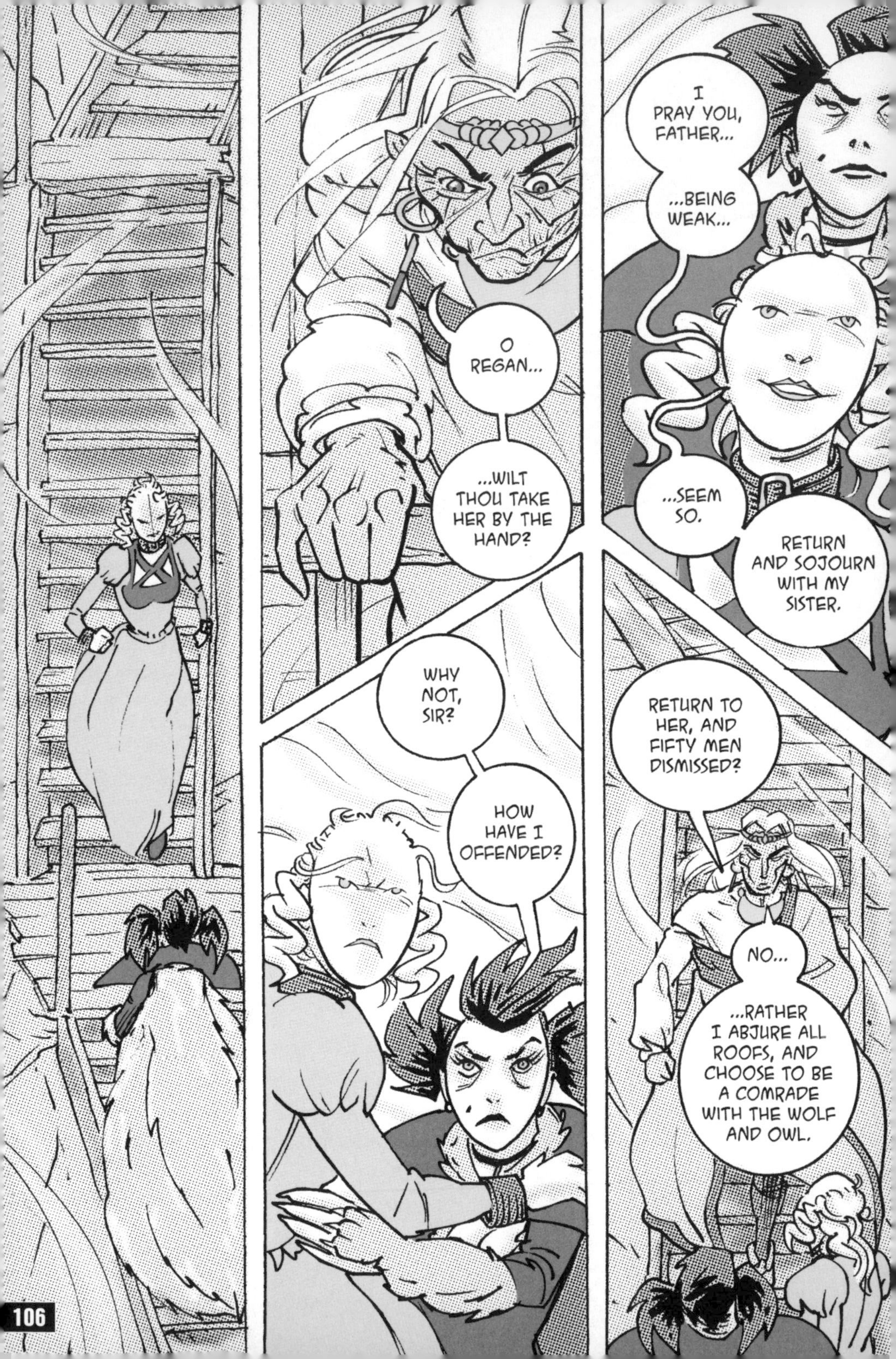
O REGAN...
...WILT THOU TAKE HER BY THE HAND?
WHY NOT, SIR?
HOW HAVE I OFFENDED?
I PRAY YOU, FATHER...
...BEING WEAK...
...SEEM SO.
RETURN AND SOJOURN WITH MY SISTER.
RETURN TO HER, AND FIFTY MEN DISMISSED?
NO...
...RATHER I ABJURE ALL ROOFS, AND CHOOSE TO BE A COMRADE WITH THE WOLF AND OWL.

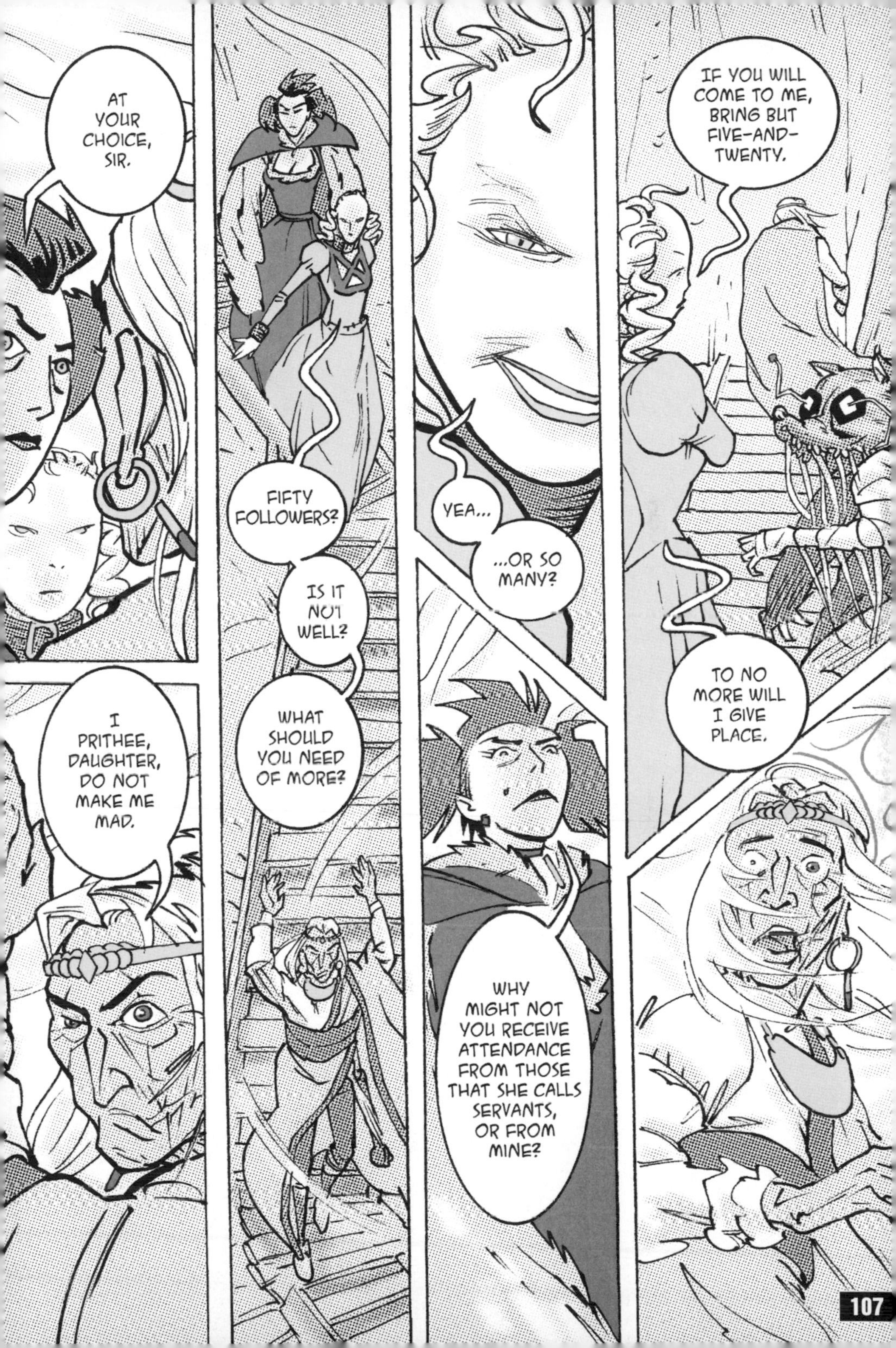
AT YOUR CHOICE, SIR.
I PRITHEE, DAUGHTER, DO NOT MAKE ME MAD.
FIFTY FOLLOWERS?
IS IT NOT WELL?
WHAT SHOULD YOU NEED OF MORE?
YEA...
...OR SO MANY?
WHY MIGHT NOT YOU RECEIVE ATTENDANCE FROM THOSE THAT SHE CALLS SERVANTS, OR FROM MINE?
IF YOU WILL COME TO ME, BRING BUT FIVE-AND-TWENTY.
TO NO MORE WILL I GIVE PLACE.

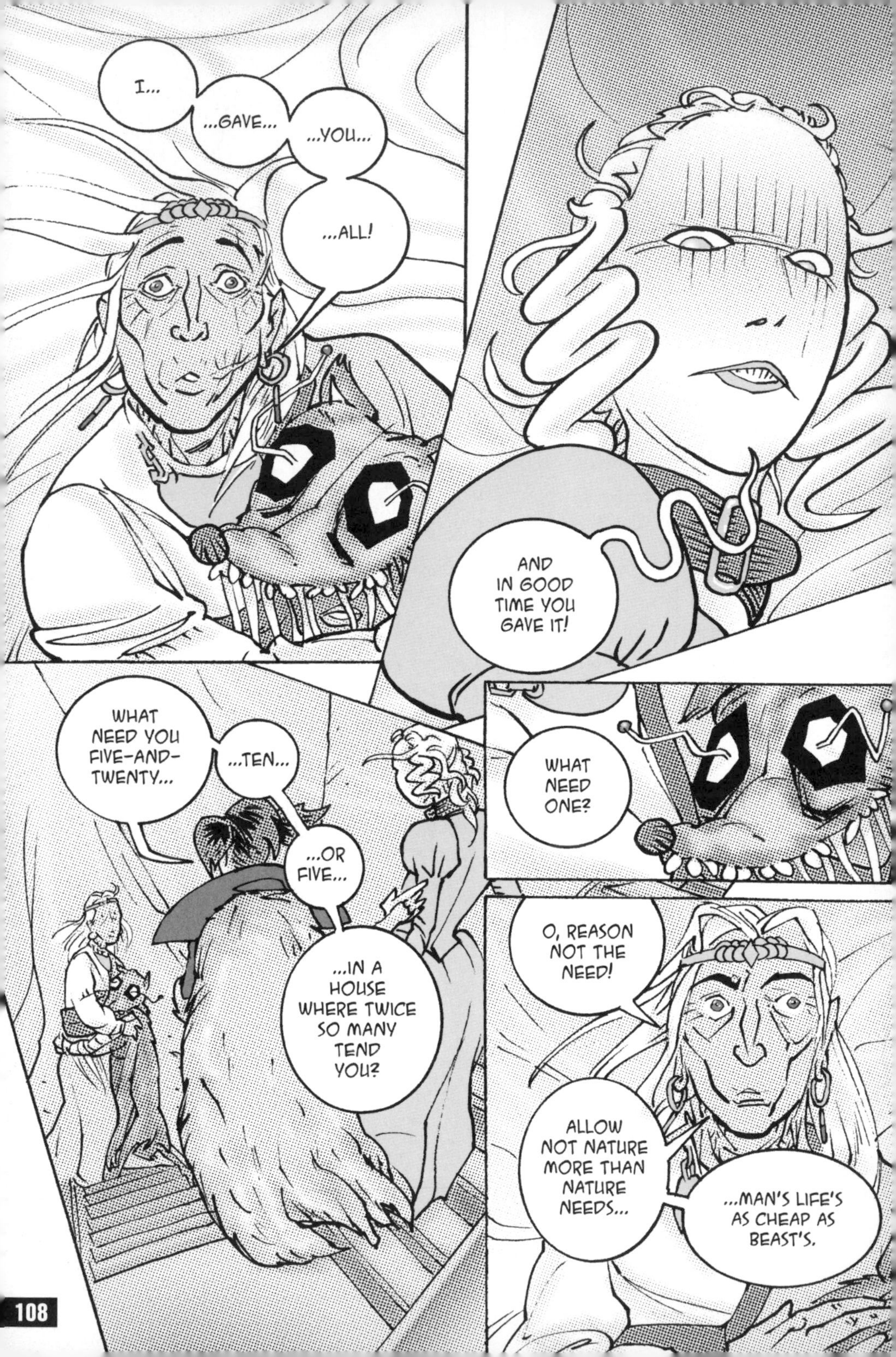
I...
...GAVE...
...YOU...
...ALL!
AND IN GOOD TIME YOU GAVE IT!
WHAT NEED YOU FIVE-AND-TWENTY...
...TEN...
...OR FIVE...
...IN A HOUSE WHERE TWICE SO MANY TEND YOU?
WHAT NEED ONE?
O, REASON NOT THE NEED!
ALLOW NOT NATURE MORE THAN NATURE NEEDS...
...MAN'S LIFE'S AS CHEAP AS BEAST'S.

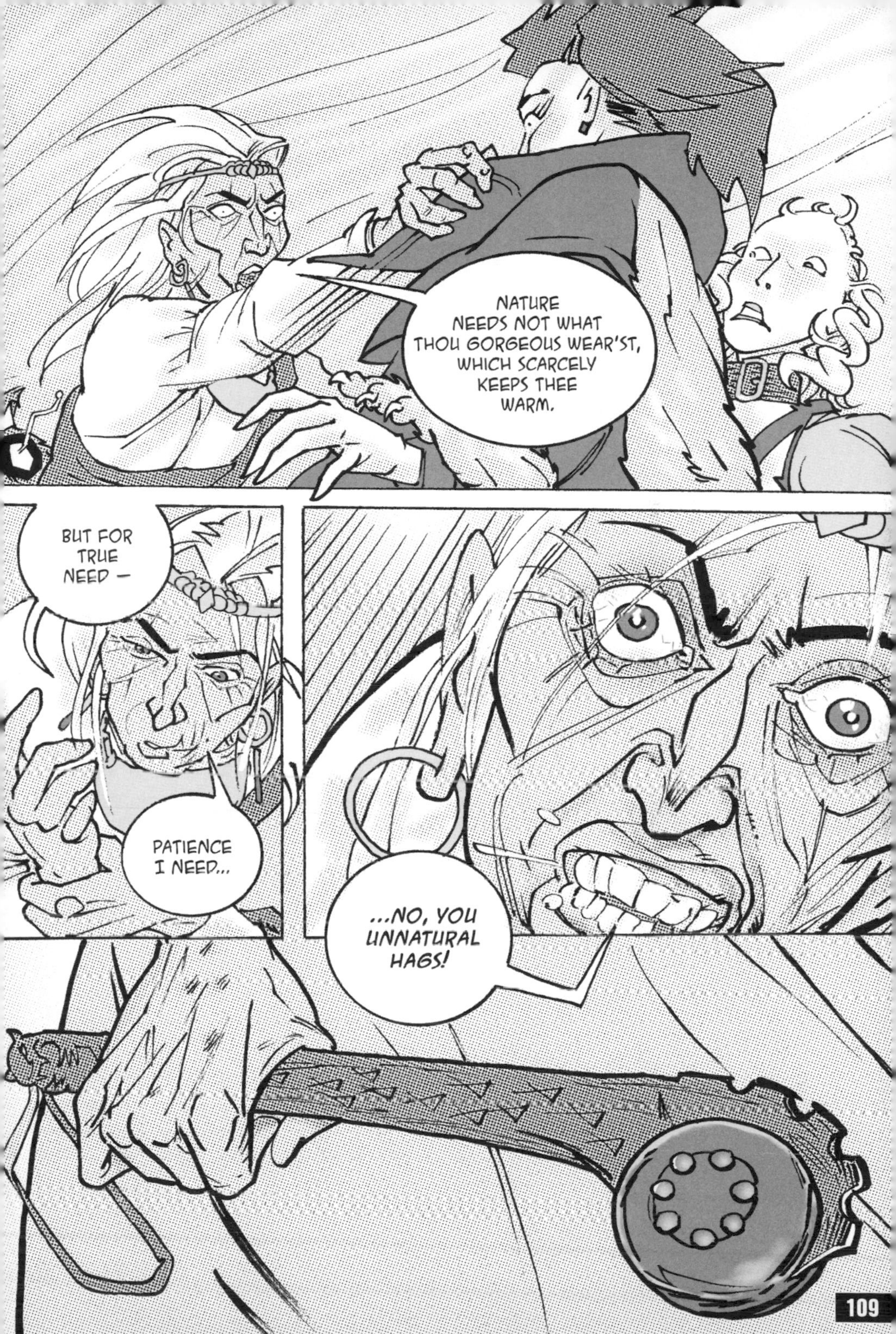
NATURE NEEDS NOT WHAT THOU GORGEOUS WEAR'ST, WHICH SCARCELY KEEPS THEE WARM.
BUT FOR TRUE NEED —
PATIENCE I NEED...
...NO, YOU UNNATURAL HAGS!

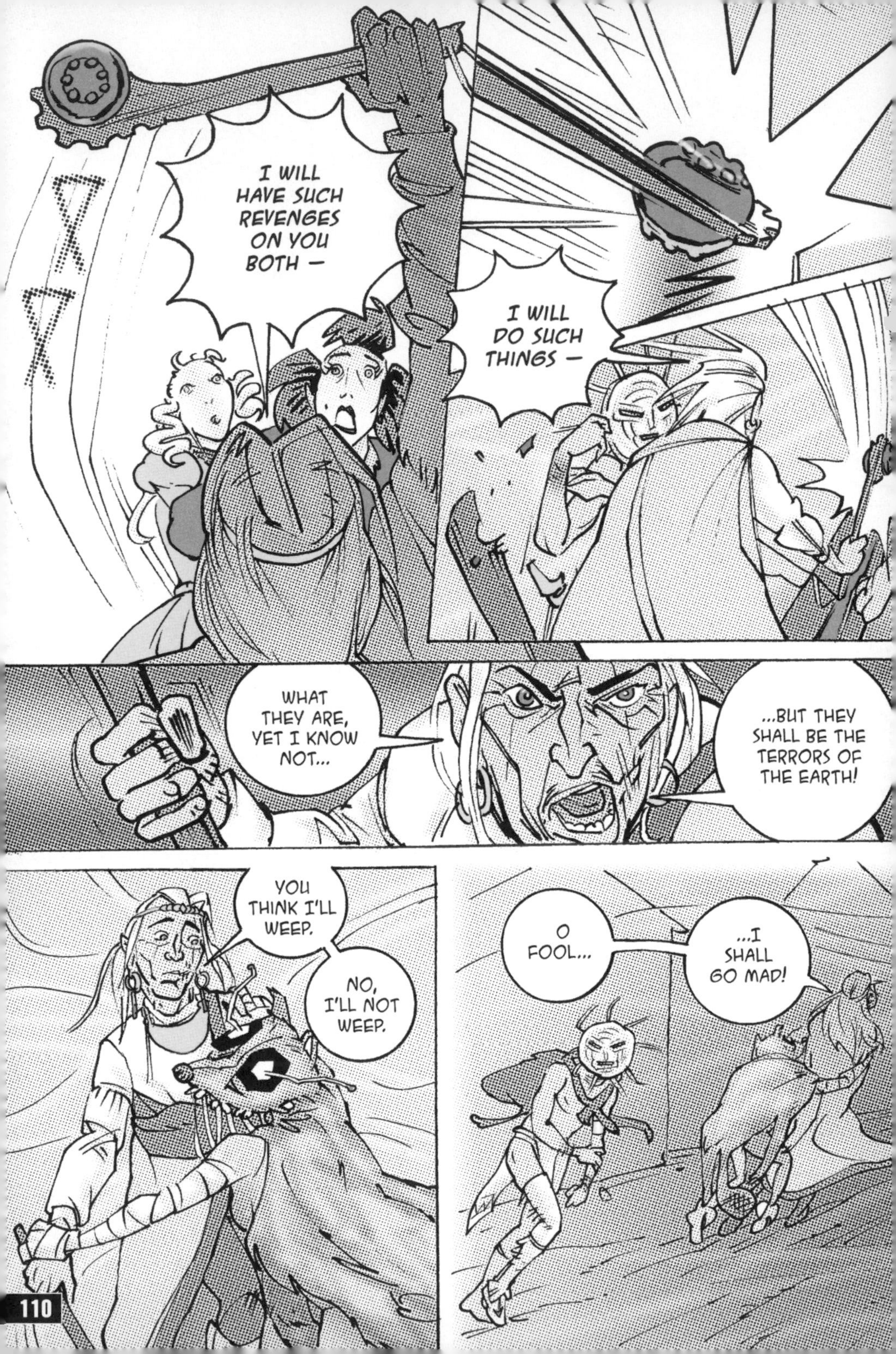

I WILL HAVE SUCH REVENGES ON YOU BOTH —
I WILL DO SUCH THINGS —
WHAT THEY ARE, YET I KNOW NOT...
...BUT THEY SHALL BE THE TERRORS OF THE EARTH!
YOU THINK I'LL WEEP.
NO, I'LL NOT WEEP.
O FOOL...
...I SHALL GO MAD!

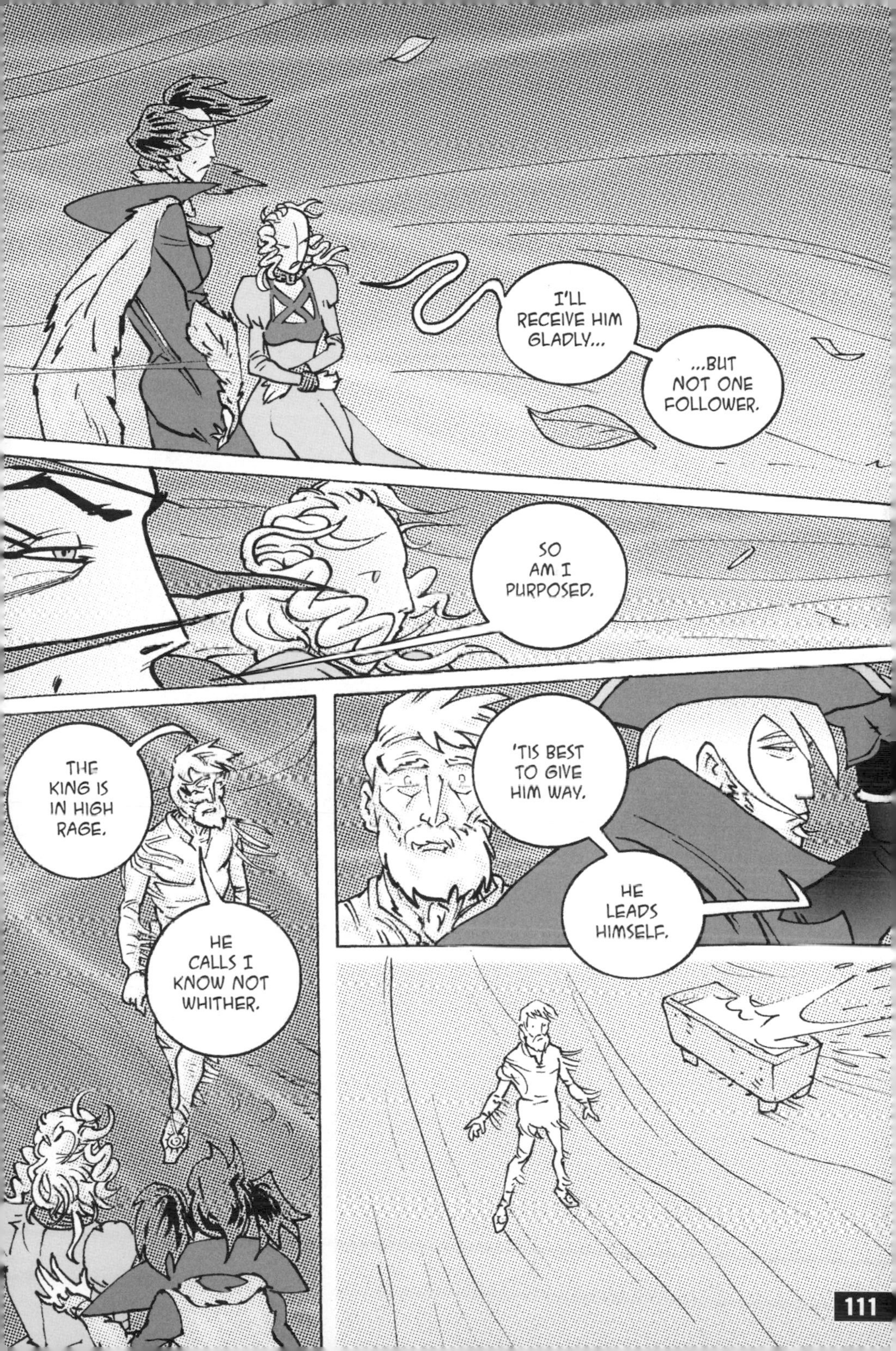
I'LL RECEIVE HIM GLADLY...
...BUT NOT ONE FOLLOWER.
SO AM I PURPOSED.
THE KING IS IN HIGH RAGE.
HE CALLS I KNOW NOT WHITHER.
'TIS BEST TO GIVE HIM WAY.
HE LEADS HIMSELF.

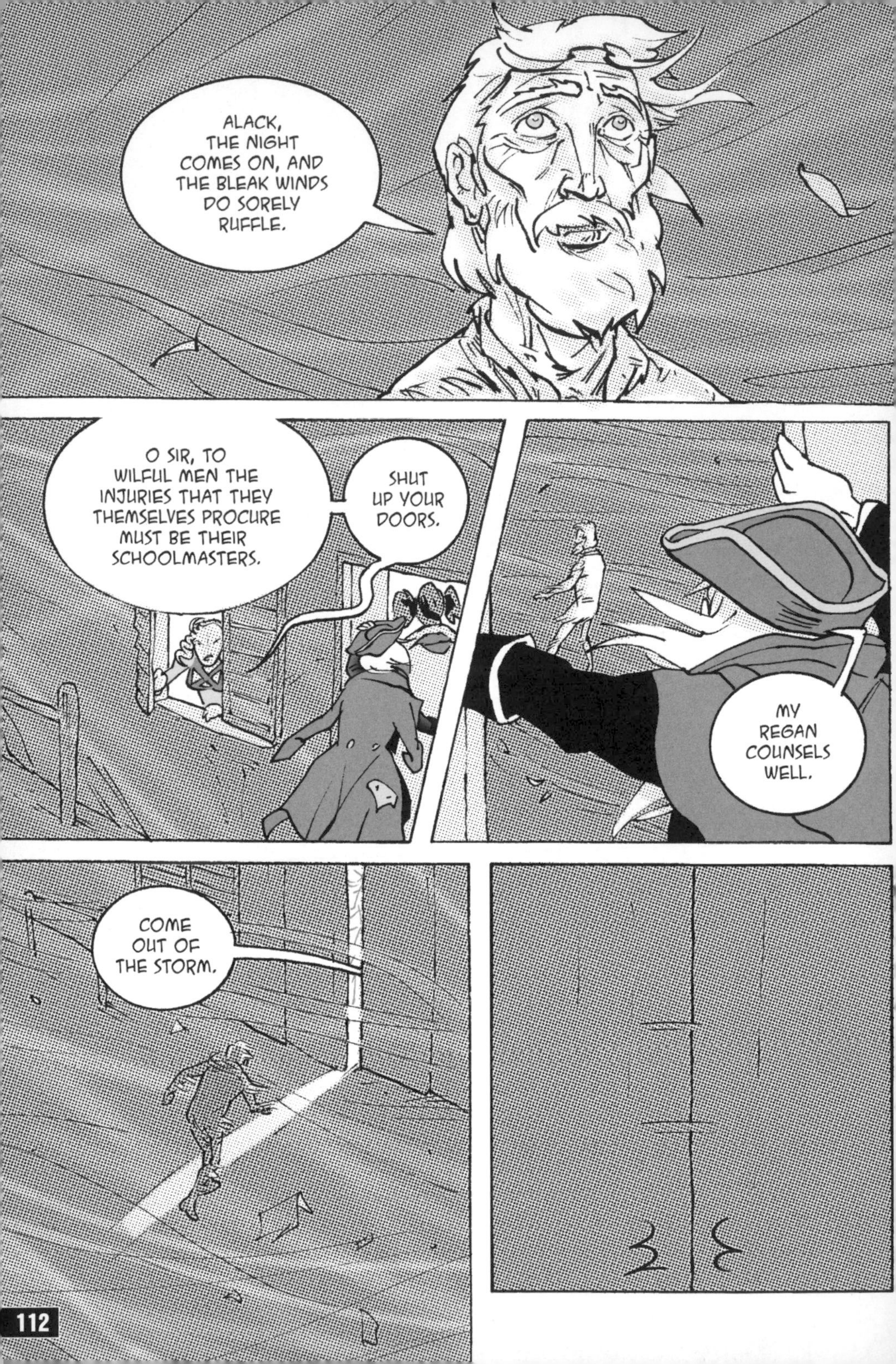
ALACK, THE NIGHT COMES ON, AND THE BLEAK WINDS DO SORELY RUFFLE.
O SIR, TO WILFUL MEN THE INJURIES THAT THEY THEMSELVES PROCURE MUST BE THEIR SCHOOLMASTERS.
SHUT UP YOUR DOORS.
MY REGAN COUNSELS WELL.
COME OUT OF THE STORM.

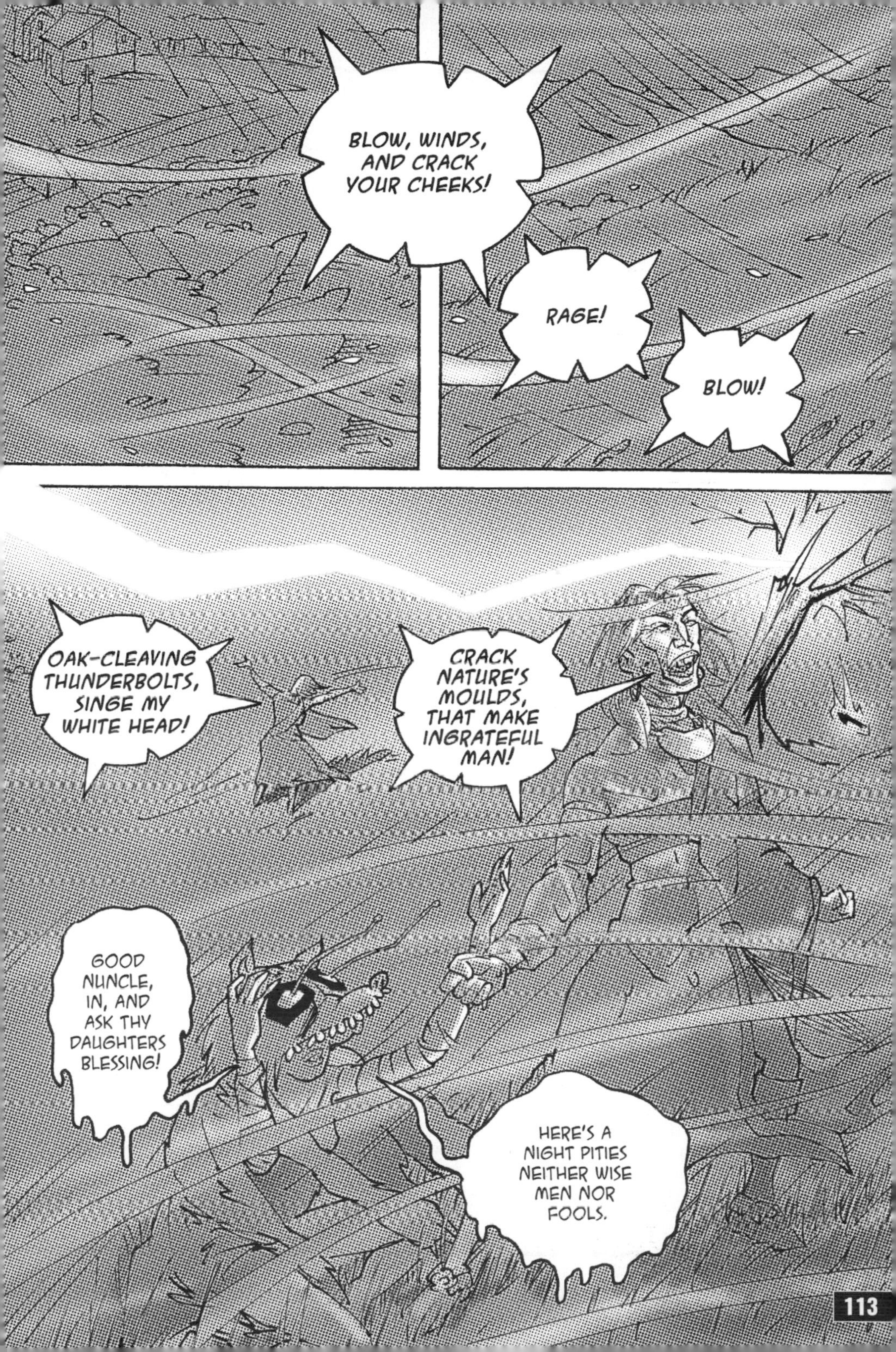
BLOW, WINDS, AND CRACK YOUR CHEEKS!
RAGE!
BLOW!
OAK-CLEAVING THUNDERBOLTS, SINGE MY WHITE HEAD!
CRACK NATURE'S MOULDS, THAT MAKE INGRATEFUL MAN!
GOOD NUNCLE, IN, AND ASK THY DAUGHTERS BLESSING!
HERE'S A NIGHT PITIES NEITHER WISE MEN NOR FOOLS.

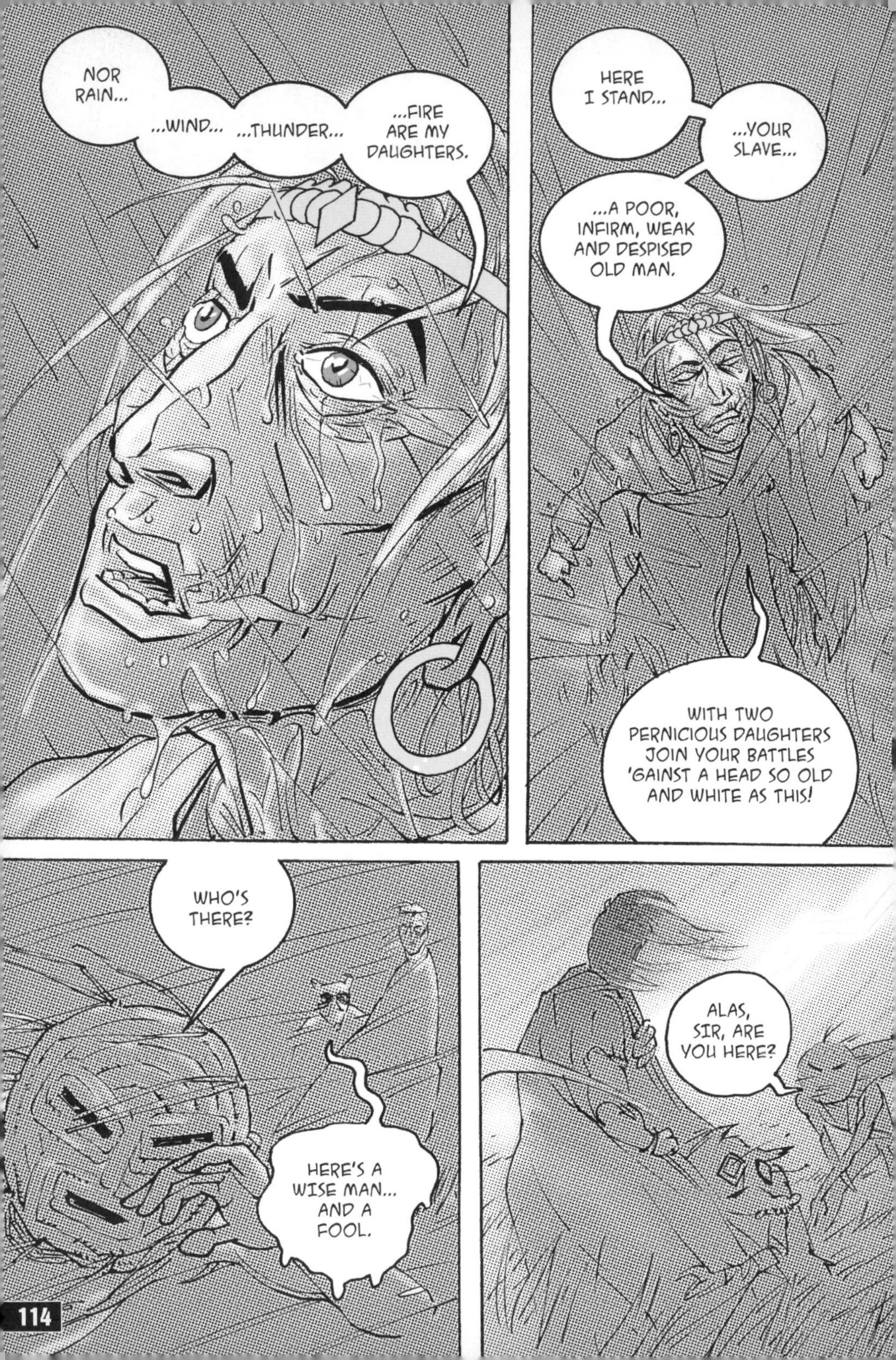
NOR RAIN...
...WIND...
...THUNDER...
...FIRE ARE MY DAUGHTERS.
HERE I STAND...
...YOUR SLAVE...
...A POOR, INFIRM, WEAK AND DESPISED OLD MAN.
WITH TWO PERNICIOUS DAUGHTERS JOIN YOUR BATTLES 'GAINST A HEAD SO OLD AND WHITE AS THIS!
WHO'S THERE?
HERE'S A WISE MAN... AND A FOOL.
ALAS, SIR, ARE YOU HERE?

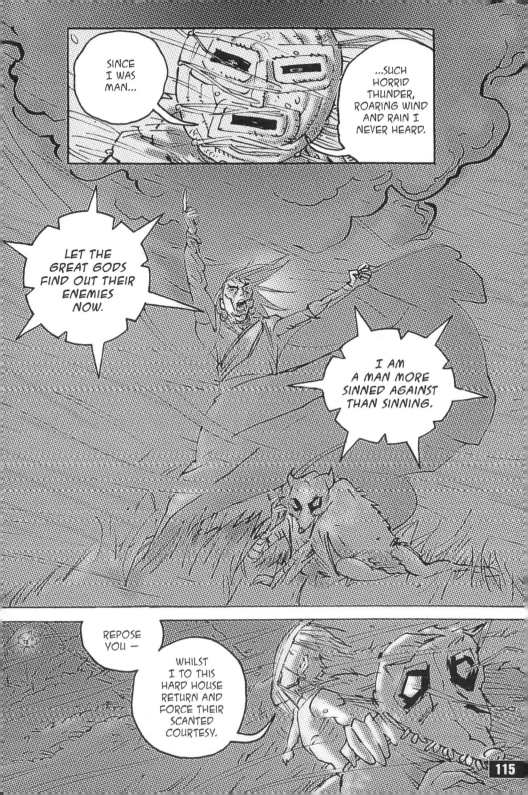

SINCE I WAS MAN...

...SUCH HORRID THUNDER, ROARING WIND AND RAIN I NEVER HEARD.

LET THE GREAT GODS FIND OUT THEIR ENEMIES NOW.

I AM A MAN MORE SINNED AGAINST THAN SINNING.

REPOSE YOU —

WHILST I TO THIS HARD HOUSE RETURN AND FORCE THEIR SCANTED COURTESY.

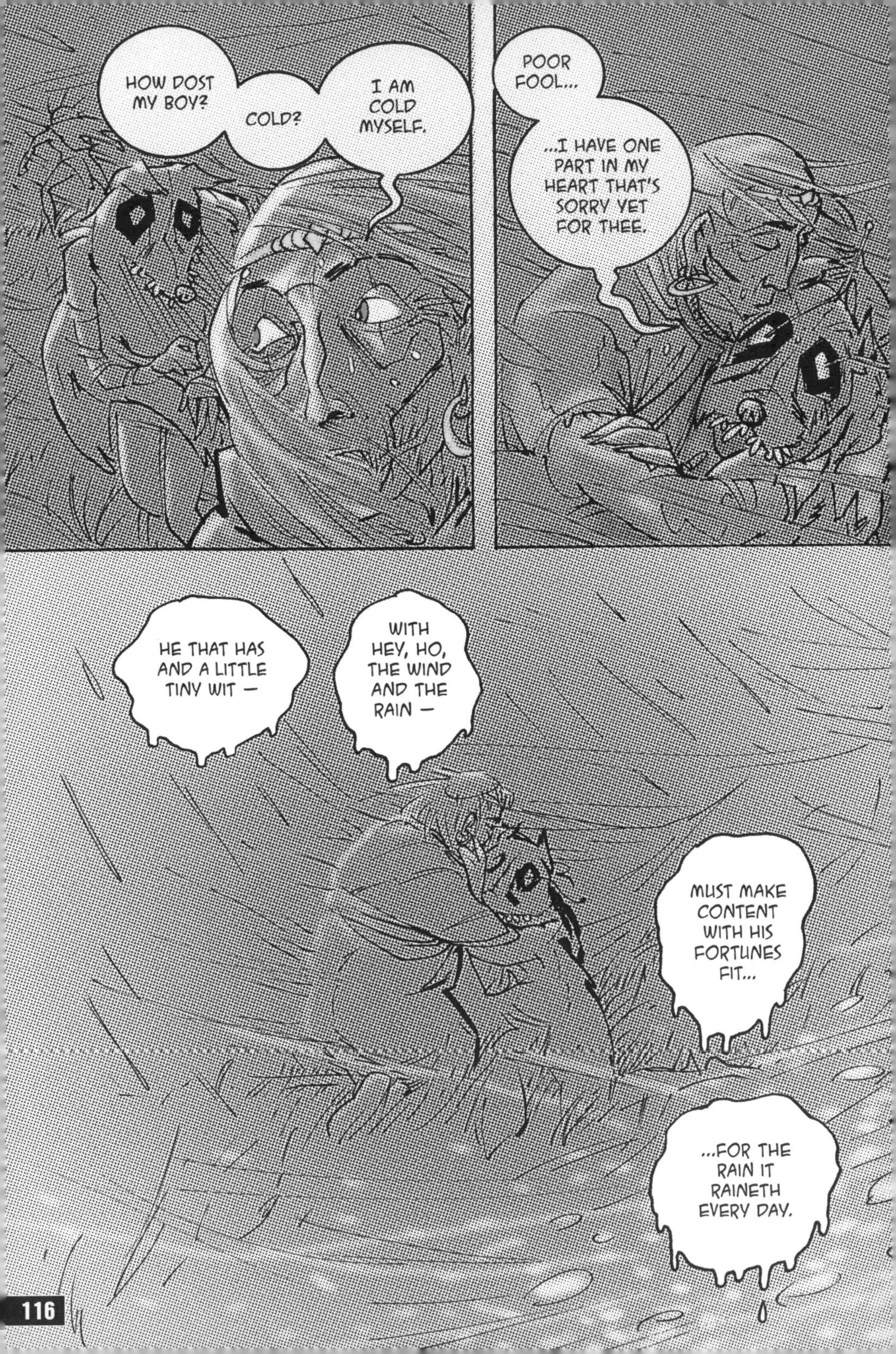

HOW DOST MY BOY?
COLD?
I AM COLD MYSELF.
POOR FOOL...
...I HAVE ONE PART IN MY HEART THAT'S SORRY YET FOR THEE.
HE THAT HAS AND A LITTLE TINY WIT —
WITH HEY, HO, THE WIND AND THE RAIN —
MUST MAKE CONTENT WITH HIS FORTUNES FIT...
...FOR THE RAIN IT RAINETH EVERY DAY.

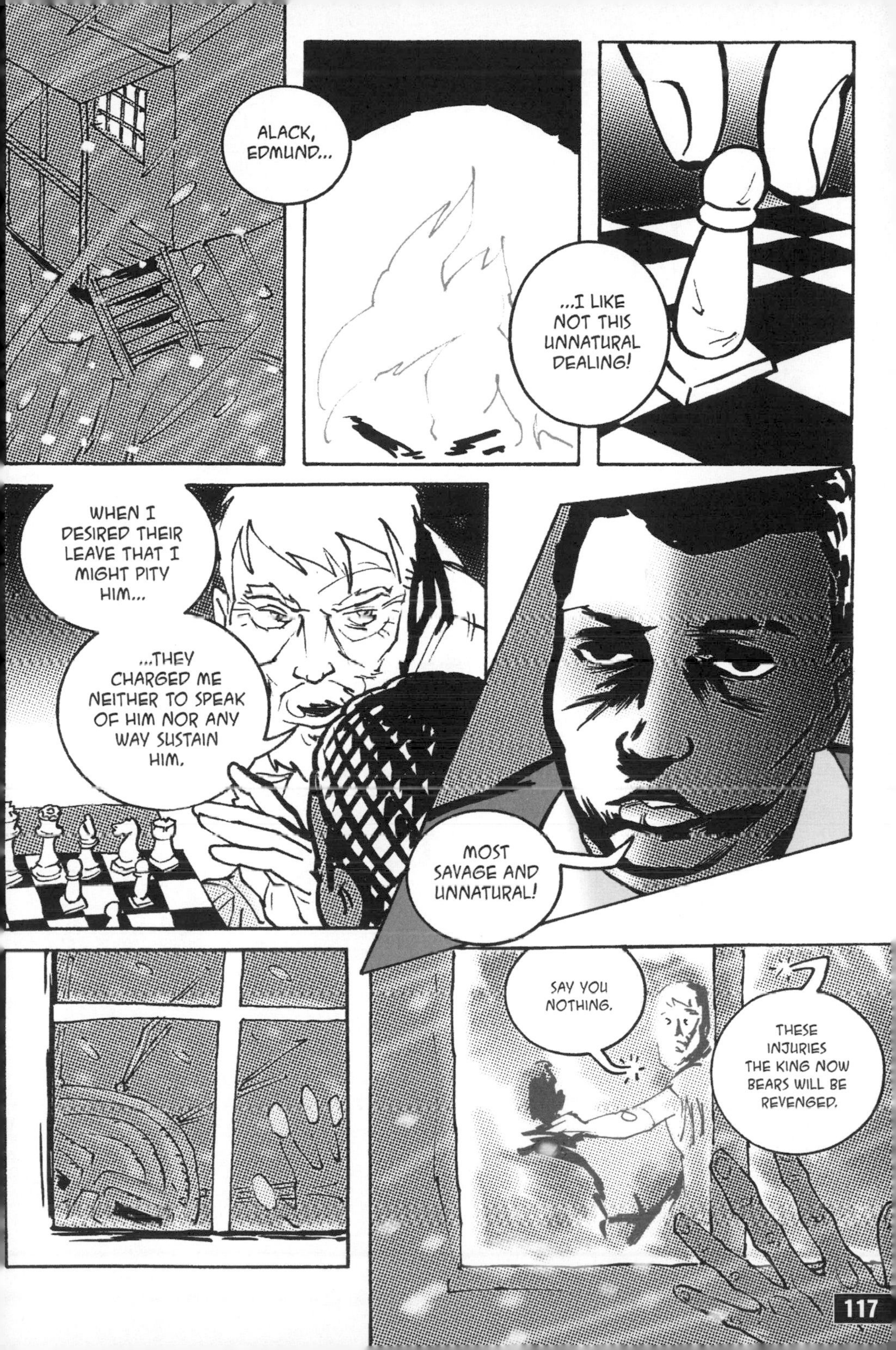
ALACK, EDMUND...
...I LIKE NOT THIS UNNATURAL DEALING!
WHEN I DESIRED THEIR LEAVE THAT I MIGHT PITY HIM...
...THEY CHARGED ME NEITHER TO SPEAK OF HIM NOR ANY WAY SUSTAIN HIM.
MOST SAVAGE AND UNNATURAL!
SAY YOU NOTHING.
THESE INJURIES THE KING NOW BEARS WILL BE REVENGED.

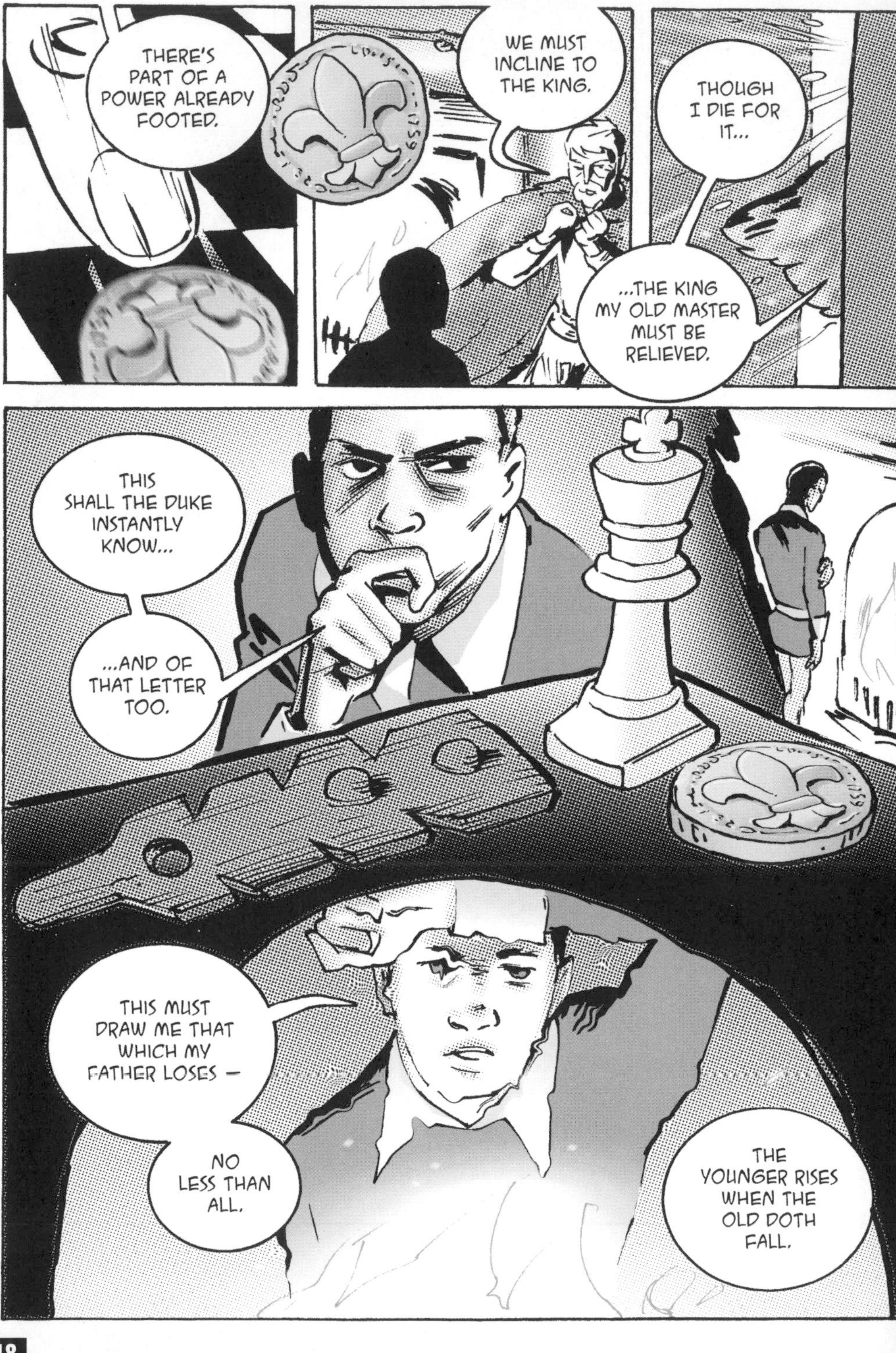

THERE'S PART OF A POWER ALREADY FOOTED.
WE MUST INCLINE TO THE KING.
THOUGH I DIE FOR IT...
...THE KING MY OLD MASTER MUST BE RELIEVED.
THIS SHALL THE DUKE INSTANTLY KNOW...
...AND OF THAT LETTER TOO.
THIS MUST DRAW ME THAT WHICH MY FATHER LOSES –
NO LESS THAN ALL.
THE YOUNGER RISES WHEN THE OLD DOTH FALL.

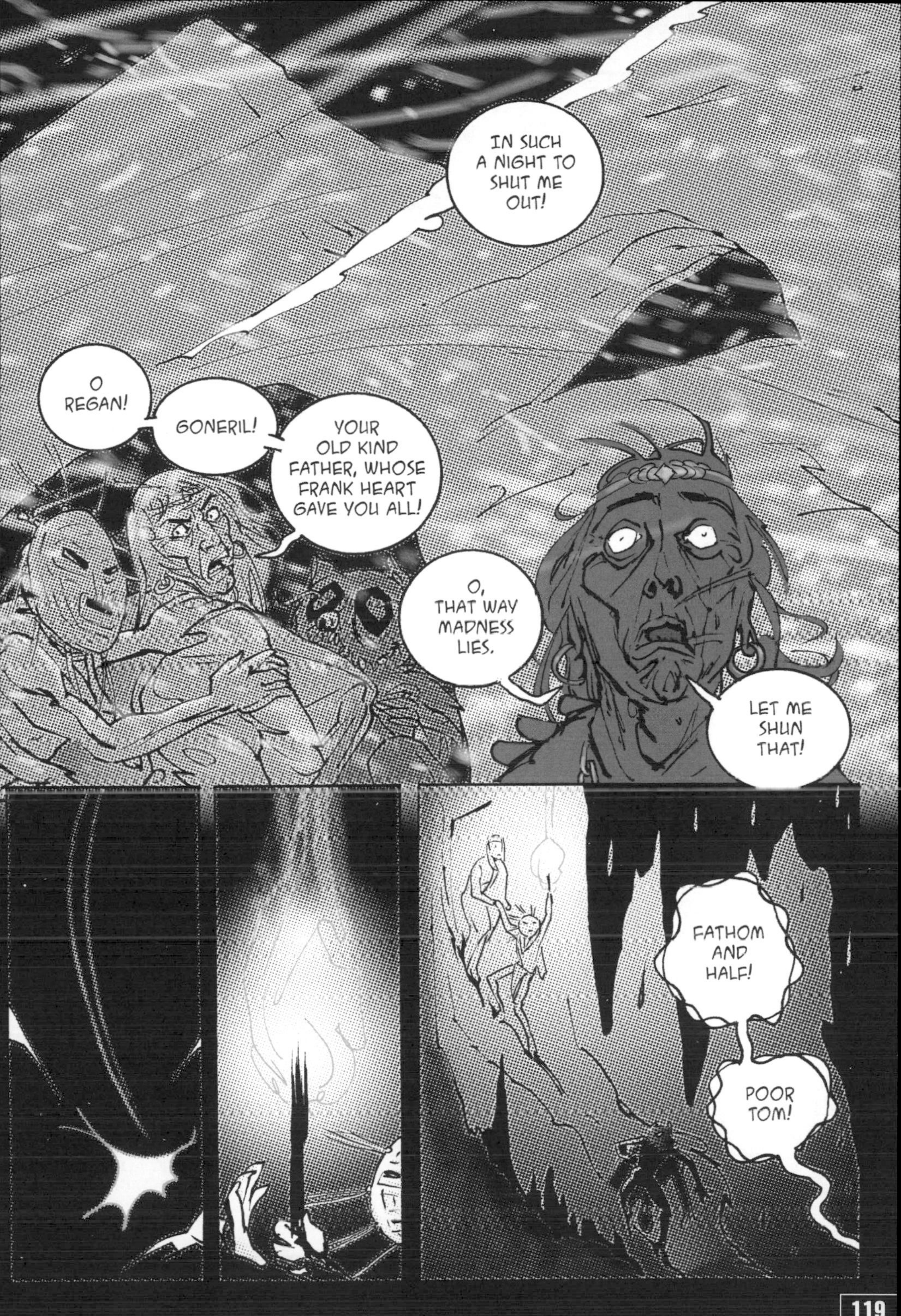
IN SUCH A NIGHT TO SHUT ME OUT!
O REGAN!
GONERIL!
YOUR OLD KIND FATHER, WHOSE FRANK HEART GAVE YOU ALL!
O, THAT WAY MADNESS LIES.
LET ME SHUN THAT!
FATHOM AND HALF!
POOR TOM!

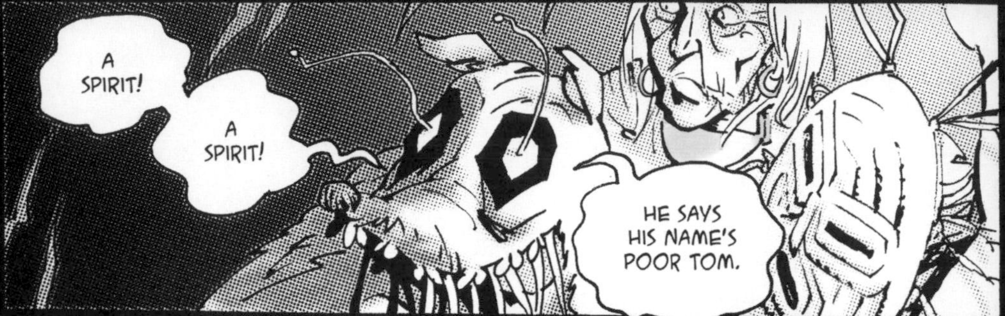
A SPIRIT!
A SPIRIT!
HE SAYS HIS NAME'S POOR TOM.
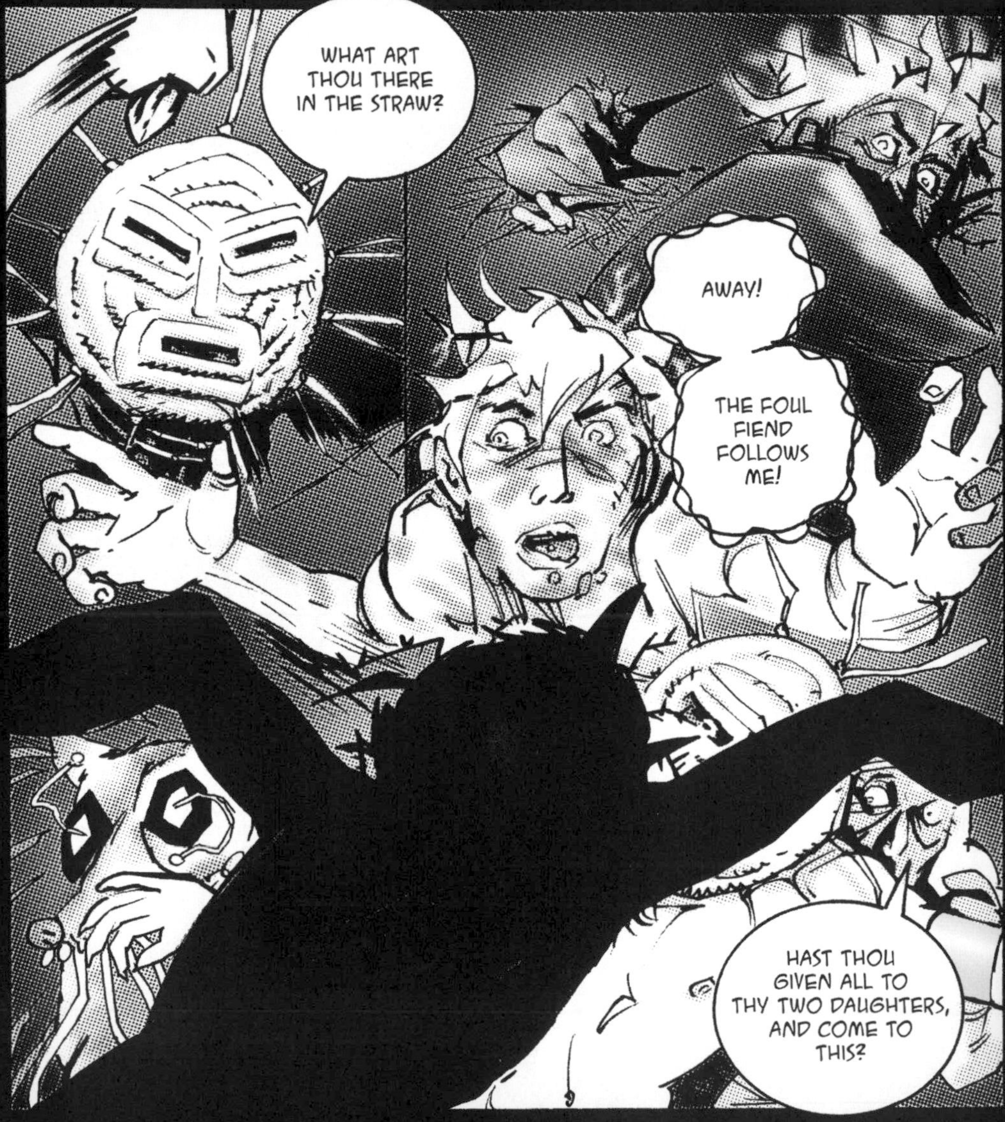
WHAT ART THOU THERE IN THE STRAW?
AWAY!
THE FOUL FIEND FOLLOWS ME!
HAST THOU GIVEN ALL TO THY TWO DAUGHTERS, AND COME TO THIS?

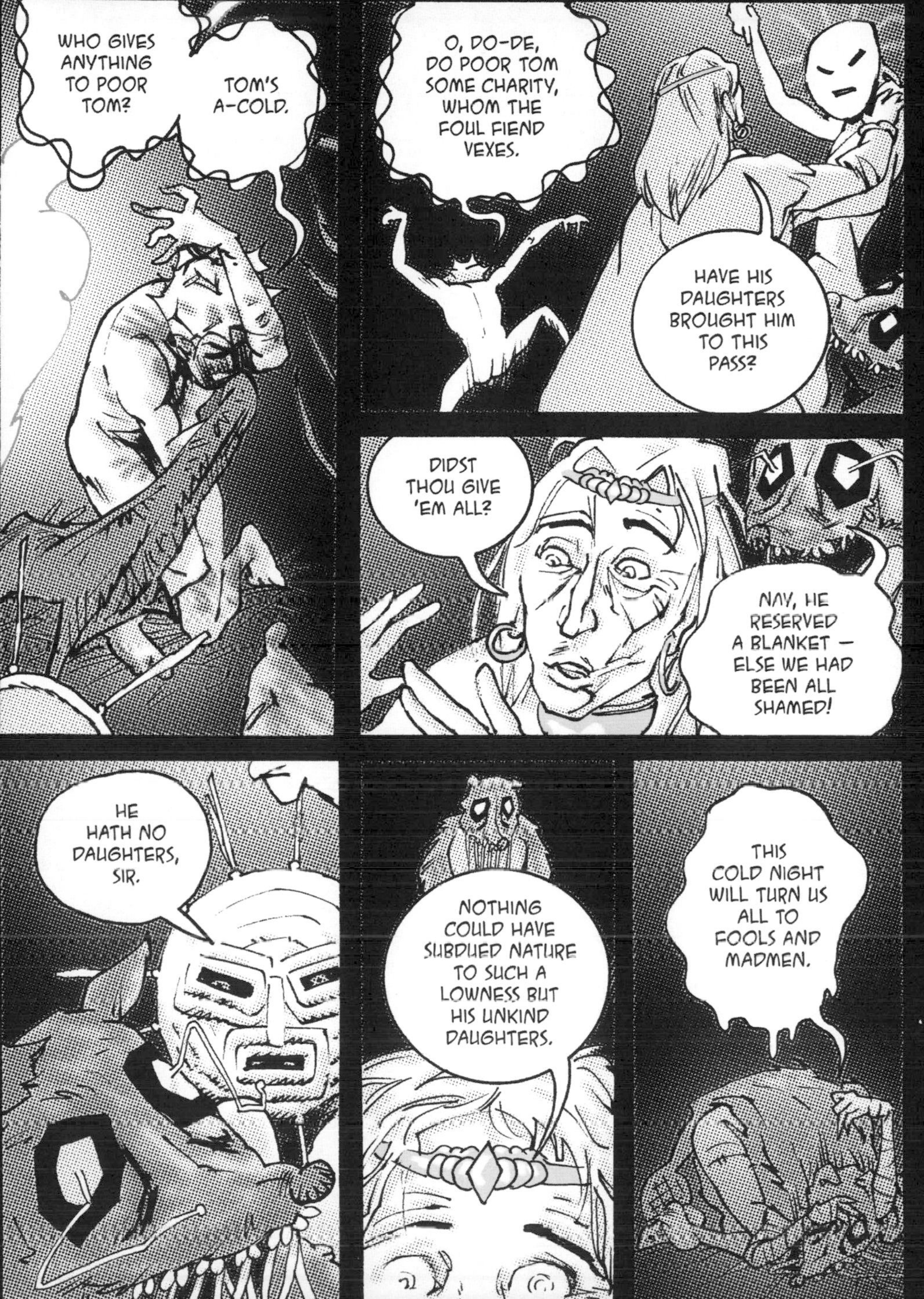
WHO GIVES ANYTHING TO POOR TOM?
TOM'S A-COLD.
O, DO-DE, DO POOR TOM SOME CHARITY, WHOM THE FOUL FIEND VEXES.
HAVE HIS DAUGHTERS BROUGHT HIM TO THIS PASS?
DIDST THOU GIVE 'EM ALL?
NAY, HE RESERVED A BLANKET — ELSE WE HAD BEEN ALL SHAMED!
HE HATH NO DAUGHTERS, SIR.
NOTHING COULD HAVE SUBDUED NATURE TO SUCH A LOWNESS BUT HIS UNKIND DAUGHTERS.
THIS COLD NIGHT WILL TURN US ALL TO FOOLS AND MADMEN.

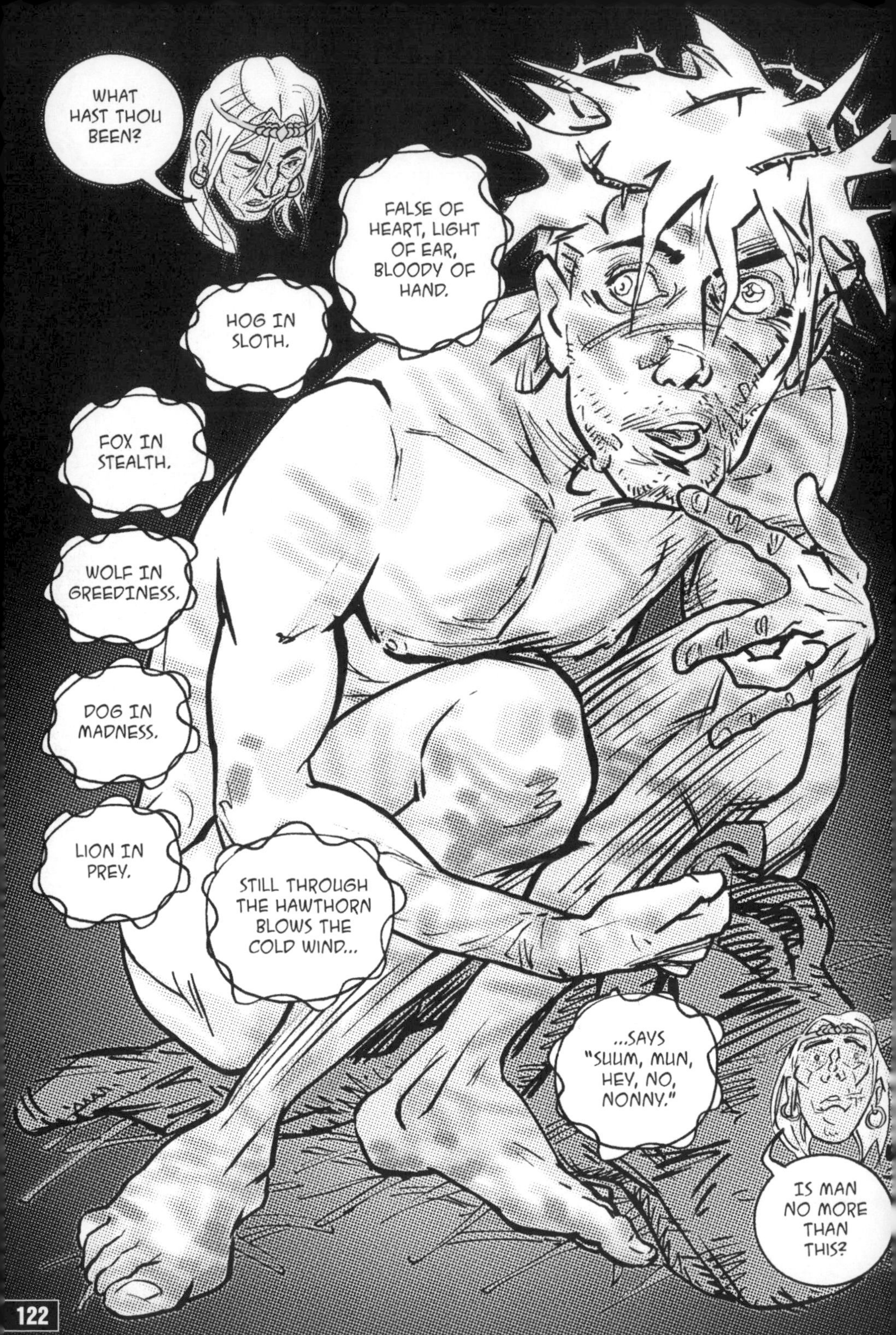
WHAT HAST THOU BEEN?
FALSE OF HEART, LIGHT OF EAR, BLOODY OF HAND.
HOG IN SLOTH.
FOX IN STEALTH.
WOLF IN GREEDINESS.
DOG IN MADNESS.
LION IN PREY.
STILL THROUGH THE HAWTHORN BLOWS THE COLD WIND...
...SAYS "SUUM, MUN, HEY, NO, NONNY."
IS MAN NO MORE THAN THIS?

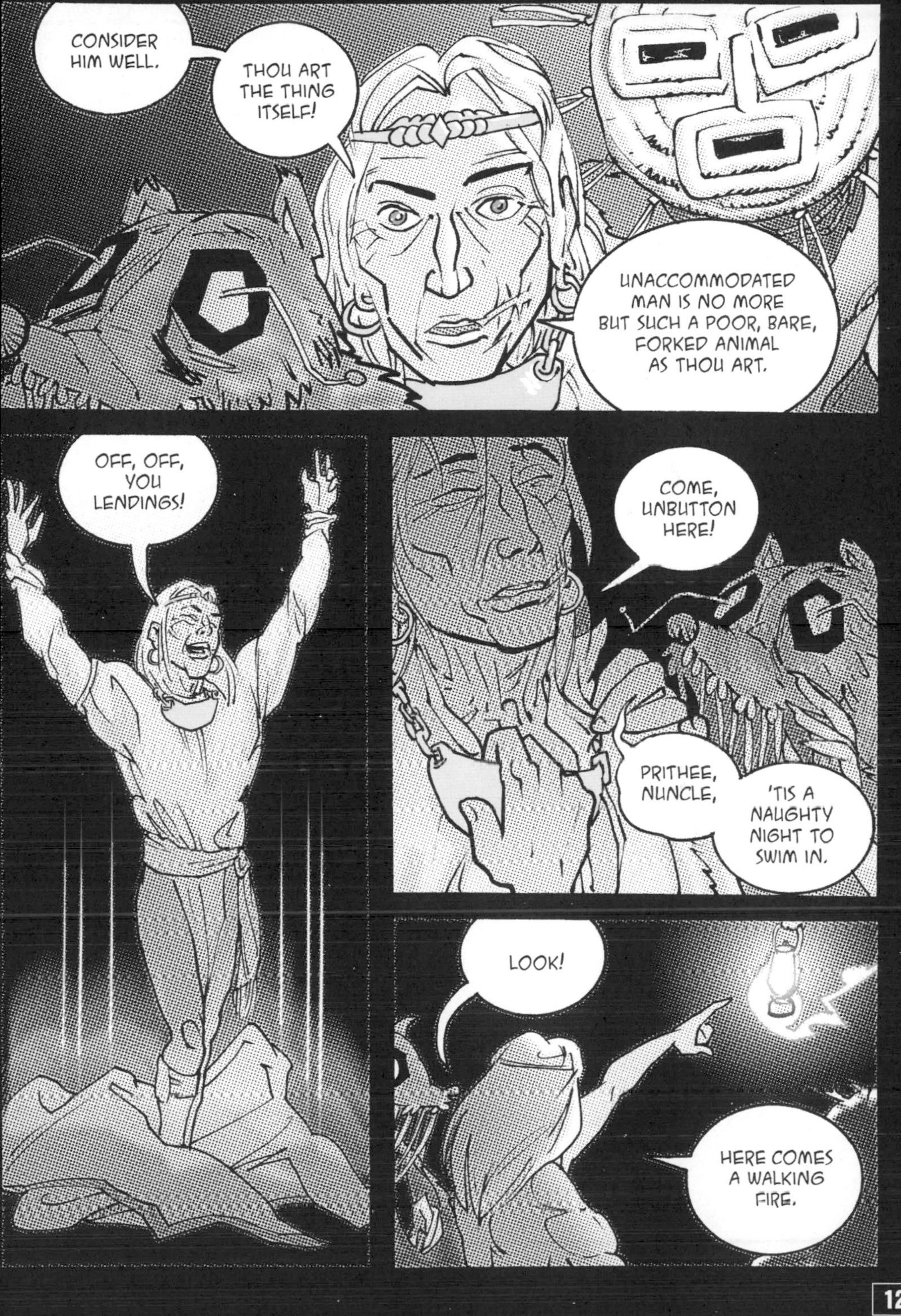
CONSIDER HIM WELL.
THOU ART THE THING ITSELF!
UNACCOMMODATED MAN IS NO MORE BUT SUCH A POOR, BARE, FORKED ANIMAL AS THOU ART.
OFF, OFF, YOU LENDINGS!
COME, UNBUTTON HERE!
PRITHEE, NUNCLE,
'TIS A NAUGHTY NIGHT TO SWIM IN.
LOOK!
HERE COMES A WALKING FIRE.

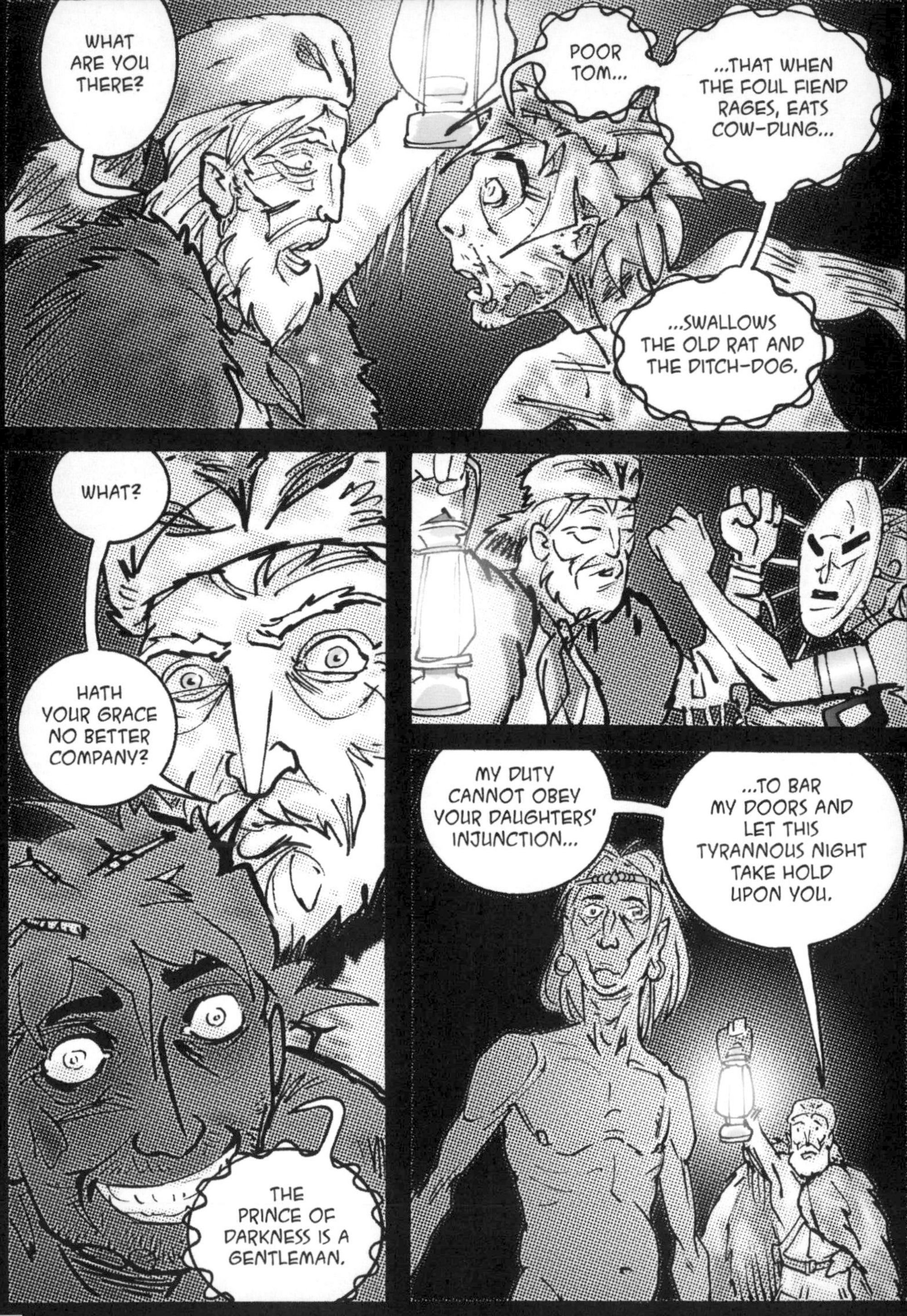
WHAT ARE YOU THERE?
POOR TOM...
...THAT WHEN THE FOUL FIEND RAGES, EATS COW-DUNG...
...SWALLOWS THE OLD RAT AND THE DITCH-DOG.
WHAT?
HATH YOUR GRACE NO BETTER COMPANY?
THE PRINCE OF DARKNESS IS A GENTLEMAN.
MY DUTY CANNOT OBEY YOUR DAUGHTERS' INJUNCTION...
...TO BAR MY DOORS AND LET THIS TYRANNOUS NIGHT TAKE HOLD UPON YOU.

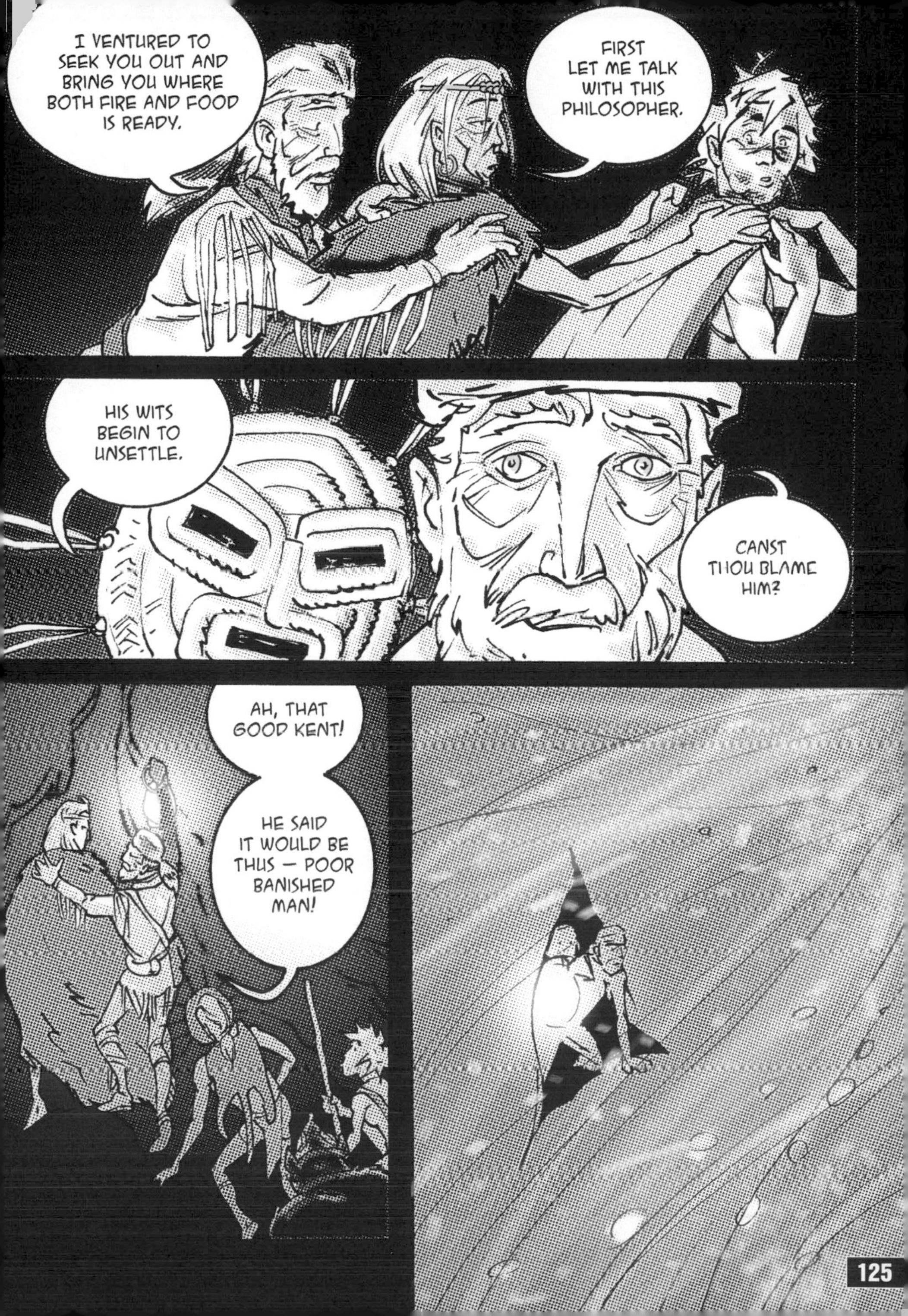
I VENTURED TO SEEK YOU OUT AND BRING YOU WHERE BOTH FIRE AND FOOD IS READY.
FIRST LET ME TALK WITH THIS PHILOSOPHER.
HIS WITS BEGIN TO UNSETTLE.
CANST THOU BLAME HIM?
AH, THAT GOOD KENT!
HE SAID IT WOULD BE THUS — POOR BANISHED MAN!

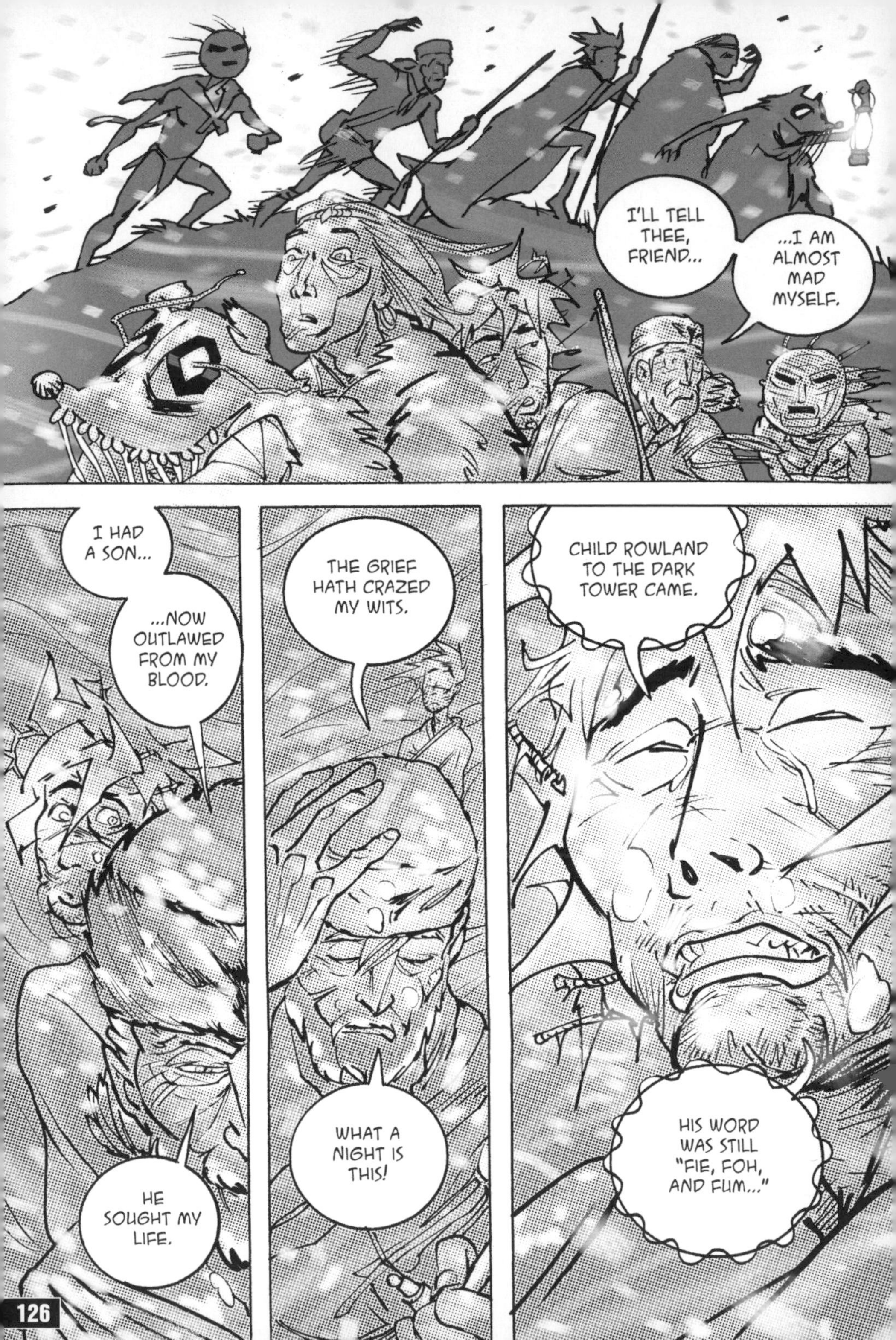
I'LL TELL THEE, FRIEND...
...I AM ALMOST MAD MYSELF.
I HAD A SON...
...NOW OUTLAWED FROM MY BLOOD.
HE SOUGHT MY LIFE.
THE GRIEF HATH CRAZED MY WITS.
WHAT A NIGHT IS THIS!
CHILD ROWLAND TO THE DARK TOWER CAME.
HIS WORD WAS STILL "FIE, FOH, AND FUM..."

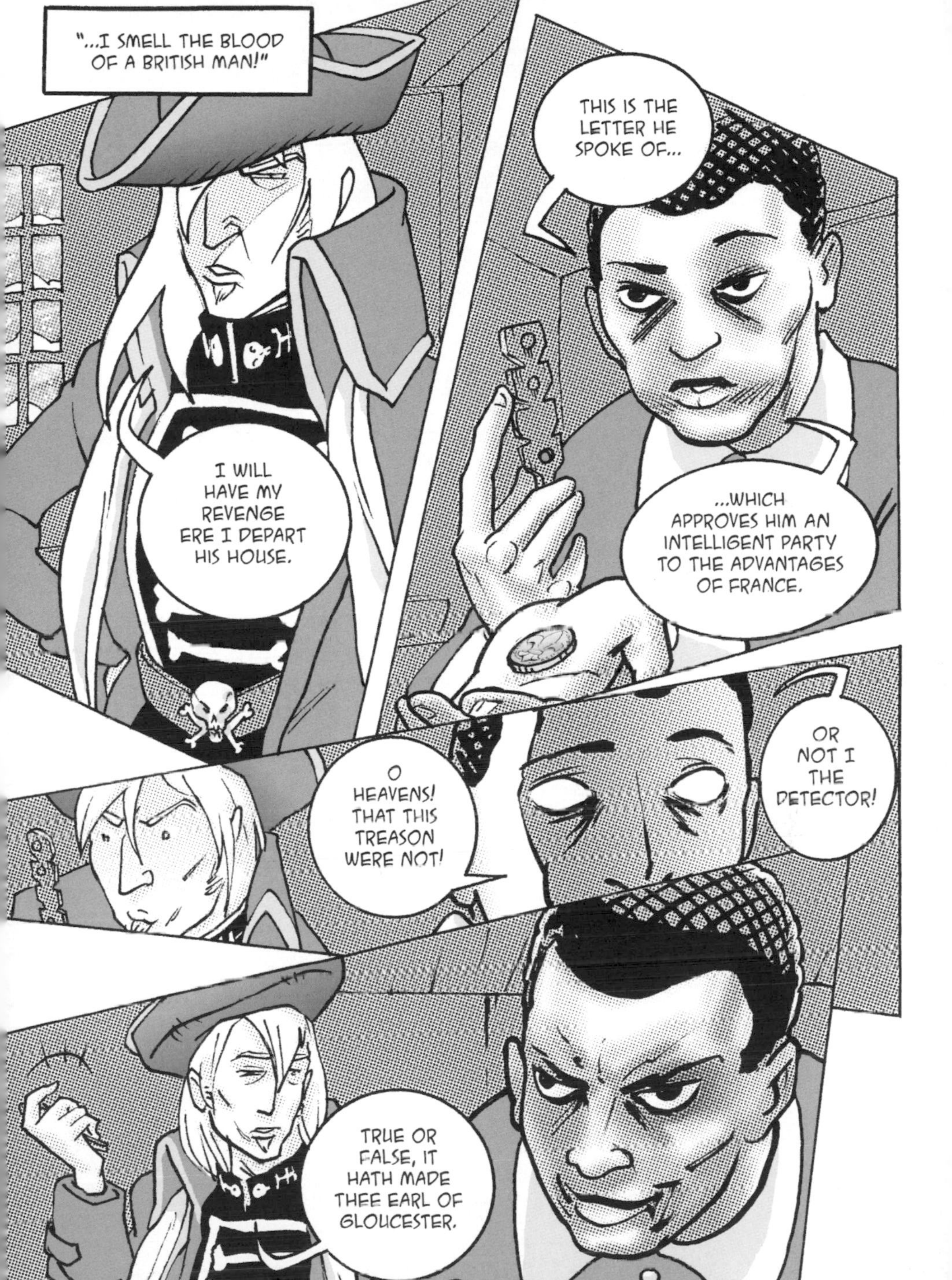
"...I SMELL THE BLOOD OF A BRITISH MAN!"
I WILL HAVE MY REVENGE ERE I DEPART HIS HOUSE.
THIS IS THE LETTER HE SPOKE OF...
...WHICH APPROVES HIM AN INTELLIGENT PARTY TO THE ADVANTAGES OF FRANCE.
O HEAVENS! THAT THIS TREASON WERE NOT!
OR NOT I THE DETECTOR!
TRUE OR FALSE, IT HATH MADE THEE EARL OF GLOUCESTER.

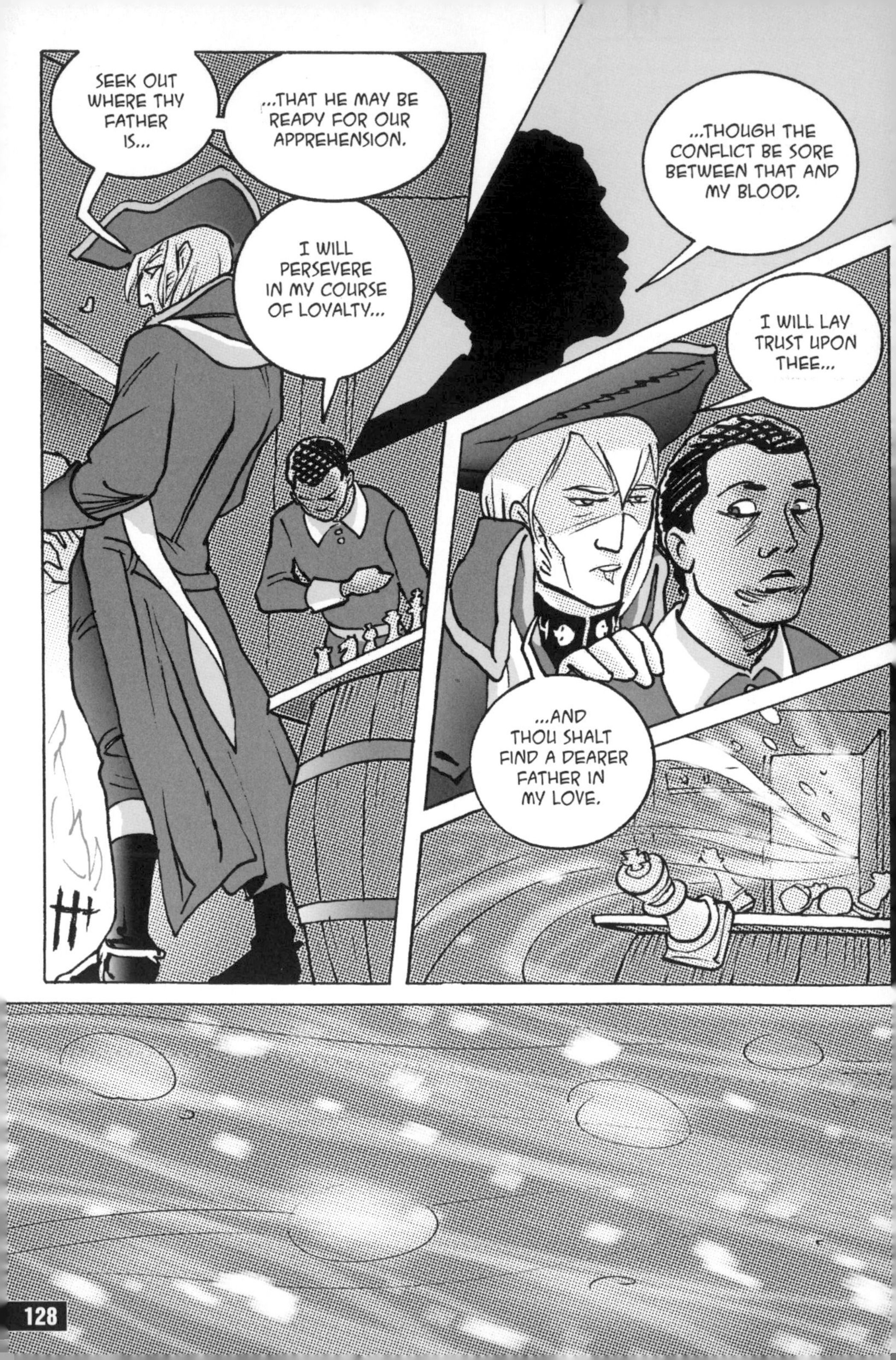
SEEK OUT WHERE THY FATHER IS...
...THAT HE MAY BE READY FOR OUR APPREHENSION.
I WILL PERSEVERE IN MY COURSE OF LOYALTY...
...THOUGH THE CONFLICT BE SORE BETWEEN THAT AND MY BLOOD.
I WILL LAY TRUST UPON THEE...
...AND THOU SHALT FIND A DEARER FATHER IN MY LOVE.

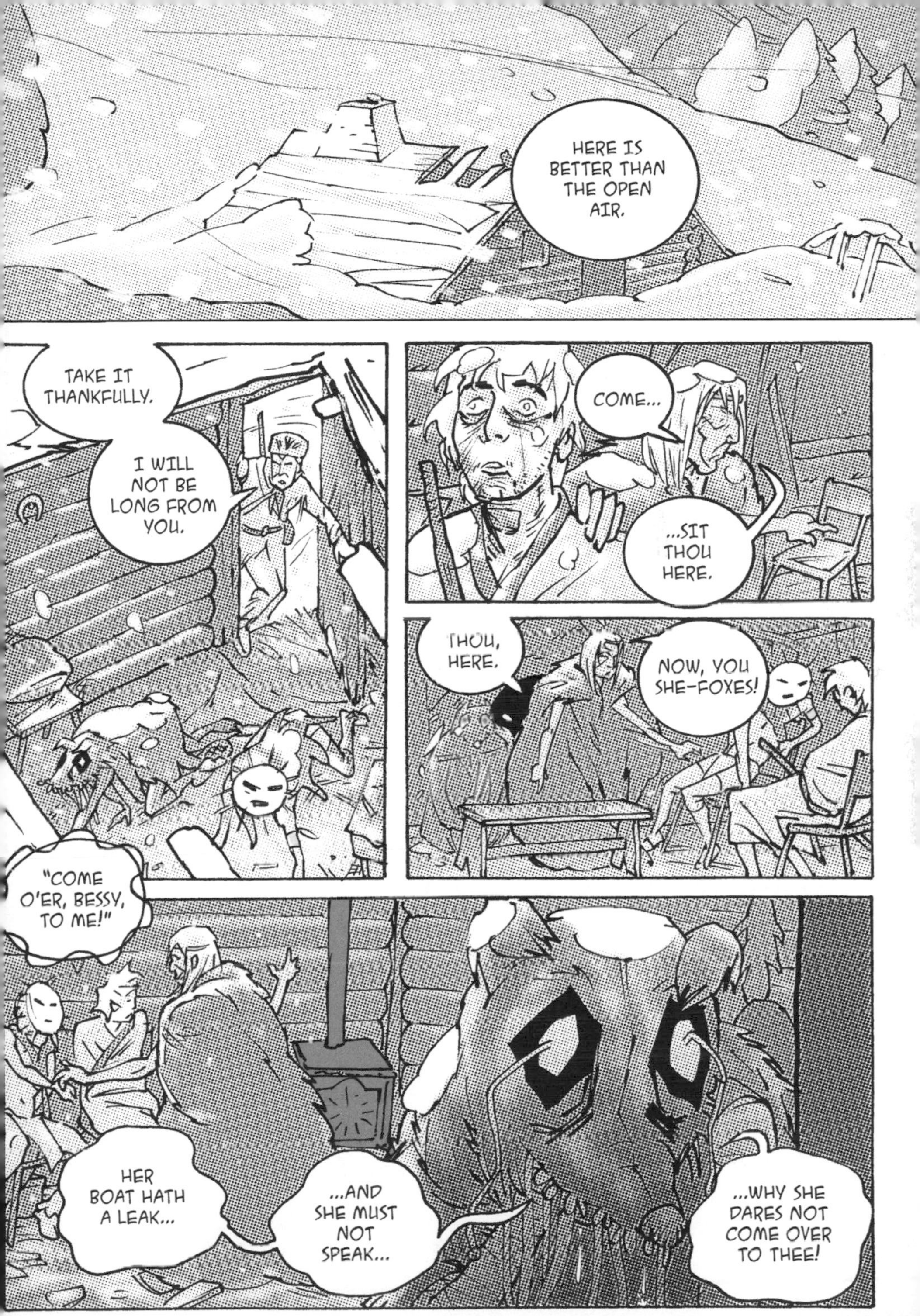
HERE IS BETTER THAN THE OPEN AIR.
TAKE IT THANKFULLY.
I WILL NOT BE LONG FROM YOU.
COME...
...SIT THOU HERE.
THOU, HERE.
NOW, YOU SHE-FOXES!
"COME O'ER, BESSY, TO ME!"
HER BOAT HATH A LEAK...
...AND SHE MUST NOT SPEAK...
...WHY SHE DARES NOT COME OVER TO THEE!

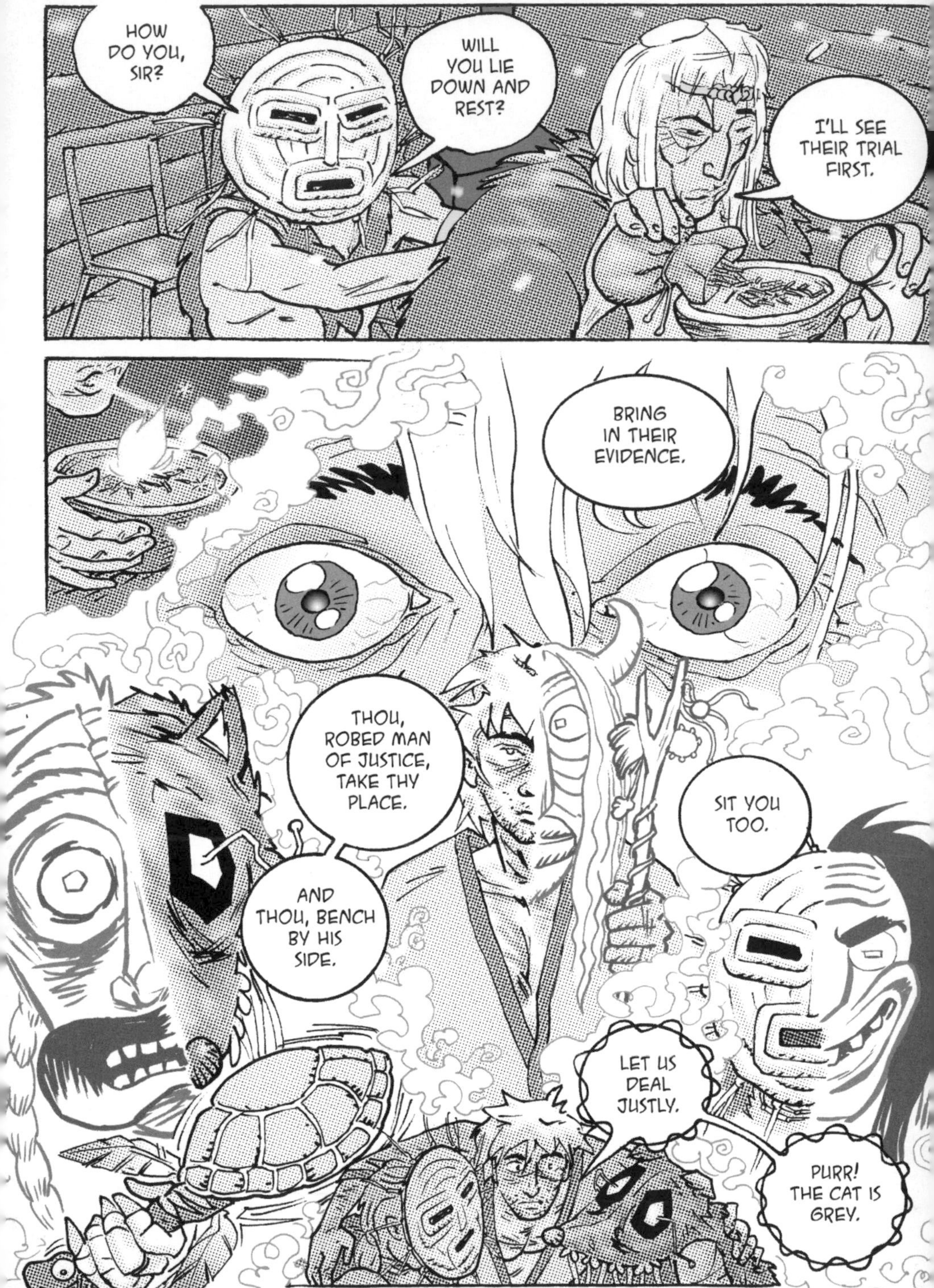
HOW DO YOU, SIR?
WILL YOU LIE DOWN AND REST?
I'LL SEE THEIR TRIAL FIRST.
BRING IN THEIR EVIDENCE.
THOU, ROBED MAN OF JUSTICE, TAKE THY PLACE.
AND THOU, BENCH BY HIS SIDE.
SIT YOU TOO.
LET US DEAL JUSTLY.
PURR! THE CAT IS GREY.

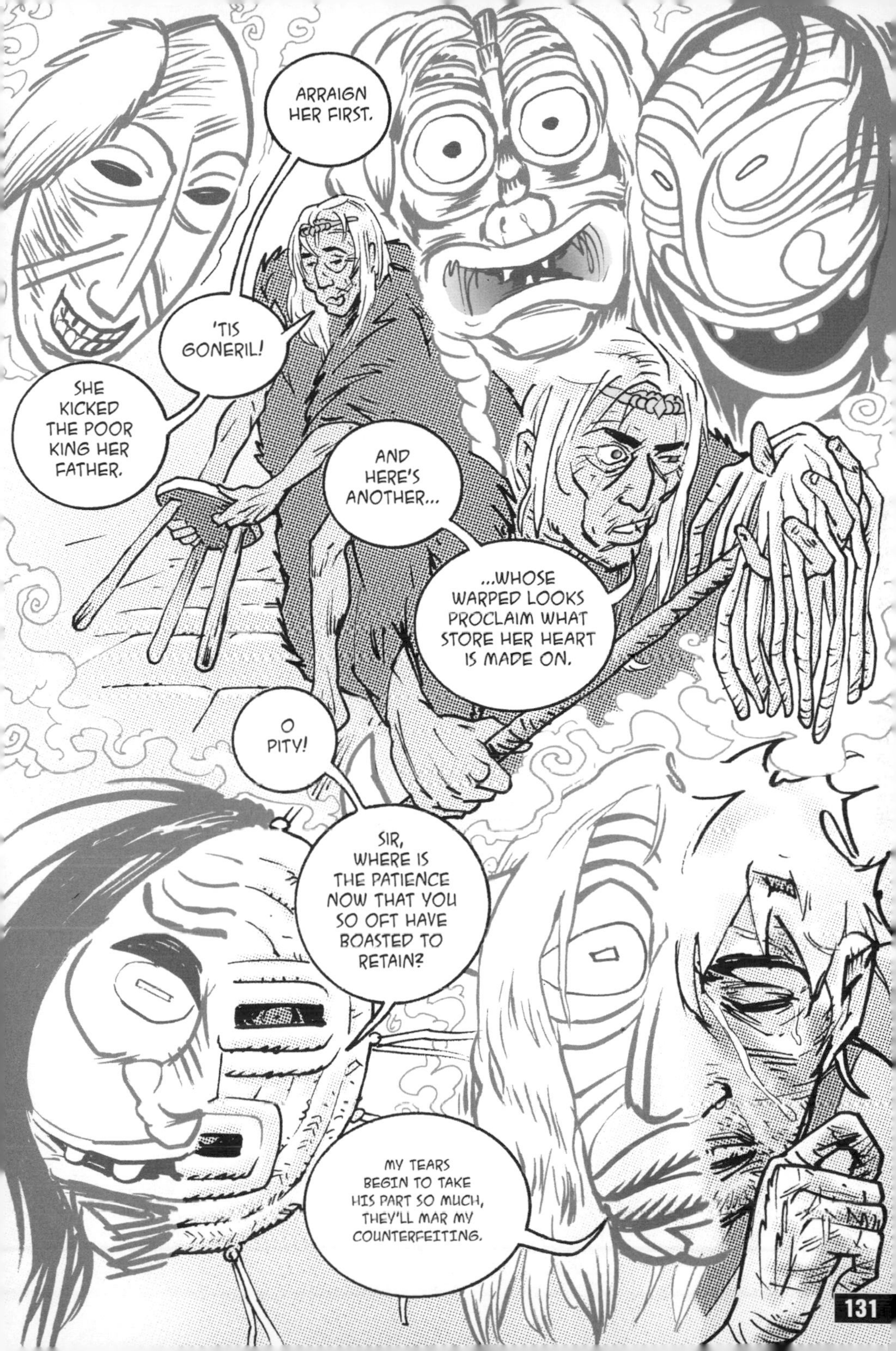

ARRAIGN HER FIRST.
'TIS GONERIL!
SHE KICKED THE POOR KING HER FATHER.
AND HERE'S ANOTHER...
...WHOSE WARPED LOOKS PROCLAIM WHAT STORE HER HEART IS MADE ON.
O PITY!
SIR, WHERE IS THE PATIENCE NOW THAT YOU SO OFT HAVE BOASTED TO RETAIN?
MY TEARS BEGIN TO TAKE HIS PART SO MUCH, THEY'LL MAR MY COUNTERFEITING.

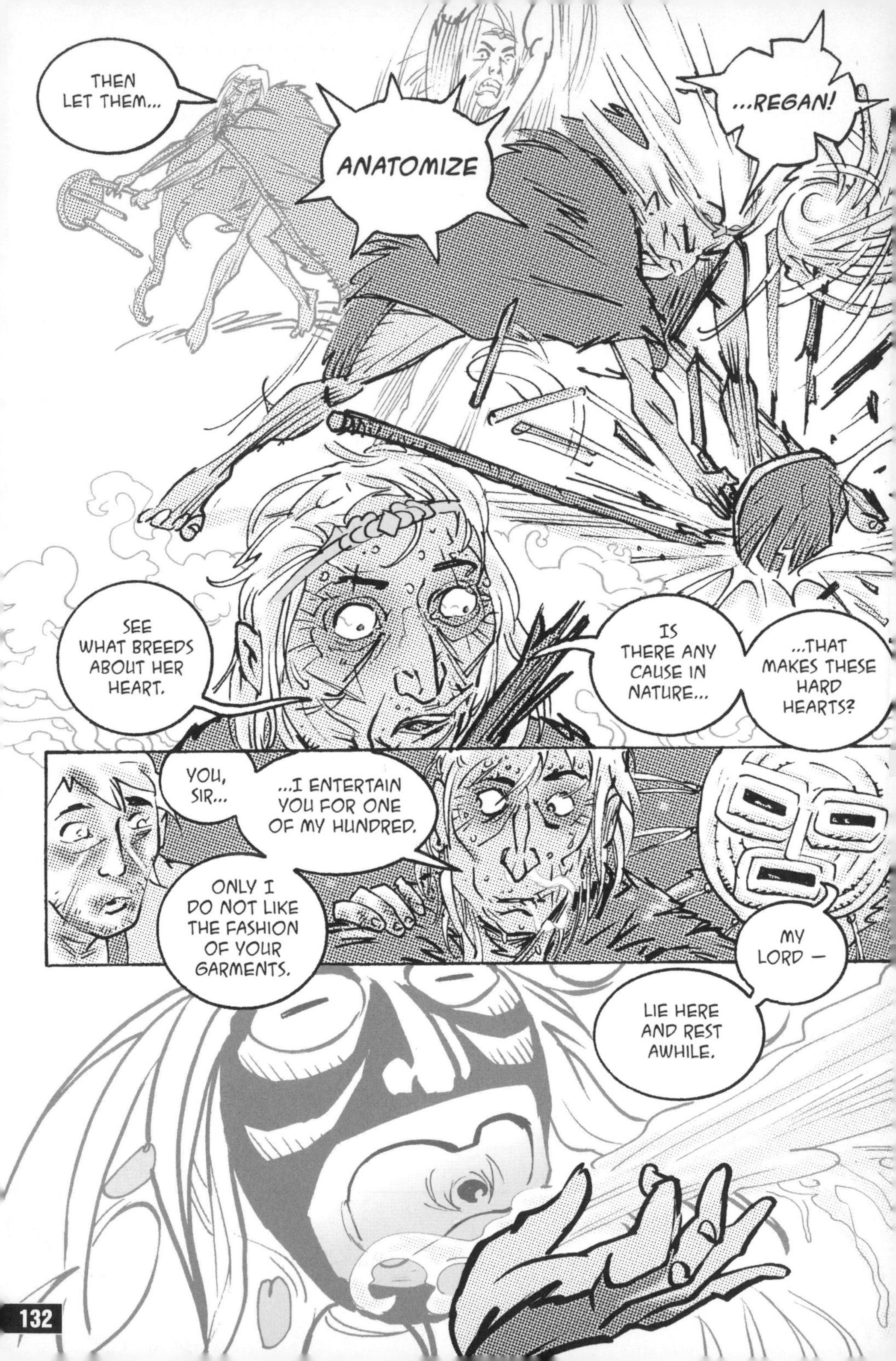
THEN LET THEM...
ANATOMIZE
...REGAN!
SEE WHAT BREEDS ABOUT HER HEART.
IS THERE ANY CAUSE IN NATURE...
...THAT MAKES THESE HARD HEARTS?
YOU, SIR...
...I ENTERTAIN YOU FOR ONE OF MY HUNDRED.
ONLY I DO NOT LIKE THE FASHION OF YOUR GARMENTS.
MY LORD —
LIE HERE AND REST AWHILE.

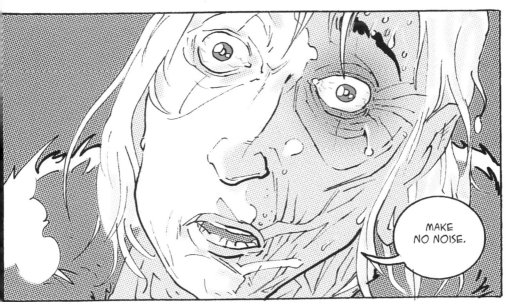

MAKE NO NOISE.

WE'LL GO TO SUPPER IN THE MORNING.

AND I'LL GO TO BED AT NOON.

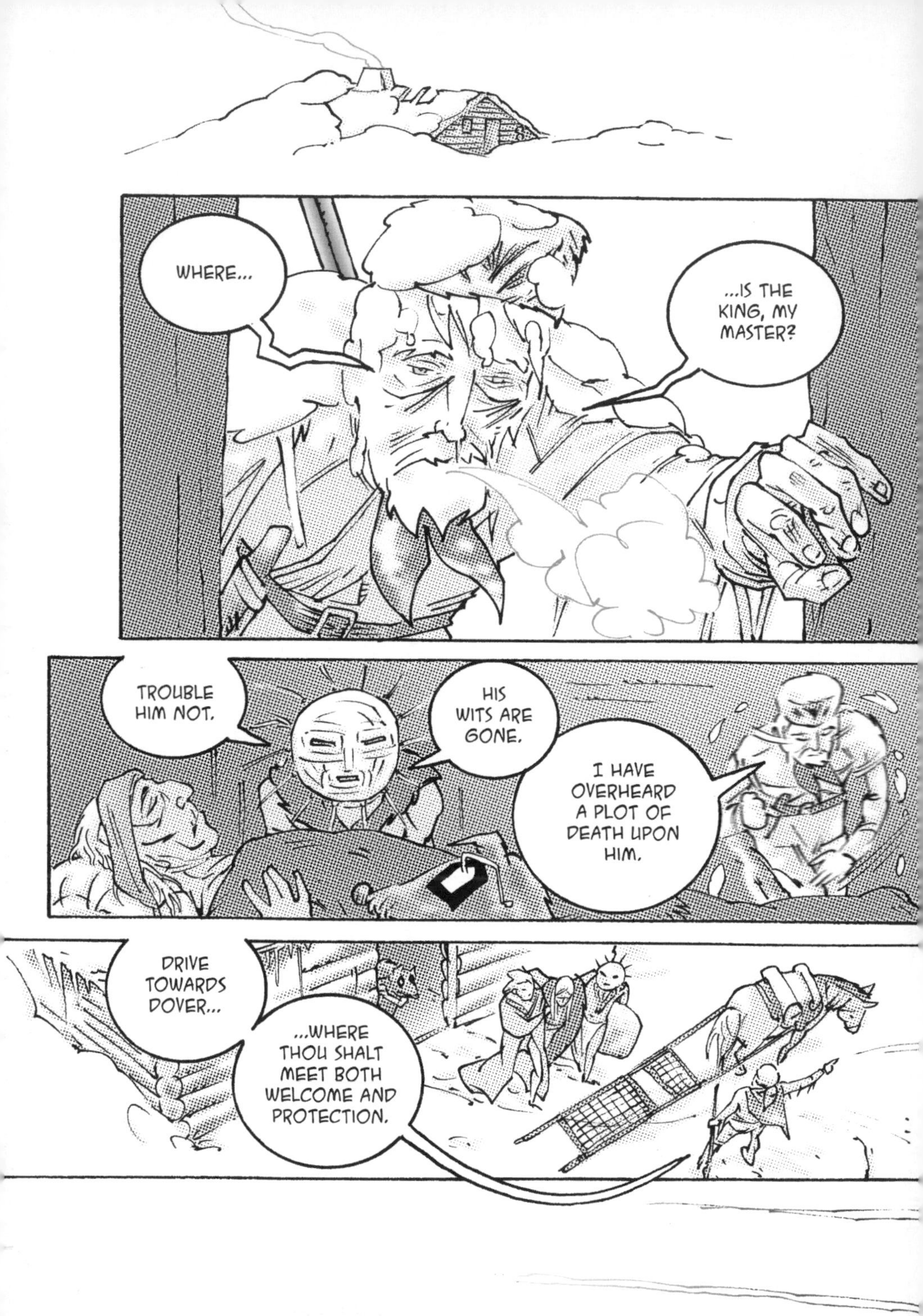
WHERE...
...IS THE KING, MY MASTER?
TROUBLE HIM NOT.
HIS WITS ARE GONE.
I HAVE OVERHEARD A PLOT OF DEATH UPON HIM.
DRIVE TOWARDS DOVER...
...WHERE THOU SHALT MEET BOTH WELCOME AND PROTECTION.

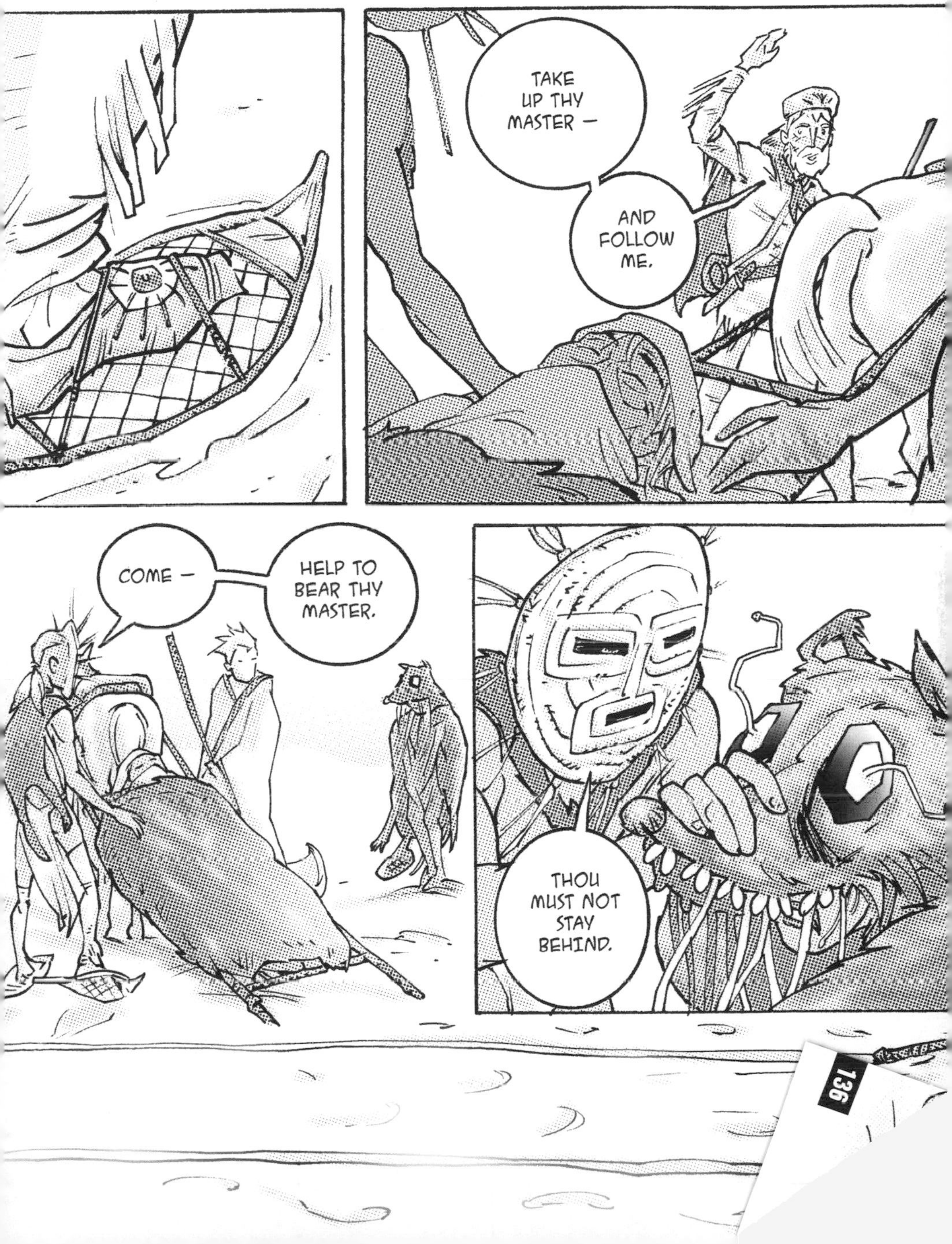
TAKE UP THY MASTER —
AND FOLLOW ME.
COME —
HELP TO BEAR THY MASTER.
THOU MUST NOT STAY BEHIND.

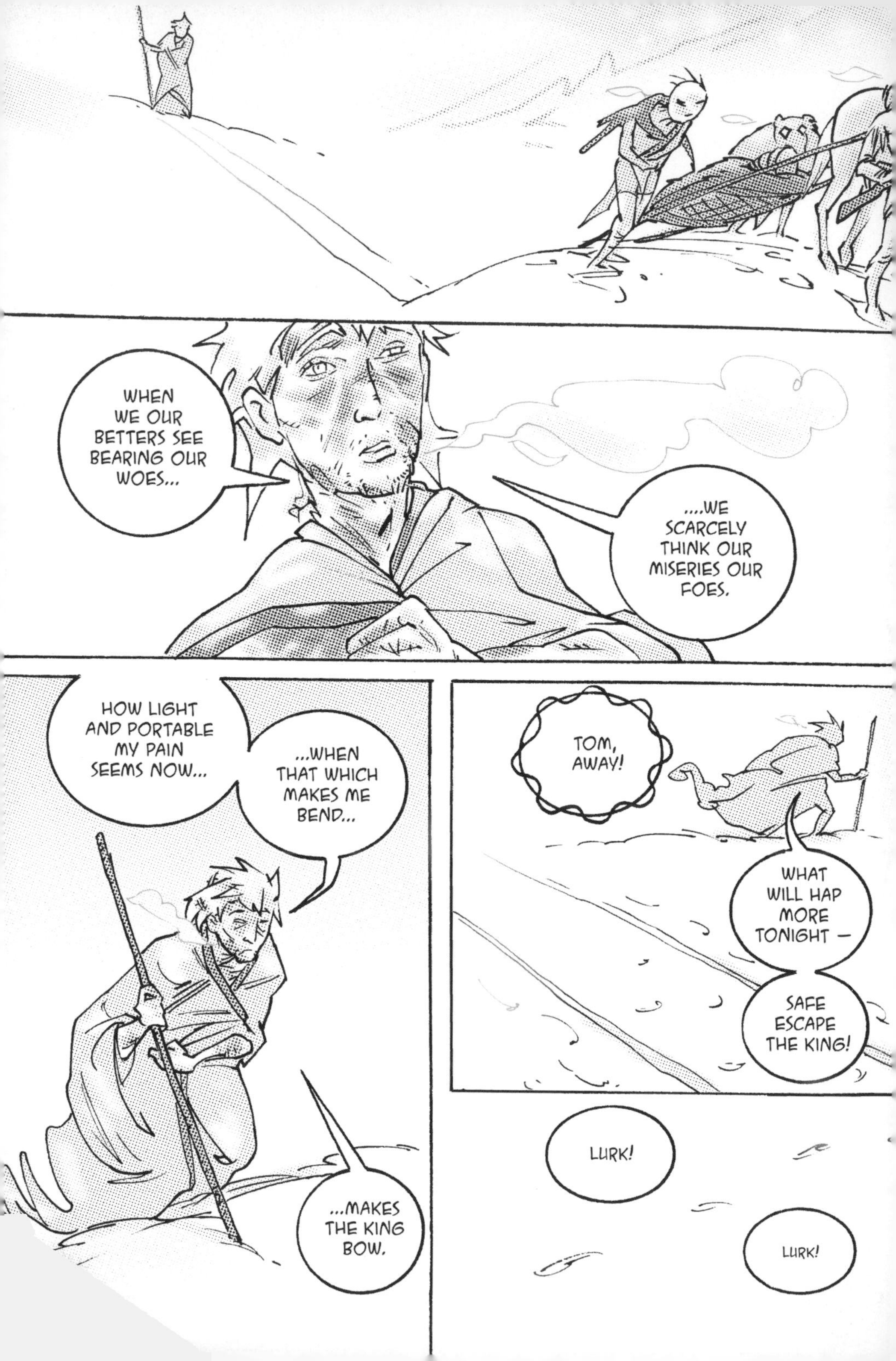
WHEN WE OUR BETTERS SEE BEARING OUR WOES...
....WE SCARCELY THINK OUR MISERIES OUR FOES.
HOW LIGHT AND PORTABLE MY PAIN SEEMS NOW...
...WHEN THAT WHICH MAKES ME BEND...
...MAKES THE KING BOW.
TOM, AWAY!
WHAT WILL HAP MORE TONIGHT —
SAFE ESCAPE THE KING!
LURK!
LURK!

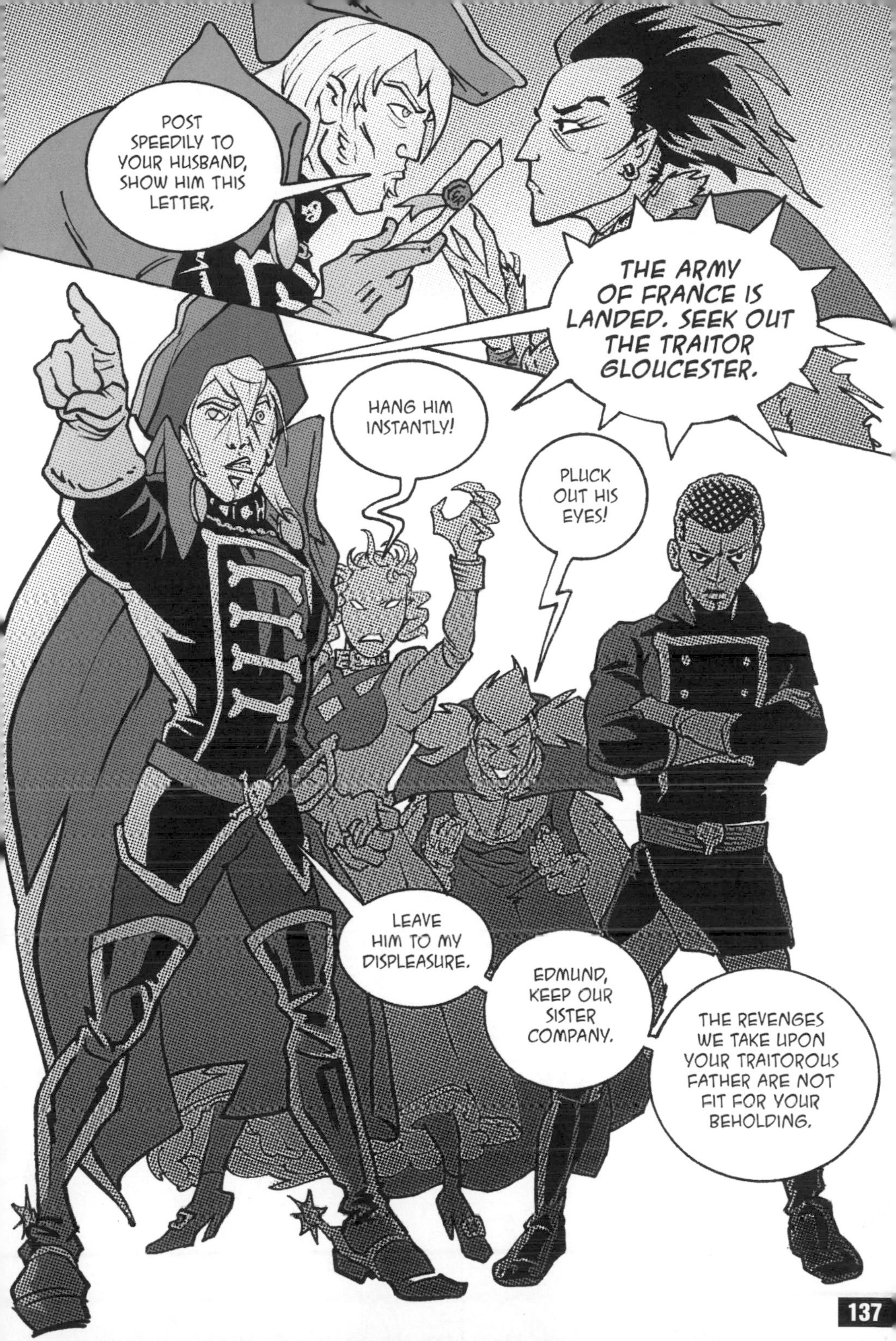
POST SPEEDILY TO YOUR HUSBAND, SHOW HIM THIS LETTER.
THE ARMY OF FRANCE IS LANDED. SEEK OUT THE TRAITOR GLOUCESTER.
HANG HIM INSTANTLY!
PLUCK OUT HIS EYES!
LEAVE HIM TO MY DISPLEASURE.
EDMUND, KEEP OUR SISTER COMPANY.
THE REVENGES WE TAKE UPON YOUR TRAITOROUS FATHER ARE NOT FIT FOR YOUR BEHOLDING.

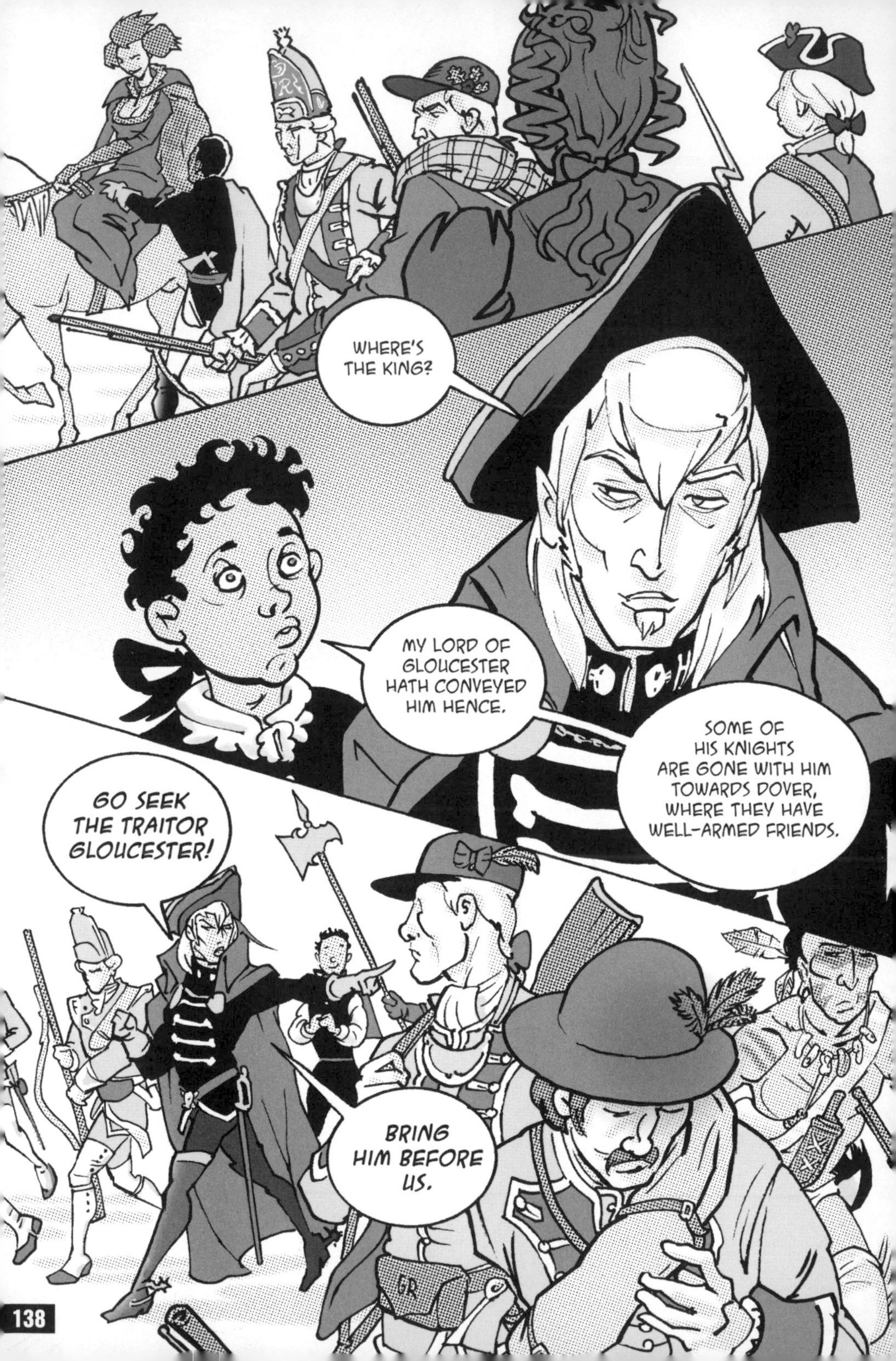
WHERE'S THE KING?
MY LORD OF GLOUCESTER HATH CONVEYED HIM HENCE.
SOME OF HIS KNIGHTS ARE GONE WITH HIM TOWARDS DOVER, WHERE THEY HAVE WELL-ARMED FRIENDS.
GO SEEK THE TRAITOR GLOUCESTER!
BRING HIM BEFORE US.
GR

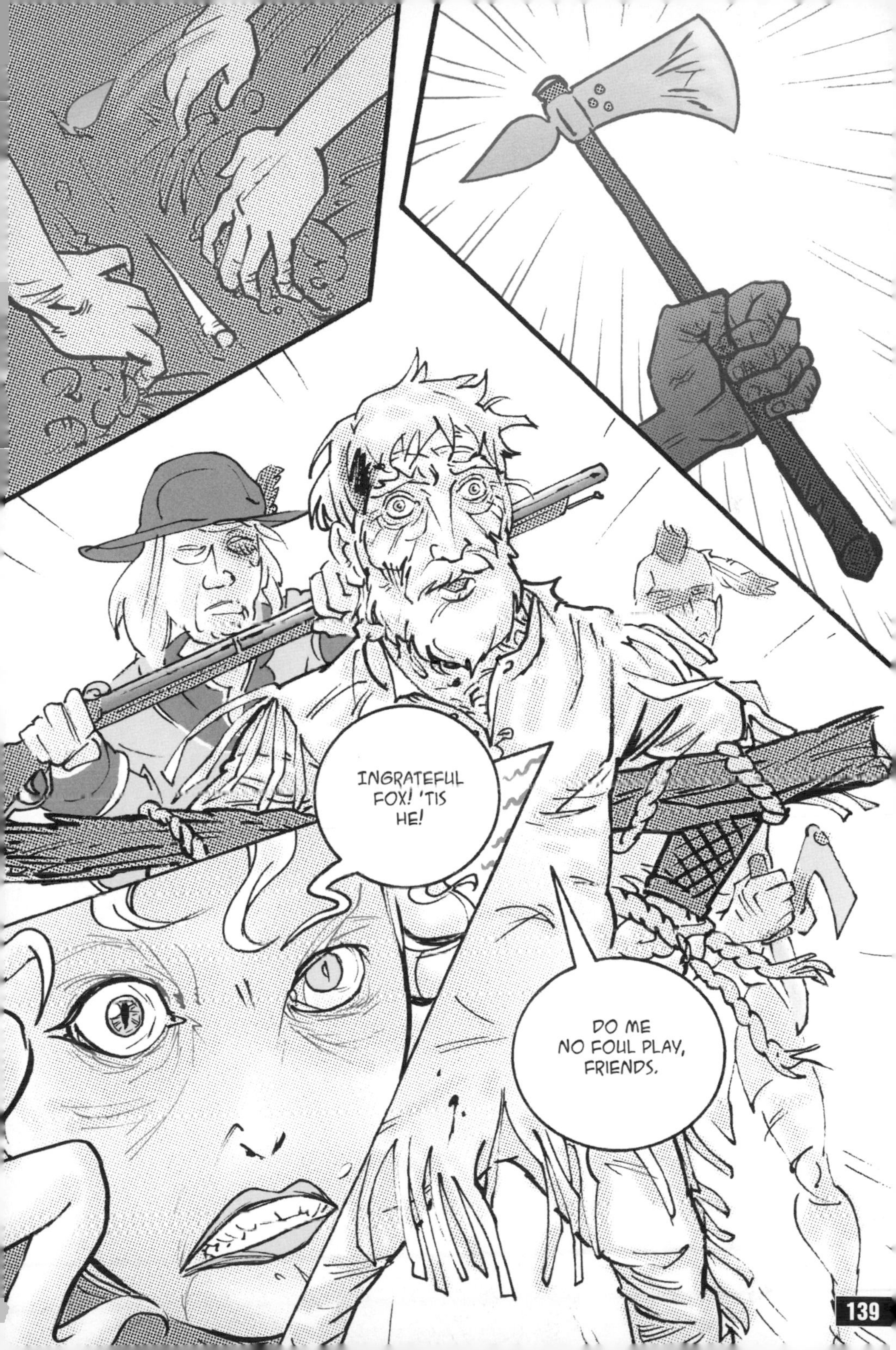
INGRATEFUL FOX! 'TIS HE!
DO ME NO FOUL PLAY, FRIENDS.

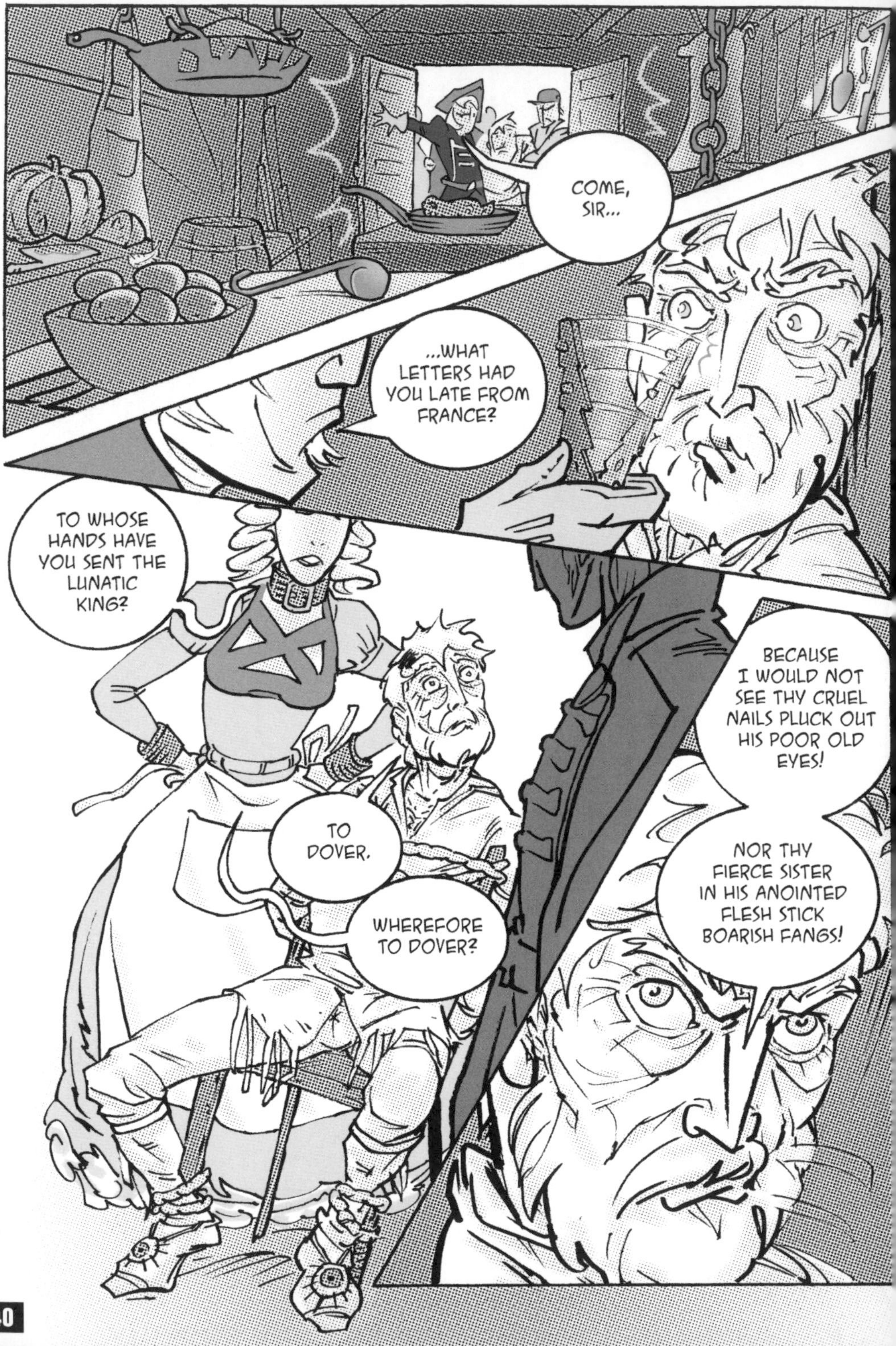

COME, SIR...
...WHAT LETTERS HAD YOU LATE FROM FRANCE?
TO WHOSE HANDS HAVE YOU SENT THE LUNATIC KING?
TO DOVER.
WHEREFORE TO DOVER?
BECAUSE I WOULD NOT SEE THY CRUEL NAILS PLUCK OUT HIS POOR OLD EYES!
NOR THY FIERCE SISTER IN HIS ANOINTED FLESH STICK BOARISH FANGS!

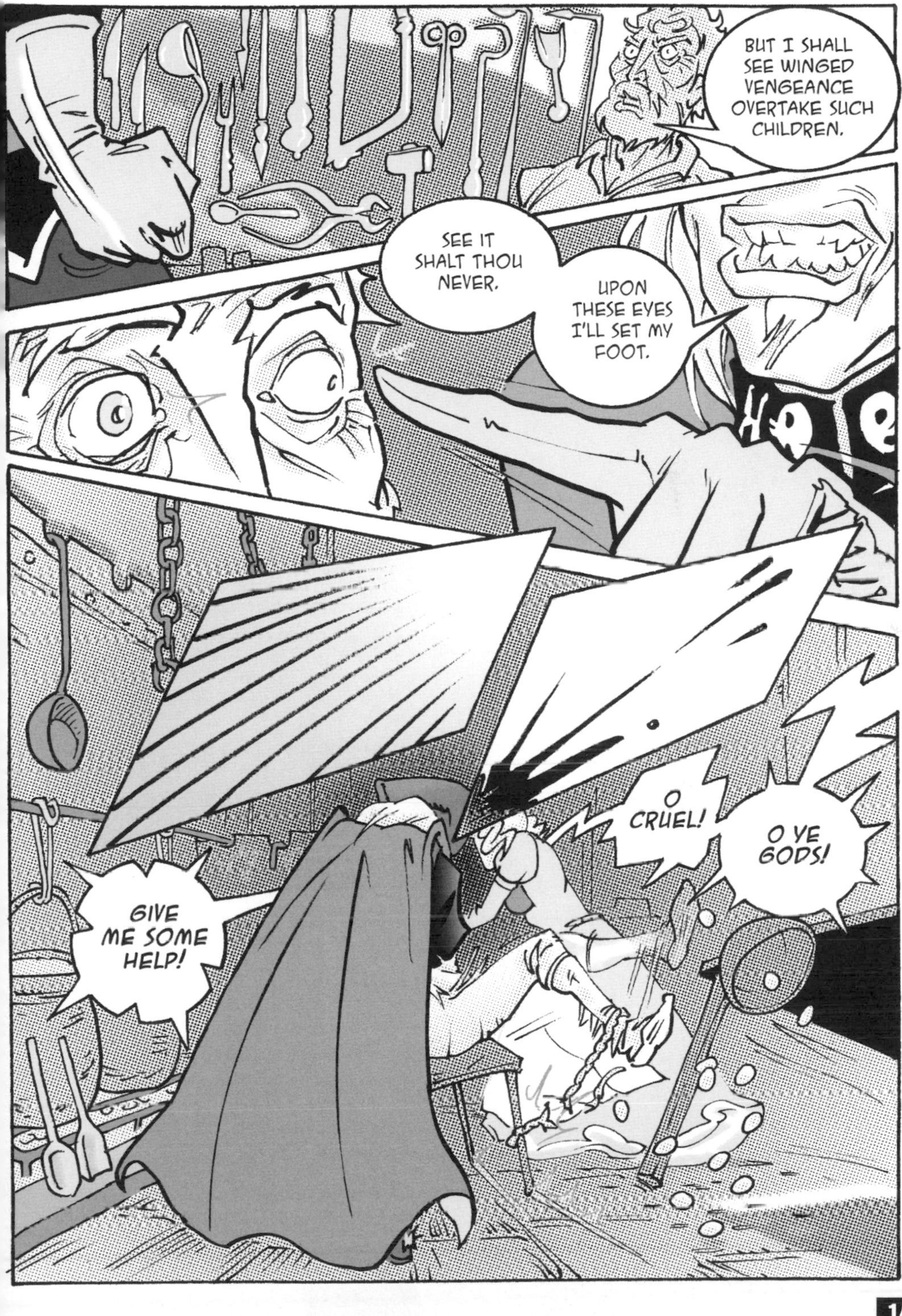
BUT I SHALL SEE WINGED VENGEANCE OVERTAKE SUCH CHILDREN.
SEE IT SHALT THOU NEVER.
UPON THESE EYES I'LL SET MY FOOT.
GIVE ME SOME HELP!
O CRUEL!
O YE GODS!

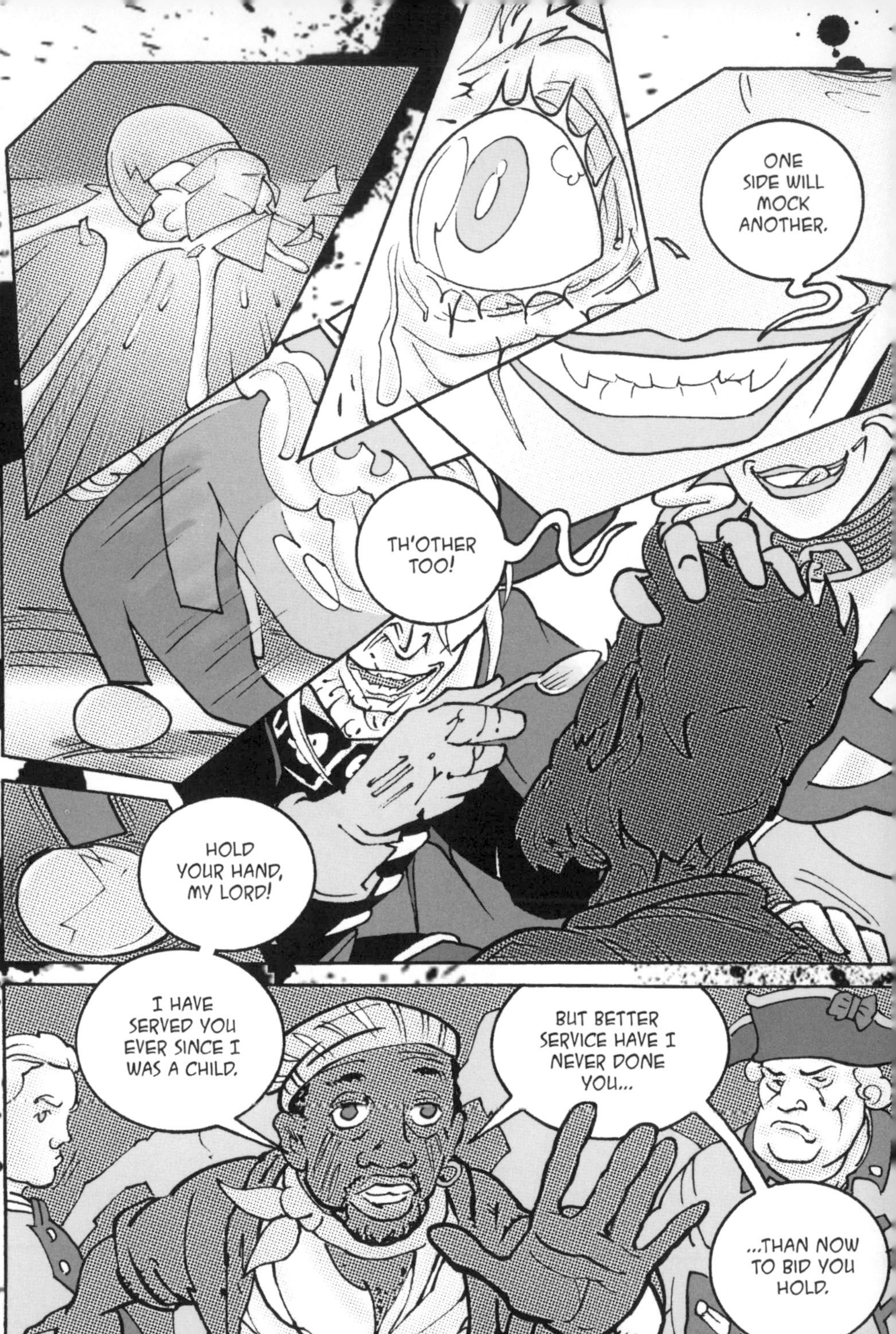
ONE SIDE WILL MOCK ANOTHER.
TH'OTHER TOO!
HOLD YOUR HAND, MY LORD!
I HAVE SERVED YOU EVER SINCE I WAS A CHILD.
BUT BETTER SERVICE HAVE I NEVER DONE YOU...
...THAN NOW TO BID YOU HOLD.

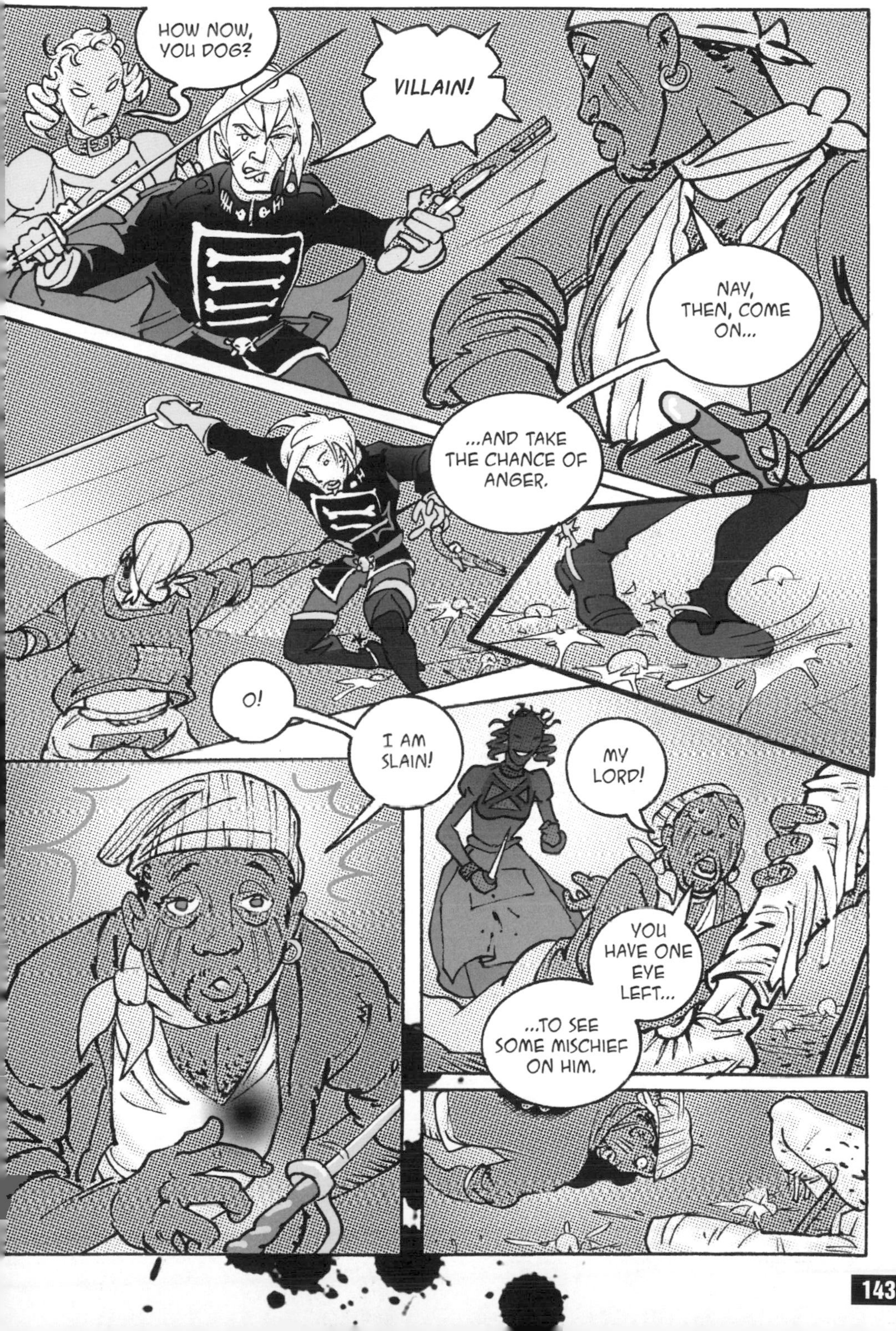
HOW NOW, YOU DOG?
VILLAIN!
NAY, THEN, COME ON...
...AND TAKE THE CHANCE OF ANGER.
O!
I AM SLAIN!
MY LORD!
YOU HAVE ONE EYE LEFT...
...TO SEE SOME MISCHIEF ON HIM.

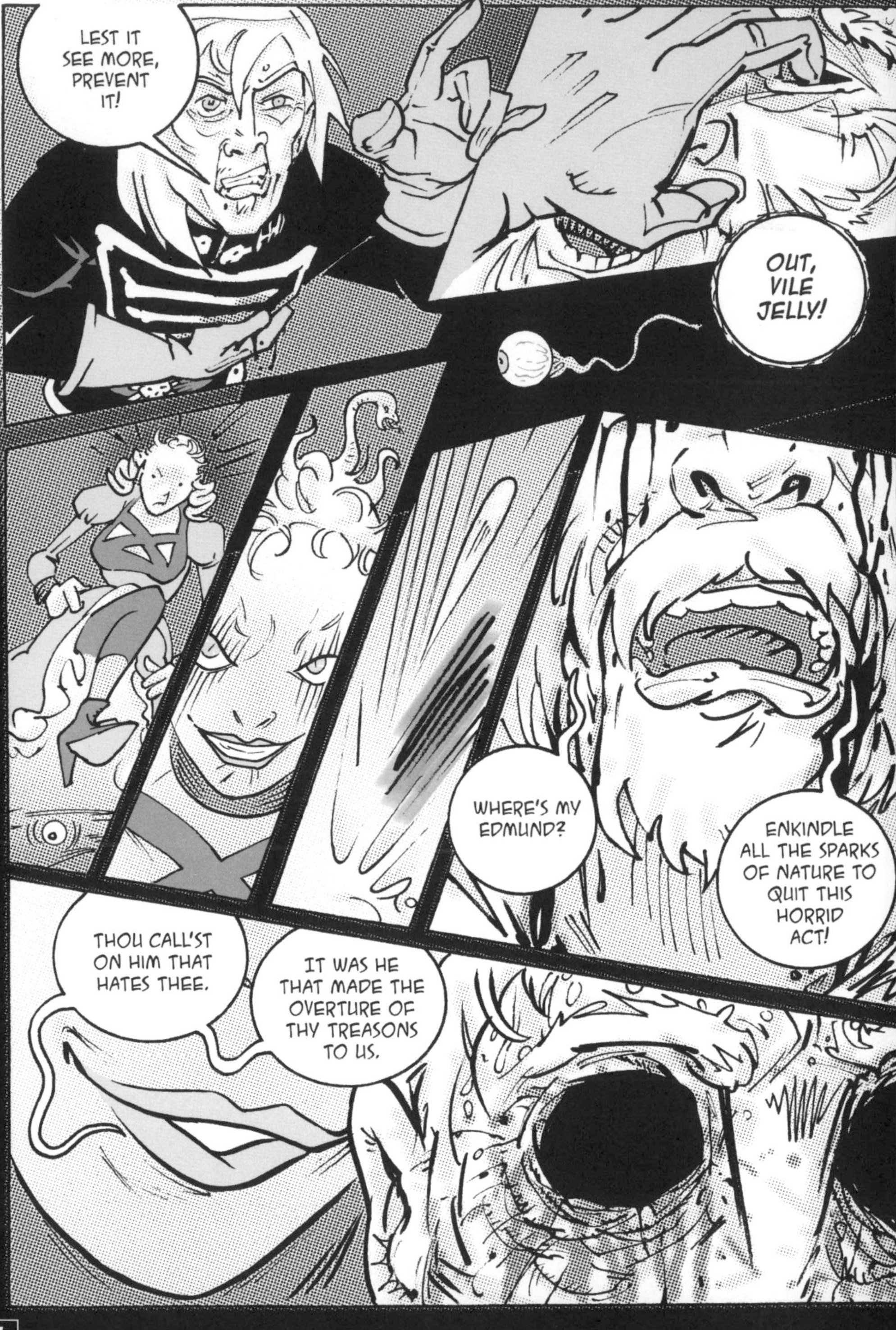
LEST IT SEE MORE, PREVENT IT!
OUT, VILE JELLY!
WHERE'S MY EDMUND?
ENKINDLE ALL THE SPARKS OF NATURE TO QUIT THIS HORRID ACT!
THOU CALL'ST ON HIM THAT HATES THEE.
IT WAS HE THAT MADE THE OVERTURE OF THY TREASONS TO US.

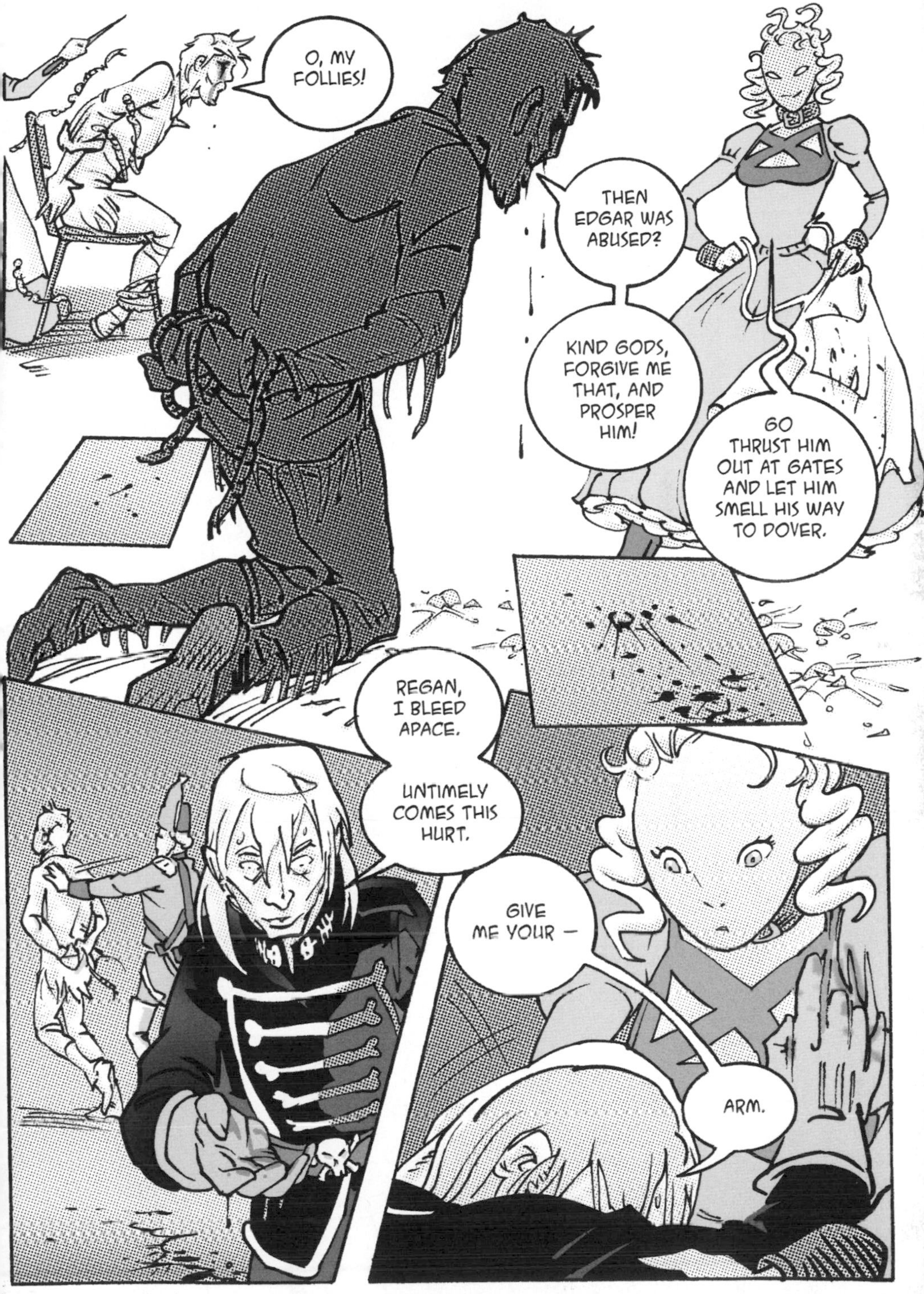
O, MY FOLLIES!
THEN EDGAR WAS ABUSED?
KIND GODS, FORGIVE ME THAT, AND PROSPER HIM!
GO THRUST HIM OUT AT GATES AND LET HIM SMELL HIS WAY TO DOVER.
REGAN, I BLEED APACE.
UNTIMELY COMES THIS HURT.
GIVE ME YOUR —
ARM.

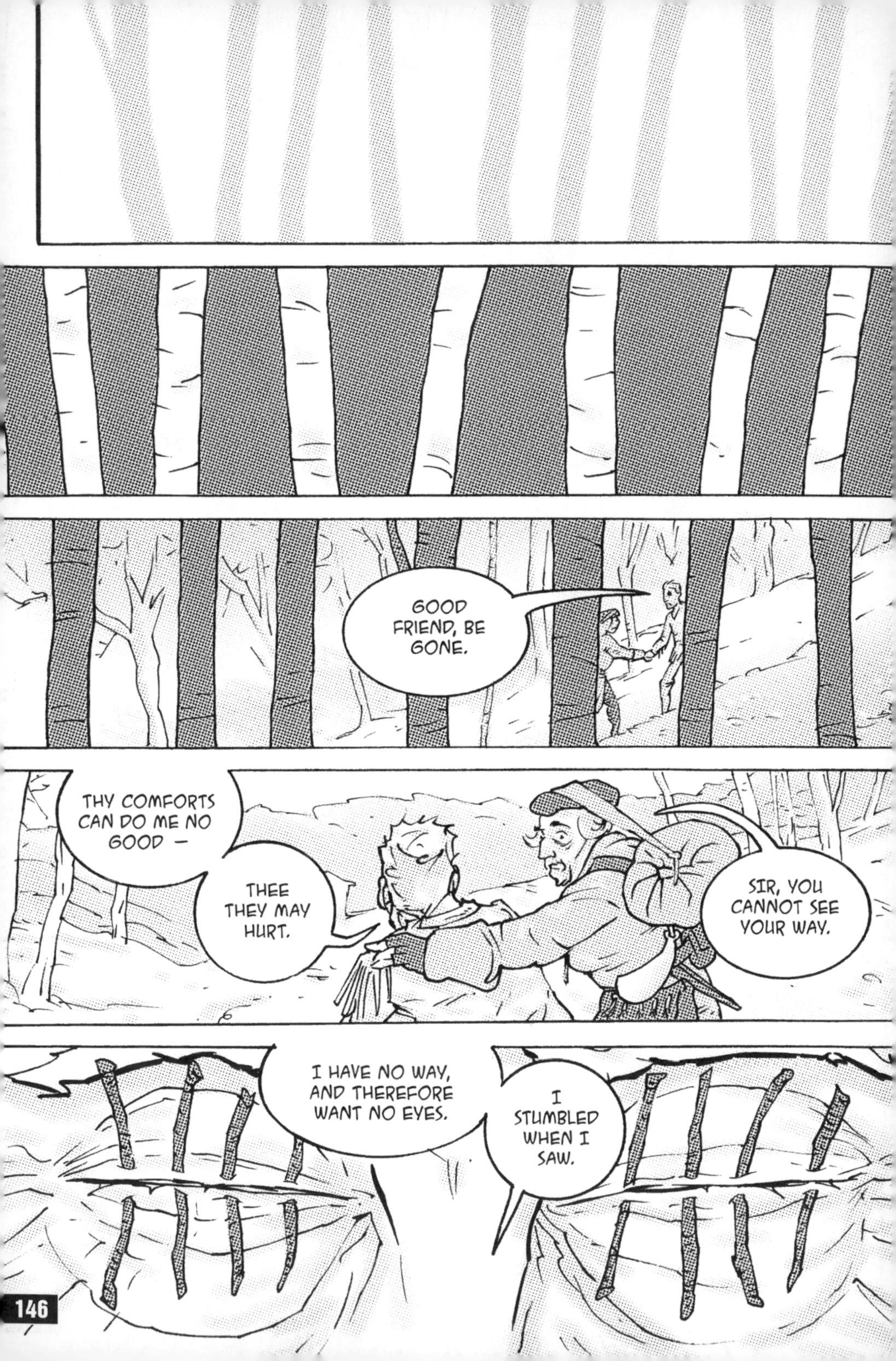
GOOD FRIEND, BE GONE.
THY COMFORTS CAN DO ME NO GOOD –
THEE THEY MAY HURT.
SIR, YOU CANNOT SEE YOUR WAY.
I HAVE NO WAY, AND THEREFORE WANT NO EYES.
I STUMBLED WHEN I SAW.

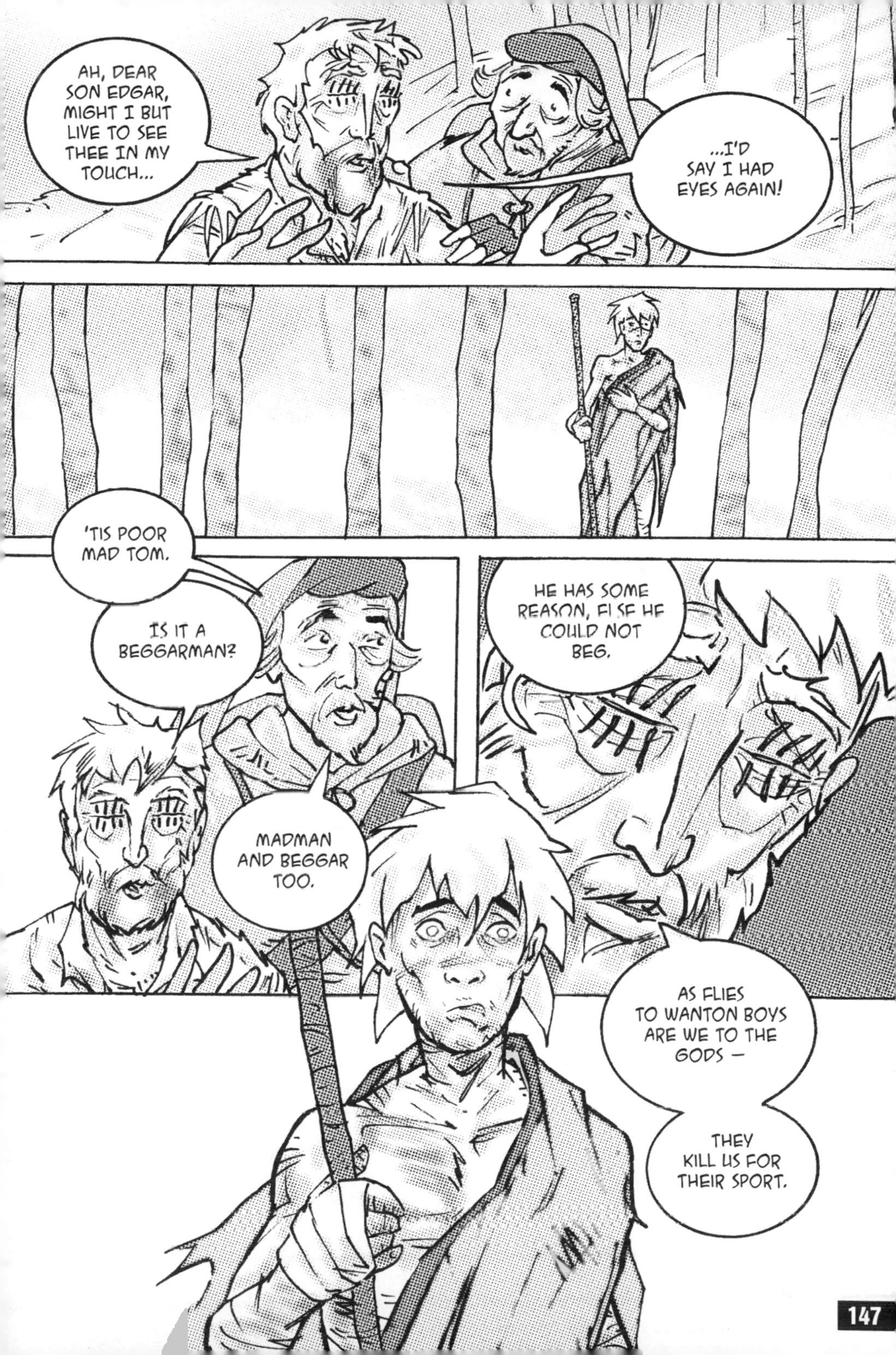
AH, DEAR SON EDGAR, MIGHT I BUT LIVE TO SEE THEE IN MY TOUCH...
...I'D SAY I HAD EYES AGAIN!
'TIS POOR MAD TOM.
IS IT A BEGGARMAN?
MADMAN AND BEGGAR TOO.
HE HAS SOME REASON, ELSE HE COULD NOT BEG.
AS FLIES TO WANTON BOYS ARE WE TO THE GODS —
THEY KILL US FOR THEIR SPORT.

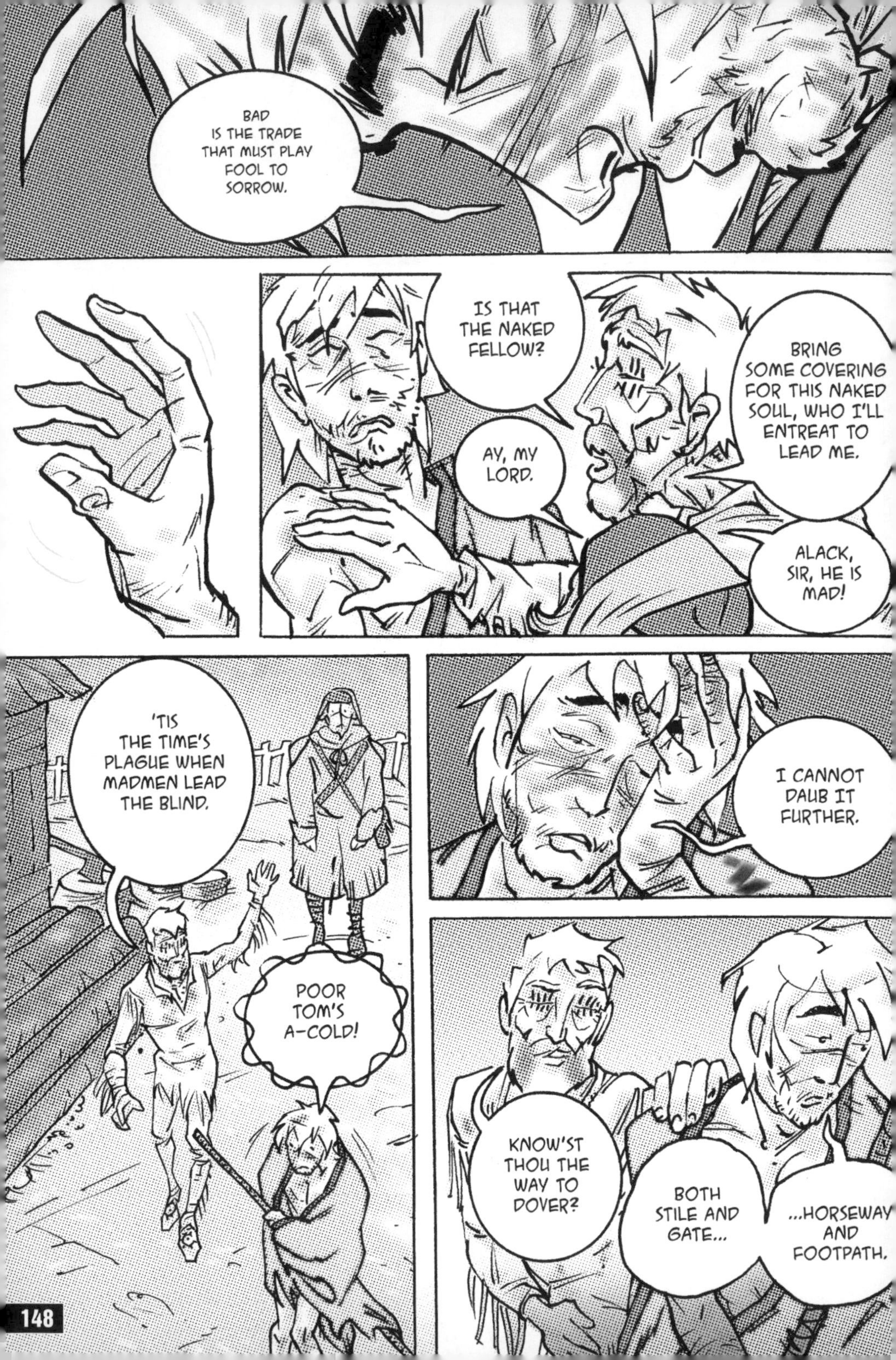
BAD IS THE TRADE THAT MUST PLAY FOOL TO SORROW.
IS THAT THE NAKED FELLOW?
AY, MY LORD.
BRING SOME COVERING FOR THIS NAKED SOUL, WHO I'LL ENTREAT TO LEAD ME.
ALACK, SIR, HE IS MAD!
'TIS THE TIME'S PLAGUE WHEN MADMEN LEAD THE BLIND.
POOR TOM'S A-COLD!
I CANNOT DAUB IT FURTHER.
KNOW'ST THOU THE WAY TO DOVER?
BOTH STILE AND GATE...
...HORSEWAY AND FOOTPATH.

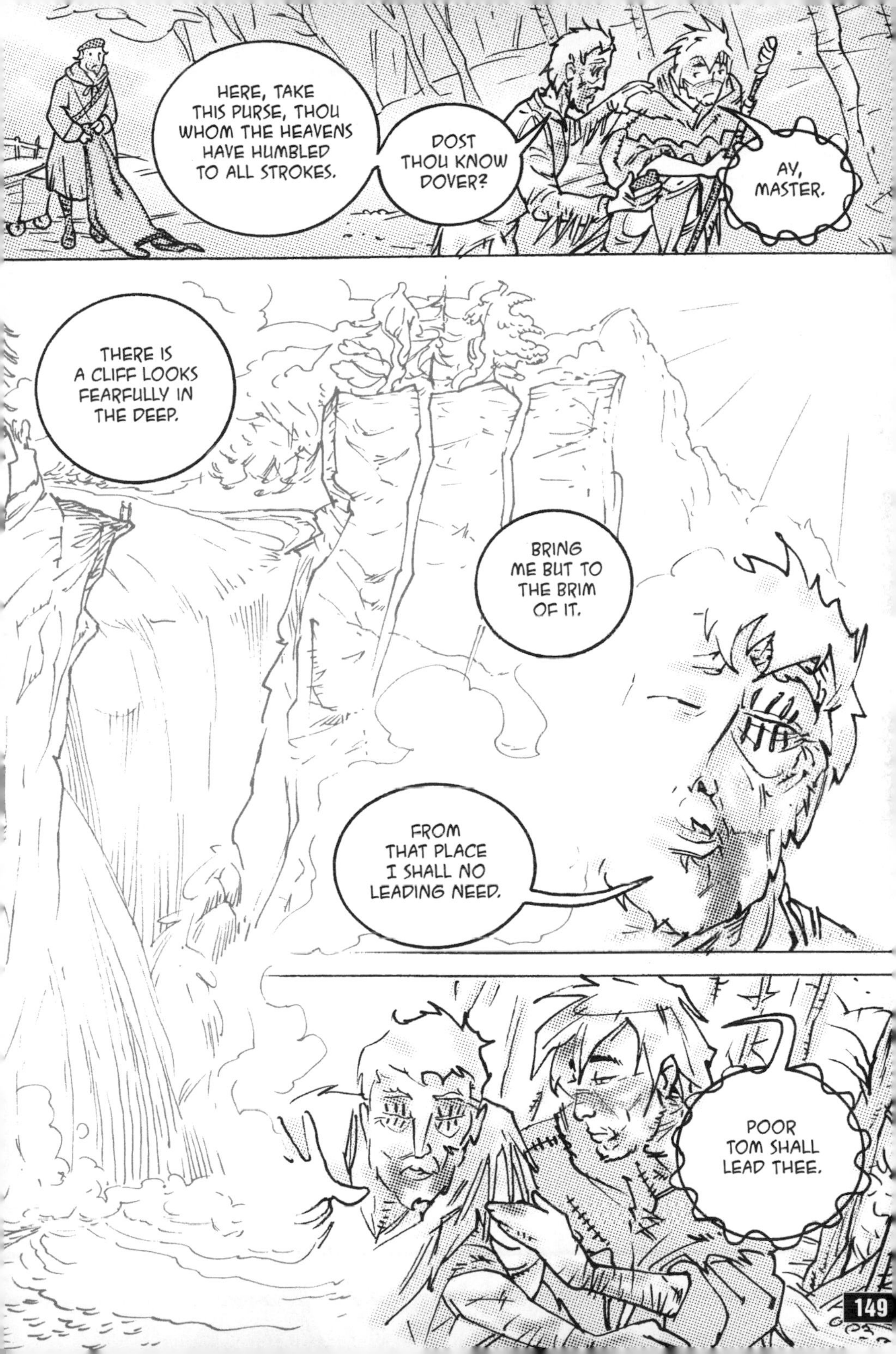
HERE, TAKE THIS PURSE, THOU WHOM THE HEAVENS HAVE HUMBLED TO ALL STROKES.
DOST THOU KNOW DOVER?
AY, MASTER.
THERE IS A CLIFF LOOKS FEARFULLY IN THE DEEP.
BRING ME BUT TO THE BRIM OF IT.
FROM THAT PLACE I SHALL NO LEADING NEED.
POOR TOM SHALL LEAD THEE.

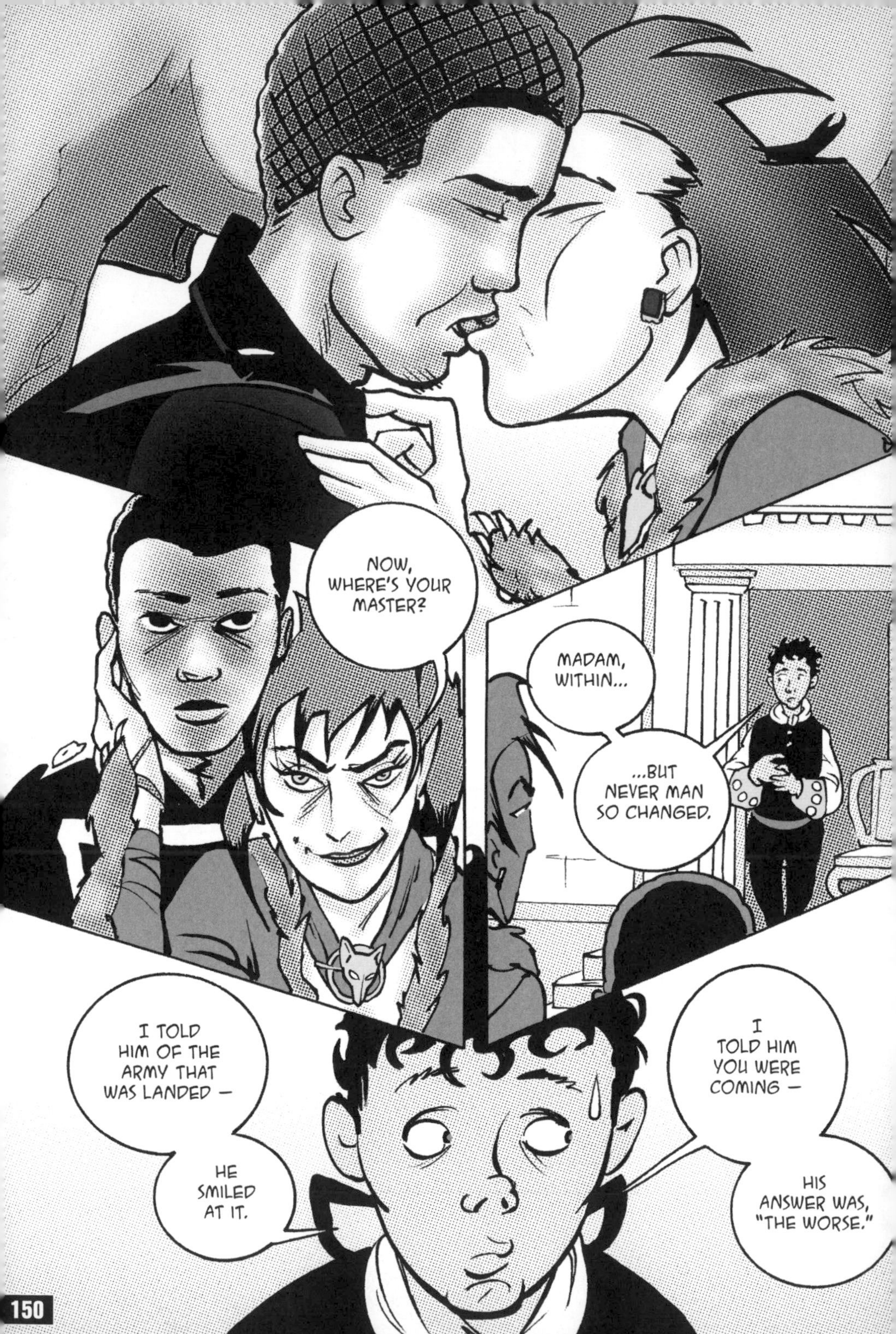
NOW, WHERE'S YOUR MASTER?
MADAM, WITHIN...
...BUT NEVER MAN SO CHANGED.
I TOLD HIM OF THE ARMY THAT WAS LANDED —
HE SMILED AT IT.
I TOLD HIM YOU WERE COMING —
HIS ANSWER WAS, "THE WORSE."

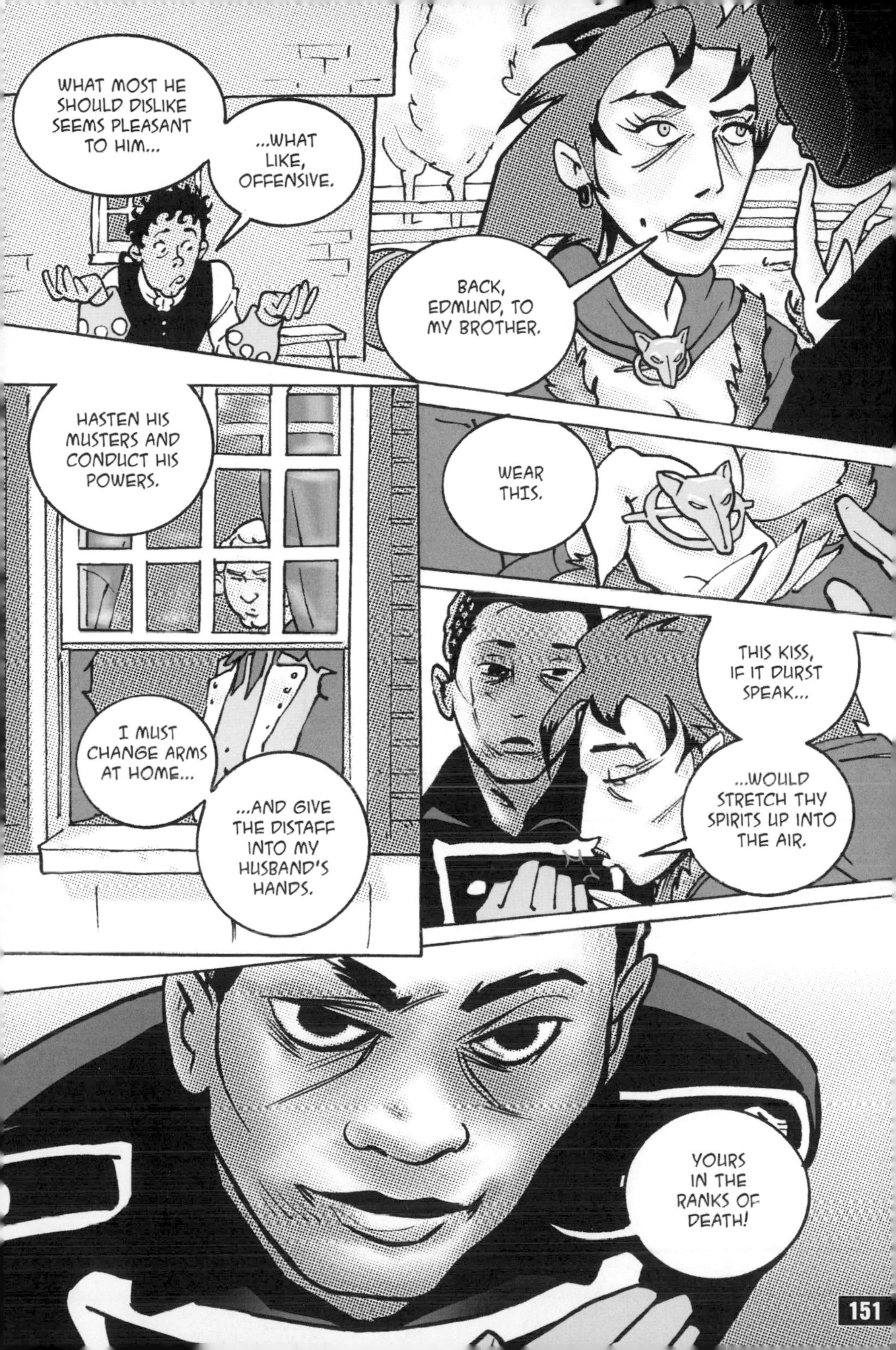
WHAT MOST HE SHOULD DISLIKE SEEMS PLEASANT TO HIM...
...WHAT LIKE, OFFENSIVE.
BACK, EDMUND, TO MY BROTHER.
HASTEN HIS MUSTERS AND CONDUCT HIS POWERS.
I MUST CHANGE ARMS AT HOME...
...AND GIVE THE DISTAFF INTO MY HUSBAND'S HANDS.
WEAR THIS.
THIS KISS, IF IT DURST SPEAK...
...WOULD STRETCH THY SPIRITS UP INTO THE AIR.
YOURS IN THE RANKS OF DEATH!

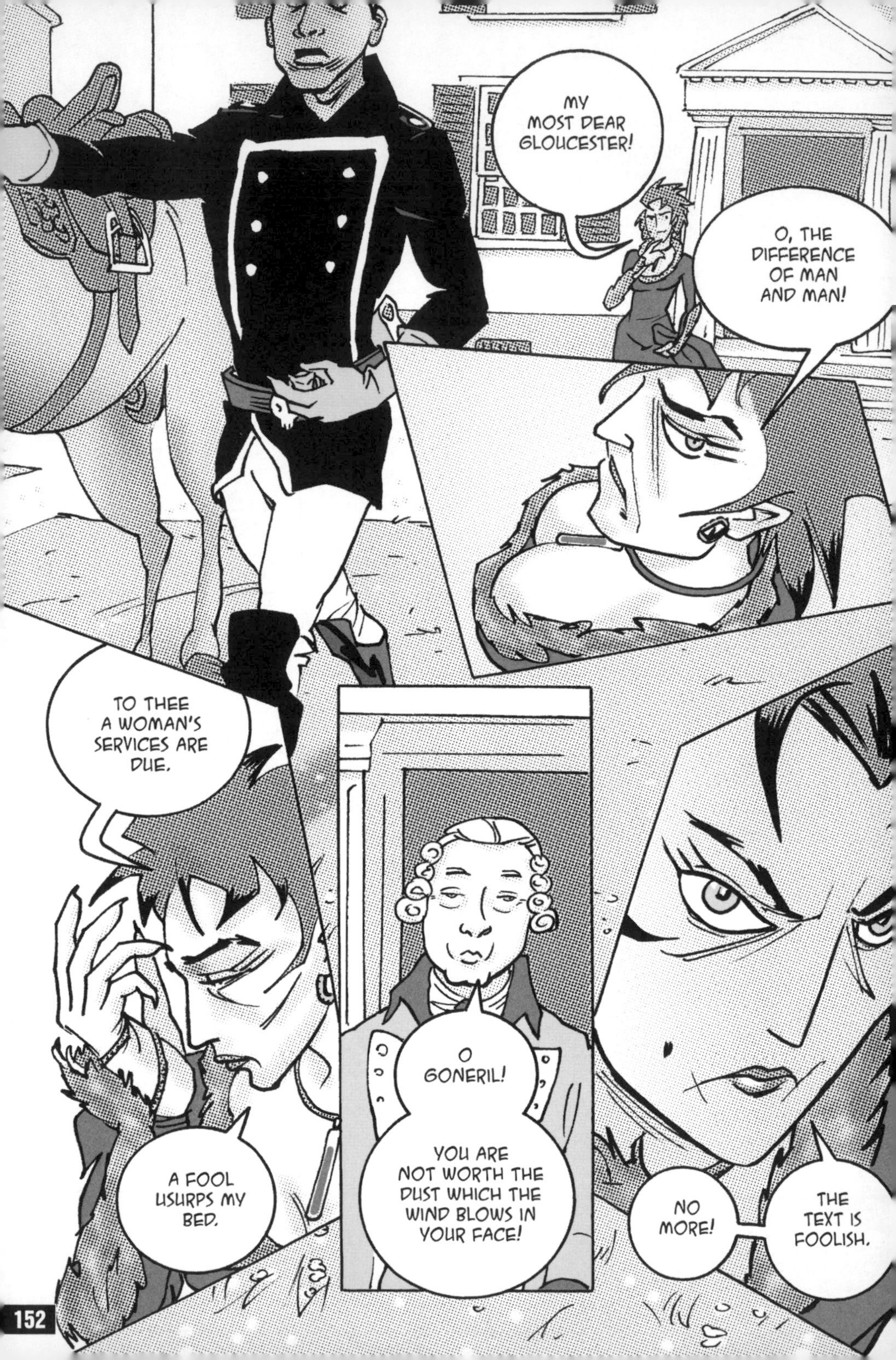
MY MOST DEAR GLOUCESTER!
O, THE DIFFERENCE OF MAN AND MAN!
TO THEE A WOMAN'S SERVICES ARE DUE.
A FOOL USURPS MY BED.
O GONERIL!
YOU ARE NOT WORTH THE DUST WHICH THE WIND BLOWS IN YOUR FACE!
NO MORE!
THE TEXT IS FOOLISH.

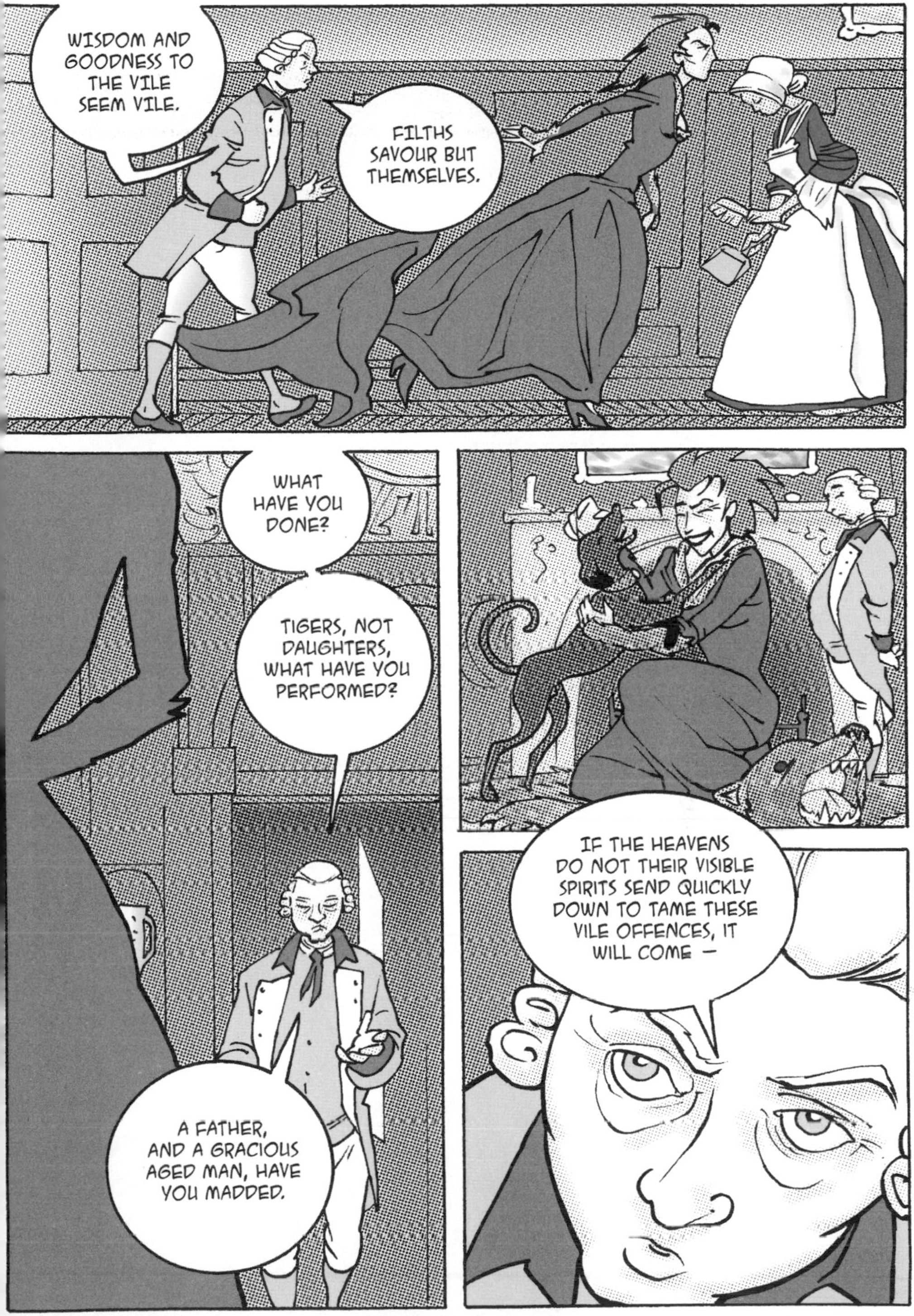
WISDOM AND GOODNESS TO THE VILE SEEM VILE.
FILTHS SAVOUR BUT THEMSELVES.
WHAT HAVE YOU DONE?
TIGERS, NOT DAUGHTERS, WHAT HAVE YOU PERFORMED?
A FATHER, AND A GRACIOUS AGED MAN, HAVE YOU MADDED.
IF THE HEAVENS DO NOT THEIR VISIBLE SPIRITS SEND QUICKLY DOWN TO TAME THESE VILE OFFENCES, IT WILL COME –

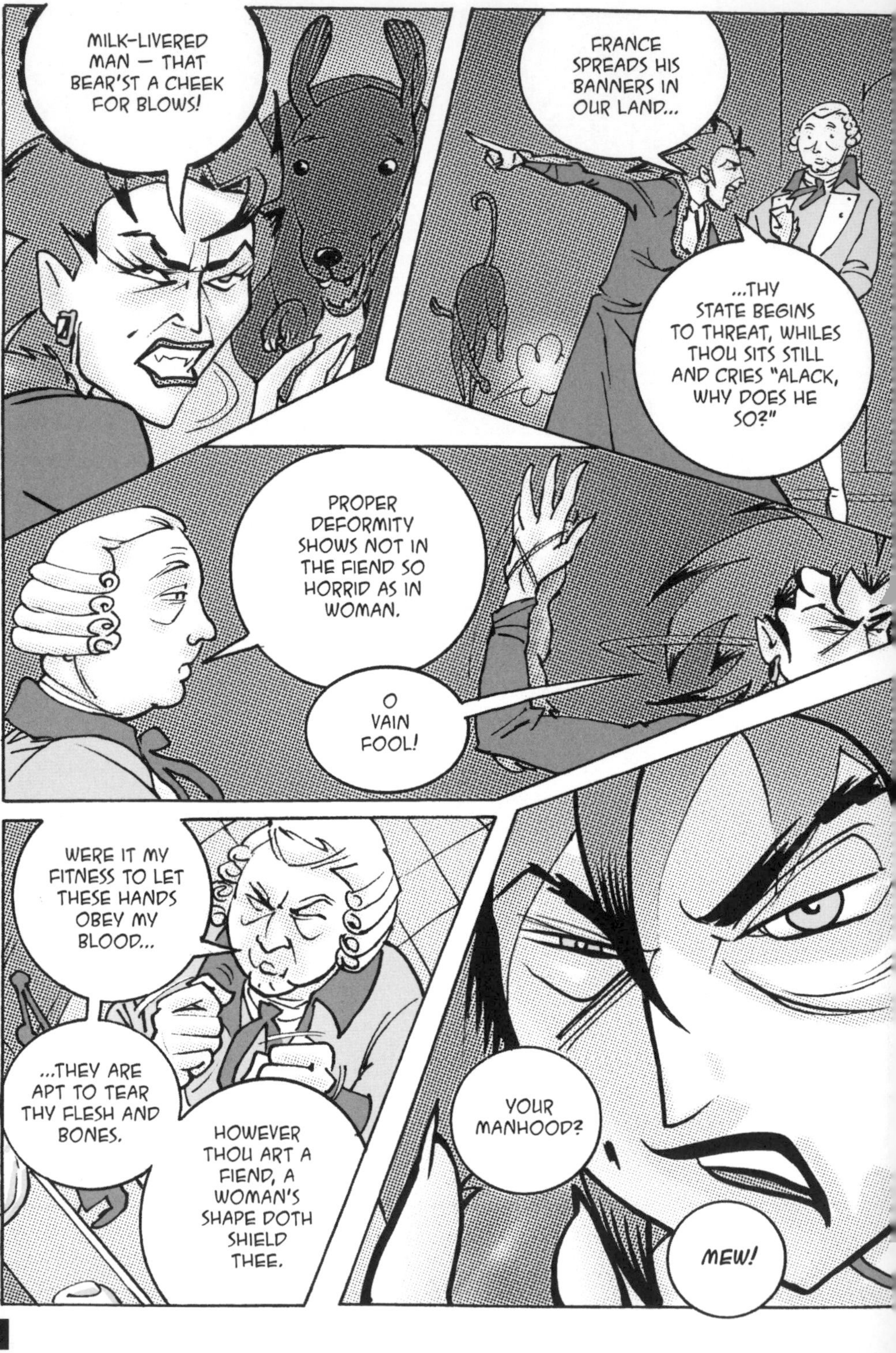
MILK-LIVERED MAN — THAT BEAR'ST A CHEEK FOR BLOWS!
FRANCE SPREADS HIS BANNERS IN OUR LAND...
...THY STATE BEGINS TO THREAT, WHILES THOU SITS STILL AND CRIES "ALACK, WHY DOES HE SO?"
PROPER DEFORMITY SHOWS NOT IN THE FIEND SO HORRID AS IN WOMAN.
O VAIN FOOL!
WERE IT MY FITNESS TO LET THESE HANDS OBEY MY BLOOD...
...THEY ARE APT TO TEAR THY FLESH AND BONES.
HOWEVER THOU ART A FIEND, A WOMAN'S SHAPE DOTH SHIELD THEE.
YOUR MANHOOD?
MEW!

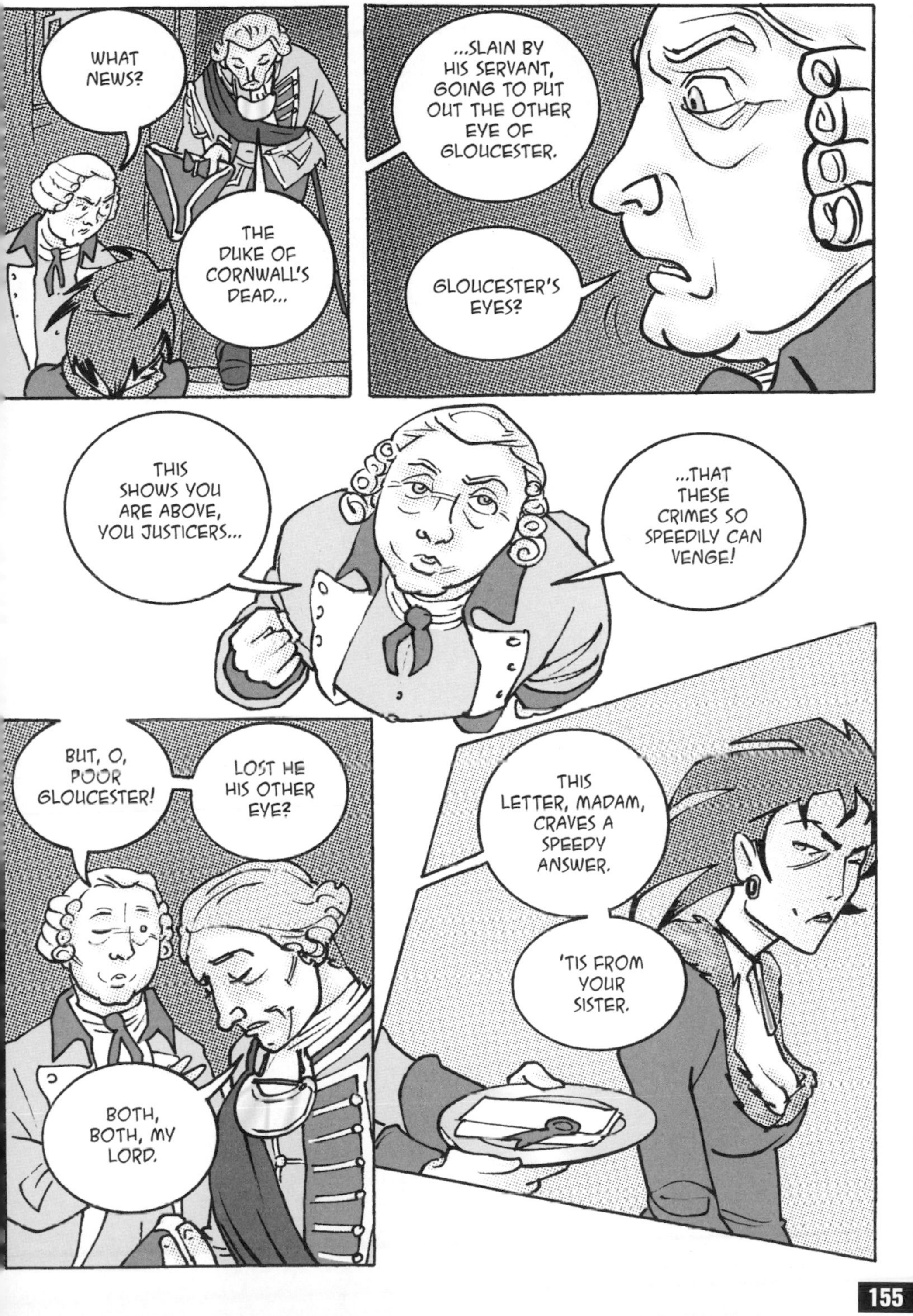
WHAT NEWS?
THE DUKE OF CORNWALL'S DEAD...
...SLAIN BY HIS SERVANT, GOING TO PUT OUT THE OTHER EYE OF GLOUCESTER.
GLOUCESTER'S EYES?
THIS SHOWS YOU ARE ABOVE, YOU JUSTICERS...
...THAT THESE CRIMES SO SPEEDILY CAN VENGE!
BUT, O, POOR GLOUCESTER!
LOST HE HIS OTHER EYE?
BOTH, BOTH, MY LORD.
THIS LETTER, MADAM, CRAVES A SPEEDY ANSWER.
'TIS FROM YOUR SISTER.

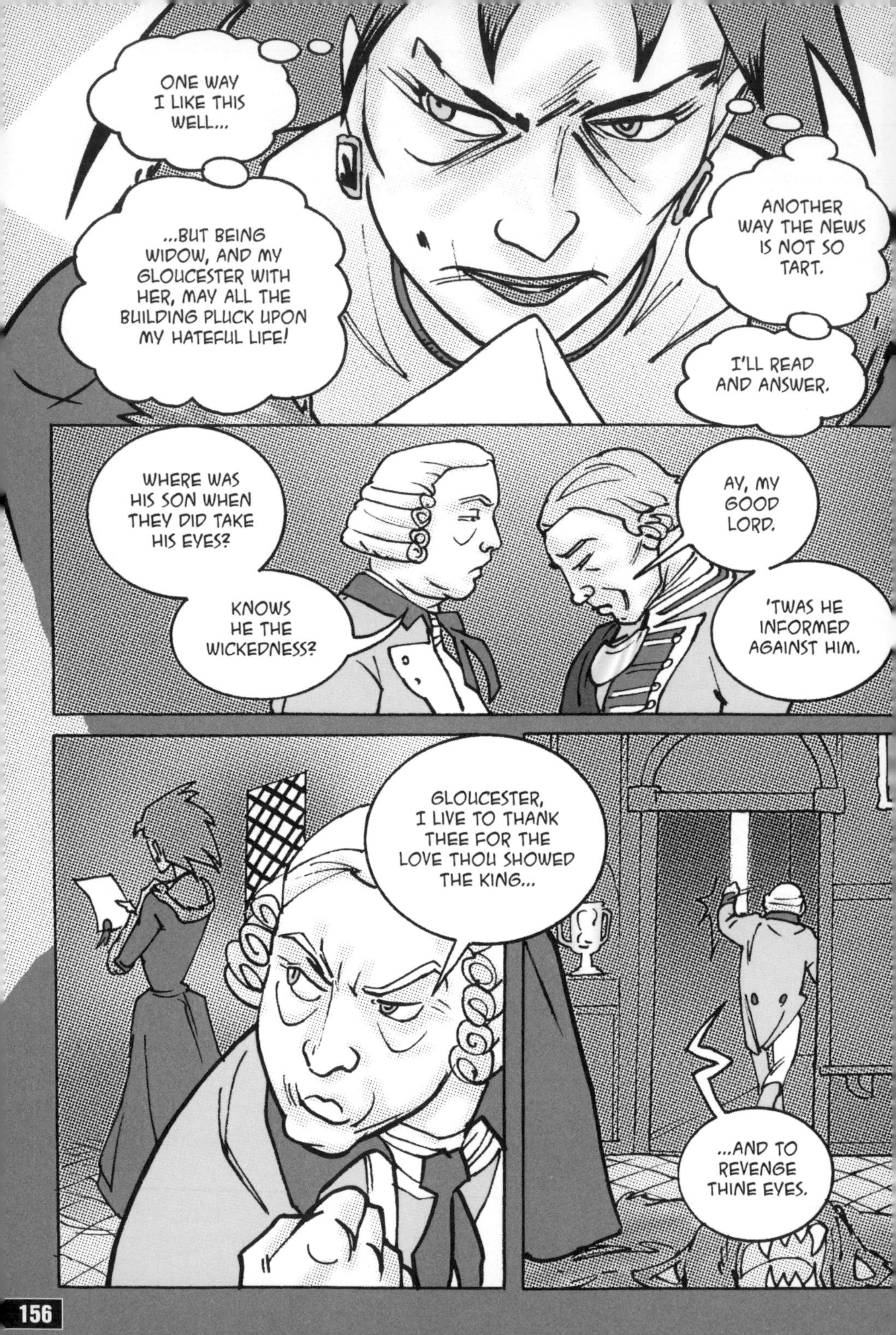
ONE WAY I LIKE THIS WELL...
...BUT BEING WIDOW, AND MY GLOUCESTER WITH HER, MAY ALL THE BUILDING PLUCK UPON MY HATEFUL LIFE!
ANOTHER WAY THE NEWS IS NOT SO TART.
I'LL READ AND ANSWER.
WHERE WAS HIS SON WHEN THEY DID TAKE HIS EYES?
KNOWS HE THE WICKEDNESS?
AY, MY GOOD LORD.
'TWAS HE INFORMED AGAINST HIM.
GLOUCESTER, I LIVE TO THANK THEE FOR THE LOVE THOU SHOWED THE KING...
...AND TO REVENGE THINE EYES.

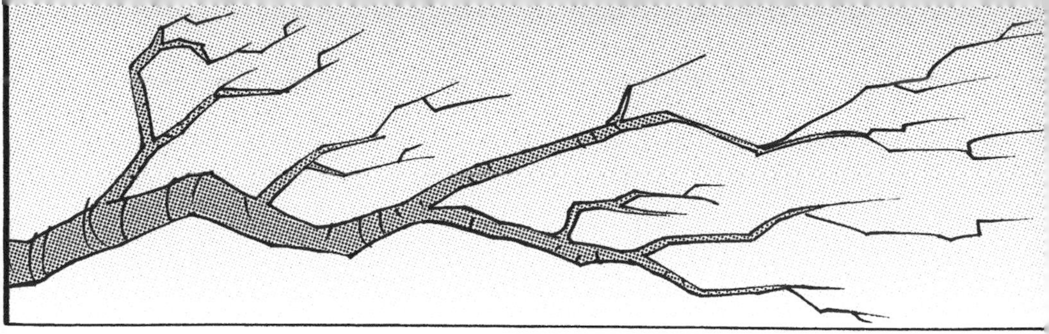
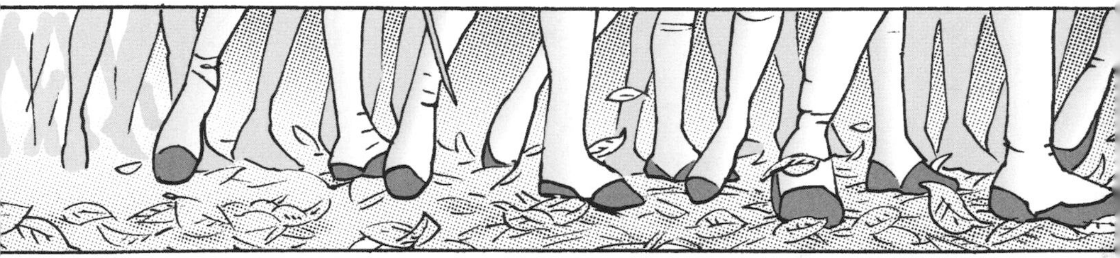
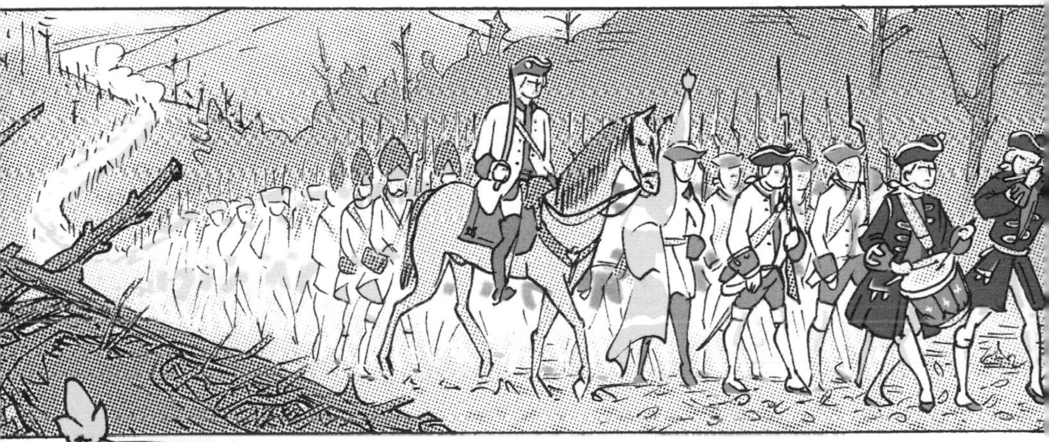
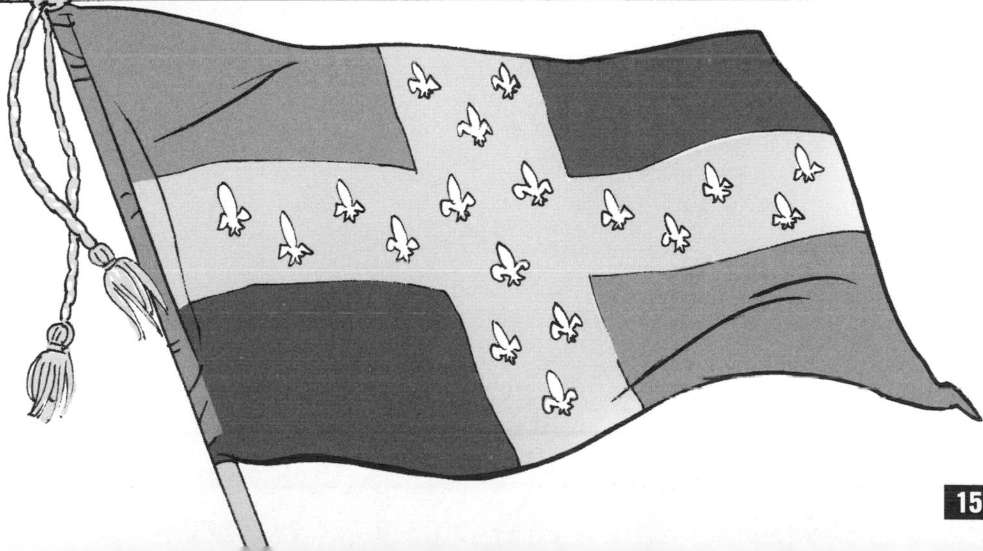

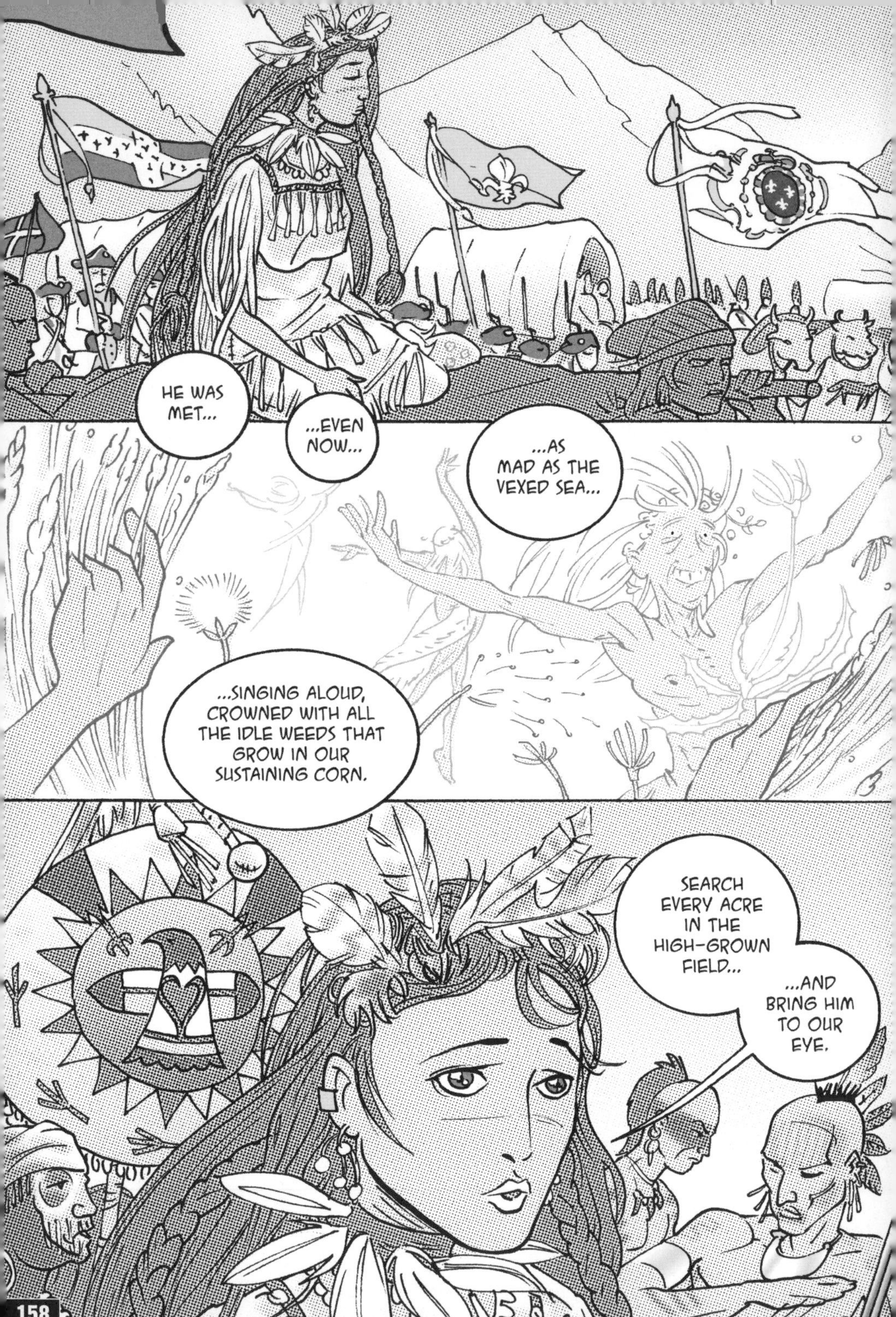
HE WAS MET...
...EVEN NOW...
...AS MAD AS THE VEXED SEA...
...SINGING ALOUD, CROWNED WITH ALL THE IDLE WEEDS THAT GROW IN OUR SUSTAINING CORN.
SEARCH EVERY ACRE IN THE HIGH-GROWN FIELD...
...AND BRING HIM TO OUR EYE.

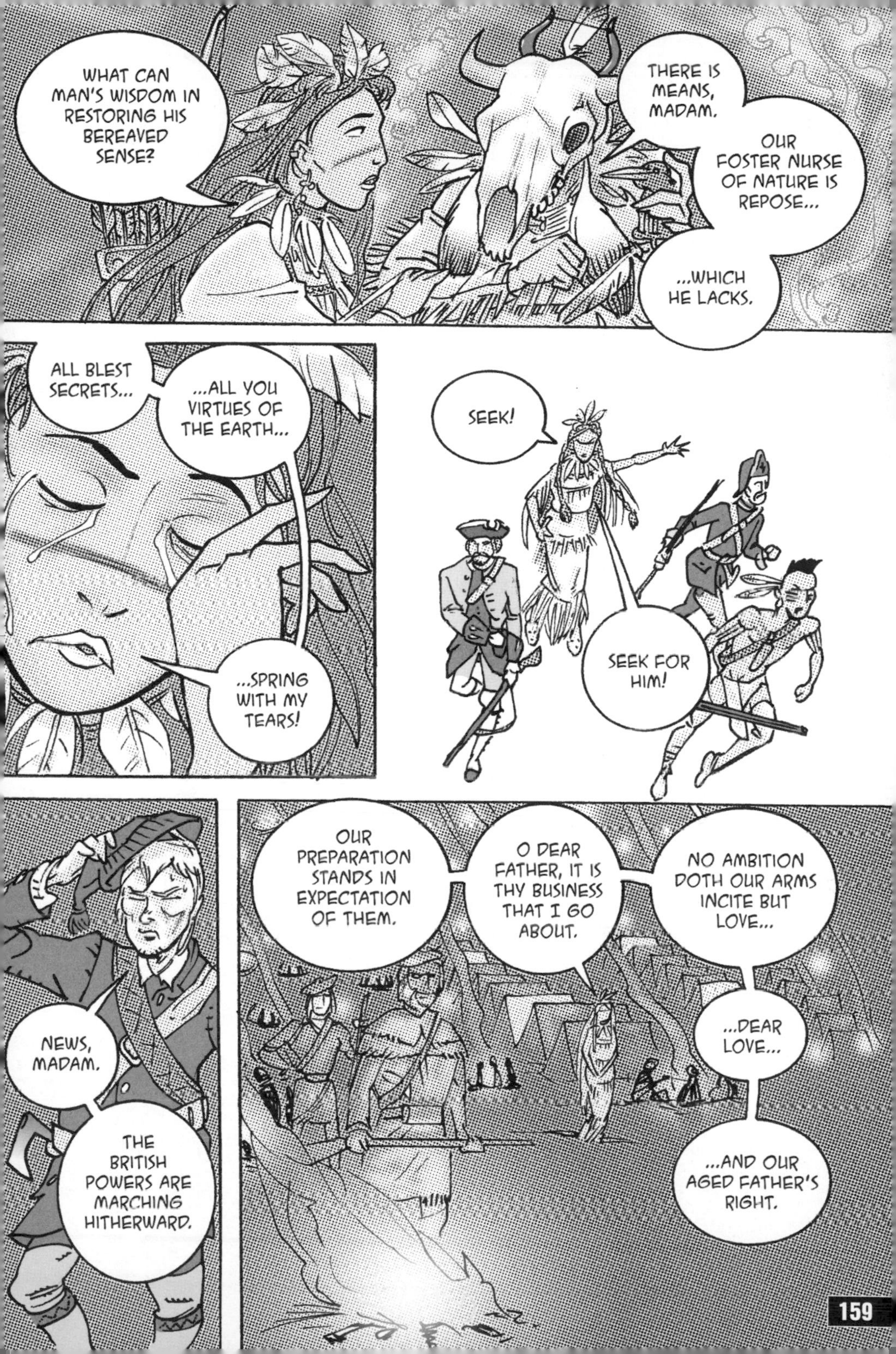
WHAT CAN MAN'S WISDOM IN RESTORING HIS BEREAVED SENSE?
THERE IS MEANS, MADAM.
OUR FOSTER NURSE OF NATURE IS REPOSE...
...WHICH HE LACKS.
ALL BLEST SECRETS...
...ALL YOU VIRTUES OF THE EARTH...
...SPRING WITH MY TEARS!
SEEK!
SEEK FOR HIM!
NEWS, MADAM.
THE BRITISH POWERS ARE MARCHING HITHERWARD.
OUR PREPARATION STANDS IN EXPECTATION OF THEM.
O DEAR FATHER, IT IS THY BUSINESS THAT I GO ABOUT.
NO AMBITION DOTH OUR ARMS INCITE BUT LOVE...
...DEAR LOVE...
...AND OUR AGED FATHER'S RIGHT.

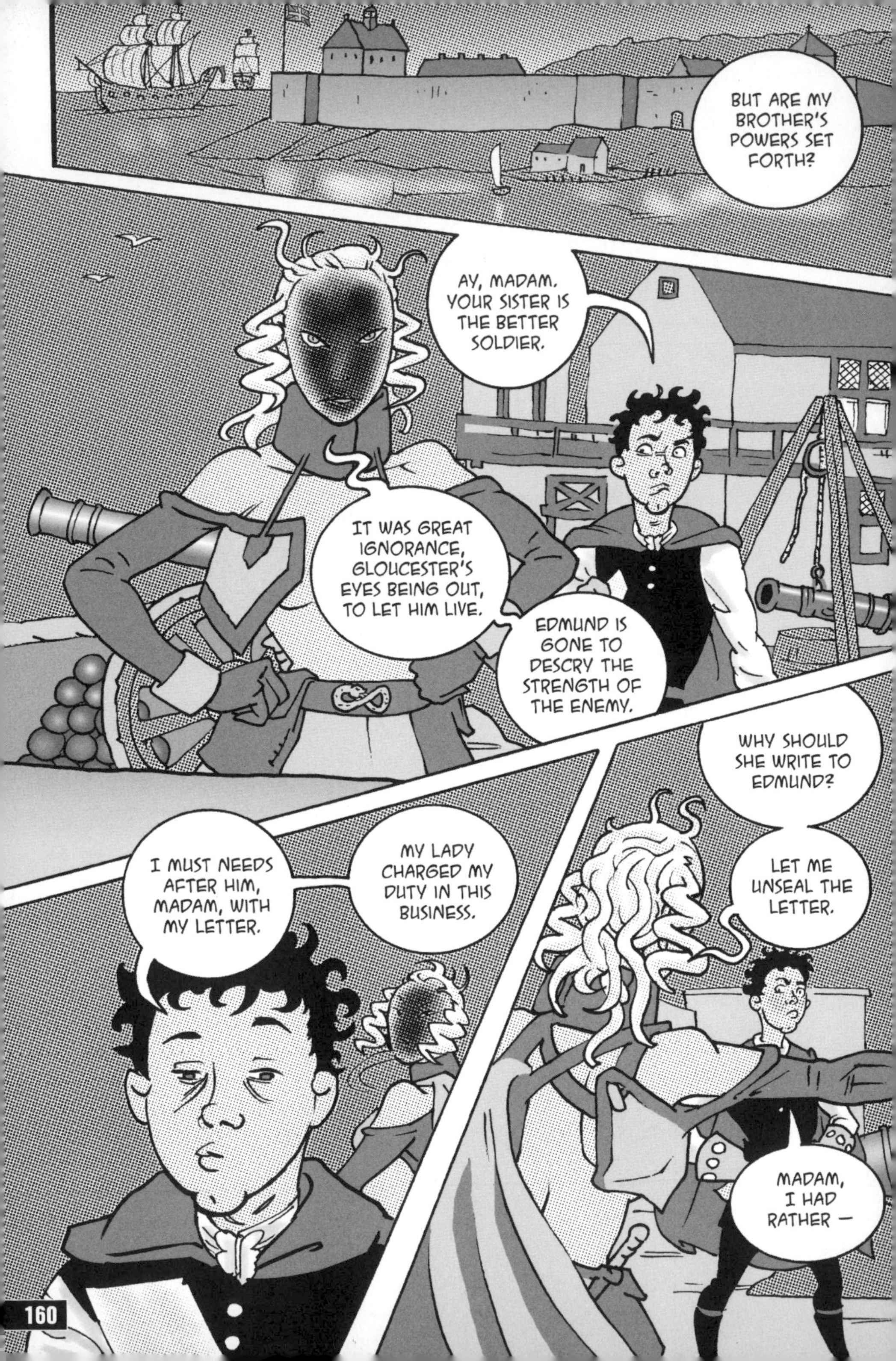
BUT ARE MY BROTHER'S POWERS SET FORTH?
AY, MADAM. YOUR SISTER IS THE BETTER SOLDIER.
IT WAS GREAT IGNORANCE, GLOUCESTER'S EYES BEING OUT, TO LET HIM LIVE.
EDMUND IS GONE TO DESCRY THE STRENGTH OF THE ENEMY.
I MUST NEEDS AFTER HIM, MADAM, WITH MY LETTER.
MY LADY CHARGED MY DUTY IN THIS BUSINESS.
WHY SHOULD SHE WRITE TO EDMUND?
LET ME UNSEAL THE LETTER.
MADAM, I HAD RATHER —

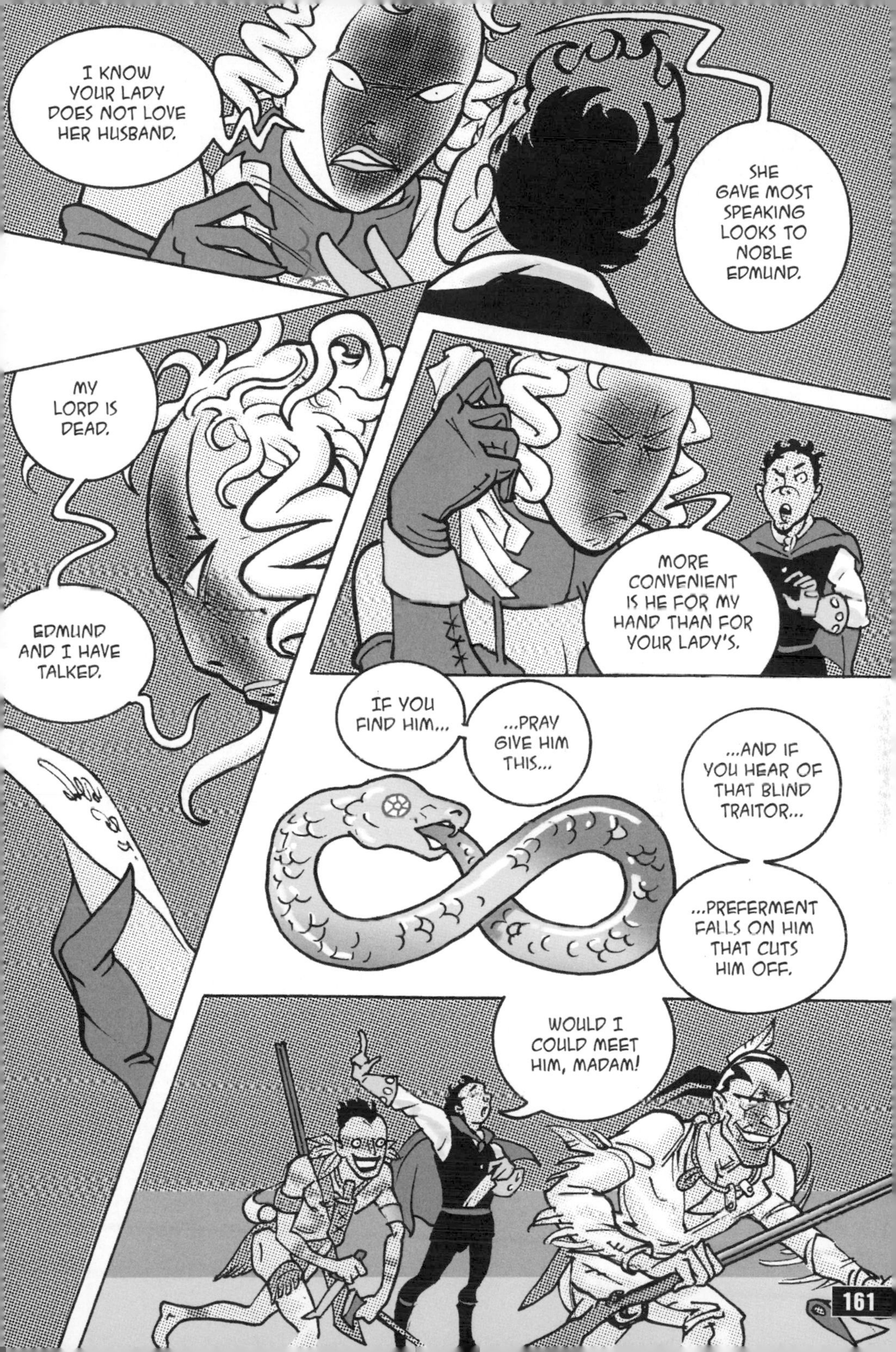

I KNOW YOUR LADY DOES NOT LOVE HER HUSBAND.
SHE GAVE MOST SPEAKING LOOKS TO NOBLE EDMUND.
MY LORD IS DEAD.
EDMUND AND I HAVE TALKED.
MORE CONVENIENT IS HE FOR MY HAND THAN FOR YOUR LADY'S.
IF YOU FIND HIM...
...PRAY GIVE HIM THIS...
...AND IF YOU HEAR OF THAT BLIND TRAITOR...
...PREFERMENT FALLS ON HIM THAT CUTS HIM OFF.
WOULD I COULD MEET HIM, MADAM!

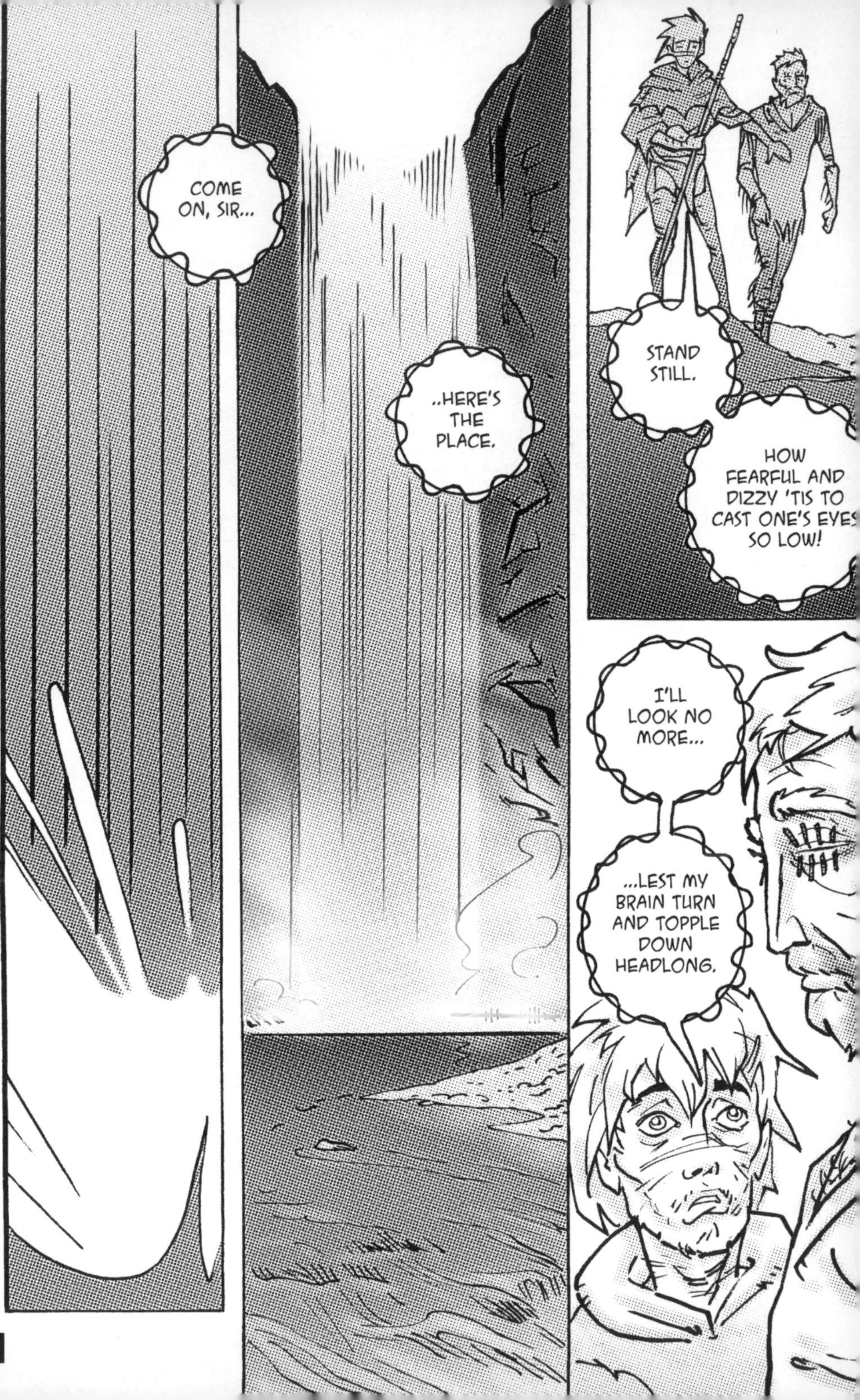

COME ON, SIR...
..HERE'S THE PLACE.
STAND STILL.
HOW FEARFUL AND DIZZY 'TIS TO CAST ONE'S EYES SO LOW!
I'LL LOOK NO MORE...
...LEST MY BRAIN TURN AND TOPPLE DOWN HEADLONG.

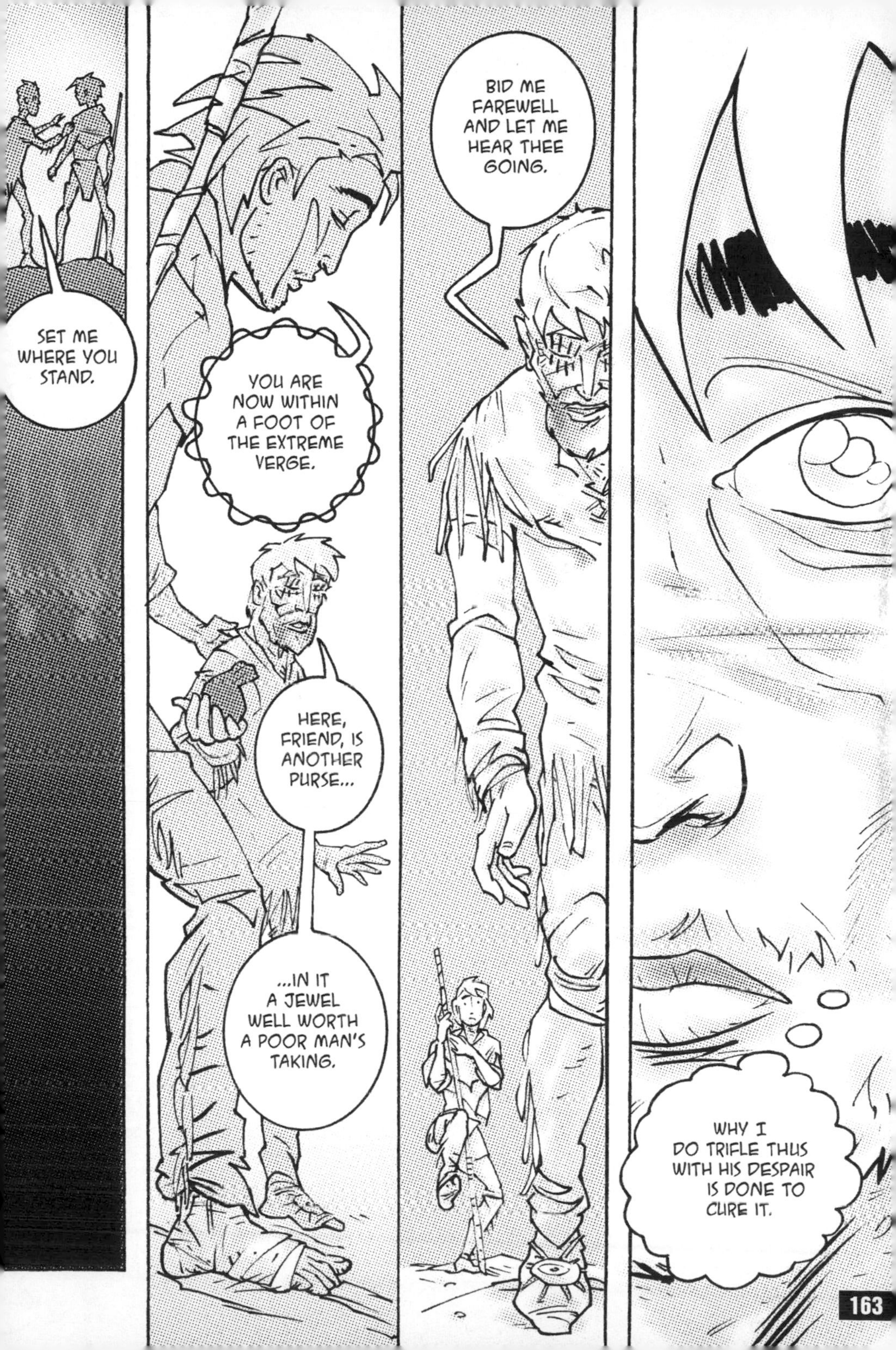
SET ME WHERE YOU STAND.
YOU ARE NOW WITHIN A FOOT OF THE EXTREME VERGE.
HERE, FRIEND, IS ANOTHER PURSE...
...IN IT A JEWEL WELL WORTH A POOR MAN'S TAKING.
BID ME FAREWELL AND LET ME HEAR THEE GOING.
WHY I DO TRIFLE THUS WITH HIS DESPAIR IS DONE TO CURE IT.

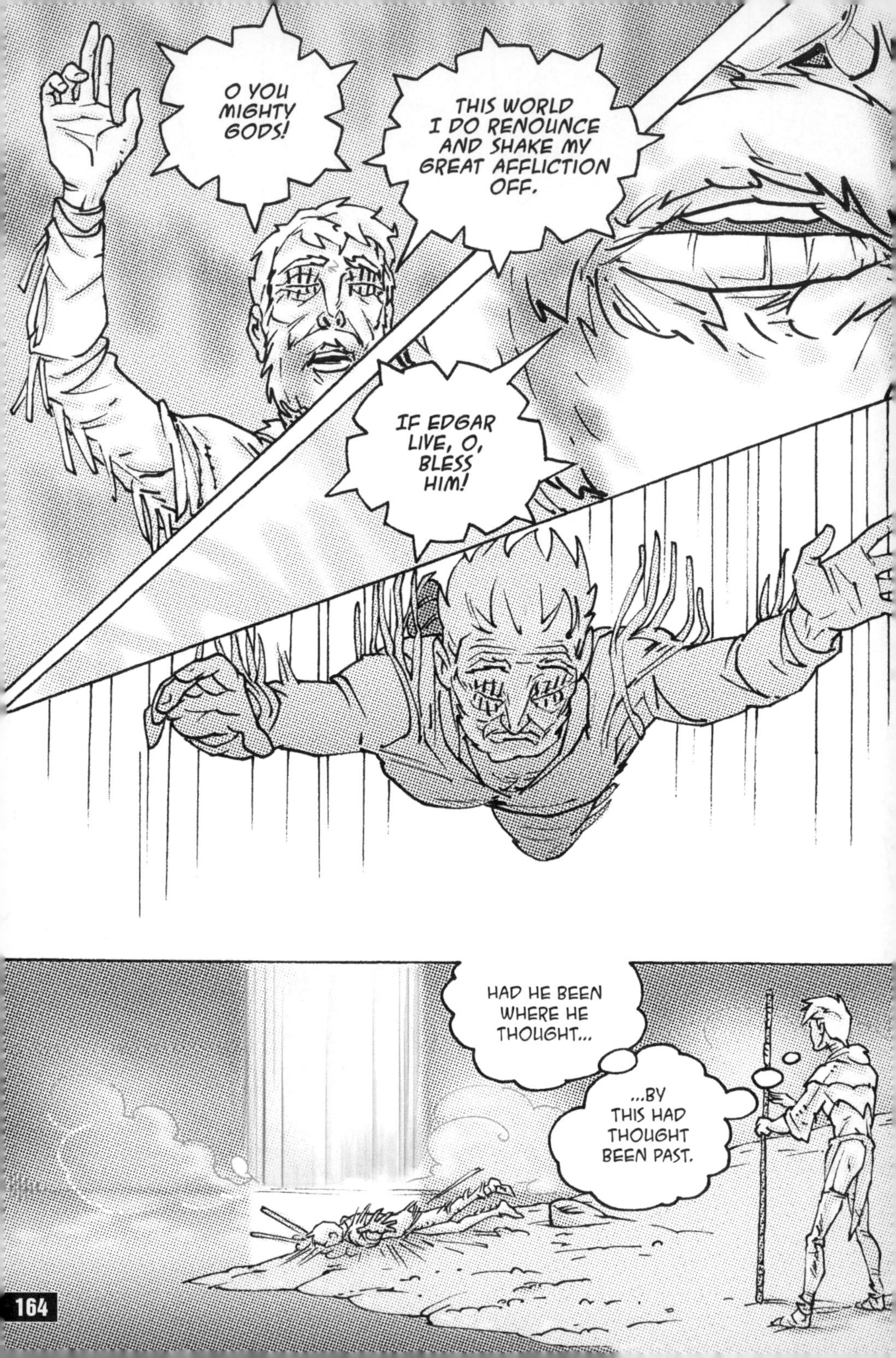
O YOU MIGHTY GODS!
THIS WORLD I DO RENOUNCE AND SHAKE MY GREAT AFFLICTION OFF.
IF EDGAR LIVE, O, BLESS HIM!
HAD HE BEEN WHERE HE THOUGHT...
...BY THIS HAD THOUGHT BEEN PAST.

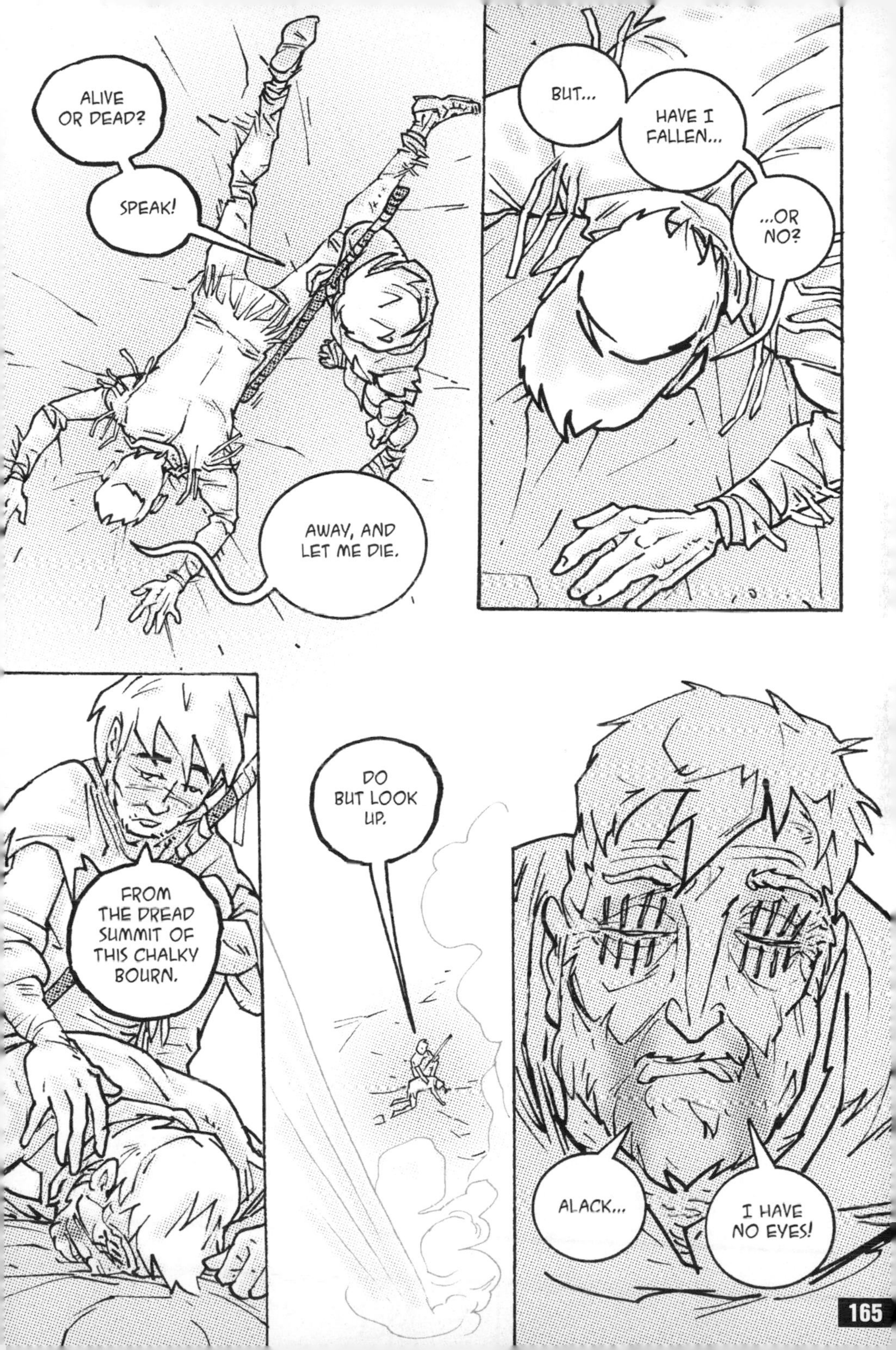
ALIVE OR DEAD?
SPEAK!
AWAY, AND LET ME DIE.
BUT...
HAVE I FALLEN...
...OR NO?
FROM THE DREAD SUMMIT OF THIS CHALKY BOURN.
DO BUT LOOK UP.
ALACK...
I HAVE NO EYES!

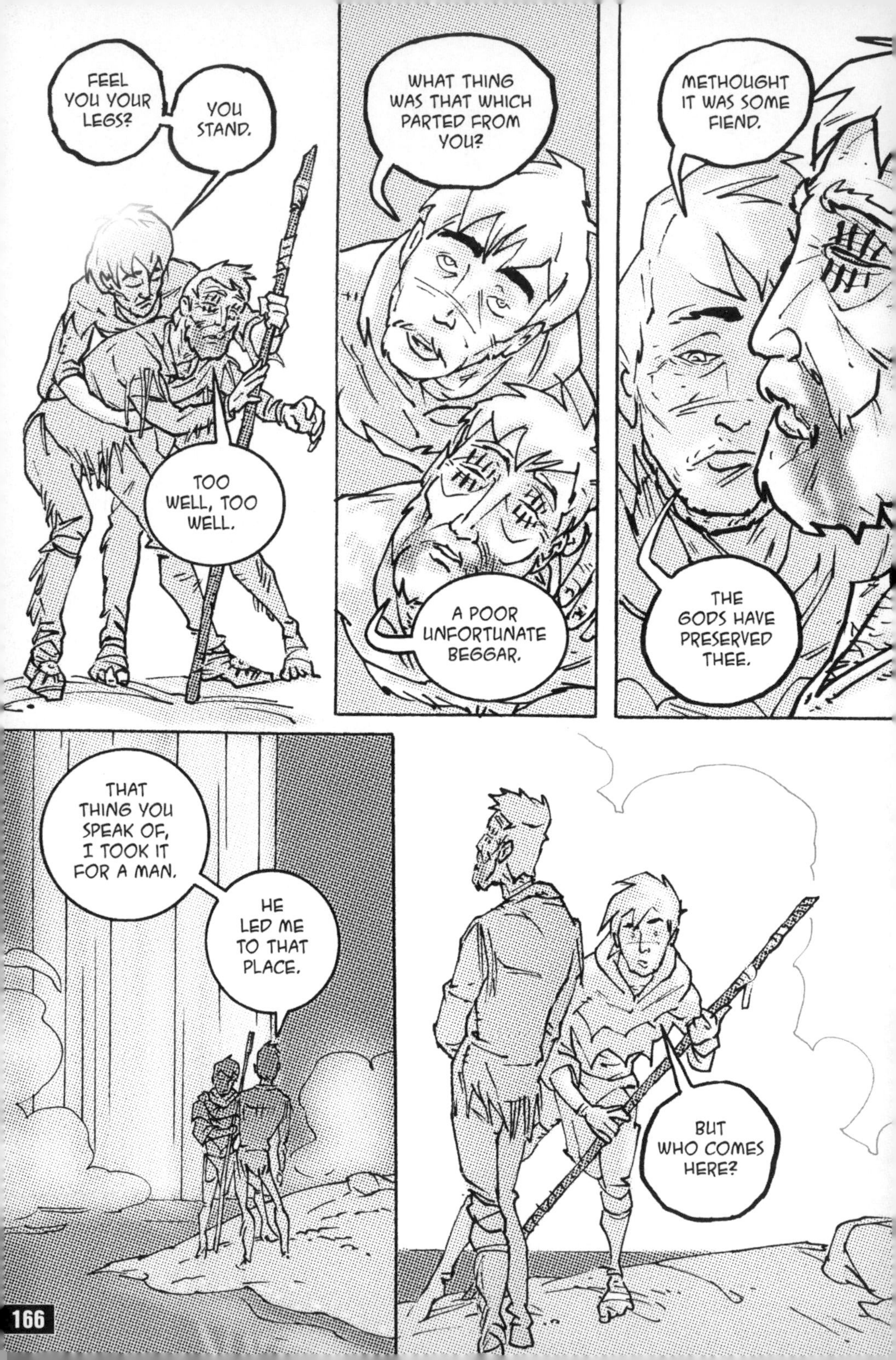
FEEL YOU YOUR LEGS?
YOU STAND.
TOO WELL, TOO WELL.
WHAT THING WAS THAT WHICH PARTED FROM YOU?
A POOR UNFORTUNATE BEGGAR.
METHOUGHT IT WAS SOME FIEND.
THE GODS HAVE PRESERVED THEE.
THAT THING YOU SPEAK OF, I TOOK IT FOR A MAN.
HE LED ME TO THAT PLACE.
BUT WHO COMES HERE?

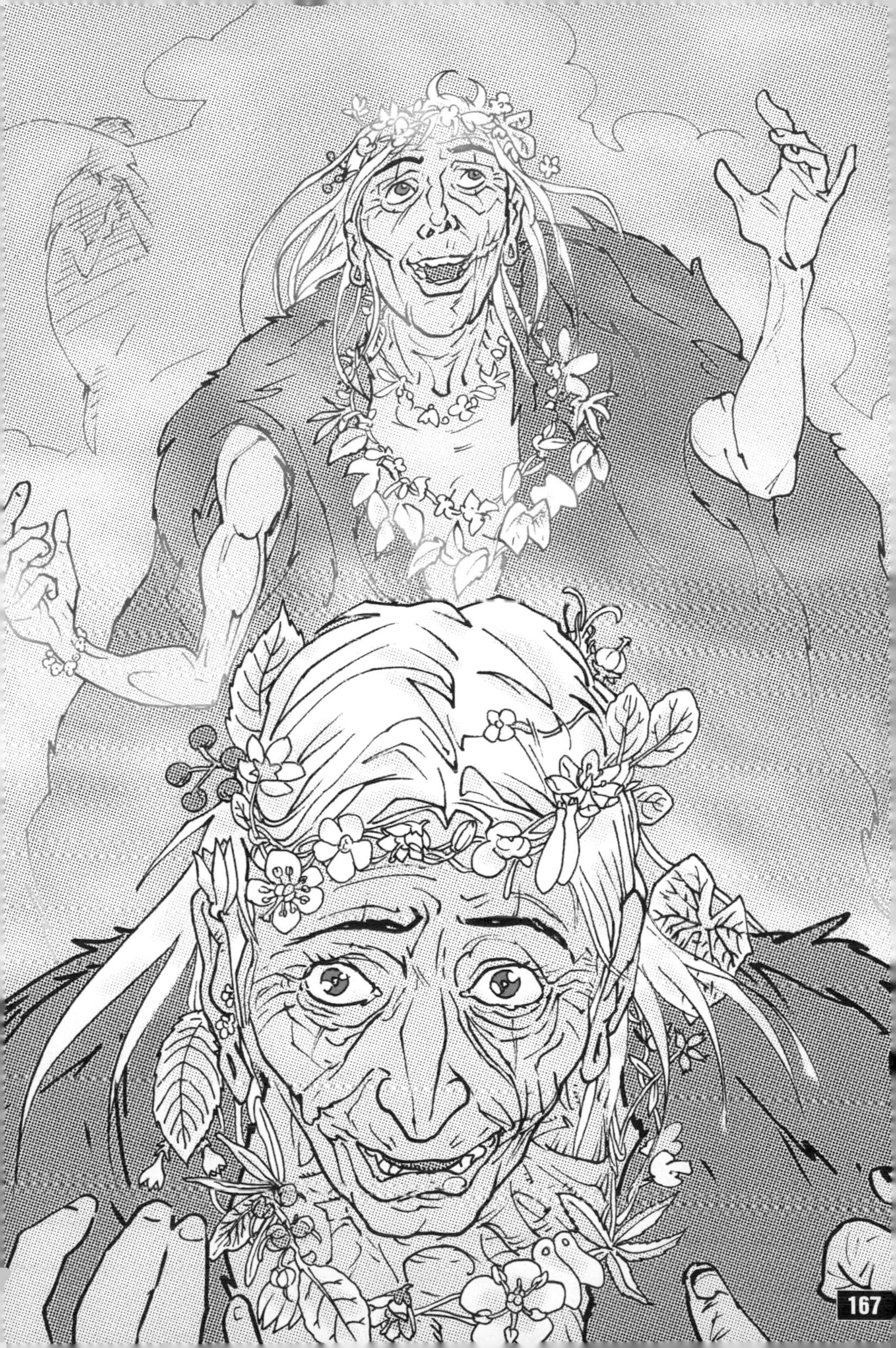

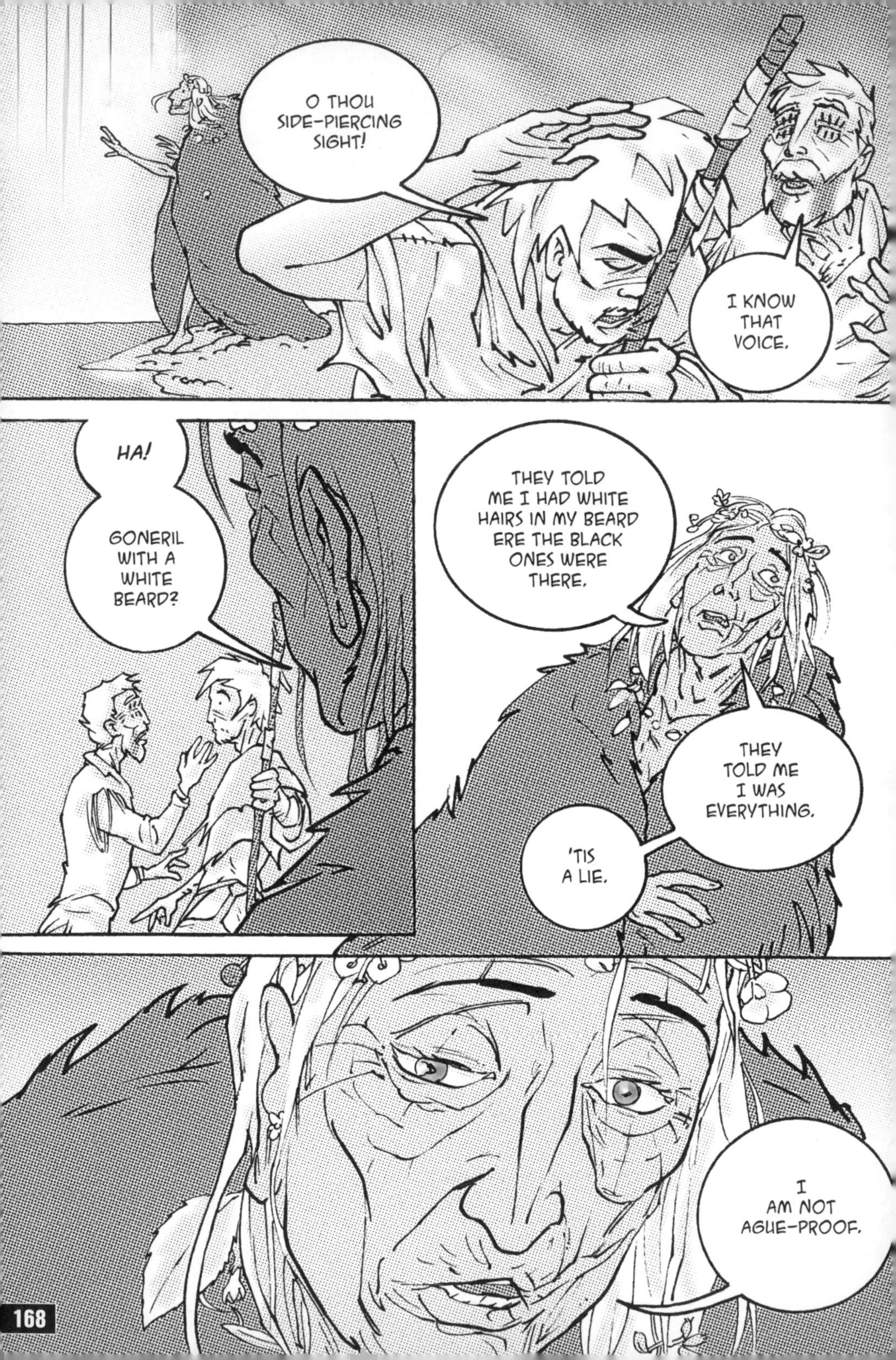
O THOU SIDE-PIERCING SIGHT!
I KNOW THAT VOICE.
HA!
GONERIL WITH A WHITE BEARD?
THEY TOLD ME I HAD WHITE HAIRS IN MY BEARD ERE THE BLACK ONES WERE THERE.
THEY TOLD ME I WAS EVERYTHING.
'TIS A LIE.
I AM NOT AGUE-PROOF.

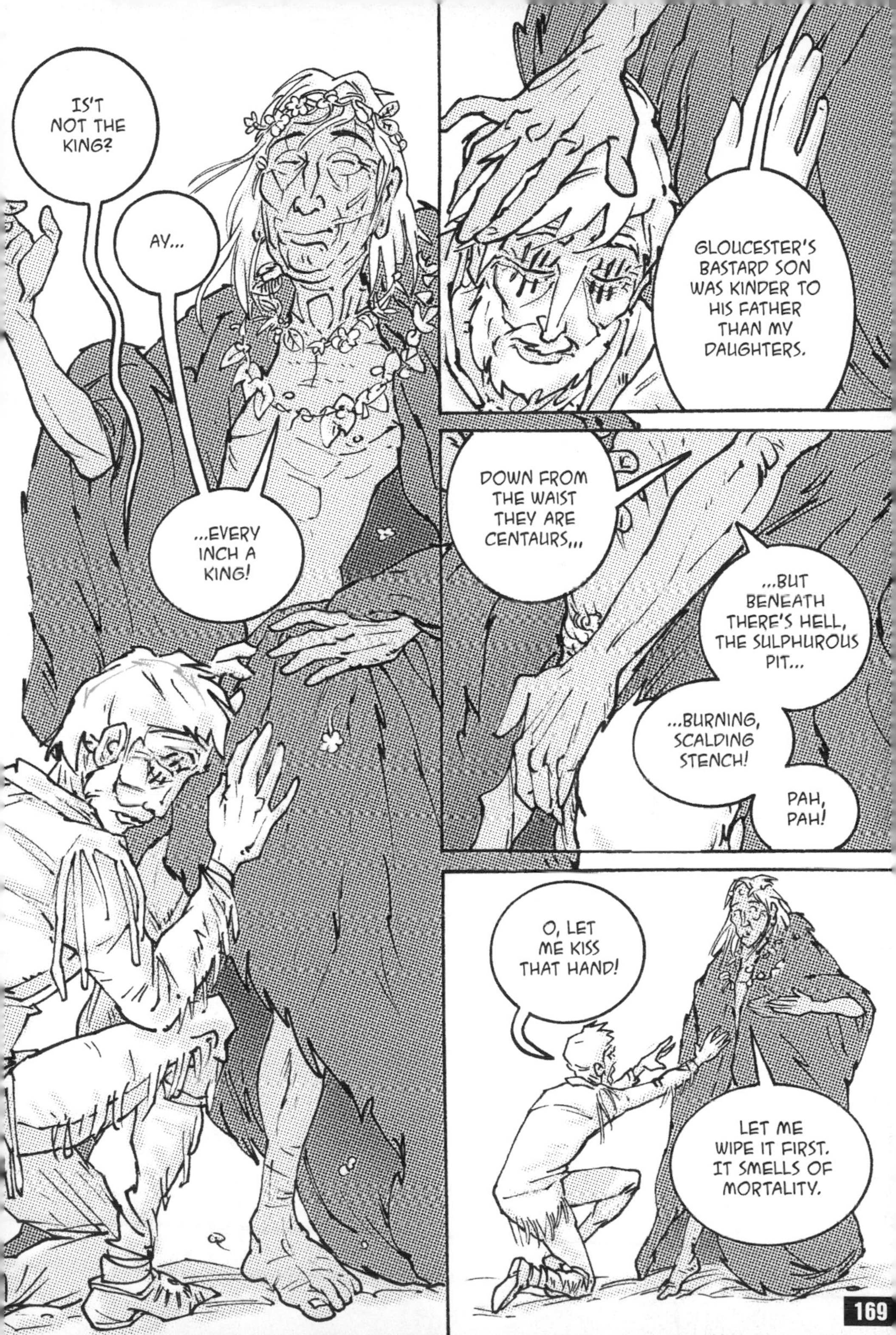
IS'T NOT THE KING?
AY...
...EVERY INCH A KING!
GLOUCESTER'S BASTARD SON WAS KINDER TO HIS FATHER THAN MY DAUGHTERS.
DOWN FROM THE WAIST THEY ARE CENTAURS...
...BUT BENEATH THERE'S HELL, THE SULPHUROUS PIT...
...BURNING, SCALDING STENCH!
PAH, PAH!
O, LET ME KISS THAT HAND!
LET ME WIPE IT FIRST. IT SMELLS OF MORTALITY.

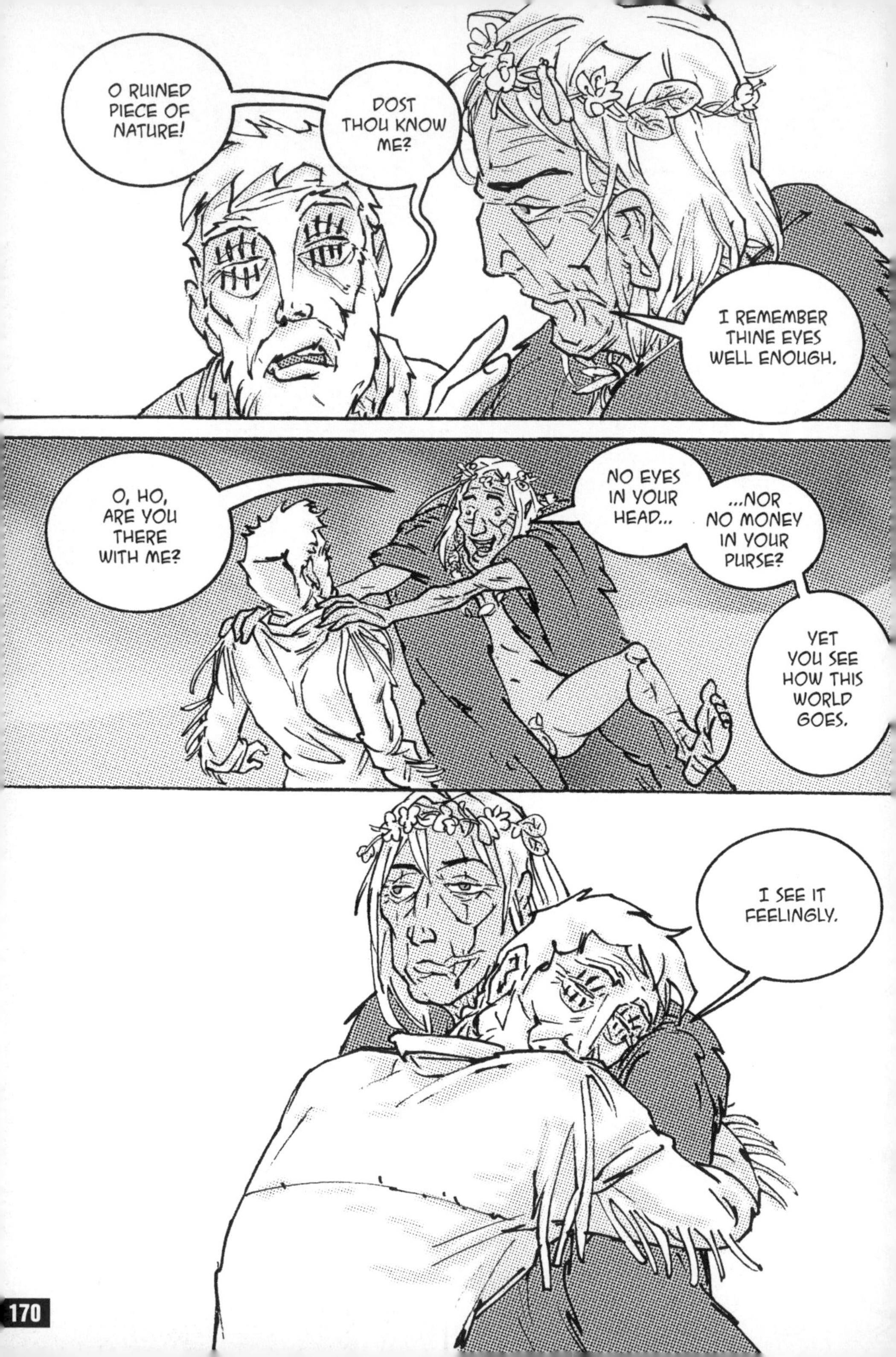
O RUINED PIECE OF NATURE!
DOST THOU KNOW ME?
I REMEMBER THINE EYES WELL ENOUGH.
O, HO, ARE YOU THERE WITH ME?
NO EYES IN YOUR HEAD...
...NOR NO MONEY IN YOUR PURSE?
YET YOU SEE HOW THIS WORLD GOES.
I SEE IT FEELINGLY.

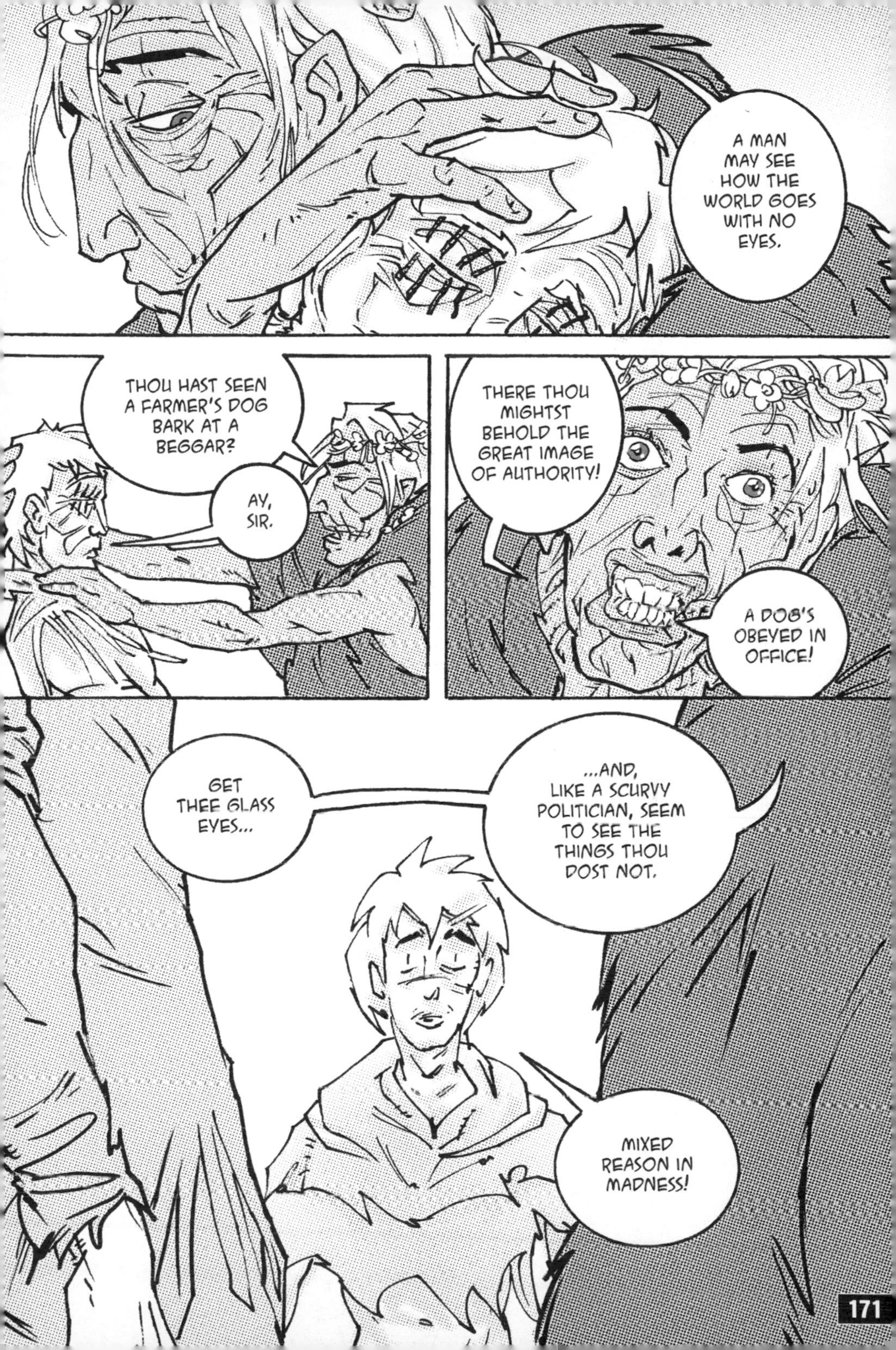
A MAN MAY SEE HOW THE WORLD GOES WITH NO EYES.
THOU HAST SEEN A FARMER'S DOG BARK AT A BEGGAR?
AY, SIR.
THERE THOU MIGHTST BEHOLD THE GREAT IMAGE OF AUTHORITY!
A DOG'S OBEYED IN OFFICE!
GET THEE GLASS EYES...
...AND, LIKE A SCURVY POLITICIAN, SEEM TO SEE THE THINGS THOU DOST NOT.
MIXED REASON IN MADNESS!

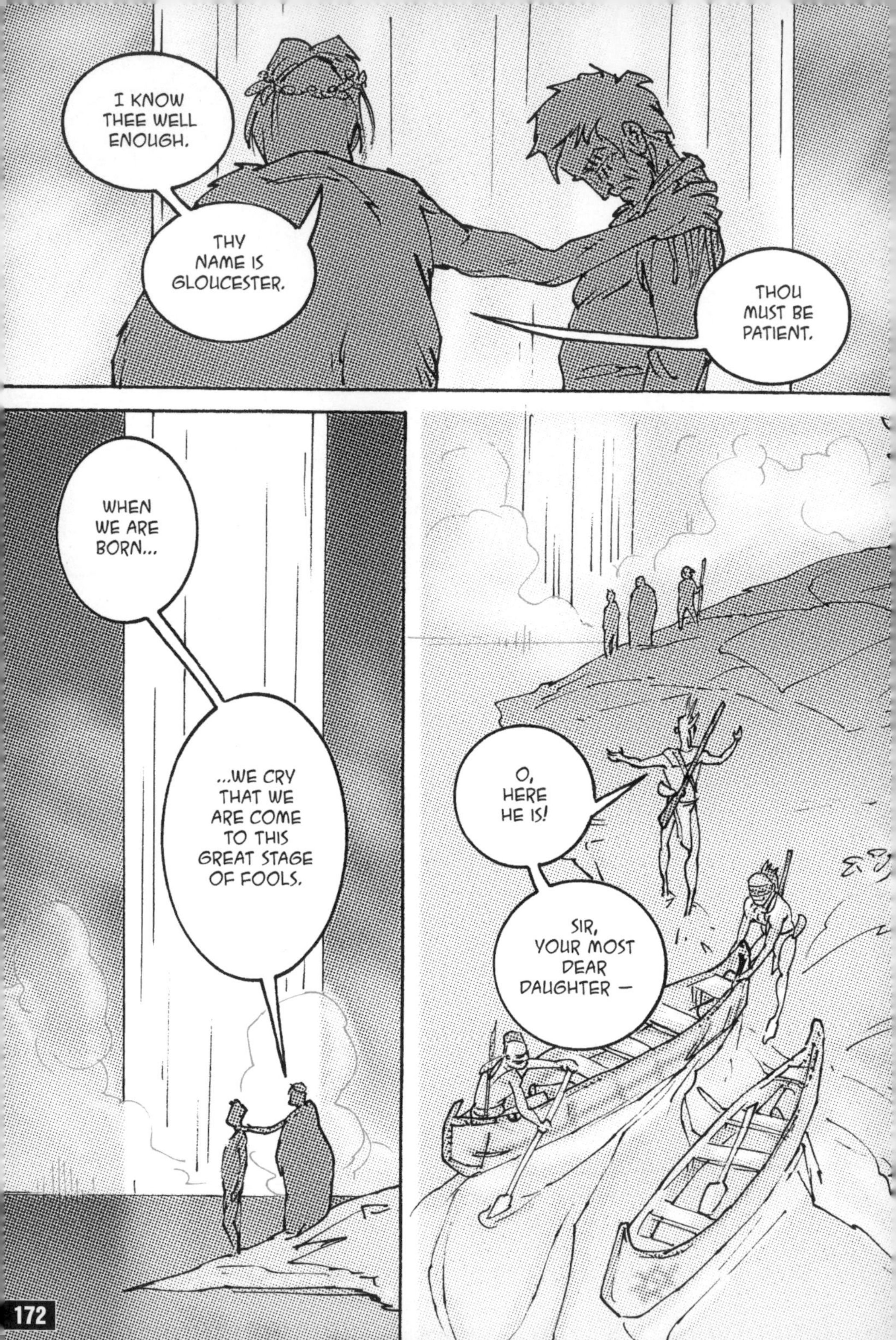
I KNOW THEE WELL ENOUGH.
THY NAME IS GLOUCESTER.
THOU MUST BE PATIENT.
WHEN WE ARE BORN...
...WE CRY THAT WE ARE COME TO THIS GREAT STAGE OF FOOLS.
O, HERE HE IS!
SIR, YOUR MOST DEAR DAUGHTER —

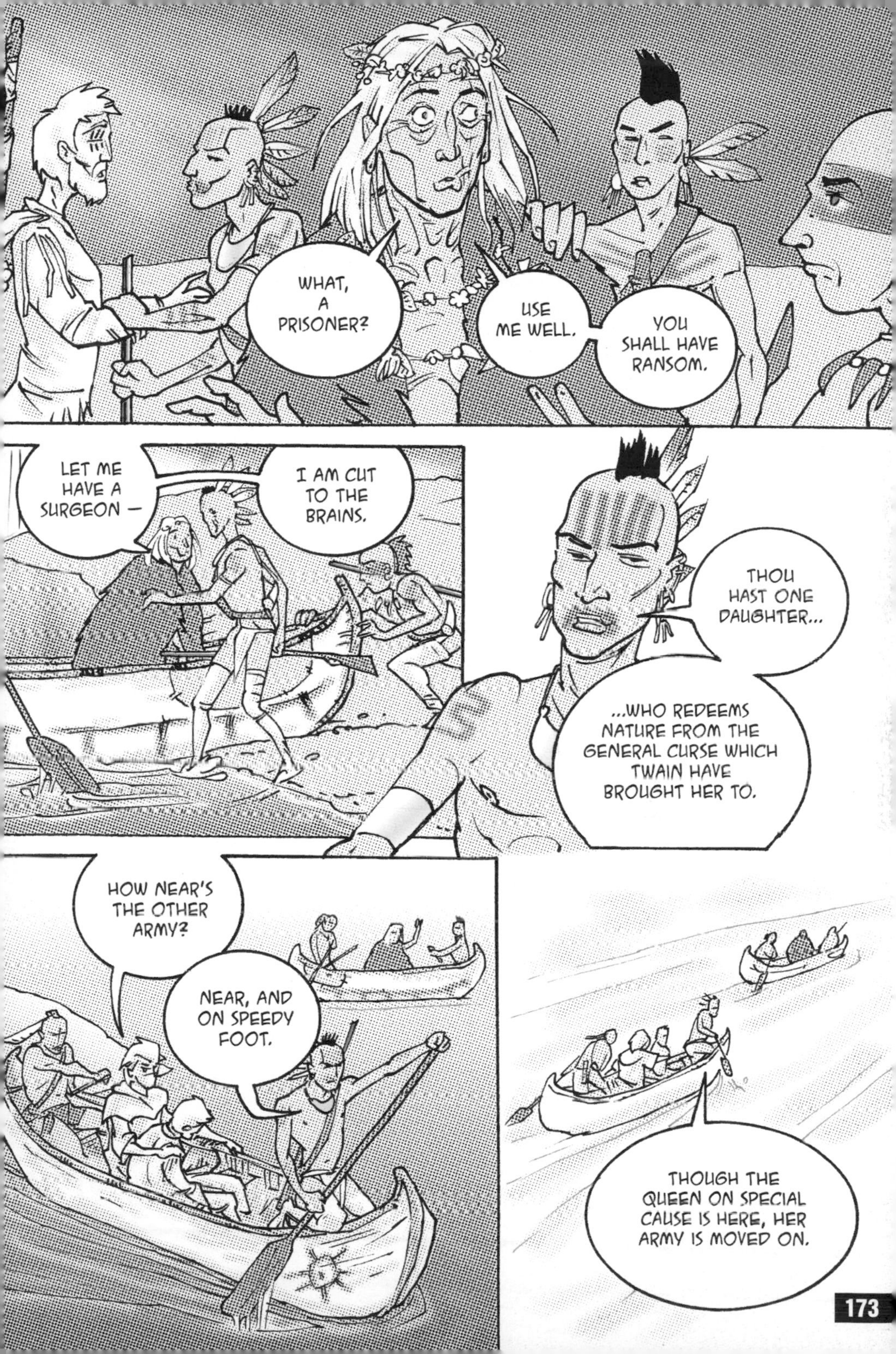
WHAT, A PRISONER?
USE ME WELL.
YOU SHALL HAVE RANSOM.
LET ME HAVE A SURGEON —
I AM CUT TO THE BRAINS.
THOU HAST ONE DAUGHTER...
...WHO REDEEMS NATURE FROM THE GENERAL CURSE WHICH TWAIN HAVE BROUGHT HER TO.
HOW NEAR'S THE OTHER ARMY?
NEAR, AND ON SPEEDY FOOT.
THOUGH THE QUEEN ON SPECIAL CAUSE IS HERE, HER ARMY IS MOVED ON.

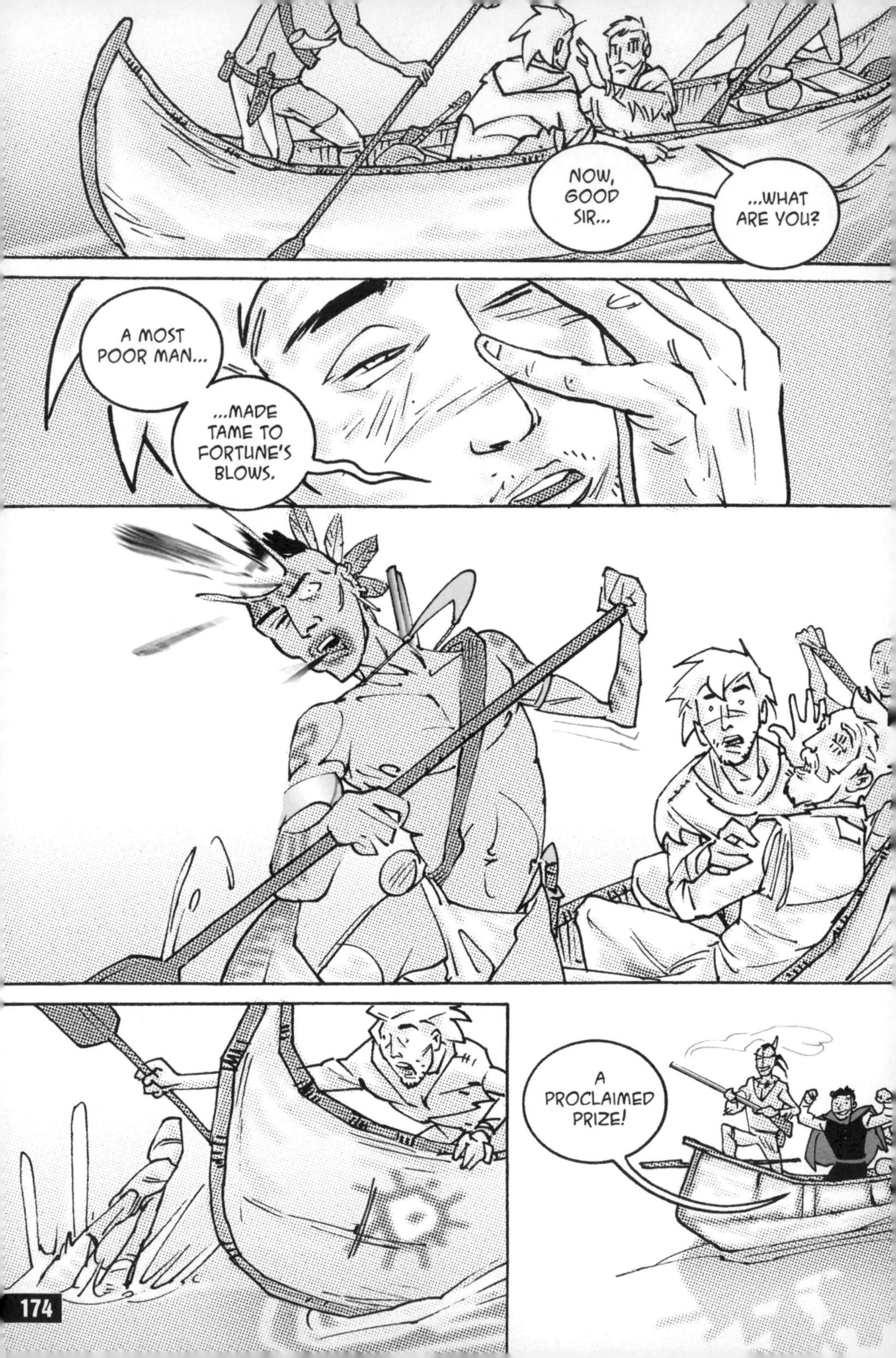

NOW, GOOD SIR...
...WHAT ARE YOU?
A MOST POOR MAN...
...MADE TAME TO FORTUNE'S BLOWS.
A PROCLAIMED PRIZE!

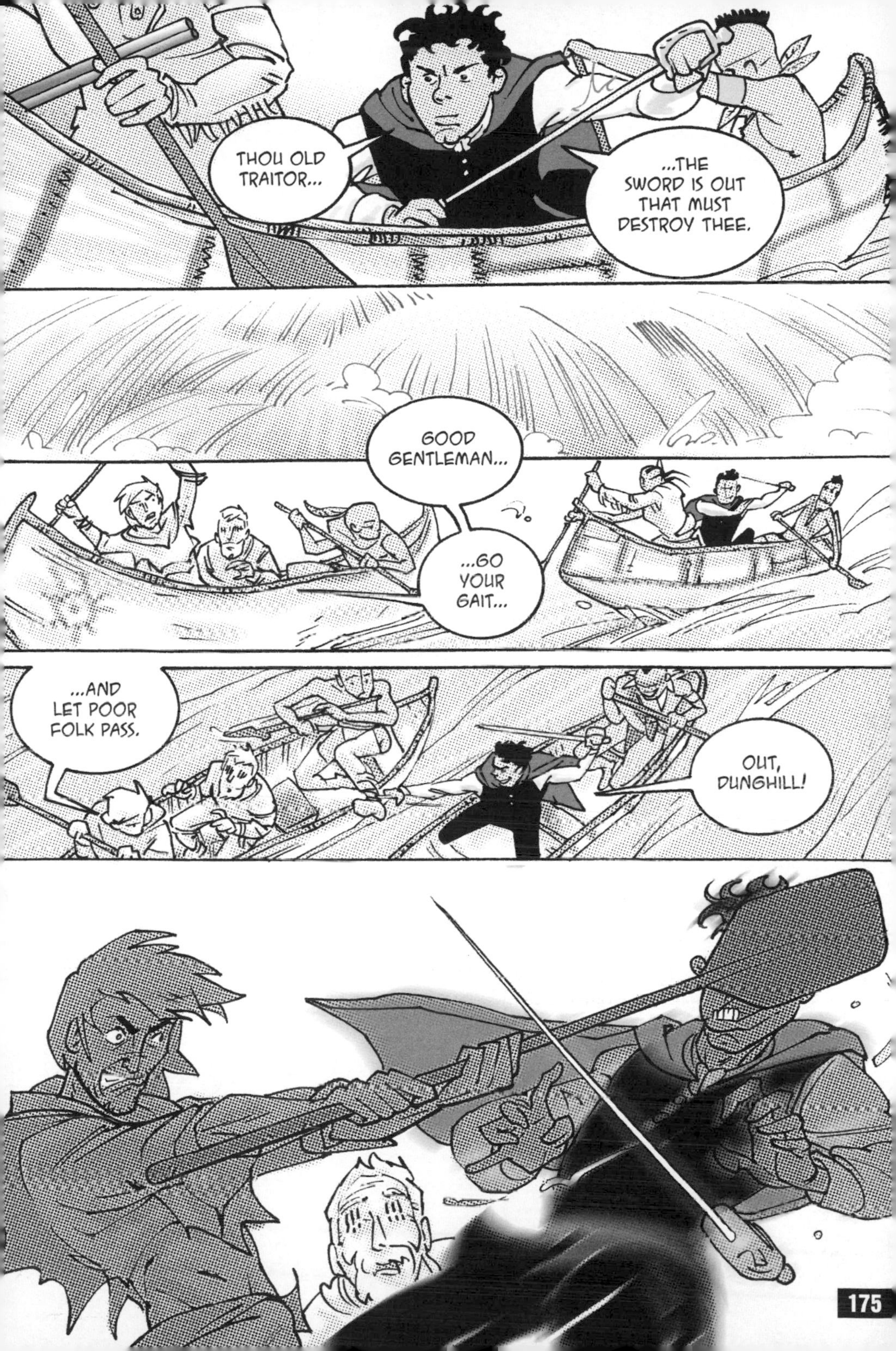
THOU OLD TRAITOR...
...THE SWORD IS OUT THAT MUST DESTROY THEE.
GOOD GENTLEMAN...
...GO YOUR GAIT...
...AND LET POOR FOLK PASS.
OUT, DUNGHILL!

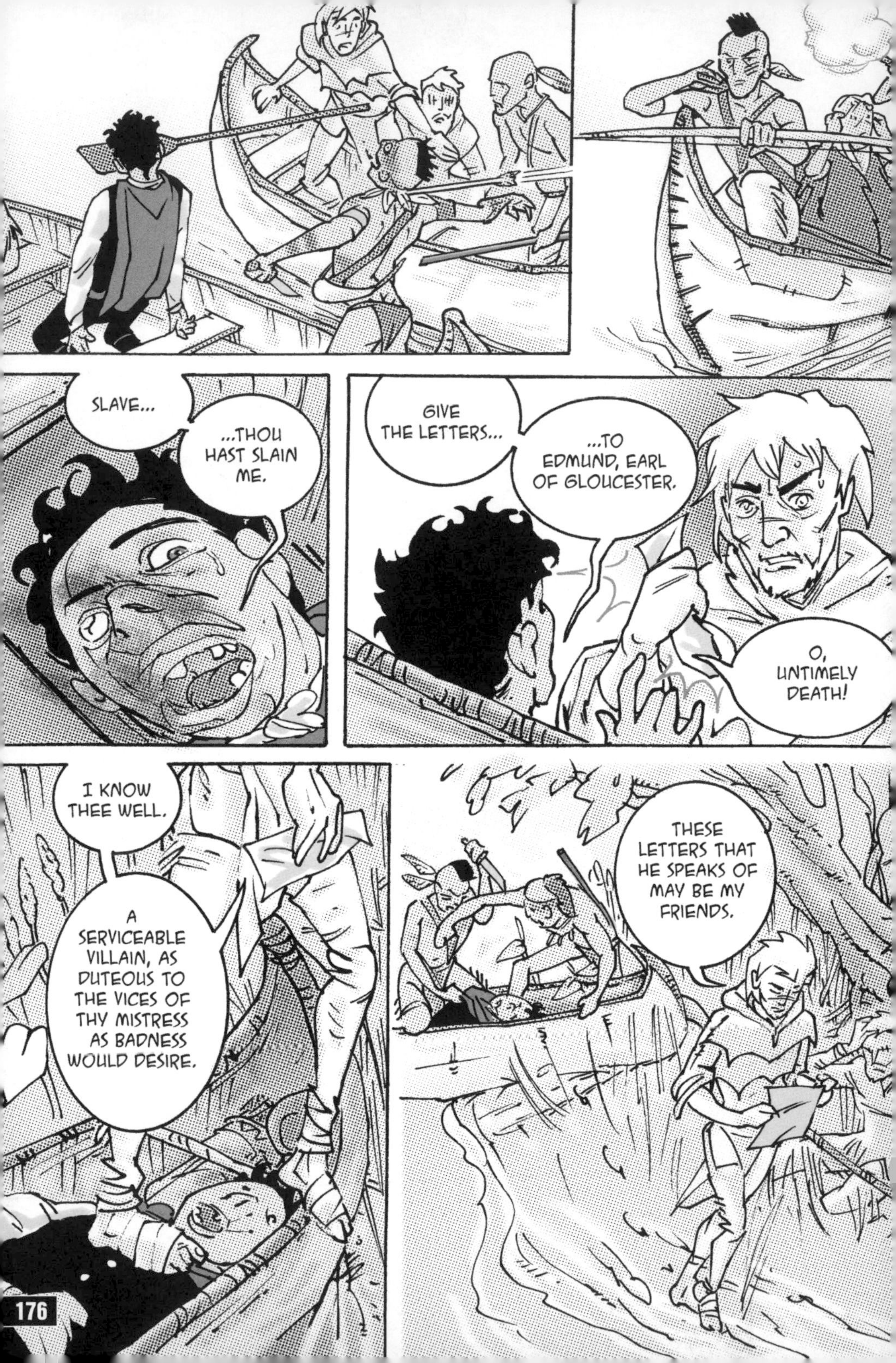

SLAVE...
...THOU HAST SLAIN ME.
GIVE THE LETTERS...
...TO EDMUND, EARL OF GLOUCESTER.
O, UNTIMELY DEATH!
I KNOW THEE WELL.
A SERVICEABLE VILLAIN, AS DUTEOUS TO THE VICES OF THY MISTRESS AS BADNESS WOULD DESIRE.
THESE LETTERS THAT HE SPEAKS OF MAY BE MY FRIENDS.

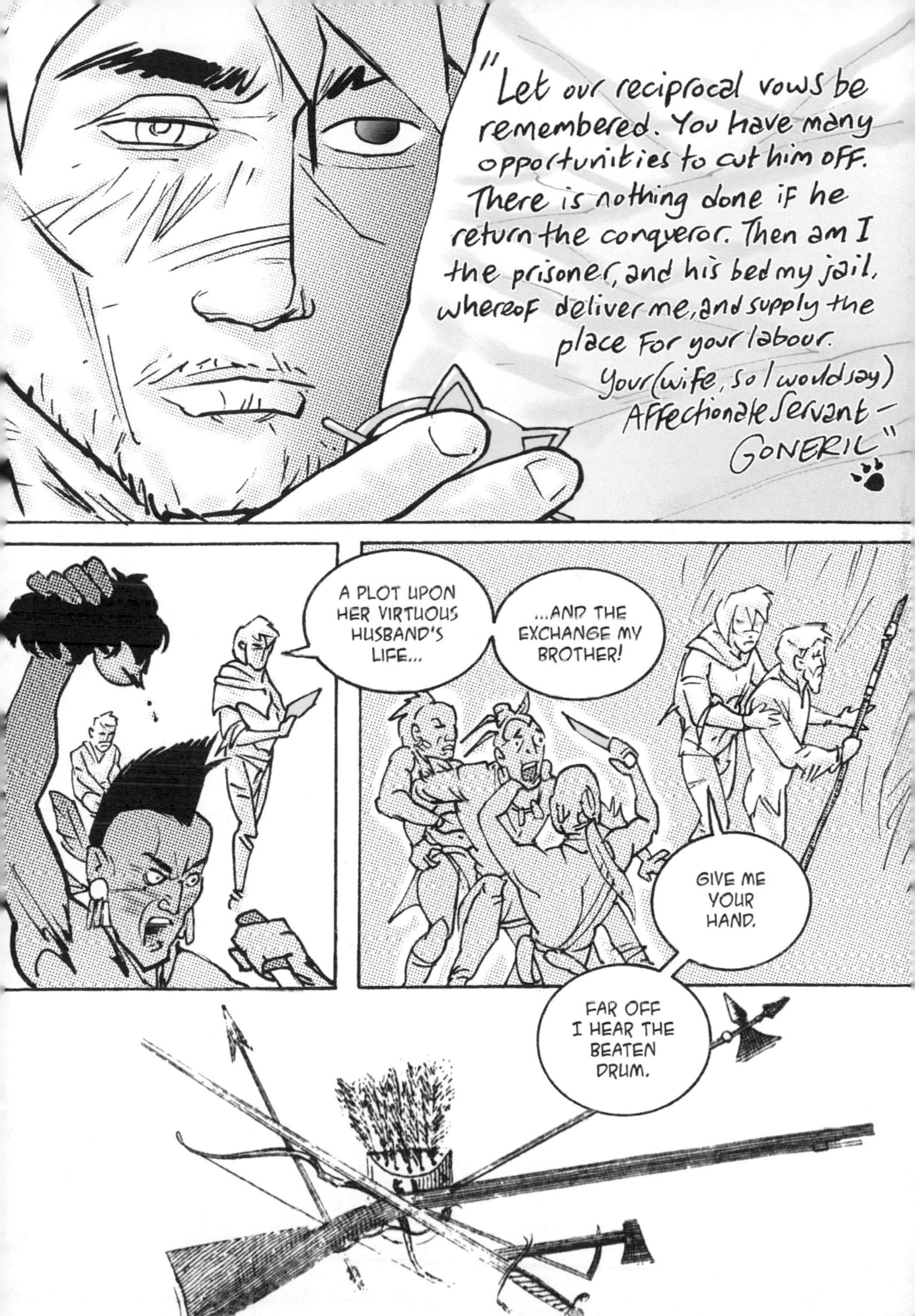
"Let our reciprocal vows be remembered. You have many opportunities to cut him off. There is nothing done if he return the conqueror. Then am I the prisoner, and his bed my jail, whereof deliver me, and supply the place for your labour.
Your (wife, so I would say) Affectionate Servant -
GONERIL"
A PLOT UPON HER VIRTUOUS HUSBAND'S LIFE...
...AND THE EXCHANGE MY BROTHER!
GIVE ME YOUR HAND.
FAR OFF I HEAR THE BEATEN DRUM.

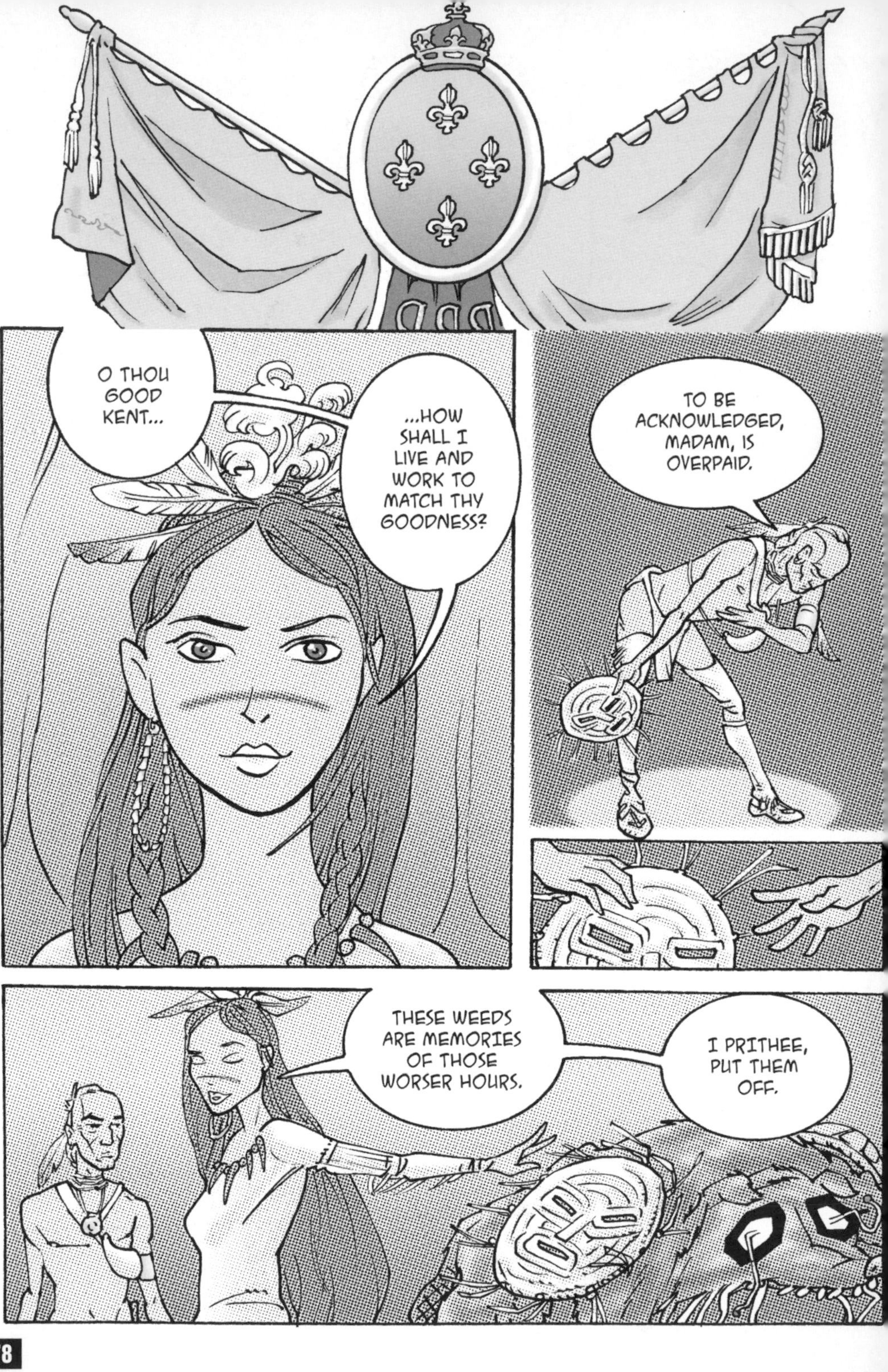
O THOU GOOD KENT...
...HOW SHALL I LIVE AND WORK TO MATCH THY GOODNESS?
TO BE ACKNOWLEDGED, MADAM, IS OVERPAID.
THESE WEEDS ARE MEMORIES OF THOSE WORSER HOURS.
I PRITHEE, PUT THEM OFF.

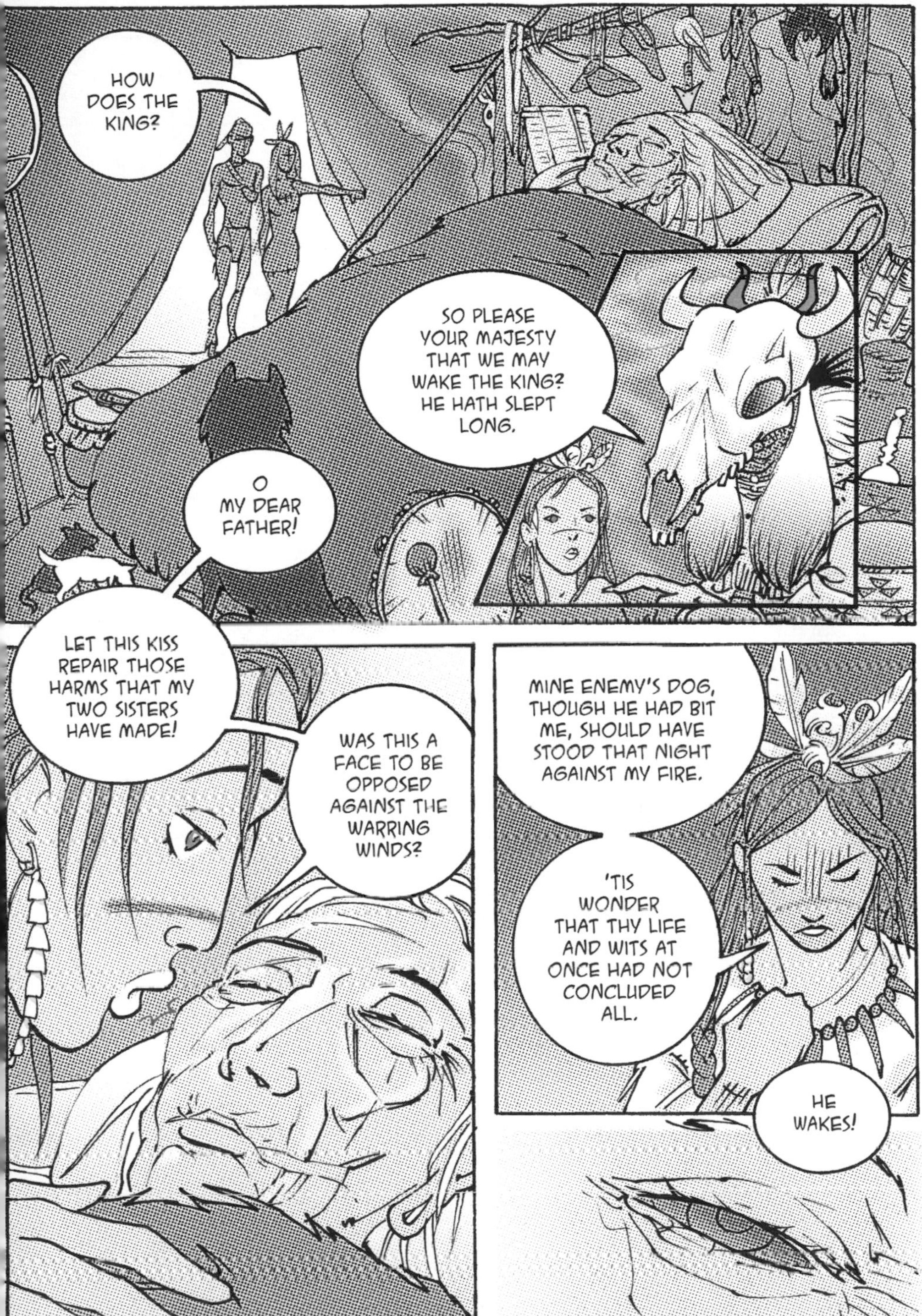
HOW DOES THE KING?
SO PLEASE YOUR MAJESTY THAT WE MAY WAKE THE KING? HE HATH SLEPT LONG.
O MY DEAR FATHER!
LET THIS KISS REPAIR THOSE HARMS THAT MY TWO SISTERS HAVE MADE!
WAS THIS A FACE TO BE OPPOSED AGAINST THE WARRING WINDS?
MINE ENEMY'S DOG, THOUGH HE HAD BIT ME, SHOULD HAVE STOOD THAT NIGHT AGAINST MY FIRE.
'TIS WONDER THAT THY LIFE AND WITS AT ONCE HAD NOT CONCLUDED ALL.
HE WAKES!

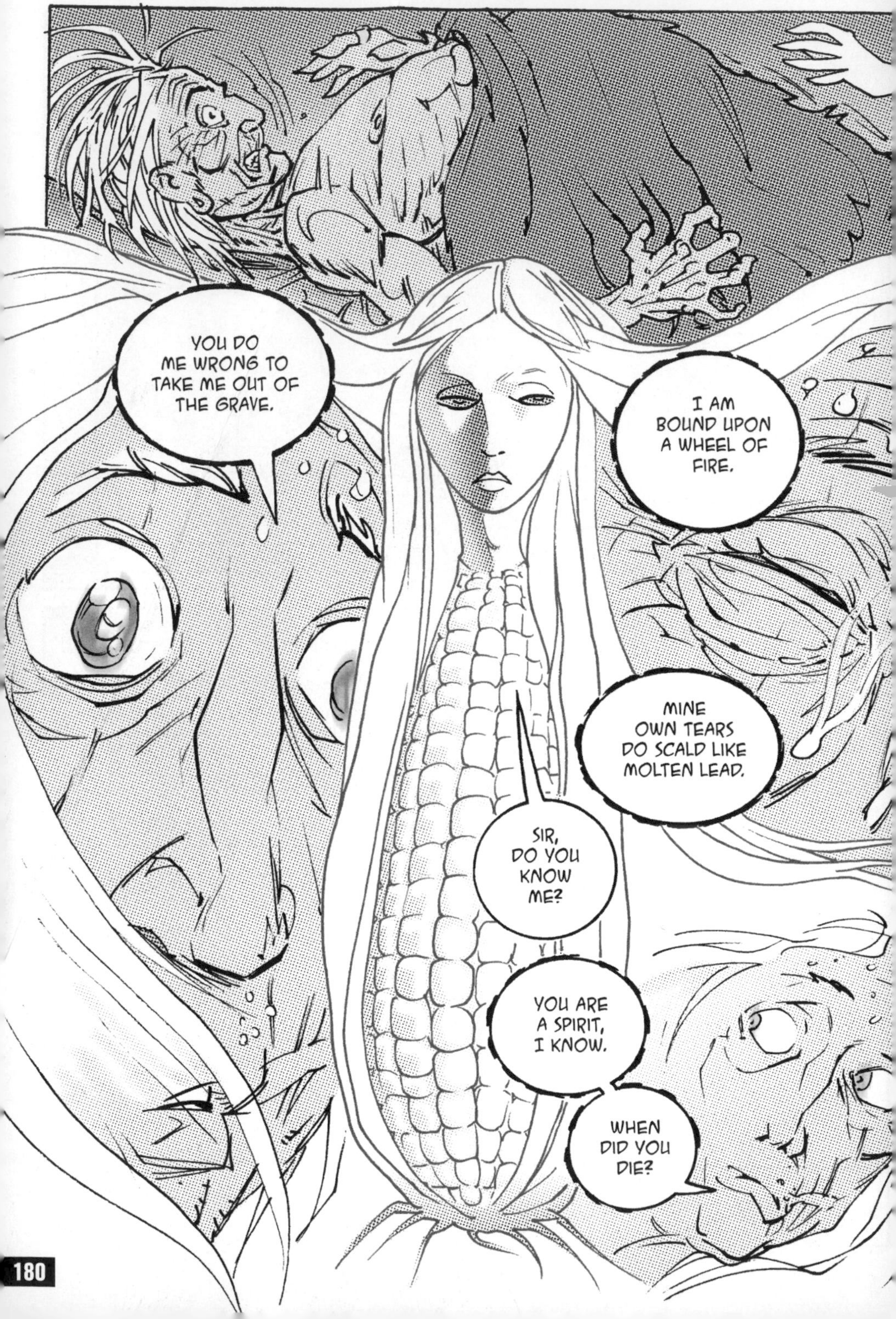
YOU DO ME WRONG TO TAKE ME OUT OF THE GRAVE.
I AM BOUND UPON A WHEEL OF FIRE.
MINE OWN TEARS DO SCALD LIKE MOLTEN LEAD.
SIR, DO YOU KNOW ME?
YOU ARE A SPIRIT, I KNOW.
WHEN DID YOU DIE?

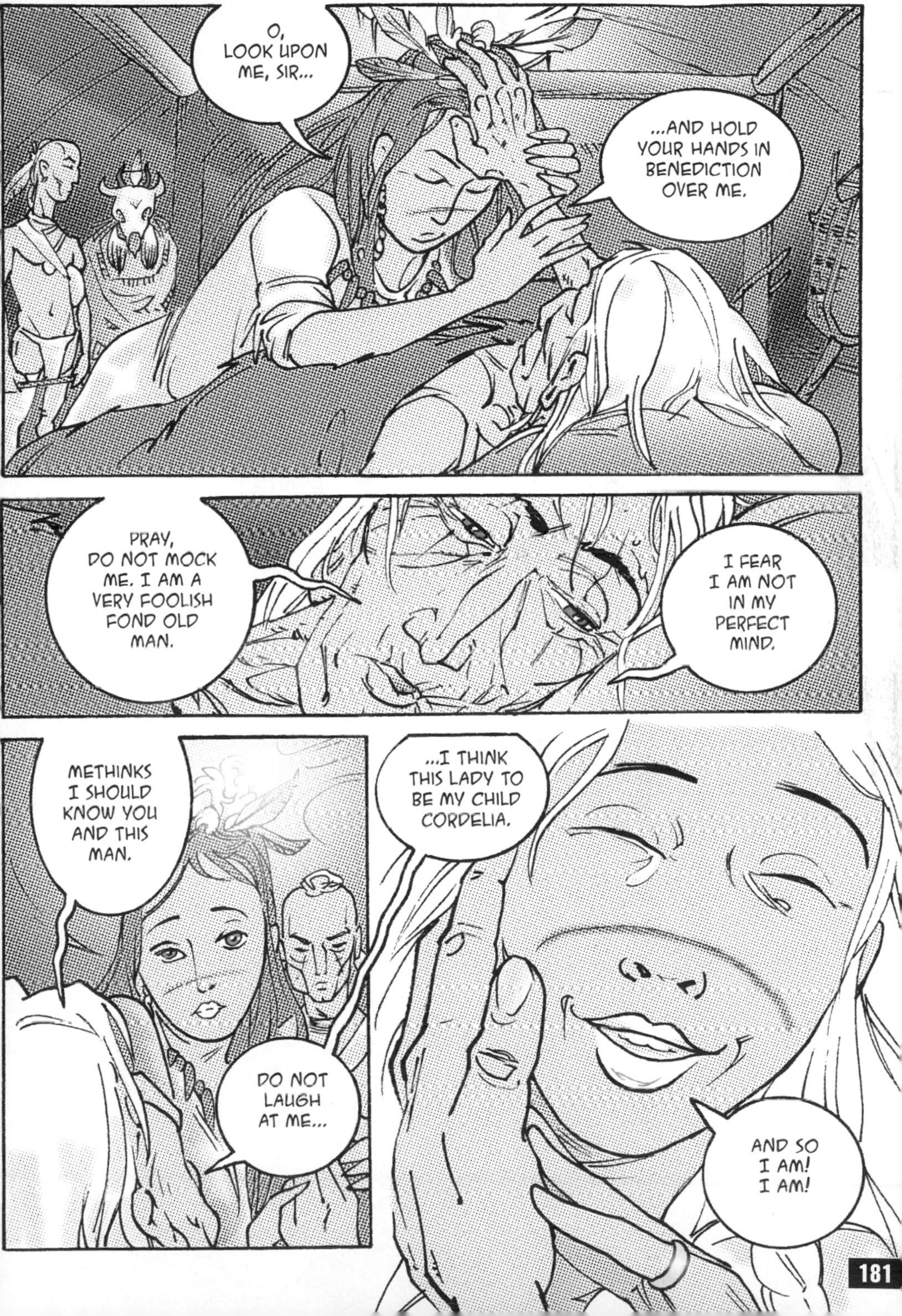
O, LOOK UPON ME, SIR...
...AND HOLD YOUR HANDS IN BENEDICTION OVER ME.
PRAY, DO NOT MOCK ME. I AM A VERY FOOLISH FOND OLD MAN.
I FEAR I AM NOT IN MY PERFECT MIND.
METHINKS I SHOULD KNOW YOU AND THIS MAN.
DO NOT LAUGH AT ME...
...I THINK THIS LADY TO BE MY CHILD CORDELIA.
AND SO I AM! I AM!

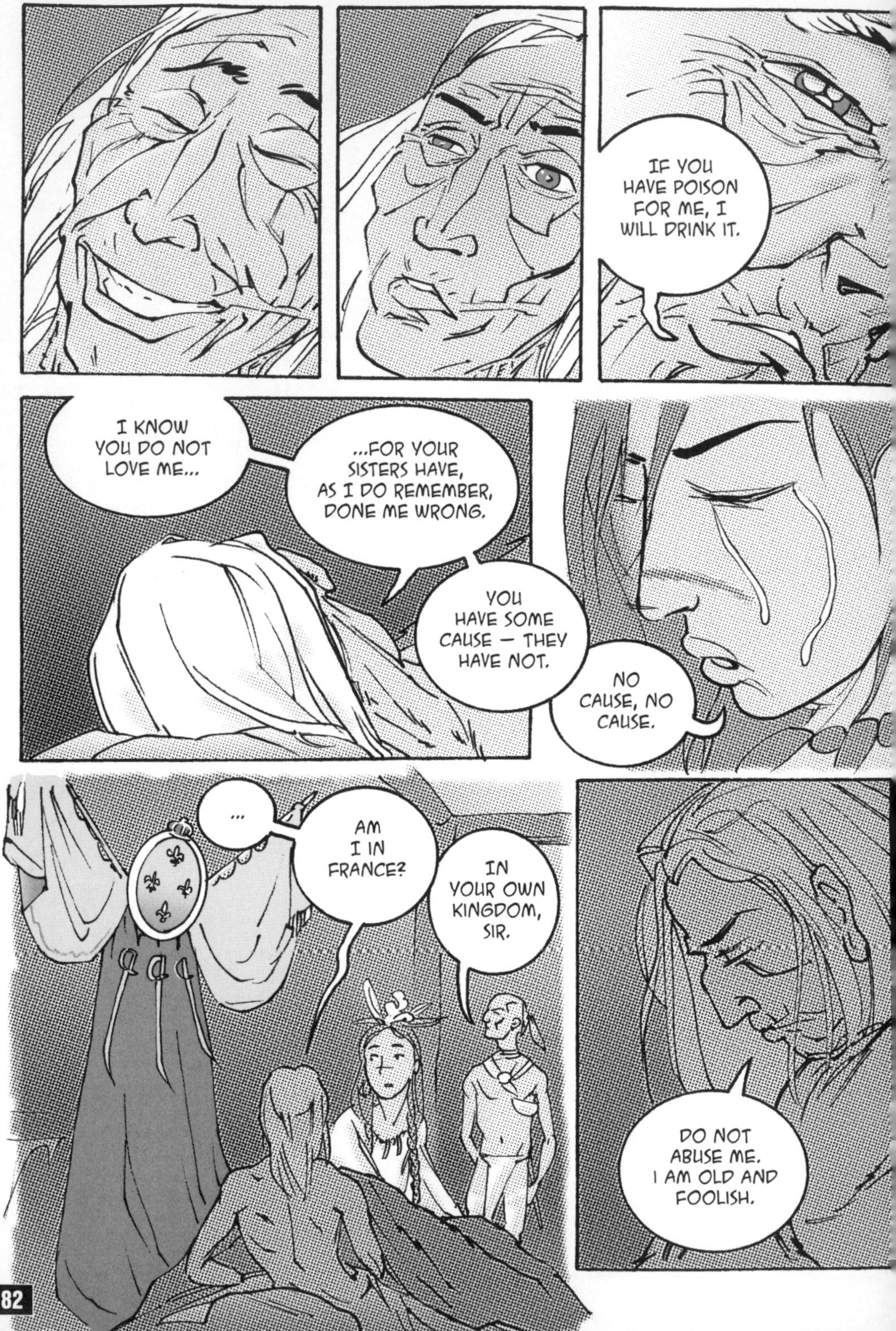
IF YOU HAVE POISON FOR ME, I WILL DRINK IT.
I KNOW YOU DO NOT LOVE ME...
...FOR YOUR SISTERS HAVE, AS I DO REMEMBER, DONE ME WRONG.
YOU HAVE SOME CAUSE — THEY HAVE NOT.
NO CAUSE, NO CAUSE.
...
AM I IN FRANCE?
IN YOUR OWN KINGDOM, SIR.
DO NOT ABUSE ME. I AM OLD AND FOOLISH.

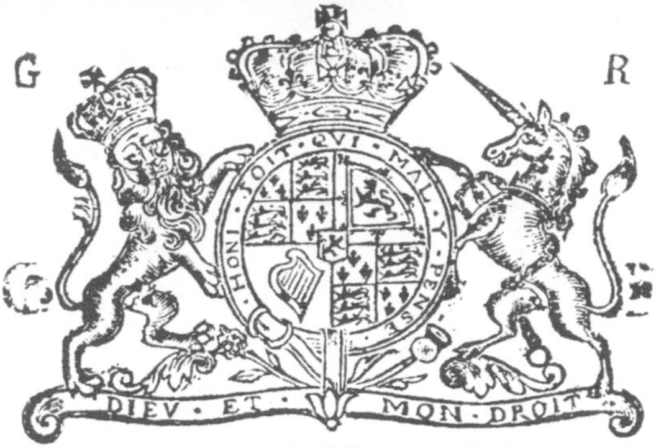
G R
HONI SOIT QVI MAL Y PENSE
DIEV ET MON DROIT

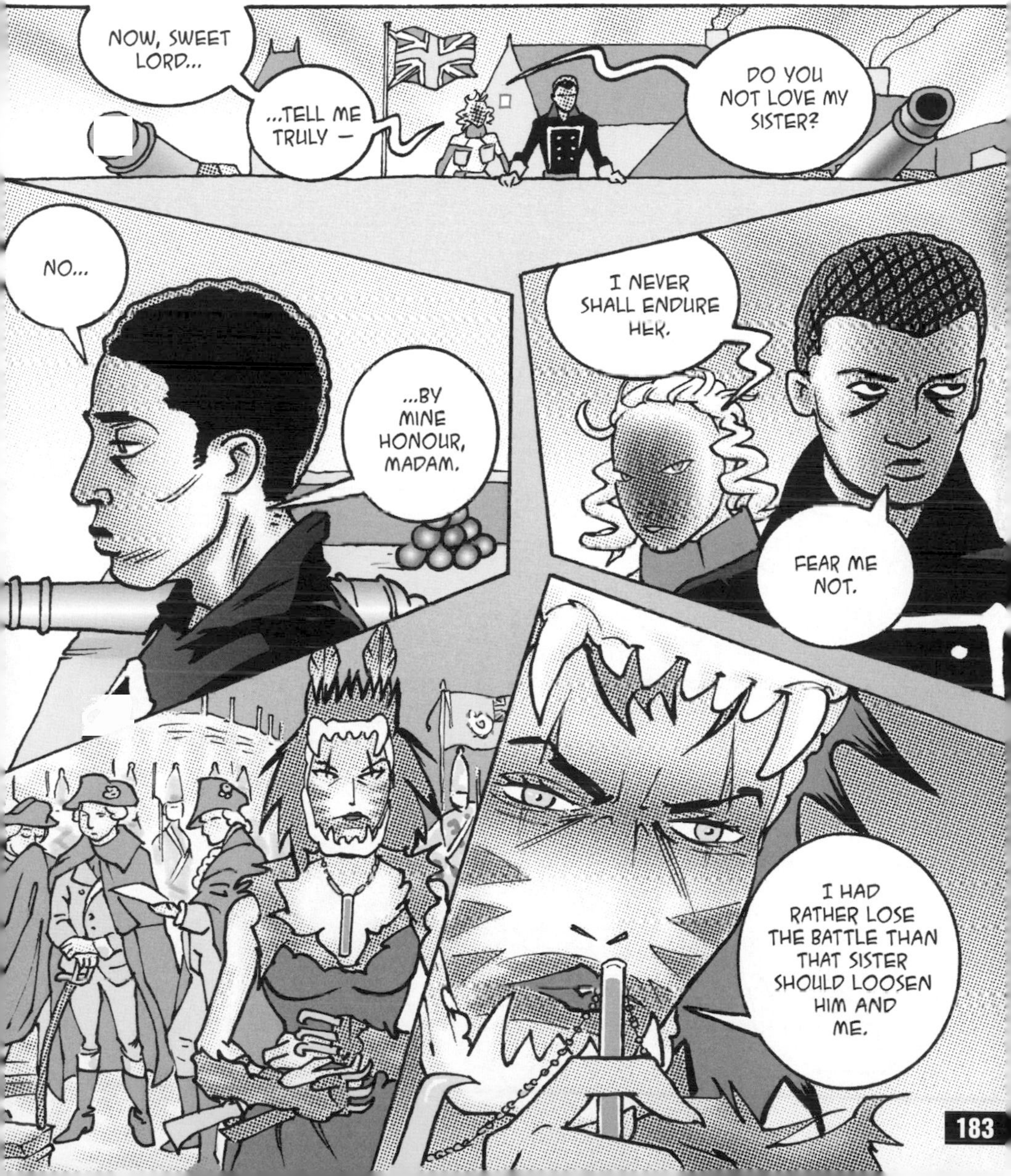
NOW, SWEET LORD...
...TELL ME TRULY —
DO YOU NOT LOVE MY SISTER?
NO...
...BY MINE HONOUR, MADAM.
I NEVER SHALL ENDURE HER.
FEAR ME NOT.
I HAD RATHER LOSE THE BATTLE THAN THAT SISTER SHOULD LOOSEN HIM AND ME.

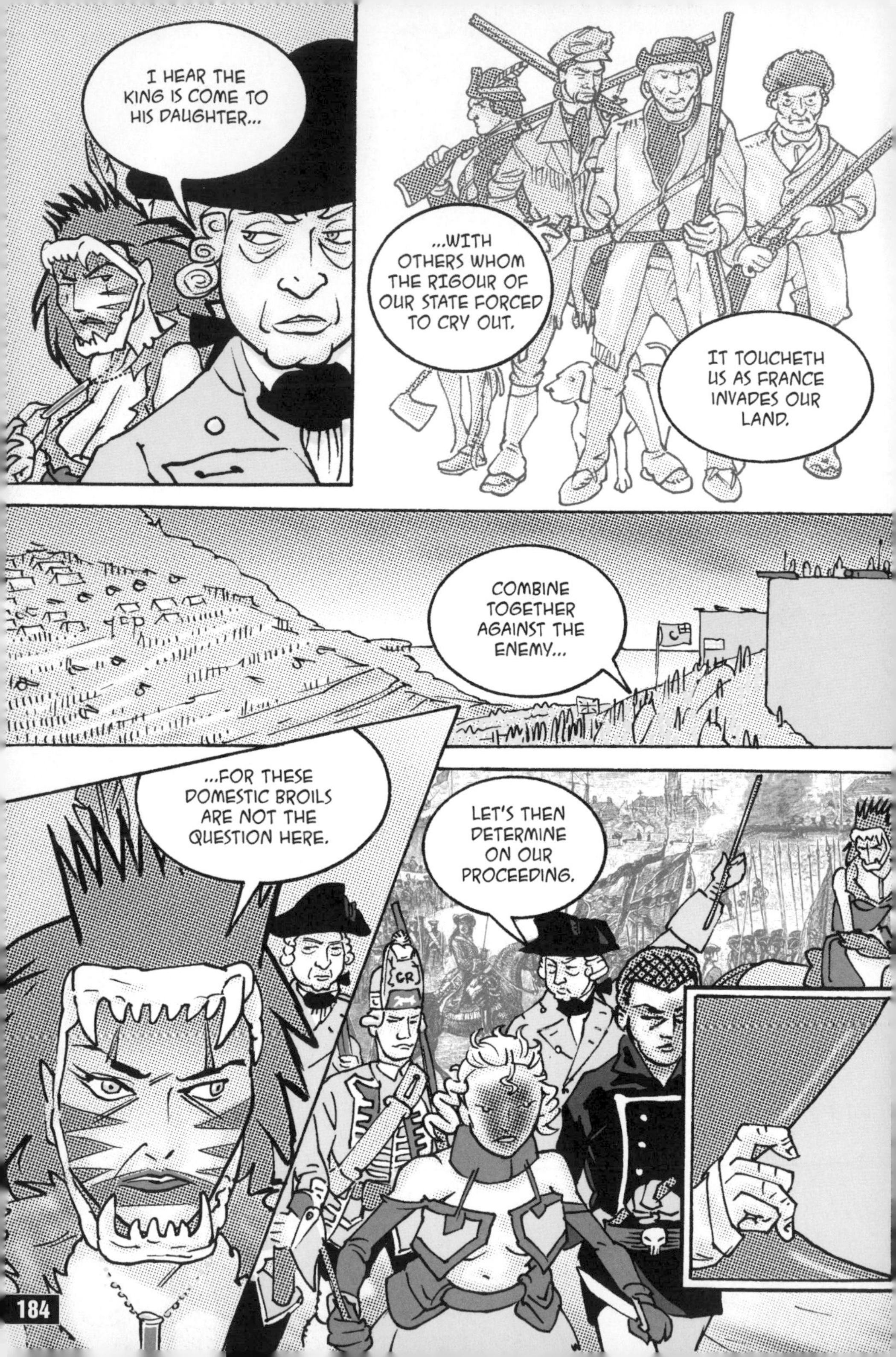
I HEAR THE KING IS COME TO HIS DAUGHTER...
...WITH OTHERS WHOM THE RIGOUR OF OUR STATE FORCED TO CRY OUT.
IT TOUCHETH US AS FRANCE INVADES OUR LAND.
COMBINE TOGETHER AGAINST THE ENEMY...
...FOR THESE DOMESTIC BROILS ARE NOT THE QUESTION HERE.
LET'S THEN DETERMINE ON OUR PROCEEDING.
GR

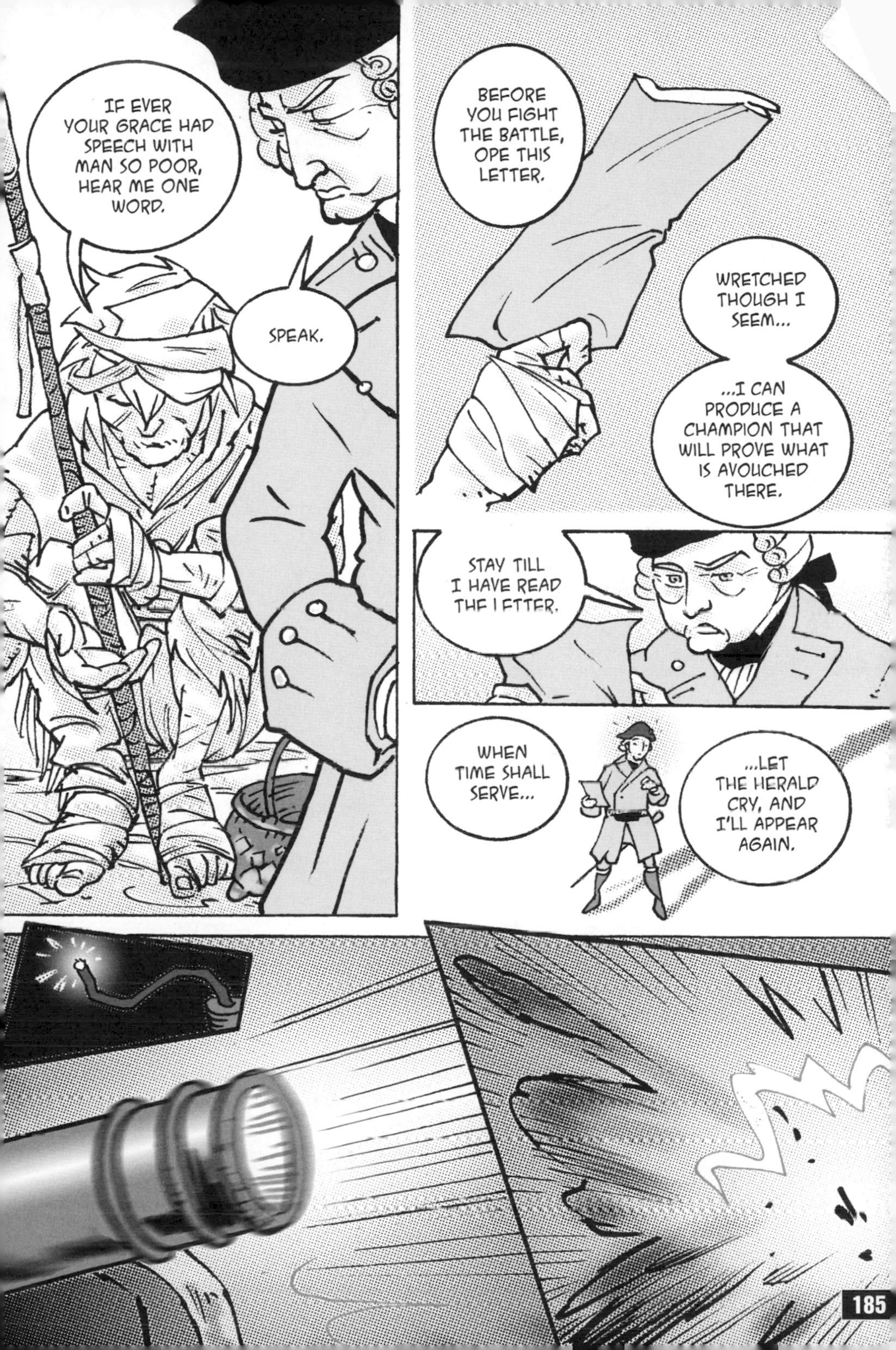
IF EVER YOUR GRACE HAD SPEECH WITH MAN SO POOR, HEAR ME ONE WORD.
SPEAK.
BEFORE YOU FIGHT THE BATTLE, OPE THIS LETTER.
WRETCHED THOUGH I SEEM...
...I CAN PRODUCE A CHAMPION THAT WILL PROVE WHAT IS AVOUCHED THERE.
STAY TILL I HAVE READ THE LETTER.
WHEN TIME SHALL SERVE...
...LET THE HERALD CRY, AND I'LL APPEAR AGAIN.

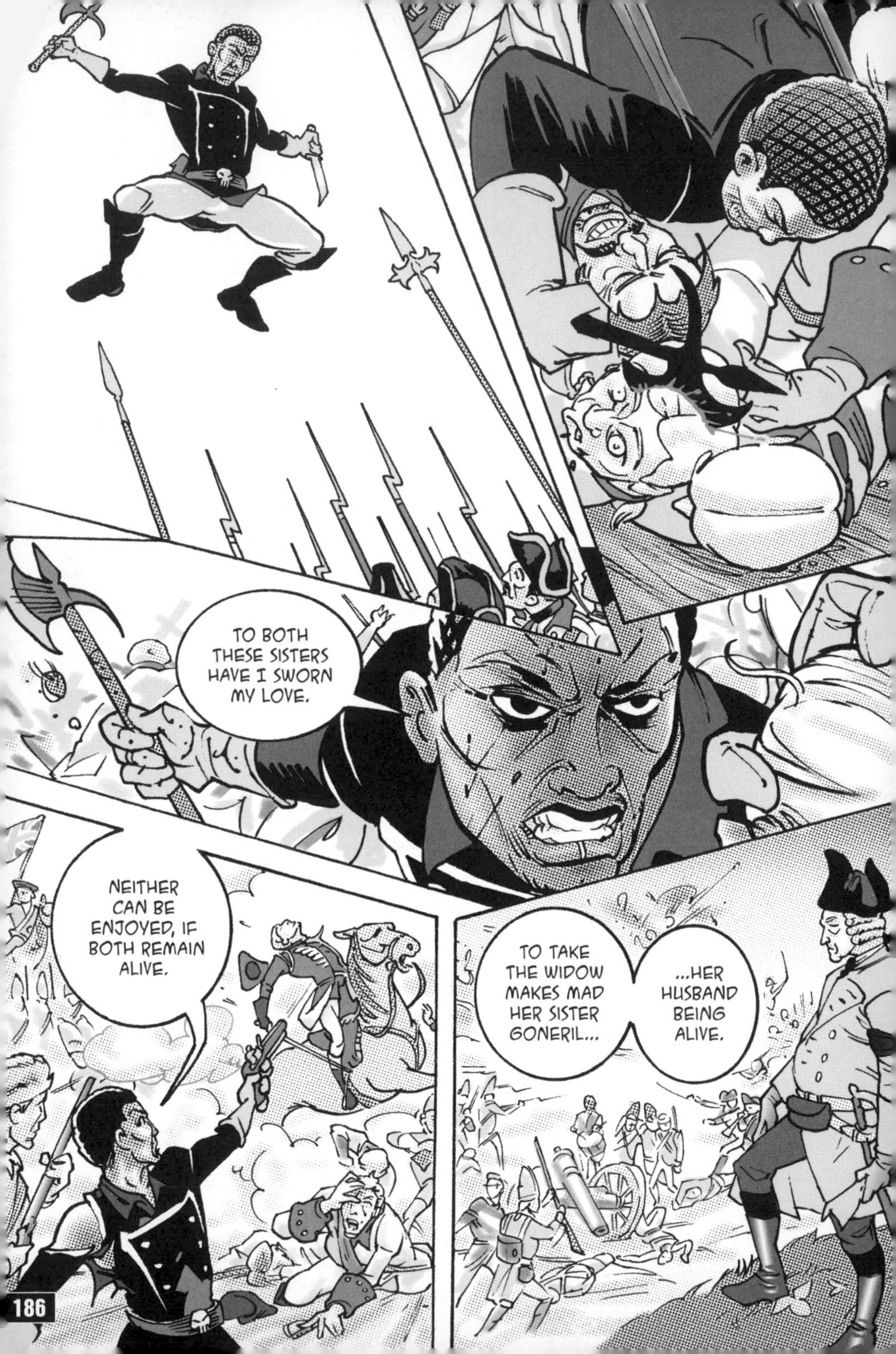
TO BOTH THESE SISTERS HAVE I SWORN MY LOVE.
NEITHER CAN BE ENJOYED, IF BOTH REMAIN ALIVE.
TO TAKE THE WIDOW MAKES MAD HER SISTER GONERIL...
...HER HUSBAND BEING ALIVE.

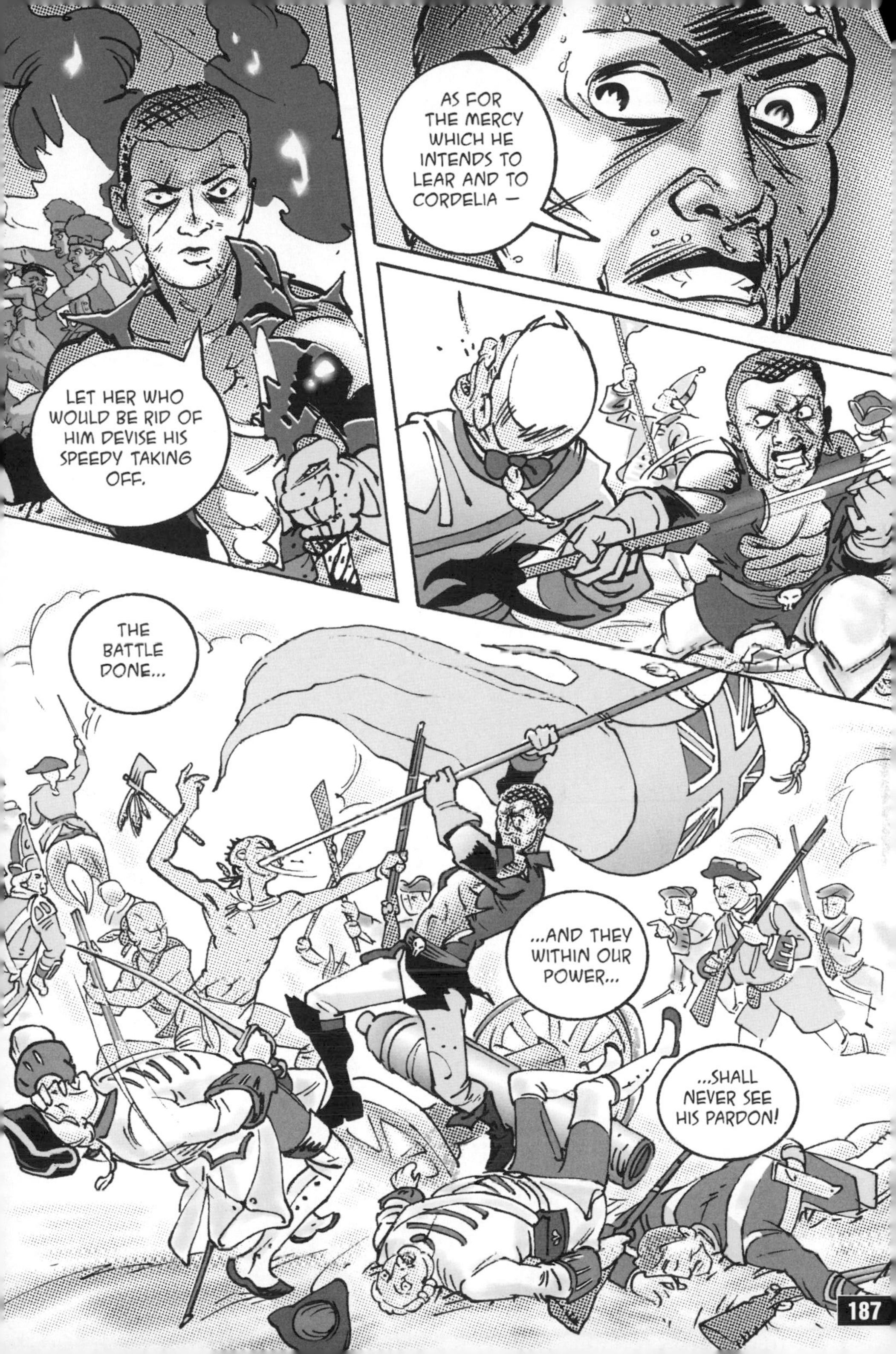
LET HER WHO WOULD BE RID OF HIM DEVISE HIS SPEEDY TAKING OFF.
AS FOR THE MERCY WHICH HE INTENDS TO LEAR AND TO CORDELIA —
THE BATTLE DONE...
...AND THEY WITHIN OUR POWER...
...SHALL NEVER SEE HIS PARDON!

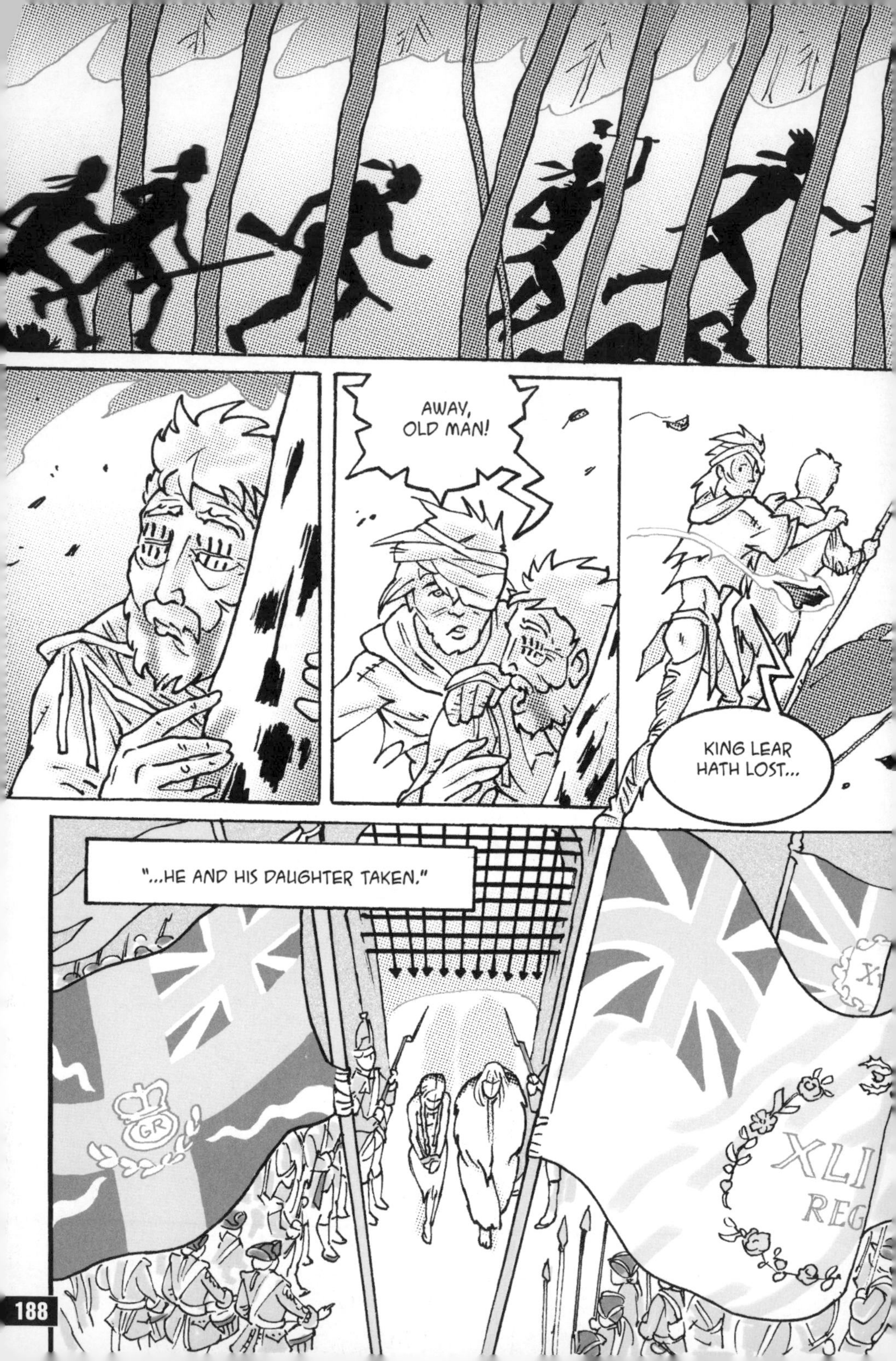
AWAY, OLD MAN!
KING LEAR HATH LOST...
"...HE AND HIS DAUGHTER TAKEN."
GR
XLI
REG

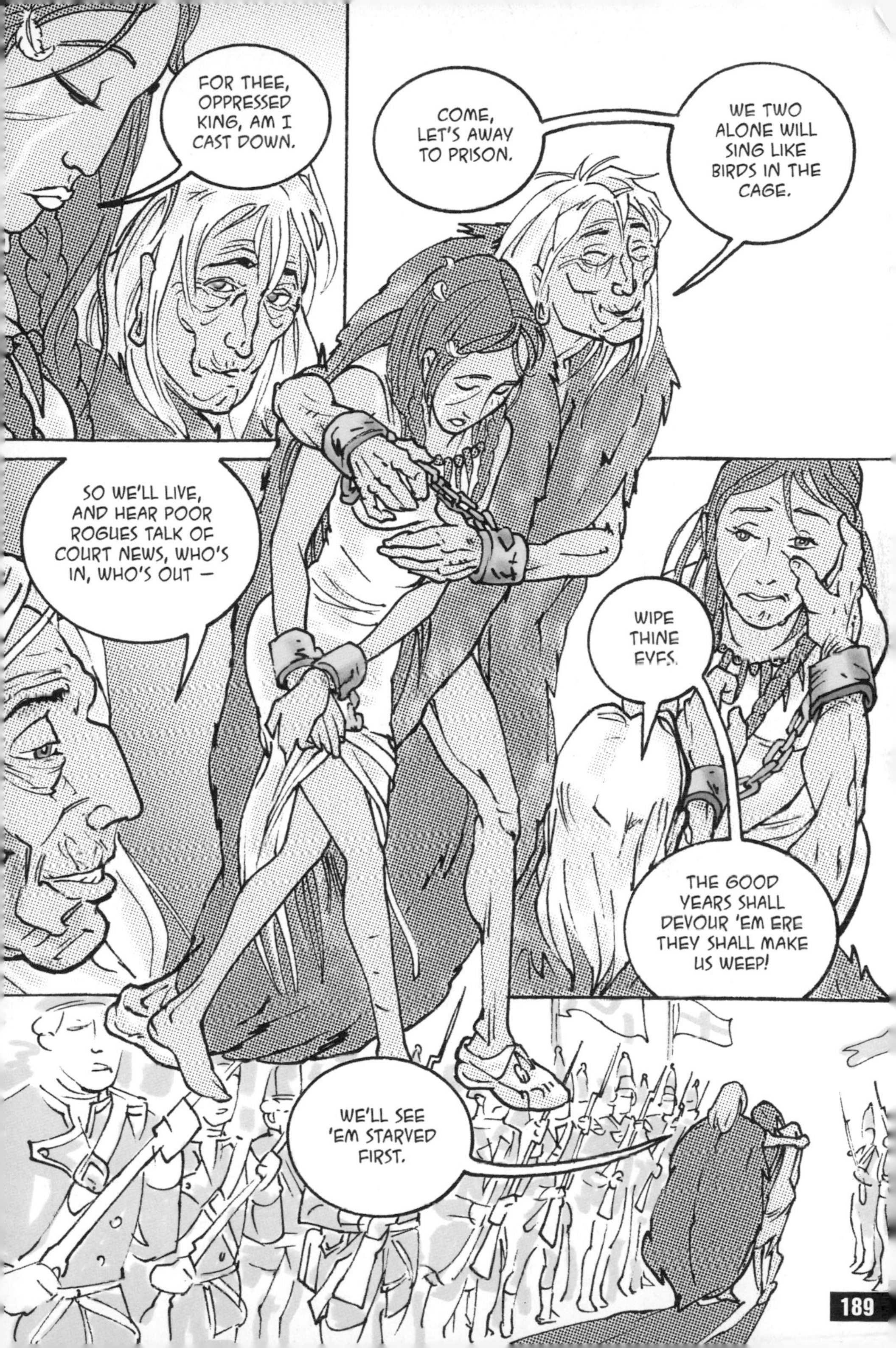
FOR THEE, OPPRESSED KING, AM I CAST DOWN.
COME, LET'S AWAY TO PRISON.
WE TWO ALONE WILL SING LIKE BIRDS IN THE CAGE.
SO WE'LL LIVE, AND HEAR POOR ROGUES TALK OF COURT NEWS, WHO'S IN, WHO'S OUT —
WIPE THINE EYES.
THE GOOD YEARS SHALL DEVOUR 'EM ERE THEY SHALL MAKE US WEEP!
WE'LL SEE 'EM STARVED FIRST.

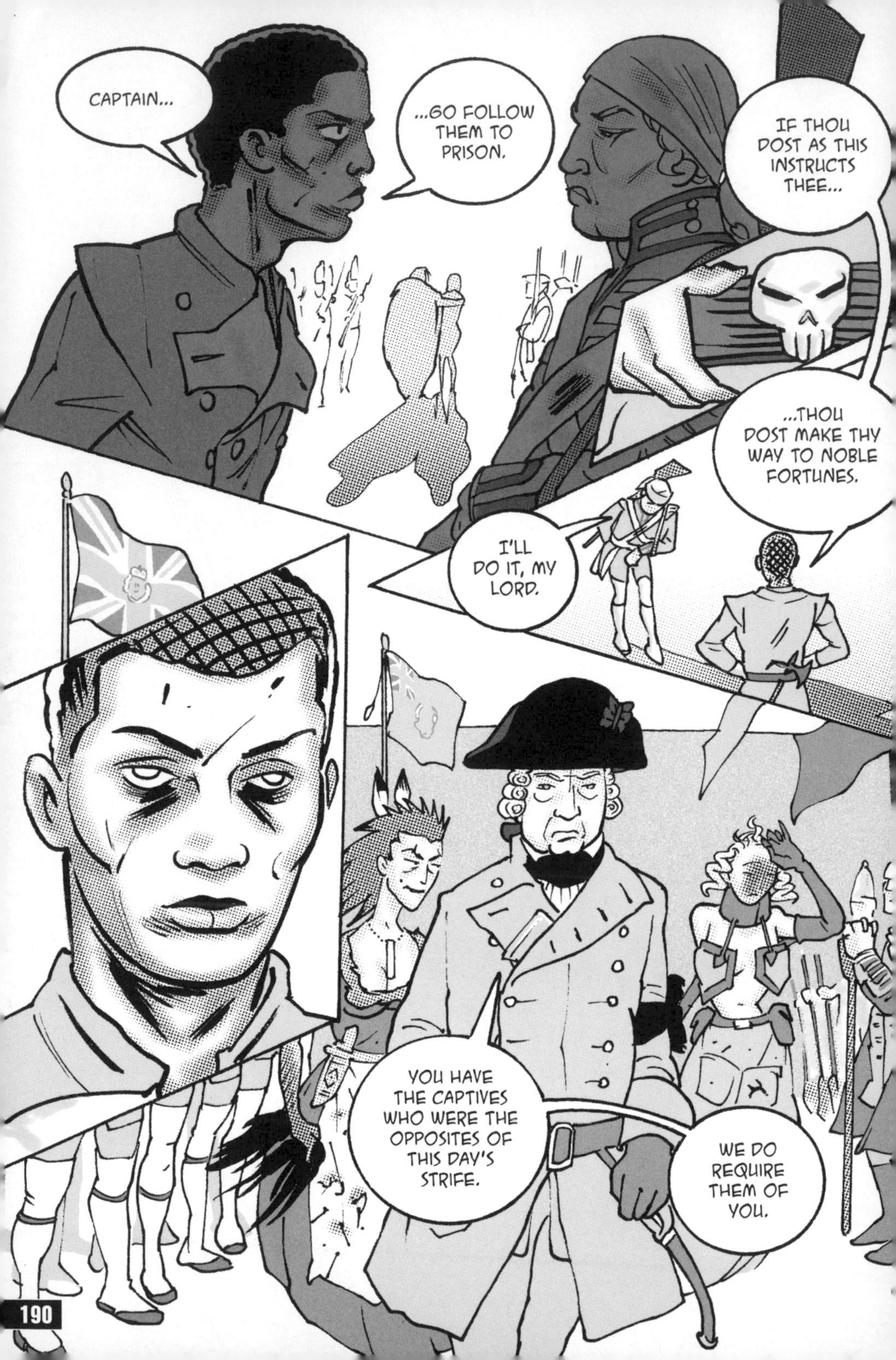
CAPTAIN...
...GO FOLLOW THEM TO PRISON.
IF THOU DOST AS THIS INSTRUCTS THEE...
...THOU DOST MAKE THY WAY TO NOBLE FORTUNES.
I'LL DO IT, MY LORD.
YOU HAVE THE CAPTIVES WHO WERE THE OPPOSITES OF THIS DAY'S STRIFE.
WE DO REQUIRE THEM OF YOU.

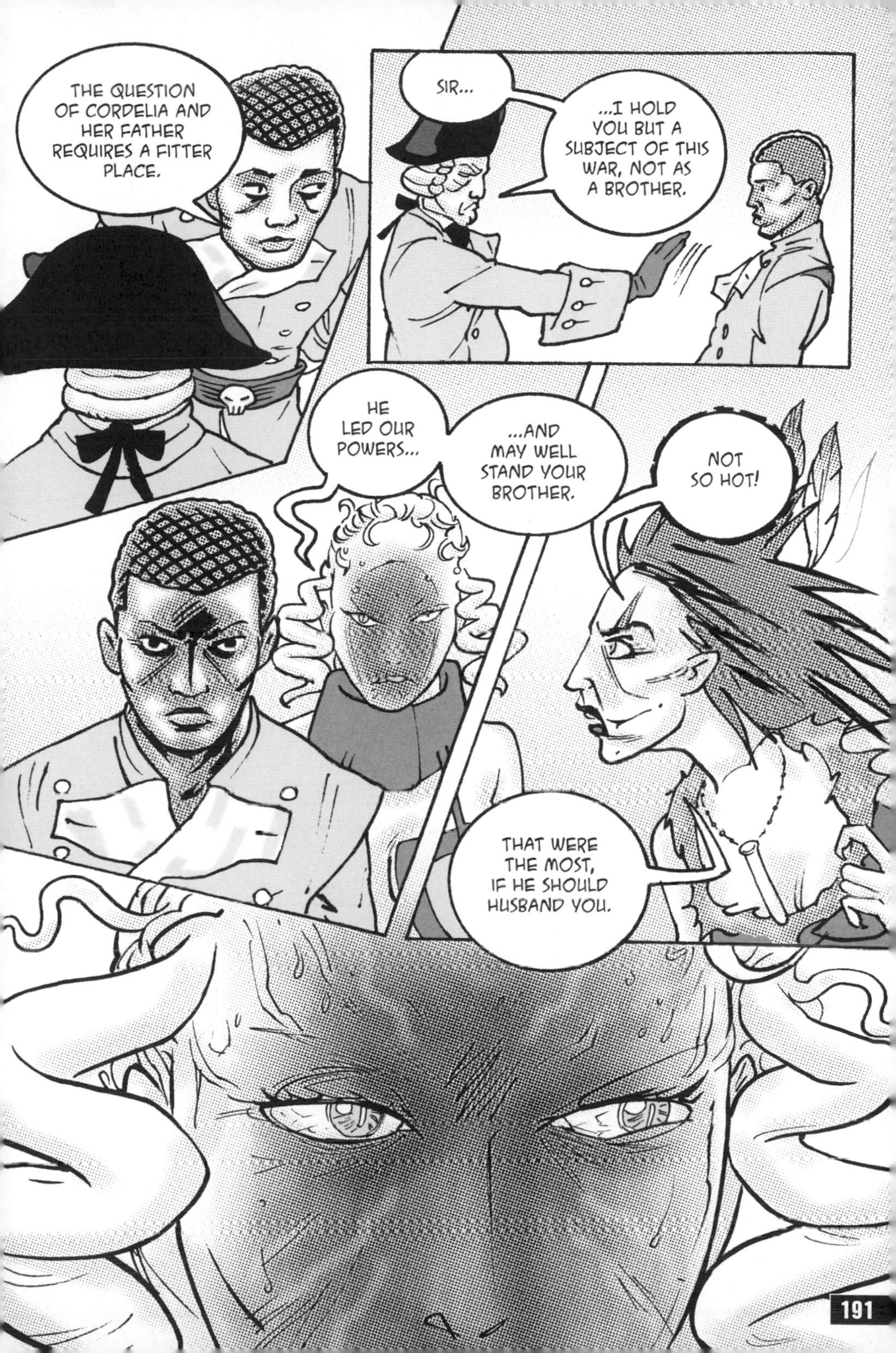
THE QUESTION OF CORDELIA AND HER FATHER REQUIRES A FITTER PLACE.
SIR...
...I HOLD YOU BUT A SUBJECT OF THIS WAR, NOT AS A BROTHER.
HE LED OUR POWERS...
...AND MAY WELL STAND YOUR BROTHER.
NOT SO HOT!
THAT WERE THE MOST, IF HE SHOULD HUSBAND YOU.

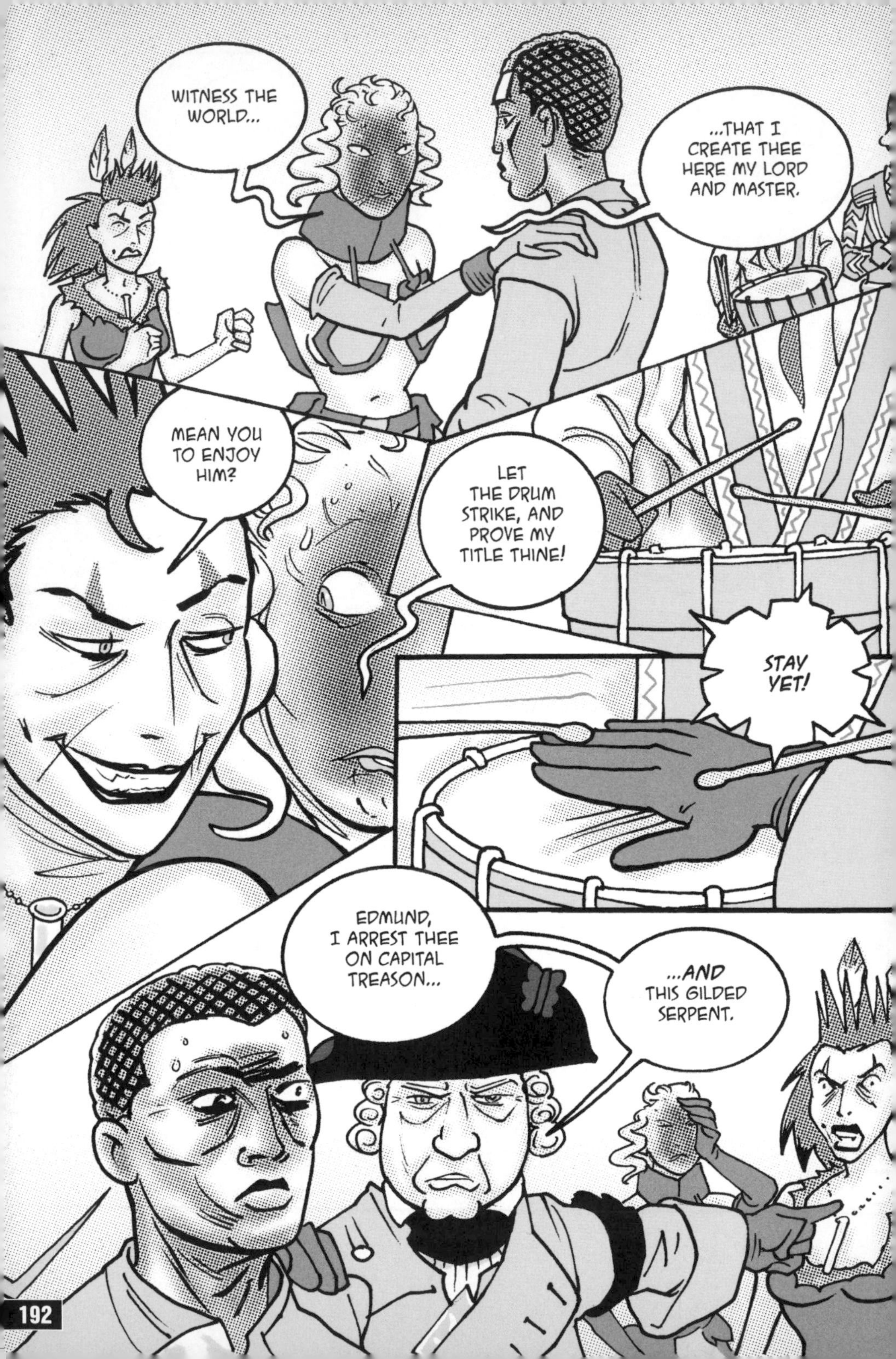
WITNESS THE WORLD...
...THAT I CREATE THEE HERE MY LORD AND MASTER.
MEAN YOU TO ENJOY HIM?
LET THE DRUM STRIKE, AND PROVE MY TITLE THINE!
STAY YET!
EDMUND, I ARREST THEE ON CAPITAL TREASON...
...AND THIS GILDED SERPENT.

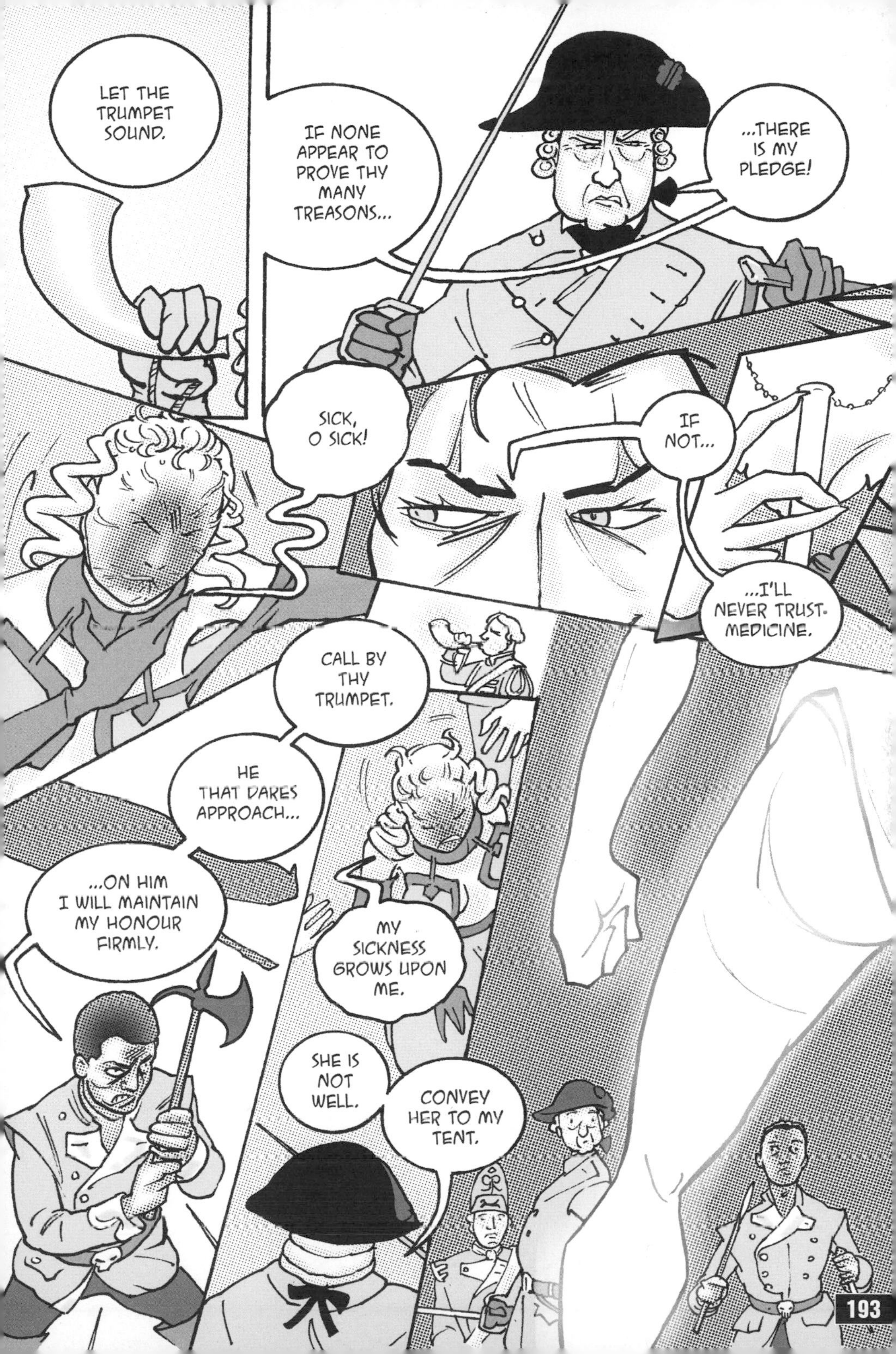
LET THE TRUMPET SOUND.
IF NONE APPEAR TO PROVE THY MANY TREASONS...
...THERE IS MY PLEDGE!
SICK, O SICK!
IF NOT...
...I'LL NEVER TRUST MEDICINE.
CALL BY THY TRUMPET.
HE THAT DARES APPROACH...
...ON HIM I WILL MAINTAIN MY HONOUR FIRMLY.
MY SICKNESS GROWS UPON ME.
SHE IS NOT WELL.
CONVEY HER TO MY TENT.

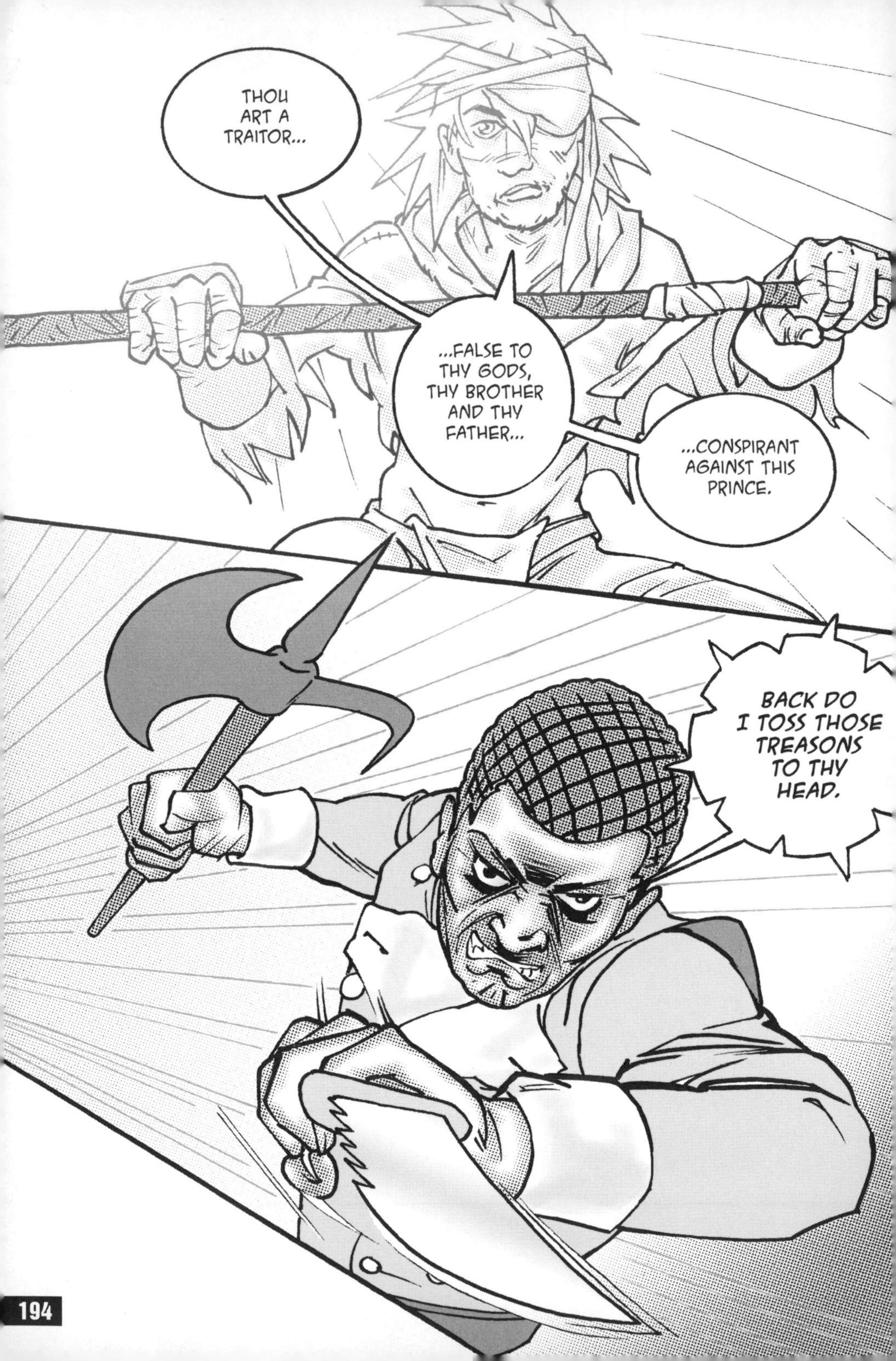
THOU ART A TRAITOR...
...FALSE TO THY GODS, THY BROTHER AND THY FATHER...
...CONSPIRANT AGAINST THIS PRINCE.
BACK DO I TOSS THOSE TREASONS TO THY HEAD.

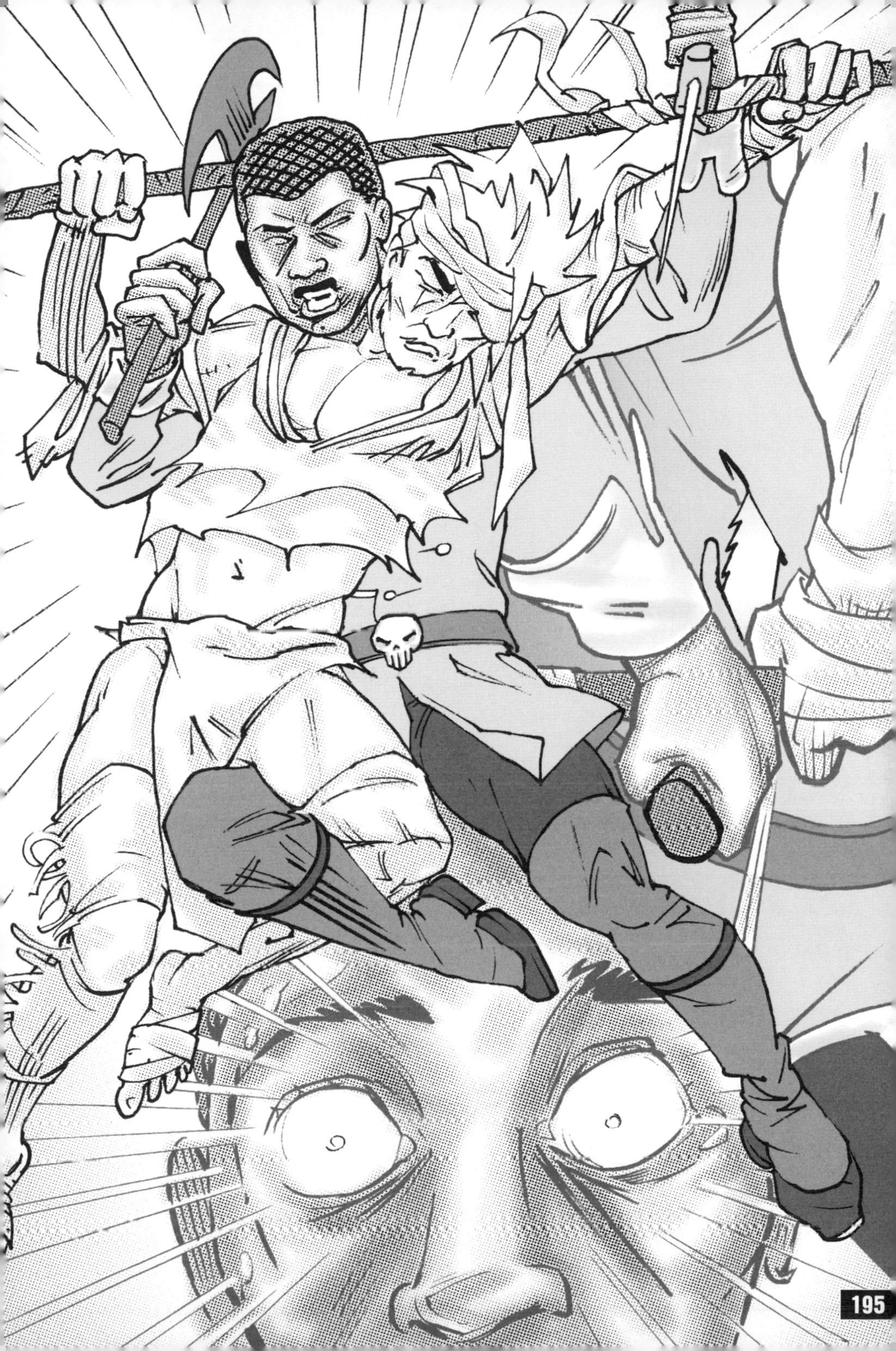

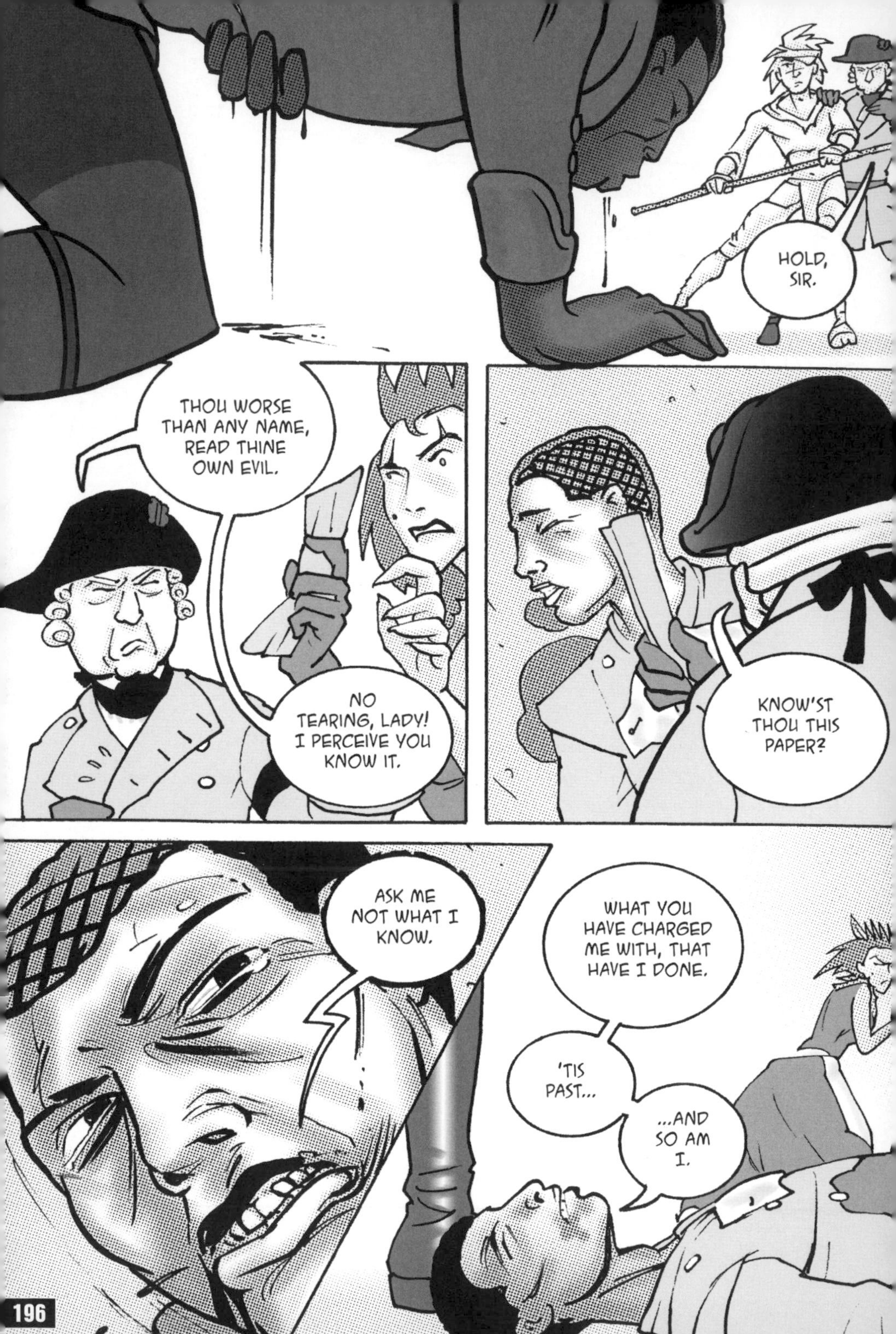
HOLD, SIR.
THOU WORSE THAN ANY NAME, READ THINE OWN EVIL.
NO TEARING, LADY! I PERCEIVE YOU KNOW IT.
KNOW'ST THOU THIS PAPER?
ASK ME NOT WHAT I KNOW.
WHAT YOU HAVE CHARGED ME WITH, THAT HAVE I DONE.
'TIS PAST...
...AND SO AM I.

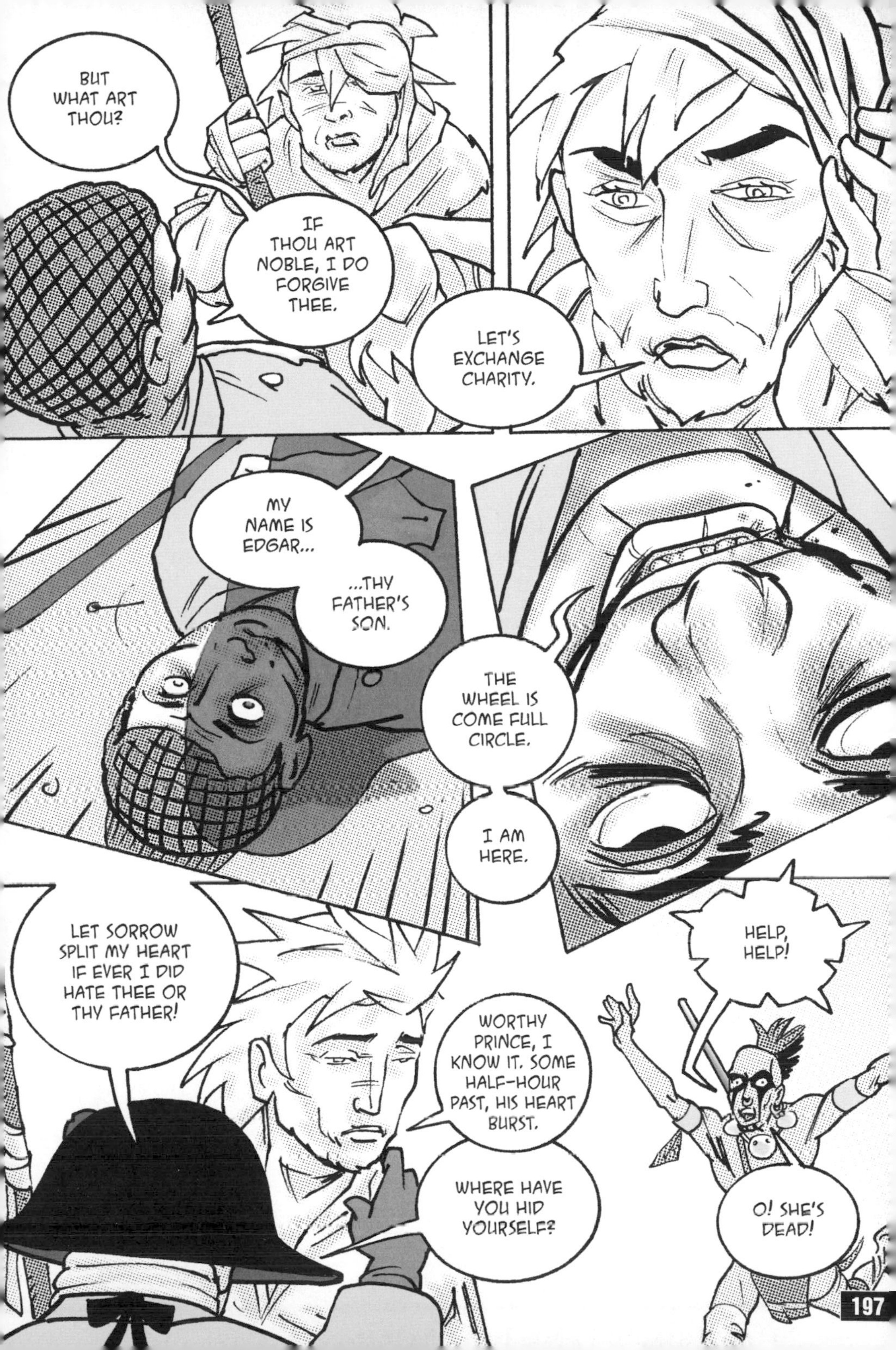
BUT WHAT ART THOU?
IF THOU ART NOBLE, I DO FORGIVE THEE.
LET'S EXCHANGE CHARITY.
MY NAME IS EDGAR...
...THY FATHER'S SON.
THE WHEEL IS COME FULL CIRCLE.
I AM HERE.
LET SORROW SPLIT MY HEART IF EVER I DID HATE THEE OR THY FATHER!
WORTHY PRINCE, I KNOW IT. SOME HALF-HOUR PAST, HIS HEART BURST.
WHERE HAVE YOU HID YOURSELF?
HELP, HELP!
O! SHE'S DEAD!

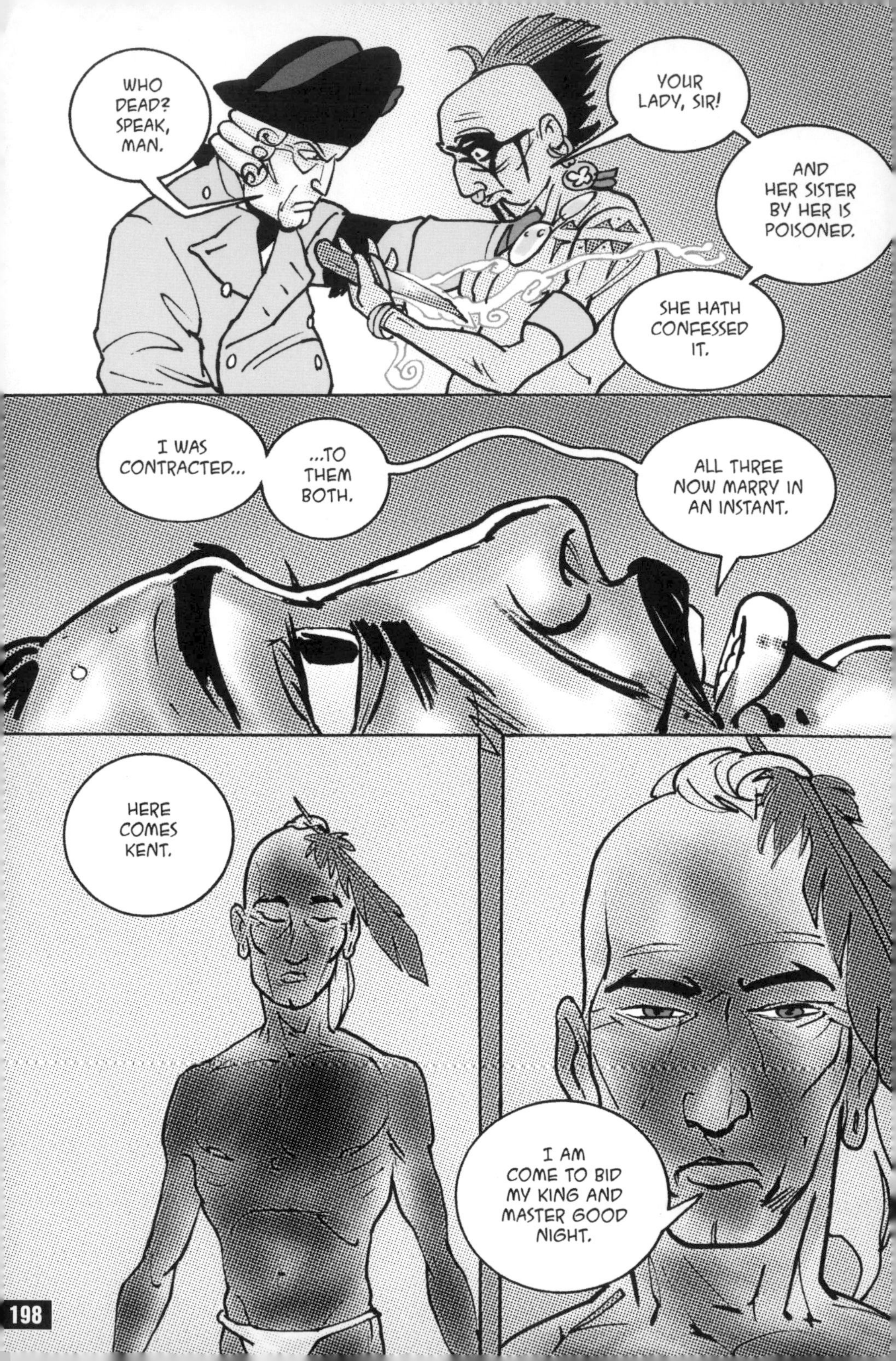
WHO DEAD? SPEAK, MAN.
YOUR LADY, SIR!
AND HER SISTER BY HER IS POISONED.
SHE HATH CONFESSED IT.
I WAS CONTRACTED...
...TO THEM BOTH.
ALL THREE NOW MARRY IN AN INSTANT.
HERE COMES KENT.
I AM COME TO BID MY KING AND MASTER GOOD NIGHT.

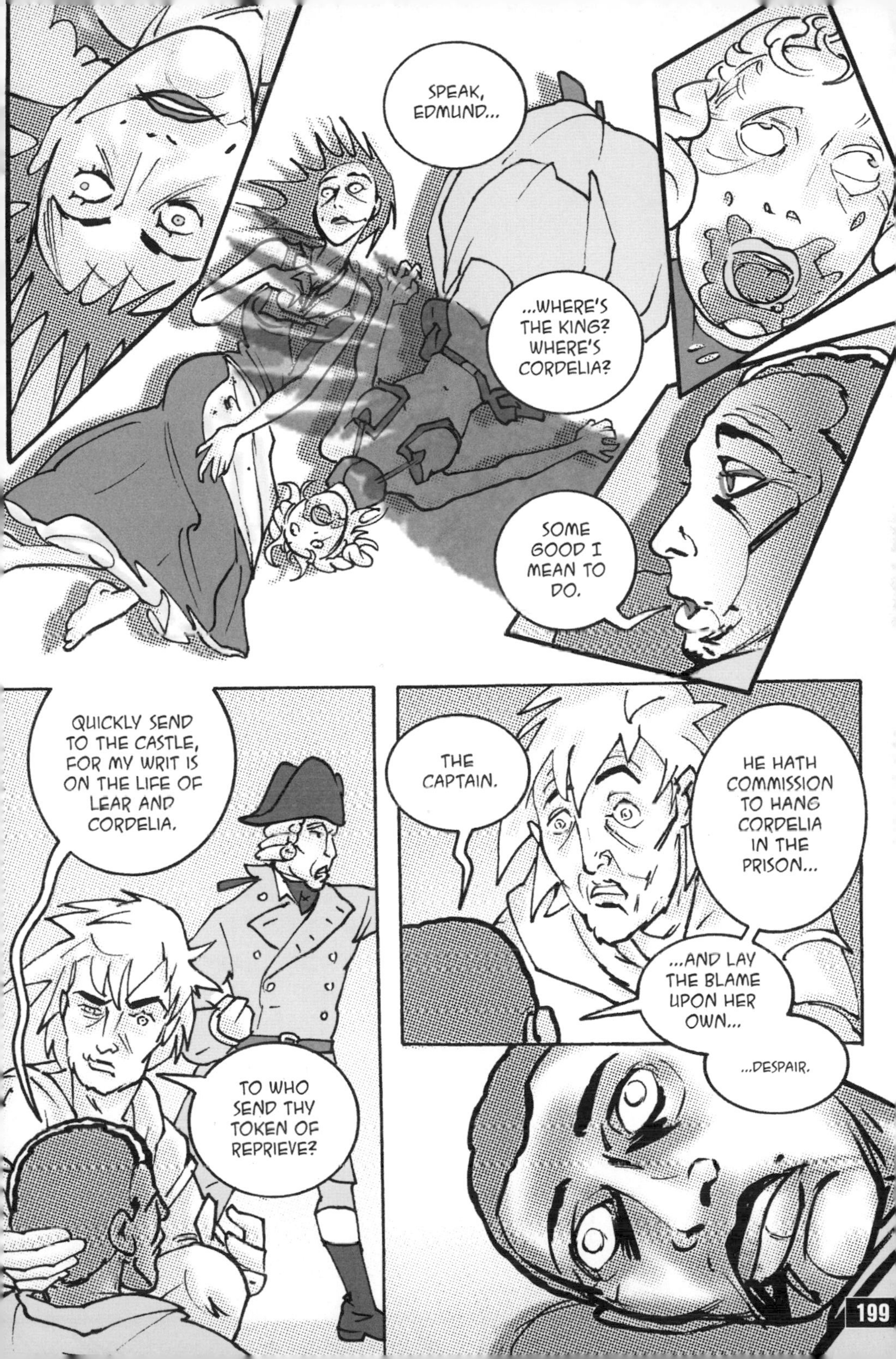
SPEAK, EDMUND...
...WHERE'S THE KING? WHERE'S CORDELIA?
SOME GOOD I MEAN TO DO.
QUICKLY SEND TO THE CASTLE, FOR MY WRIT IS ON THE LIFE OF LEAR AND CORDELIA.
TO WHO SEND THY TOKEN OF REPRIEVE?
THE CAPTAIN.
HE HATH COMMISSION TO HANG CORDELIA IN THE PRISON...
...AND LAY THE BLAME UPON HER OWN...
...DESPAIR.

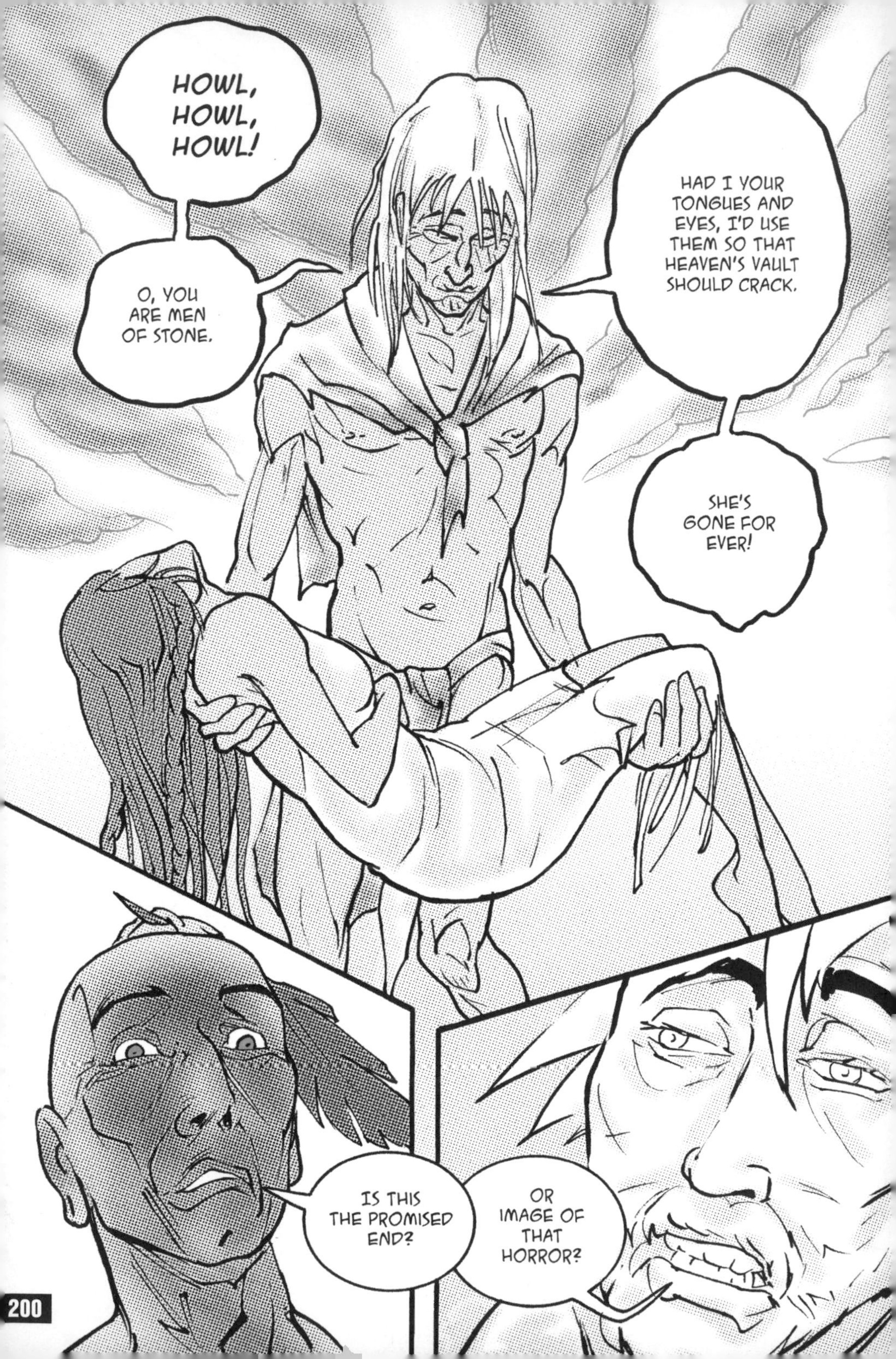
HOWL, HOWL, HOWL!
O, YOU ARE MEN OF STONE.
HAD I YOUR TONGUES AND EYES, I'D USE THEM SO THAT HEAVEN'S VAULT SHOULD CRACK.
SHE'S GONE FOR EVER!
IS THIS THE PROMISED END?
OR IMAGE OF THAT HORROR?

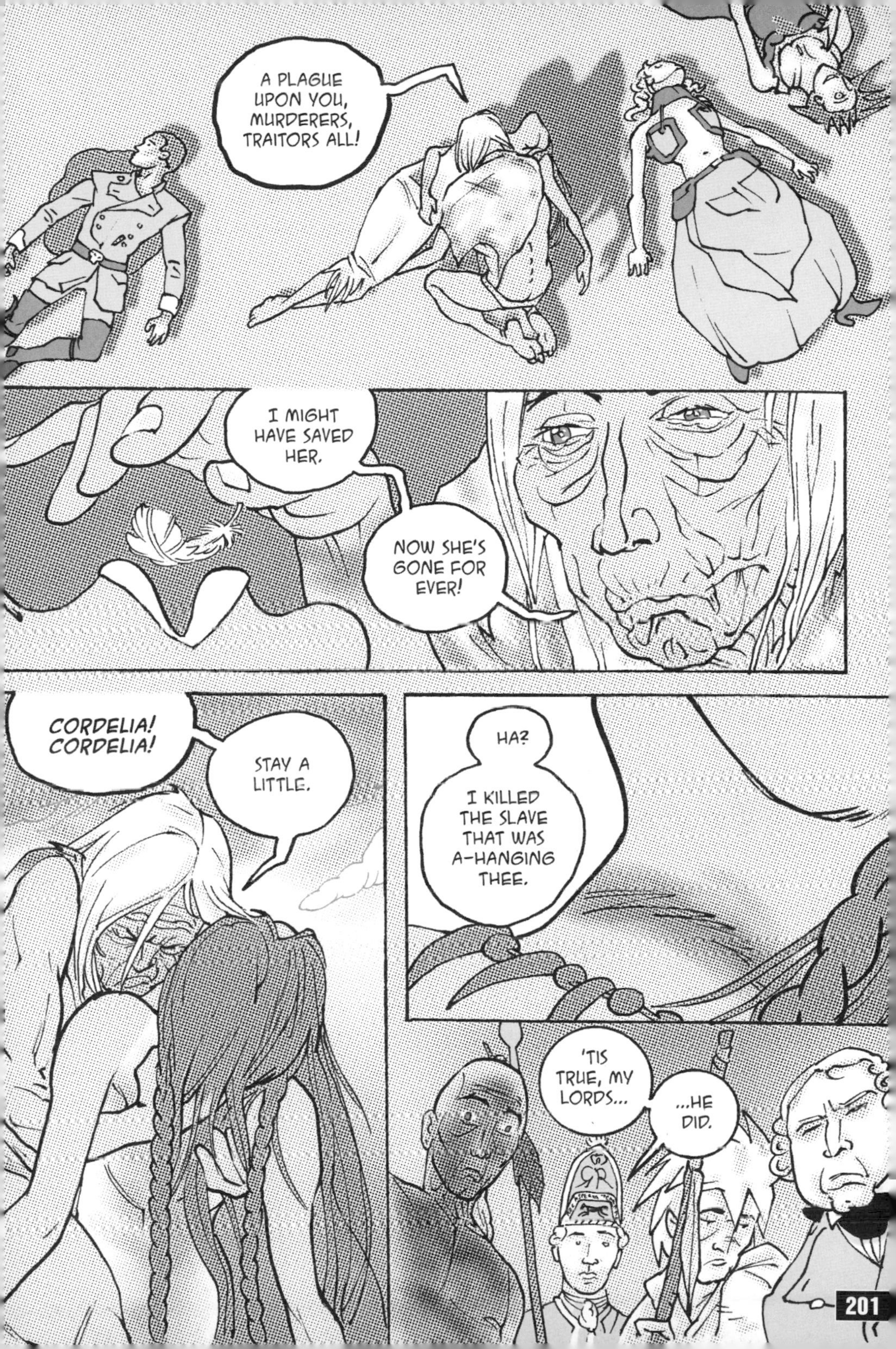
A PLAGUE UPON YOU, MURDERERS, TRAITORS ALL!
I MIGHT HAVE SAVED HER.
NOW SHE'S GONE FOR EVER!
CORDELIA! CORDELIA!
STAY A LITTLE.
HA?
I KILLED THE SLAVE THAT WAS A-HANGING THEE.
'TIS TRUE, MY LORDS...
...HE DID.

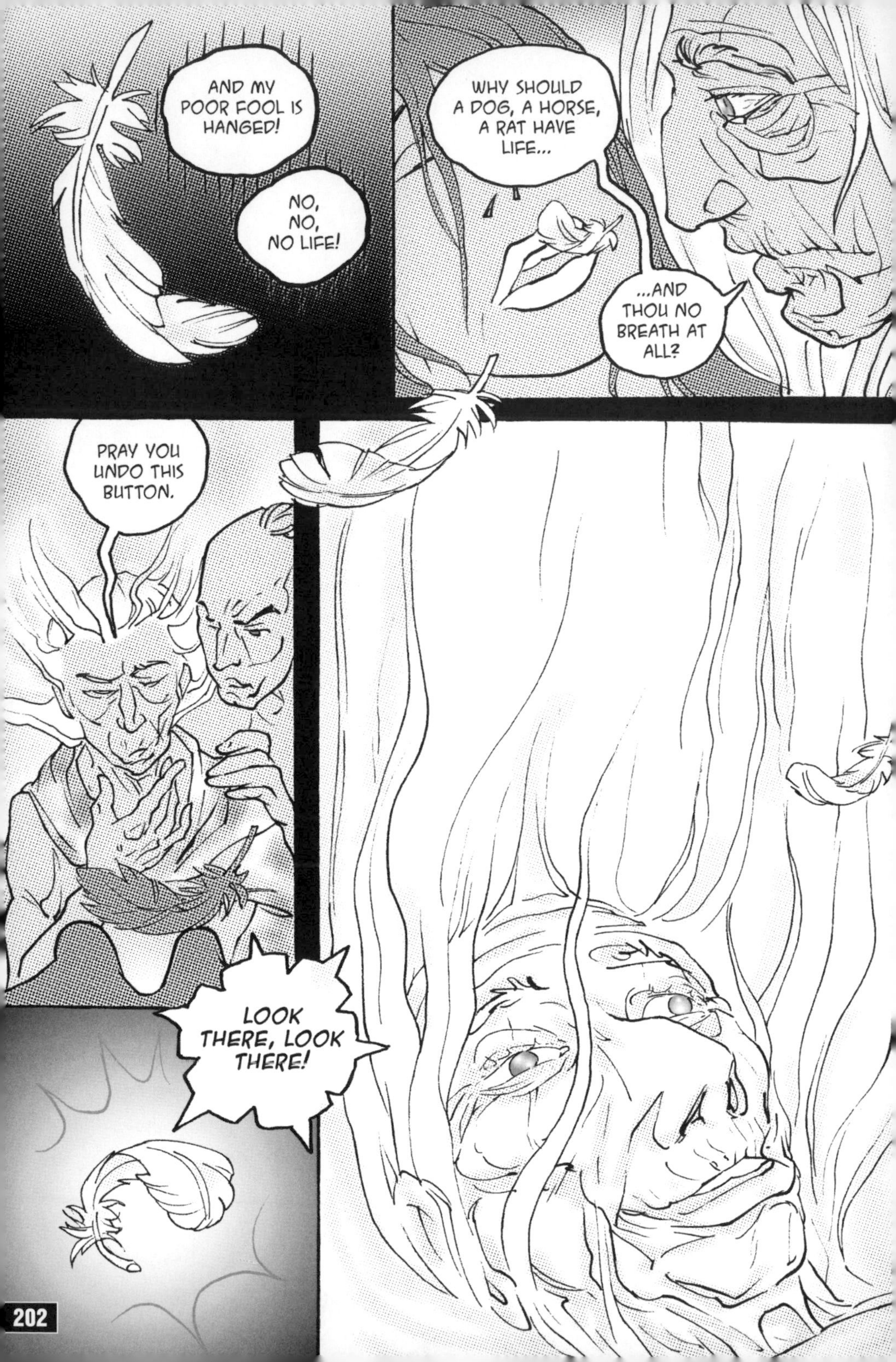
AND MY POOR FOOL IS HANGED!
NO, NO, NO LIFE!
WHY SHOULD A DOG, A HORSE, A RAT HAVE LIFE...
...AND THOU NO BREATH AT ALL?
PRAY YOU UNDO THIS BUTTON.
LOOK THERE, LOOK THERE!

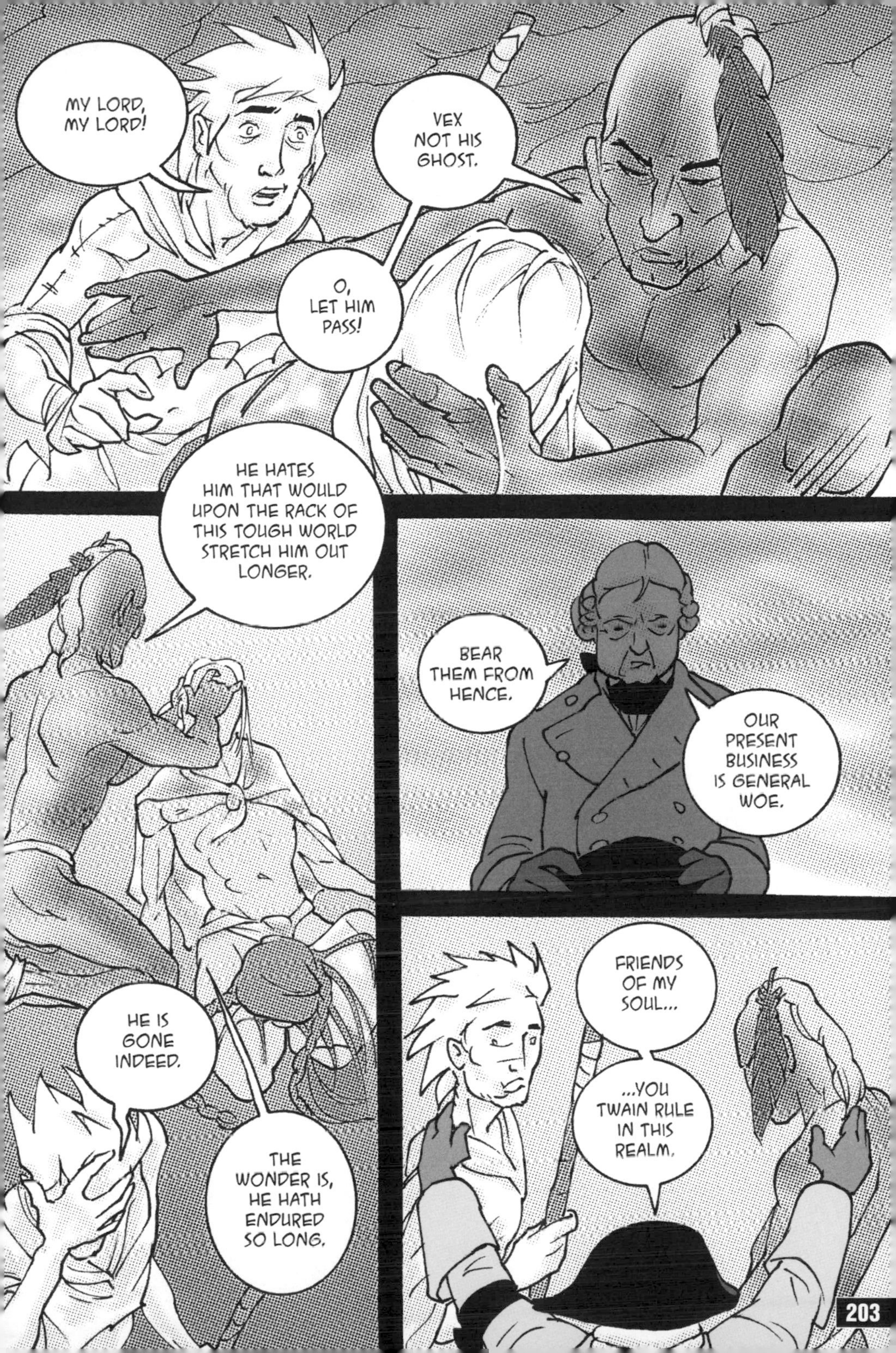

MY LORD, MY LORD!
VEX NOT HIS GHOST.
O, LET HIM PASS!
HE HATES HIM THAT WOULD UPON THE RACK OF THIS TOUGH WORLD STRETCH HIM OUT LONGER.
HE IS GONE INDEED.
THE WONDER IS, HE HATH ENDURED SO LONG.
BEAR THEM FROM HENCE.
OUR PRESENT BUSINESS IS GENERAL WOE.
FRIENDS OF MY SOUL...
...YOU TWAIN RULE IN THIS REALM.

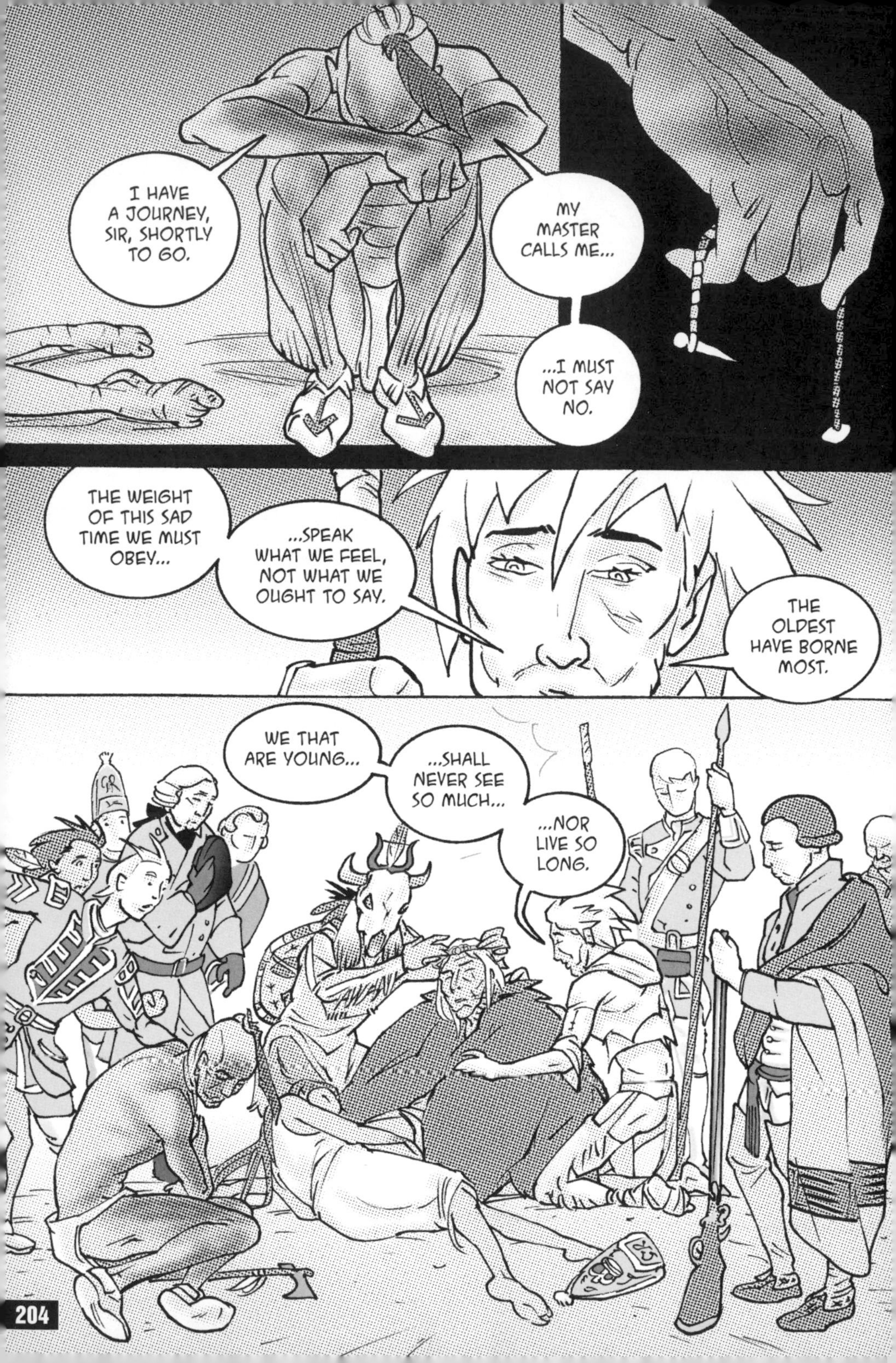
I HAVE A JOURNEY, SIR, SHORTLY TO GO.
MY MASTER CALLS ME...
...I MUST NOT SAY NO.
THE WEIGHT OF THIS SAD TIME WE MUST OBEY...
...SPEAK WHAT WE FEEL, NOT WHAT WE OUGHT TO SAY.
THE OLDEST HAVE BORNE MOST.
WE THAT ARE YOUNG...
...SHALL NEVER SEE SO MUCH...
...NOR LIVE SO LONG.
GR

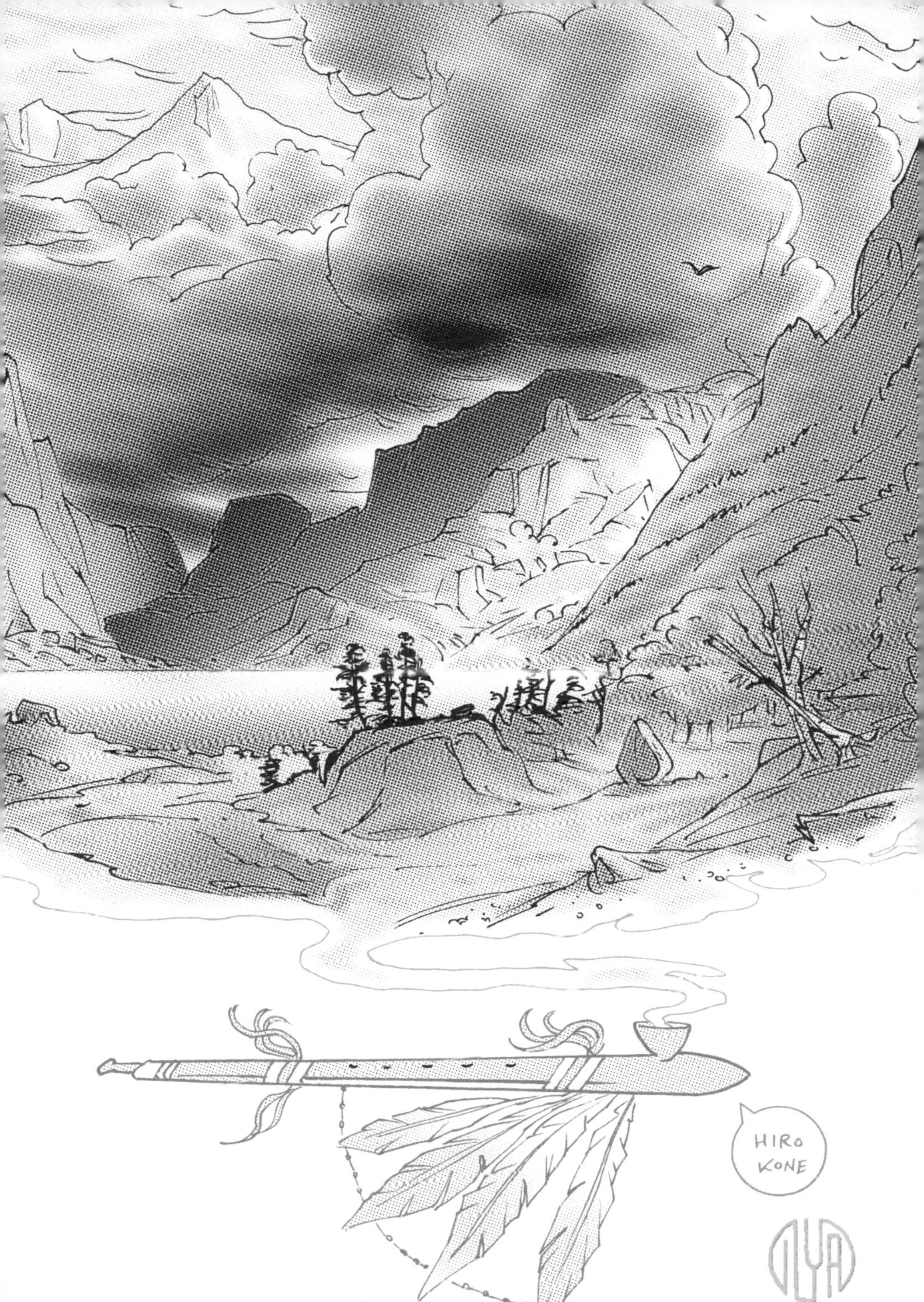
HIRO
KONE

PLOT SUMMARY OF KING LEAR

Old King Lear has three daughters: Goneril (wife of Albany), Regan (wife of Cornwall), and Cordelia (who has two suitors, Burgundy and France). Gloucester – Lear's counsellor, like him a widower – has two sons: Edgar, and the illegitimate Edmund. Lear has decided to abdicate, and divide his kingdom between his daughters, promising the largest portion to the one who loves him most. Goneril and Regan effusively declare their love, but Cordelia is revolted by this "love-test", replying that she loves him as any daughter should love a father. This enrages Lear, who disinherits her. Kent attempts to intervene – but is banished from the court. Burgundy withdraws his marriage offer, but Cordelia accepts that of France, and they leave together.

Now powerless, Lear is at the mercy of his elder daughters. When Goneril criticizes his behaviour, Lear angrily leaves to join Regan – but he is rapidly running out of friends. Only the Fool (his enigmatic court-jester) and the ever-faithful Kent (who has disguised himself to aid his master) stay loyal. When Kent arrives at Gloucester's castle, where Regan and Cornwall are staying, he is set in the stocks for insulting Goneril's servant Oswald. Lear is enraged at this – but then driven to madness when his two daughters unite against him. A storm breaks and he rages into the night, with only the Fool and Kent for company.

Meanwhile, Edmund has effected his plan to steal Edgar's inheritance by turning Gloucester against him. Edgar has fled, disguising himself as the madman "Poor Tom", and is seeking shelter in a countryside hovel during the storm when Lear, the Fool, and Kent arrive. Appalled at Regan and Goneril's behaviour, Gloucester seeks them out to offer the shelter of his castle. But Edmund betrays his father, and when Gloucester returns home, he is savagely punished by having his eyes put out. Kicked out of his own house, he is placed in the charge of the madman "Poor Tom" (his own disguised son Edgar). Assuming further rôles for his blind father, Edgar counsels him against despair.

Gloucester's blinding proves the turning-point: Cornwall is killed by an outraged servant (leaving Regan free to court Edmund); Albany vows revenge against Goneril (who has her eyes on Edmund herself); and Edgar kills Oswald when he tries to capture Gloucester. Cordelia lands with the French army, and is reunited with Lear, whom her doctor restores to sanity. But the French lose the battle, Cordelia and Lear are captured, and the terrible final phase begins.

Jealous of her relationship with Edmund, Goneril poisons Regan. In single combat, Edgar fatally wounds Edmund, to whom he reveals his identity, relating Gloucester's death from the shock at learning who "Poor Tom" really was. Goneril commits suicide. The dying Edmund reveals that he has ordered Lear and Cordelia's execution – but it is too late: Lear now enters with Cordelia's corpse, mad again with grief, and dies raving. Kent renounces the world; Lear's kingdom passes to Albany and Edgar.

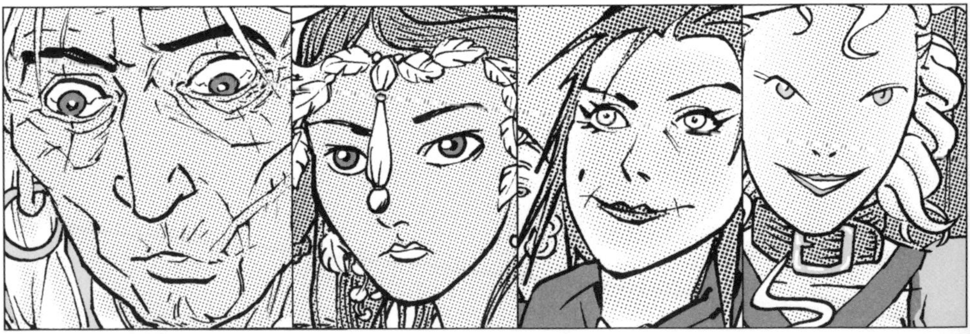

A BRIEF LIFE OF WILLIAM SHAKESPEARE

Shakespeare's birthday is traditionally said to be the 23rd of April — St George's Day, patron saint of England. A good start for England's greatest writer. But that date and even his name are uncertain. He signed his own name in different ways. "Shakespeare" is now the accepted one out of dozens of different versions.

He was born at Stratford-upon-Avon in 1564, and baptized on 26th April. His mother, Mary Arden, was the daughter of a prosperous farmer. His father, John Shakespeare, a glove-maker, was a respected civic figure — and probably also a Catholic. In 1570, just as Will began school, his father was accused of illegal dealings. The family fell into debt and disrepute.

Will attended a local school for eight years. He did not go to university. The next ten years are a blank filled by suppositions. Was he briefly a Latin teacher, a soldier, a sea-faring explorer? Was he prosecuted and whipped for poaching deer?

We do know that in 1582 he married Anne Hathaway, eight years his senior, and three months pregnant. Two more children — twins — were born three years later but, by around 1590, Will had left Stratford to pursue a theatre career in London. Shakespeare's apprenticeship began as an actor and "pen for hire".

He learned his craft the hard way. He soon won fame as a playwright with often-staged popular hits.

He and his colleagues formed a stage company, the Lord Chamberlain's Men, which built the famous Globe Theatre. It opened in 1599 but was destroyed by fire in 1613 during a performance of *Henry VIII* which used gunpowder special effects. It was rebuilt in brick the following year.

Shakespeare was a financially successful writer who invested his money wisely in property. In 1597, he bought an enormous house in Stratford, and in 1608 became a shareholder in London's Blackfriars Theatre. He also redeemed the family's honour by acquiring a personal coat of arms.

Shakespeare wrote over 40 works, including poems, "lost" plays and collaborations, in a career spanning nearly 25 years. He retired to Stratford in 1613, where he died on 23rd April 1616, aged 52, apparently of a fever after a "merry meeting" of drinks with friends. Shakespeare did in fact die on St George's Day! He was buried "full 17 foot deep" in Holy Trinity Church, Stratford, and left an epitaph cursing anyone who dared disturb his bones.

There have been preposterous theories disputing Shakespeare's authorship. Some claim that Sir Francis Bacon (1561–1626), philosopher and Lord Chancellor, was the real author of Shakespeare's plays. Others propose Edward de Vere, Earl of Oxford (1550–1604), or, even more weirdly, Queen Elizabeth I. The implication is that the "real" Shakespeare had to be a university graduate or an aristocrat. Nothing less would do for the world's greatest writer.

Shakespeare is mysteriously hidden behind his work. His life will not tell us what inspired his genius.

MANGA SHAKESPEARE

Praise for *Manga Shakespeare*:

ALA Quick Pick
ALA Best Books for Young Adults
New York Public Library Best Book
for the Teen Age

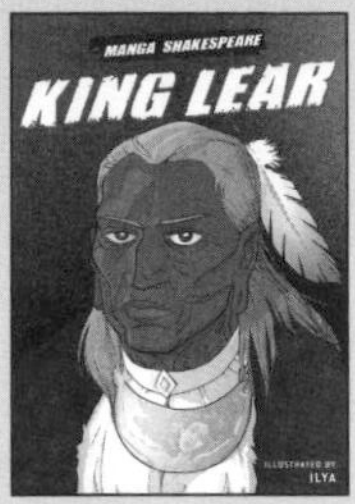
MANGA SHAKESPEARE
KING LEAR
ILLUSTRATED BY
ILYA

978-0-8109-4222-6
$10.95 paperback

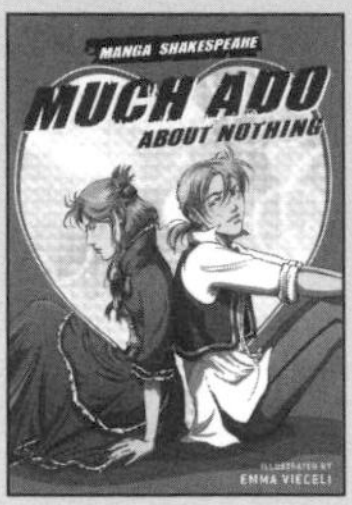
MANGA SHAKESPEARE
MUCH ADO
ABOUT NOTHING
ILLUSTRATED BY
EMMA VIECELI

978-0-8109-4323-0
$10.95 paperback

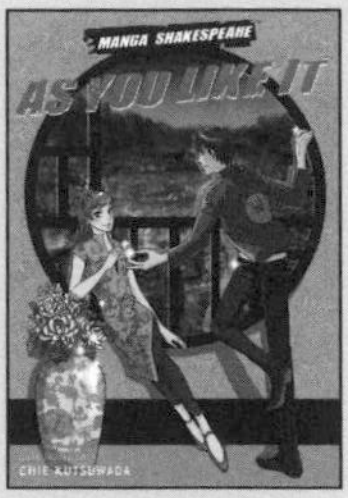
MANGA SHAKESPEARE
AS YOU LIKE IT
CHIE KUTSUWADA

978-0-8109-8351-9
$10.95 paperback

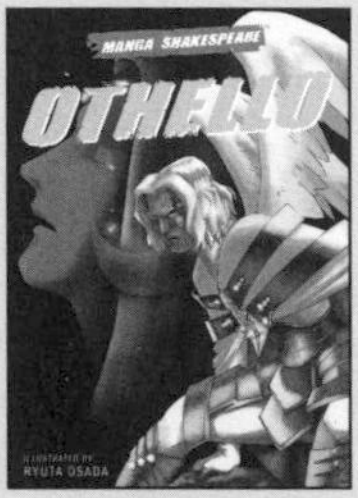
MANGA SHAKESPEARE
OTHELLO
ILLUSTRATED BY
RYUTA OSADA

978-0-8109-8350-2
$10.95 paperback

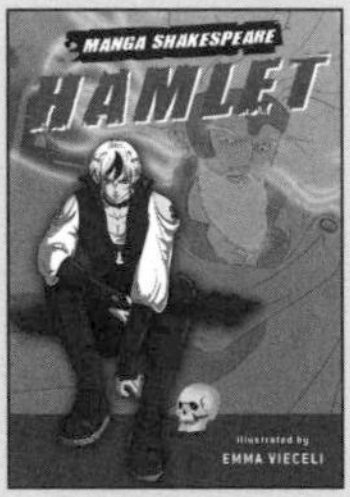
MANGA SHAKESPEARE
HAMLET
Illustrated by
EMMA VIECELI

978-0-8109-9324-2
$10.95 paperback

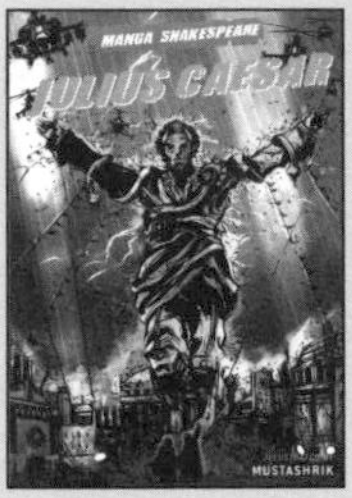
MANGA SHAKESPEARE
JULIUS CAESAR
MUSTASHRIK

978-0-8109-7072-4
$10.95 paperback

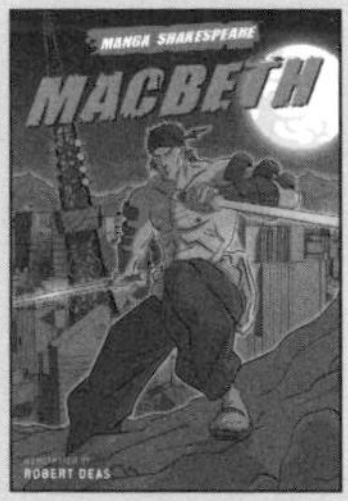
MANGA SHAKESPEARE
MACBETH
ROBERT DEAS

978-0-8109-7073-1
$10.95 paperback

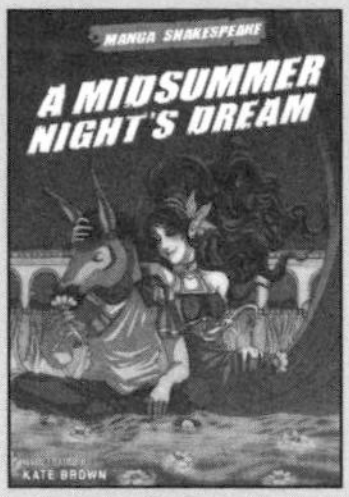
MANGA SHAKESPEARE
A MIDSUMMER NIGHT'S DREAM
KATE BROWN

978-0-8109-9475-1
$10.95 paperback

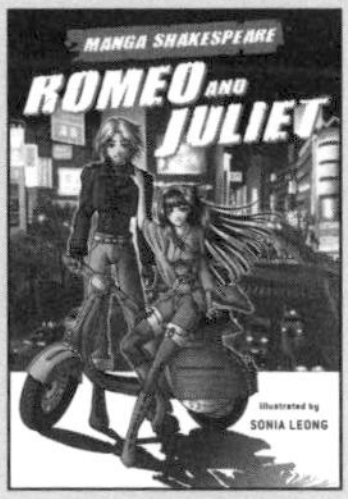
MANGA SHAKESPEARE
ROMEO AND JULIET
Illustrated by
SONIA LEONG

978-0-8109-9325-9
$10.95 paperback

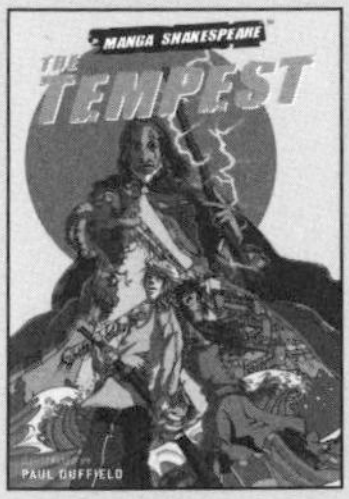
MANGA SHAKESPEARE
THE TEMPEST
PAUL DUFFIELD

978-0-8109-9476-8
$10.95 paperback

AMULET BOOKS, AVAILABLE WHEREVER BOOKS ARE SOLD | WWW.AMULETBOOKS.COM

Send author fan mail to Amulet Books, Attn: Marketing, 115 West 18th Street, New York, NY 10011, or in an e-mail to *marketing@hnabooks.com*. All mail will be forwarded. Amulet Books is an imprint of ABRAMS.